# The Blue-Eyed Girl

# The Blue-Eyed Girl

William Goodson

RED SQUARE PRESS
North Tustin, California

Cover illustration by Polly Lockman
Interior design by JM Shubin, ShubinDesign
Typeface: Sabon

CATALOGING DATA:
The Blue-Eyed Girl
By William Goodson
Fiction

ISBN 978-0-9760398-2-2

For every woman who knows this story.

"...by force, fear, or fraud."
S. Jean Heriot Emans
Donald Peter Goldstein
*Pediatric and Adolescent Gynecology*
1977

# The Blue-Eyed Girl

# Epilogue, Part II

It's a sunny afternoon in New York City, but I'm stuck on the other side of the world where it's night. I stare at the dark and cannot sleep. I will doze fitfully before dawn, but tomorrow I will be exhausted. In the afternoon, I will wander through my house, and at the end of the day, when everyone else sleeps, I will lie awake again.

For months now, I know only that when it's sunny in New York, I cannot leave the night—and I dream that I could return to America.

Food has no taste. I do not have the energy to exercise. My muscles have aged. My silk jacket hangs off a thin man. I have grown a beard because I do not like to look at myself to shave.

My name is Sayiid Algedda. I am a diplomat. I have retired, but I remain an observer of nations in the sense that a lawyer is always a lawyer, and a policeman is always a policeman. I used to manage the secrets of nations. As I have learned, a diplomat who cannot control secrets is useless. A diplomat who has his own secrets is a liability.

My dream was to live in New York City, so after I had signed my last official document, we settled there as expatriates. I was vigorous and looked younger than most of my colleagues. Then her letter arrived.

Americans typically overlook many aspects of history—how we have come to be where we are—and I often thought that only Arabs and Jews remember forever. But when I received the letter, I learned that Americans can remember, and what followed underscored the importance of secrets and how one can never be certain their secrets are truly secure.

She sent it as an "open letter" to our entire staff, and a copy quickly found its way to the Internet. On the surface, the content was not embarrassing and would not have driven me out of the United States. On the contrary, the letter and the photographs with it hinted at a story that is valued, almost mythical, in America. If they had been seen from that perspective, they should have helped me be accepted, as I had always wanted. But the way they were sent suggested a different, more complex meaning.

My closest colleague understood why the letter was sent, but he officially chose to be ignorant. He assumed interest in the letter would fade, and it would quickly be forgotten. However, as luck would have it, there was a lull in other news, and first other Arab diplomats, and then the entire diplomatic community, began to speculate about the identity of the woman who had written the letter—and why.

The afternoon the letter and photographs went viral on the Internet, I received a call on my cell phone. I did not recognize the caller I.D., but my number was closely guarded, so I thought the call might be important.

It was the annoyingly chipper voice of a reporter named

Daisy who had once interviewed me about my college years in America. I guessed she was looking at her computer screen because she asked, "You're much younger here. Was this snapshot made when you were in school?"

"I cannot remember."

"Suppose for a moment these pictures are from a girl you knew. Do you think she's trying to embarrass you?"

I paused to suggest her call had interrupted something more important. "You must excuse me. I cannot talk right now."

"Okay." But she bargained, "One more question?"

"Certainly." Anything to get her off the phone politely.

"Did you really do that?"

Our ambassador flew up from Washington that night and came to my home unannounced. I met him in my robe. He asked me, "What should we do about this?"

I told him it would blow over, and if it did not, I would file a lawsuit to silence her. He had other ideas.

"People gossip about you because you live in New York," he said. "The rumors will stop if you are not here. The Minister and I have discussed this. We suggest that you leave the United States and return home."

"Suggest?" I asked.

I boarded a plane that night, and silently stole away. First Class was booked, so I had to fly Business. It was raining, and the glow of New York was quickly lost in the clouds below me.

Twenty-four hours later I was at home. I could not tell my friends how gossip started by a woman hounded me out of America, so I did not explain my return.

Now, as is our custom, they call on me at my home, or I visit them. We sip tea and discuss politics, but as they tactfully do not ask about the letter, the story I cannot tell boils through my mind and drags me to a montage of other places until a voice or a motion jerks me back. Then I blink and find everyone trying to understand the strange malady that made me stare blankly away from the conversation.

I forget the letter when I can, but forgetting is a luxury. When I see a plane flying west, when an imam rails against America, when I see a wisp of uncovered hair on a woman on the street, I remember. I still have my passport, but only as a courtesy. The Minister has suggested—that euphemism again—I should not try to leave the country.

My story might embarrass the King, but my pain does not come from embarrassment. I am alone with memories of events I wish I could remove from my life. I want to know why she chose to send this letter now. What difference could it possibly make after so many years?

# 1. Pride

My first trip to the United States was to attend Thomas Penn College in Jackson City, Missouri, a suburb of Kansas City. An American education was the culmination of a plan suggested to me ten years earlier by a business friend of my father.

In the 1950s, our King was thrilled by increasing oil revenue and decided to launch a national airline, similar to Al Italia, Air France, and SAS. He asked Trans World Airlines, commonly called TWA, to be our partner in this project. TWA executives tried to thwart our effort to create a competitor for passengers in the Middle East until they realized that Westerners would always prefer a Western airline. An Arab airline created a convenient *de facto* segregation of all but the most affluent Arab leadership.

The King assigned the project to a Prince, his cousin, the Minister of Commerce. The Prince dreamed like the King, but he lacked understanding of airplanes, buildings, schedules, or management. My father, on the other hand, was an engineer who piloted small planes and managed our local airport.

The Prince delegated the responsibility to my father.

Everett Hartwood, senior vice president of TWA, was assigned as liaison to help establish our airline. He had the final word on all operational decisions, but orders were issued by my father in the name of the Prince.

On an early trip to the desert, Mr. Hartwood and his wife were guests in our home. My older brother, Jabir, who usually greeted guests with my father, was not at home that evening.

In preparation for their visit, my father spent several hours discussing American barbecue etiquette with my mother. It was unprecedented for women to mingle with male guests, but my father told my mother she would be the hostess, women would be in the company of the men, and she would pour lemonade. My mother was upset, but said nothing. She believed her head should be covered in the presence of a man who was not a relative and that drinks should be poured by servants. However, my father had been to America and would not consider anything else.

Mrs. Hartwood entered our house wearing a wrap on her head as was required of women everywhere, even in the back seat of a chauffeur driven car. Once she was certain she was not being watched, she threw off the scarf in frustration, "I will never get used to this!"

My father let her words settle for a moment and then replied softly, "I am sorry we have made you uncomfortable. It is our custom. Many people will be unhappy if anything is changed. Some think it helps with the heat." He caught my mother's eye and nodded toward the lemonade. "I cannot say."

Mother did not move, so father pointed to the glasses on the tray, and said to Mrs. Hartwood, "Here, have a cool drink...please."

Mother finally picked up the tray, and as she offered a glass to Mrs. Hartwood, father changed the subject. "Our son has been studying English."

"Oh, has he?" said Mr. Hartwood.

I entered the conversation. "Yes, sir. I am pleased to meet you."

"I am pleased to meet you," he replied.

"My name is Sayiid Algedda."

"My name is Everett Hartwood." He extended his hand.

"We are having hot weather," I continued.

"You can say that again," added Mrs. Hartwood.

"What do you want to be when you grow up?" he asked me.

"I want to be an ambassador."

"And why is that?

"My father has pictures of many lands. I want to see them."

I doubt my English was as good as I remember, but we did establish that I would like to travel.

"Then you should study in the United States," Mr. Hartwood concluded. "I can help arrange that."

To my parents, their son demonstrated what he had learned from his language tutor. However, as clearly as a child could conceive it, this was the beginning of my plan.

Over the course of many visits, my mother became comfortable sharing her home with the Hartwoods and would even talk to Mr. Hartwood in the hall alone while they waited for my father. Eventually other Arab couples joined us. The women were awkward at first, as though they had compromised themselves by socializing with men, but since the behavior was known only to those in the group, it bound them together rather than driving them apart. The Prince knew of these evenings but excused them as a necessary part of doing business with the Americans. Any man, especially an American, worked more effectively if his wife was happy.

My parents assumed I would go to university in Cairo and live with cousins who would monitor my progress and assure that I represented the family well. But I pointed out to my father it was necessary to understand America in order to get ahead. For example, not only did our airline fly their planes, but our pilots trained in America. To study outside of America would have been trying to learn by looking in a mirror.

Mr. Hartwood may not have recognized my argument as his own, but, in fact, he had said every word I was repeating, a few phrases at a time. I had memorized each thought and assembled them piece by piece into my dream.

I was not fluent enough in English to begin college in the United States, so after consultation with Mr. Hartwood, my father sent me to an American school in Bern, Switzerland for an additional year of preparation. Jabir lived in Germany a few hours away by train. I hated that he would supervise me, but I loved being in Europe.

Going to Switzerland was my first long flight. A little over an hour after takeoff, the stewardess was serving an elderly lady. As the purser squeezed past the stewardess in the aisle, he whispered something to her. She quickly excused herself and stepped to the galley where, in one graceful motion, she removed the scarf that wrapped all her head except her face. The purser then announced on the intercom, "Gentlemen, if you look out on either side of the plane, the blue you see is the Mediterranean. We are now in international airspace."

Other women looked out the window and then unwrapped their heads and shook their hair free. Husbands, or their required male relative escorts, largely ignored this transformation, but I gawked. I had never seen a woman's hair like that.

I was in Bern from October to May. Most of the students

lived with their parents. I was one of eight boarding students who lived in a building adjacent to the clock tower. It was cold, and the women and girls wore long sleeves and stockings, but their hair and faces were uncovered, and I could see female forms through their sweaters and skirts.

At night in the boarding students' house I learned about women's bodies. An American named Brad had copies of *Playboy* magazine. It was the first time I had seen a picture of what a woman looked like under the long robes that my sister and cousins put on at about age twelve. I marveled at nipples, breasts, and bare asses.

We loved the cartoons and read "The Playboy Advisor" although it often required a collective effort to decipher what was being described. It was the blind leading the blind, but I was more blind than the others because, in all of my previous experience, women past puberty had always been wrapped in heavy dark cloth.

I returned home for a summer in the desert, then flew to London, New York, and Kansas City on TWA a month before school started. Mr. Hartwood suggested Penn College because Quakers welcomed international students, even non-Christians, and it was easy to enroll me because he was a generous alumnus. My father believed that the conservative Midwest would have morals like the desert. I arrived early to learn about the city before school started.

The Hartwoods met me at the airport and took me to their home in suburban Leawood, Kansas. Their daughters, Kristen and Carol, smiled and shook my hand, but they were dressed for the hot day and all I could see were breasts in loose, white blouses. Madras shorts were in fashion that summer, and their legs were tan from hours in the sun.

Mr. Hartwood might have been politely ignoring my gawking, but it is more likely that he did not realize how startled I was to talk to half-dressed, sexually mature girls. In the desert, these girls would be women who were kept in wraps except when each was shown to the man who was to become her husband. It was unthinkable to introduce your half-naked daughter to a man, but I was about to experience more. He suggested we take a swim.

I said I did not have a bathing suit, but Mr. Hartwood rummaged in their pool house and found a set of swim trunks that were fortunately several sizes too large. As I came out, Carol and Kristen raced out of the house. For a moment, I thought they were naked, but then I realize they wore two-piece bathing suits. Their suits were much more modest than bikinis several years later—the bottom fully covered each girl's ass, the waist was at her waist, and the top was the same outline as a stock Sears and Roebuck bra—but the bare, living skin was beyond anything I had ever dreamed of seeing.

My body responded, and I jumped into the pool to hide myself. The girls jumped in the other side of the pool and splashed each other before they maneuvered to splash me from two sides. I splashed one way and then the other, but I got more water in my face than they did. Then Carol jumped on my shoulders from behind, pushed my head down, and yelled, "Got you!"

Her wet breasts shaped to my back. Instinctively I reached behind myself and grabbed her ass. To anyone else, it might have looked like part of wrestling as we tumbled down in the water, but I hung on too long for her to think that. As we stood up, she glared at me, while her father stood on the deck and yelled, "That's right, Sayiid! You're getting the hang of it."

Even in the cool water, it took my body some time to relax, but that night I had an even bigger surprise. I was reading a copy of National Geographic when a bell rang. Mrs.

Hartwood opened the front door herself and admitted a boy she called Sam. They talked about his summer job building swimming pools, and then she led him into the living room and introduced us. She explained how my father worked with Mr. Hartwood. Then Carol skipped down the stairs, took Sam's hand, and started for the door.

Mrs. Hartwood caught her daughter's eye, "Twelve o'clock?"

"Yes," Carol replied reluctantly.

Then she and Sam were gone. Mrs. Hartwood stepped to the window and watched them get into his car and drive away.

"They will be married?" I asked.

"Heaven's sake, no. They're way too young. They're just dating. We hope she'll graduate from college before she gets married. I'm not certain she'll even care about Sam then. She'll meet lots of boys in college."

In Bern, Brad had told me about the American custom of dating, but it seemed so improbable that I thought he was making it up. I could not comprehend that such a successful society allowed girls to be alone with many different boys. Each boy would do what he wanted with her. In the desert, a woman meets the man she will marry, and he is the only man who will touch her all of her life. She belongs to this man. Her life is easier because she knows whom she is to love. She cannot initiate a divorce. A man can feel secure because this woman belongs to him.

I thought about this as I lay in bed. The Hartwoods, who were guests in my parents' home, let their daughter drive out for the evening with a man, without a chaperone. They were not dishonored by their daughter's behavior. Like the expanse of green fields I had flown over, I could never convince anyone in the desert that these things were real.

I was still awake when I heard voices through the open window and looked down on the driveway. I could see Carol and Sam in the front seat of his car. They kissed, but when he touched her blouse, she pushed his hand away. The tone of her voice changed, but my English was not practiced enough to distinguish the words. She slid across the seat and waited while he hurried around to open the door for her. I thought she was upset, but at the door to the house, she stood on her toes and gave him a touch of a kiss.

At breakfast the next morning, Mrs. Hartwood asked Carol if she had had a good time at the movies. "Oh, yes." She smiled. "Sam asked me to go to Riverside with him Saturday."

"Riverside?"

"The racetrack in Riverside."

"What did you tell him?"

"Yes, if it's all right with you."

"I don't know. Maybe you should ask your father." Mrs. Hartwood looked at me and added, "Maybe you should ask Sayiid to go with you." And she said to me, "Drag races are something really American."

After lunch, Mr. Hartwood took me to visit TWA headquarters. I shook hands with engineers and senior pilots who smiled because their jobs depended on working with my father. From there we went to the Kansas City Municipal Airport where Mr. Hartwood took me up to the tower and pointed out the operations. Two 707 jets sat on the ramp near the end of the runway. He explained that the planes did not have enough power to get up to take off speed in hot weather on the short runway, but new engines and a longer runway were coming soon.

I listened politely.

That night the Hartwoods took me to an outdoor amphitheater to see the musical *Milk and Honey*. They were so excited to show me their city that they did not consider the personal implications of this story about Jews putting their so-called "promised land" in the middle of an Arab country. It briefly depicted Zionists herding Arabs off their land, but the emphasis was on "Shalom" and other Yiddish phrases that sanitized the violence of the creation of Israel.

The room I slept in shared a bathroom with Carol and Kristen. I listened as they showered and brushed their teeth. Then the light under the door flicked off, and I heard the other door close. I imagined them in transparent gowns like the models in *Playboy*, but they were real women just a door away. I repeated to myself that Americans thought of them as girls, but my body responded to the fact that in the desert they would be married and doing things to make them mothers.

On Saturday night I went to the drag races with Sam and Carol. It was in a poor area near the airport. No one would live there who could afford someplace different, and people hurried through going somewhere else.

The racetrack was a dirt oval with rusted portable bleachers. While Sam stood in line to get tickets, Carol told me it was the first time she had been there. "One of the guys Sam builds pools with races here. We decided to see what it's like."

Sam came back with the tickets and casually took her hand. I watched them many times when I visited the Hartwoods. Then Carol went to college, and I never saw Sam with her again. It was difficult to comprehend that a woman might kiss a man and be touched by him, and then be passed along to another man, and perhaps yet another man.

I was equally amazed that Sam's father was president of a bank. How could a wealthy man allow his son to do common labor building swimming pools even for a summer? In the desert, every job a man has ever done remains part of who he is. If a man has done dirty work, that dirt stays in his skin, and if you must touch him, you always wash your hands afterwards.

The three of us wore white tennis shoes and shorts. Others wore mostly jeans, T-shirts and scuffed old leather shoes. There were some dark-skinned people. Carol told me they were Mexican.

When I went to get a Coke, a Mexican girl stood beside me, and seeing my dark skin, spoke to me in Spanish, "*Es el coche de mi hermano.*"

I looked at her blankly, and when she realized I was not Mexican, she asked where I was from. I decided to continue a story I had fabricated for Brad in Switzerland. "I am a prince visiting friends of my family."

"Wow. A real prince?"

"Of course." And so I met Tina. She curtseyed with a pretend skirt held out from her sides, and we talked before I rejoined Sam and Carol. As we were leaving, I saw her across the parking lot. She whispered something to a girl beside her and pointed to me. She was so gullible I almost laughed.

In September, I moved into a room in the second oldest building at Penn College. The campus was located on a slight rise just off US 71 highway south of Kansas City, the highest place for miles.

I was assigned a roommate from Kansas City, Larry Davis. We had little in common on the first day and even less after that. As a devout Baptist, he was constantly trying to decide if rooming with me was his call to convert a Muslim or a test of his faith. We spoke cordially, but we never developed the mythical friendship that bonds men who meet in college.

Another Arab student, Mohammed or Mo, as I called him, was also a freshman. Our fathers were acquainted, but we had never met. My father had suggested that Mo attend Penn so that we could support each other as we tried to understand America. Like all Arabs in the United States, Mo and I agreed we had come to America—in ascending order of importance—to study, to learn about American life, and to bring back an American wife. An American wife would be exotic; lacking family for support she would be totally compliant in the desert, and our kids would automatically have American passports. There was another Arab, a junior named Fhad, but he was Shiia and I am Sunni. That was sufficient reason to hate each other.

Shortly after classes began, there was a meeting for freshmen to explain campus clubs called "societies." A few days later, the clubs had parties that were open to everyone. After that, the parties required an invitation. I went with Larry to the initial meeting and tagged along to a few of the parties. He was invited to join one of the clubs. I was not, but I didn't see the point of the clubs anyway. That was a natural separation of our ways.

The night Larry went to the second party, Mo and I compared our impressions of Penn and decided our American roommates were part of the experience. Like me, Mo was there to study America rather than to study classes. I told him about swimming with the Hartwoods' daughters. He would have thought that I was lying except girls walked all over the Penn campus in shorts and short-sleeved blouses. Half-naked women were a pleasure of American life.

It rained at the end of September, and girls wore long pants and jackets. Then it cleared, was amazingly warm, and shorts and short-sleeved blouses reappeared.

On Wednesday night, a sophomore put stereo speakers in an open second floor dormitory window. I sat outside and listened. Two girls approached, and some guys spoke to them. The girls put their books on the steps near where I sat, and the couples began to dance, bouncing their bodies in rhythm with the music. Other girls arrived, and more guys came out of the dorm until there were perhaps seventy-five or even one hundred students.

A neighbor complained, so a campus policeman made the student turn down the music. This caused shouting from the students. The officer and the student negotiated a compromise. The music could stay on until 8:30.

When the music stopped, students grumbled, but dispersed. Many couples came inside. The entry hall of the dormitory was a long room with a television and a piano at opposite ends, far enough apart that they could be used at the same time almost without interfering with each other.

A mutt dog we all knew as "Dog" wandered around the entry hall when the door was left ajar. No one ever fed Dog, but it was joked there were fewer rabbits in the bushes since Dog had shown up.

Dog found an old ball under a table and brought it to me. I tossed it aimlessly across the room. Dog brought the ball back. I threw it again. Dog brought it back, but I did not pick it up. Then Dog started sniffing my legs as dogs do and finally he started sniffing between my legs.

I picked up Dog's front paws, and he panted in my face. I balanced both paws on one hand and rubbed his chest with my other hand. Then I scratched my foot on his stomach, near his ribs at first and then toward his cock until he got a hard-on.

"God, Sayiid, that's gross!"

I looked up and saw Larry's pained face.

"What's gross?" I asked.

"What you're doing with that dog," he replied.

"I'm not doing anything with Dog," I retorted.

He looked at my foot. "Oh, yeah?"

"No," I said calmly. I loved frustrating him by not responding to him.

When the American president was assassinated, I tried to understand why students were so upset. The man had been president for less than three years, they had a new president within a few hours, and the dead man was only going to be president for one or maybe five more years at the most.

It was not like the death of the King. When a king dies, it is never certain who will be the next king. It may be peaceful; or there may be fighting, slaughter of opposition leaders, and difficult times to find food and gasoline. There is much more reason to be afraid when a king dies.

I spent Thanksgiving with the Hartwoods. Sam took Carol out on Friday and Saturday night, and I watched when he brought her home. This time she did not push him away when he rubbed her blouse. But she pushed him away when he put his hand on her leg.

I got excited watching them, to use the American term, "make out", in the front seat of his car. I had seen the James Bond movie, *Dr. No*, and understood how to approach a woman with kisses and a firm hand. When Carol came in and I heard her in the bathroom, that excitement was difficult to control.

Two weeks after the New Year, we had final examinations. This was my first experience with exams that I was not guaranteed to pass. In the desert, my tutors assured I would pass. In Switzerland, they needed me to succeed so that other Arabs would send their children. It was a novelty to study, even a little bit. As it was, I could answer most questions from my own experience, or with German, using what I had picked up in Bern. I have a good ear for languages.

In second semester English, we read John Updike's novel, *Rabbit, Run*, about Rabbit Angstrom, a fictional high school basketball star. I have seen the subsequent books about Rabbit, but the graphic sex at the beginning of the series is what I recall. It explained what happened after the cameras faded in a 007 movie.

I memorized every word that Updike wrote, and sex became the focus of my education. It did not cross my mind that if I did these things in the desert, I could be whipped, or even stoned. I did wonder what went through the minds of the girls in the class as they read the same book.

Spring in Missouri is a time of rapid change. Green blades sprout in the middle of last year's dried grass, the beginnings of leaves appear on trees, and a short white flower called a crocus blooms overnight. When the wind comes from the South, the hints of green become a flood of leaves, and girls wear short skirts again.

Mo and I tried to talk to girls at Penn. They were polite, but they quickly remembered a forgotten book or an urgent meeting.

As it became clear we would never find the American wives of our fantasies, we talked about how good it would feel to put our hand under the skirts we saw around us. Of course, we spoke in Arabic so we could smile as we discussed the prospect of fingering the panties of each girl who walked by.

Our embassy staff in Washington said they needed to spend a lot of money to demonstrate Arab wealth and validated their policy by assuring that as Arabs we went through similar amounts of money in the Midwest. The result was my generous allowance from the King's government and enough extra money to buy a car. This opened the world of the Midwest to Mo and me. We drove like madmen on the new interstate highways, and we had new friends because we could drive the seven miles to Kansas where almost every student could legally buy beer with 3.2 percent alcohol—so-called "three-two beer."

One of our new friends, Lane Radnor, persuaded me to drive a group to Fritz's, a bar on the opposite side of the metropolitan area that was popular with Penn students. We drove through a shopping area called the Plaza, past a medical center, and north on Rainbow Boulevard. As Lane directed me, I recognized it as the way Sam had driven to the racetrack.

Fritz's was a dark room with a wooden floor and fifteen or so round tables. Lane went to the counter to get a pitcher of beer but instead he got into a conversation with Fritz. They looked at our table, and Mo and me in particular, before Lane came back.

"Hey, Sayiid," he said in a joking way, "say something in Arab talk for Fritz. He was a little uncertain about you being here until I told him you weren't...well...well that you're an Arab."

I smiled at Lane. Then I called out in my best Arabic at the top of my voice as I improvised something that could be loosely translated as:

In the name of God the Compassionate,
Who made the Arabs to enjoy the best olives,
And who made all the white skinned people,
with leftovers,
From the place where camels stay, for days at a time.

Mo could hardly keep from laughing. Everyone in the bar

waited to see what would happen. Then Fritz put a pitcher of beer on our table. "On the house," he said. "I was in the desert during the war (it was always mysterious whose side Fritz had been on), and we heard guys chanting like that from all those little towers. Just didn't expect one of you here."

Fritz turned to a table at the back, "Hey, Al. This is one of the guys who'll be selling you oil when Oklahoma runs out."

The trip to Fritz's showed me how easily I could drive to Riverside, so on Saturday night, Mo and I went to the drag races. We blended in, and no one questioned us when we ordered beer at the concession stand.

"How's your highness?" I heard behind me. It was Tina.

"Pretty well," I smiled. "This is my friend Mo. He's trained in judo. He protects me. Say, 'Hi', Mo."

"Hi," he played along.

We talked, and I started walking along the fence. Tina walked with me, and as we got away from Mo and the crowd, I rested my hand on her shorts under the loose tail of her T-shirt and squeezed the bare skin at her waist. I rubbed her sweat, and she snuggled toward me. "Tell me about the desert," she said.

"It is hotter than Kansas City, but very dry. Your perspiration dries to salt before you feel wet, and your skin tastes salty." I told her I would be back the next week, and she should bring a friend to keep Mo company.

"You really pulled it off with the girl," Mo said, when we were driving back that night.

"Leave it to me," I said.

Saturday night, Tina brought a friend, Mori. We watched the races, but it cooled after the sun went down, and we drifted back to my car. Mori suggested we get hot chocolate.

I gave Mo a twenty-dollar bill and asked him to let us know when the last race was coming up. Mo took the hint and said to Mori, "Let's get something to eat."

As they walked away, Tina rubbed her shoulders, and I suggested it would be warmer in my car. She agreed. I opened the back door and touched her butt as she got in. She wiggled, but did not push me away.

It would be difficult to convey my pleasure of exploration that night. Every moment was a surprise. She kissed me and pushed her tongue between my lips. I slid one hand under her blouse and rubbed her breast. Then I touched her leg like Sam had done to Carol. Tina threaded her fingers in my hair, but she did not push my hand away. By the time I realized she set no limits, Mo rocked the car.

The next weekend it rained, and the track was too muddy to race. But a week later, it was clear again. I persuaded Mo not to come along. He extracted some trivial compensation in the bargain.

I met Tina in the parking lot. We kissed in the back of my car, but the cooler weather made the windows fog up, and a guard shone his light in.

"I've got an idea," Tina said. "Let's go." She directed me along the river to a two-lane road that ran parallel to the runway of the Kansas City Airport, but on the side away from the terminal. "It's up here," she pointed, "on the left."

We parked in a lot by the airport fence. Several other cars had windows in various states of being fogged. She slid toward me and helped me unbutton her blouse. I kissed her neck, but I had other parts of Updike's writing in mind.

I rubbed her leg, and she kissed me more as I unzipped her jeans and rubbed her stomach through her panties. I slid my hand down and rubbed the cloth between her legs. As I did, she touched my crotch. I did not expect a girl would touch a boy, and I gasped. "Did I hurt you?" she asked.

"Oh, no," I replied as I wrapped my fingers over the top of her panties and reached deep, down into her hair.

She put her fingers on my head to balance her kiss on my mouth. Then she looped her fingers over her waistband and said, "Let me help," as she slid her panties and jeans down.

I burned as I undid my belt and my trousers. Her jeans held her knees, but she pushed them down to her ankles and so she could spread her legs. I was so excited, I came almost as soon as the tip of my penis touched her, but I learned what Updike had been writing about.

On the way back, I answered her questions about the desert.

"That was my first time with a man," she said.

"There wasn't any blood," I replied. At least I knew that.

She gave me a story about falling when she was ten years old, and then she said I would like her mother when I met her. I felt a chill, but as I left her off, I told her I would be back next week.

When we met the next week, she asked me if I had a rubber. I did not know what that was, and when she explained, I did not like the idea.

"Maybe we should just kiss tonight," she said.

"You said you loved me." I had ached for this all week.

"I know, but..."

I was thinking. "All right. Let's sit in the back and kiss at least."

"I guess that'd be okay..."

We slid over to the back seat. I kissed her. Then I reached under her skirt, and she enjoyed my fingers between her legs. Gradually, I wrapped my finger over her panties to pull them down. She hesitated for a moment, and then said like she was deciding, "A little would be okay. Wouldn't it?"

I had already slipped my shoes off, and it was easy to slide my trousers off. She did not object, but when I faced her and pushed her legs apart, she said, "That's more than a little. Let's wait 'til you get a rubber."

"How can I believe you love me if you push me away?" I pushed two fingers through her hair, and she made a sound. Then I pushed into her, and we began to move, awkwardly, but enough that I got very hard and finally came. And I learned that no matter what a girl says, you just keep trying.

There was a flash of light as the car beside us backed out and turned before it drove away. For a moment I thought I could see the shadow of a girl adjusting her blouse in that car, too.

I was a prince. I had seduced a girl who was a virgin, or claimed to be. But that detail didn't matter. I wasn't going to see her again anyway. We had finals in two weeks. After finals, I went home.

My father guessed from my comments that my prayers had lapsed. He discussed this with Mr. Hartwood and decided to rent an apartment near campus where Mo and I could pray in our own space.

A distant cousin Wahiib would share this space with us in the fall. I was related to Wahiib by marriage, but he was a cousin by blood to the King, close enough that he could talk to the King if he wished. There was also another guy from the desert named Ali.

My father had told Wahiib and Ali's fathers that Penn was a good place and encouraged them to send their sons, as well. He assumed we would maintain our own customs better if we prayed in a kind of Arab unity.

Wahiib was to room with me, and Ali would room with Mo. Mo and I would be the older brothers who already knew their way around. I liked this plan because if I introduced

Wahiib to America, he would see me as a source of knowledge and it would create a sense of authority in our relationship that would be useful to further my career.

My father was right that I liked American ways, but I could already see that if I immigrated to America, I would be an outsider. If I were a diplomat, however, I would be an honored guest. That was an easy decision.

In October, Lane took us to a horse show called the American Royal, a tradition left over from when the city had been a major place for slaughter of cattle. The Royal was held in a part of downtown Kansas City with rows of empty wooden cattle pens. I asked Lane what the area was called. "The West Bottoms," he replied.

"Like a girl's ass?" I asked.

"Huh?" he looked puzzled.

"A bunch of cattle pens and a girl's ass. *Bottoms.* You call them the same thing." I was almost laughing in his face, but he was so used to the words that he was slow to see the joke.

Once a year, thousands of people had a parade, went to the Bottoms, and spent a week showing horses in an old wooden building with a dirt floor. The air was punctuated in places with the smell of fresh animal shit, but beneath that was the smell of old cattle shit that had become less pungent and more part of the dirt and the wood. The place had the feeling that when everyone went home, it would still smell like this earthy mixture of traces of animals and dried hay and the work of bacteria breaking it all down very slowly.

My favorite event was calf roping. Local folks explained the rules to me. A man waits on his horse. A calf is released and the man chases the calf on his horse while trying to throw a rope around its neck. When the rope is around the calf's neck, he pulls it tight. Then the man jumps off his horse, runs over to the calf, and throws it off balance. Once the calf falls on its side, and before it can recover and stand up again, the man gets on top of the calf's legs and holds them until he has tied three legs together with three throws of a rope. The man shows he is done by holding his hands in the air.

A good man does this in thirty seconds. A champion does it in about ten seconds. Sometimes the rope snaps the calf's neck, but that just adds an element of chance. I could have watched calf roping for hours.

We were by the animal pens when Mo pulled my shirt and pointed across the barn. "Isn't that the girl from the races?" he said.

He was right. Tina was talking with an older guy and pointing at me. I did not want to see her, but it seemed wiser to stand and smile.

The older guy walked over with her. "This is my brother, Manuel," she said. He did not say anything. "This is Sayiid."

I held my hand out. Manuel thought for a moment and then took my hand. But he did not shake my hand; he gripped it.

"How'd you know my sister?" he asked.

"I've talked to her at Riverside, at the races," I replied.

He continued to look at me. "Where do you go to school?"

"What do you mean?"

"Your high school. What school you go to?"

I realized then that Tina was younger than I thought. In the desert, this would be no problem, but high school girls in America were not expected to get married or even be, what was their word, "involved." "I graduated," I invented. "I went to high school in St. Louis."

"What you doin' messing with my sister?"

"We just talked."

He gripped my hand, tight enough to hold me and cause discomfort, but not tight enough to injure me. I looked into his eyes, and I guessed he was wondering how well I knew his sister. Then he released my hand, turned Tina away with an arm on her shoulder and walked away. She tried to look back, but he did not let her look back enough for me to see her face.

Neither Wahiib nor Ali had ever seen a girl who was old enough to have her monthly flow who was not also wrapped head to toe in black, and their responses were very different. Ali observed girls' bodies he had only dreamed of, and he wanted to experience what had been placed in front of him. Wahiib, also watched, but he was cautious as he made decisions. Their different approaches to America played out clearly in October on my twenty-first birthday.

The apartment was listed as furnished, which meant an old bed, a worn sofa and carpet, and a built-in table and benches in the kitchen. Friday night, after prayers, I gathered everyone with a flourish, opened the refrigerator and produced a six-pack of Coke and some of the sour cream dip Americans liked. Grabbing potato chips I had stashed in the high cabinet over the stove, I said, "Hey, let's eat."

Mo and Ali opened the chips, and I passed Cokes. Wahiib was quiet. "What's up, Wahiib?" I asked him

"I don't know. Should we be having snacks here?" He looked across the room at the prayer rugs we had folded away.

"Because we prayed here?" I asked him.

"Yes."

"So what? My father prays at home before we eat."

"But we are in this place to pray," he insisted.

"We're here so we can be good Arabs in the land of infidels. Nothing more!" I levered the church key into the top of a Coke can and tried to hand it to him. He would not take it, so I handed it to Ali and opened another for Mo.

"It's okay," added Mo. "I agree with Sayiid."

Ali took a gulp of Coke and held up his can in assent.

Wahiib accepted the second can I offered, took a tentative sip, and then held the can and watched us devour the chips and sour cream dip.

In November, I again had Thanksgiving with the Hartwoods. While Mrs. Hartwood and their girls were serving pie and ice cream, Mr. Hartwood asked me if my apartment was satisfactory.

"Yes, it is a good place."

"You've met other students, haven't you?" Mr. Hartwood assumed that everyone made lifelong friends in college.

"I've met some guys in class," I replied.

"Hmmm. That all? I'll have to look into that," he said.

I led our group on expeditions around the city. We sampled Mexican food on Southwest Trafficway, Italian food at Jasper's in Waldo, and hamburgers at various drive-ins. Owners were uncertain how to respond to us. Sometimes they took us for Negroes and were abrasive. Sometimes they thought we were Mexican and, at Mexican restaurants at least, gave us better service. We talked among ourselves in Arabic, and the sound of Arabic was so unfamiliar that it marked us as foreigners rather than immigrants.

One evening we stopped at the M and M Bakery, a delicatessen at the corner of 31st and Prospect run by two old Jews. They were short and stocky, and she had a blue number tattooed on the inside of her forearm. We had been there before. They were polite, but never friendly.

As we talked in Arabic about what cookies we wanted, a guy about our age started talking to us in Arabic, too. I was suspicious at first but soon learned that Khalid, that was his name, lived in Kansas City and that his father was an engineer at the Ford plant. He also introduced us to his brother, Masoud, who was waiting outside in their car. "I never leave my car alone around here. Too much temptation for the neighborhood boys," he warned.

Khalid and Masoud lived in the southeast part of the city because their father said it had the best high school. Their father had emigrated from Mindanao. He had been educated in Turkey. Their mother was from Syria, and she had returned to Syria to care for her parents when their father had brought his sons to his new job in the United States. The Ford Company expected a Filipino and did not know what to do with an Arab.

Khalid talked about the Negro students at Southeast High School, and how he and Masoud had found friends among the darker students who showed them the bars and music in the middle of the city. Technically it was in the middle on the east side of the city, but no one had thought to call it the "Middle East"—yet.

Mousad and Kahlid introduced me to the Horseshoe Bar on Troost where Milt Abel played string bass and Bettye Miller played the piano and sang. I enjoyed the blues, the dark room, and the fact that even though I was the only one who was twenty-one years old, they let me buy drinks for all of us.

After the near miss with Tina's brother, I was not as daring in approaching girls. Masoud and I talked about this as we listened to jazz.

"It's kind of a shit place that way." He summarized his experiences in the Midwest over the last eight years: "The white girls think you're too dark, and most of them won't even talk to you. Well, sometimes an Italian girl will at least talk to you. The colored girls are more friendly, but my dad goes nuts if he thinks I have even looked at one."

Impulsively, I asked if he had ever dated a Black girl.

He grinned as though I had caught him with his pants down. "I kissed one once." He seemed to enjoy the opportunity to think about a person he had driven from his mind long ago. "I had a class with her my junior year. We came to this dance with friends, but we ended up dancing together. I kissed her just a bit in a slow dance, then the lights came on. My dad was waiting to pick me up, and he saw me with her. Praise God, he did not see me kiss her. All the way home he ranted that he would never see me with her or anyone like her ever again."

I listened sympathetically, but I wondered why he had not set his sights on a white American girl. They could not all be that snooty.

I brought pizza to our apartment most Friday nights. Near the end of the year, I brought some beer, too. Wahiib insisted it was against Islam to drink any alcohol. I argued it was our obligation to learn about the infidels. He worried that someone at home would find out, but I said it was like the women with the men when the Hartwoods visited my parents. It was what was necessary to complete our education.

"We are future leaders. We need to understand Americans and Europeans. They drink, so we need to understand drinking. What is it that my wonderful roommate used to say?" I pretended to be thinking. "Oh, I know. Larry would get on his Baptist righteousness kick and say it was like a priest talking about sex. Can you imagine a man telling a man or woman about sex if he hadn't had sex himself? Do you want me to tell you about sex, Wahiib?"

Eventually, Wahiib stopped arguing against alcohol use. It was harder to lead Wahiib than Ali or Mo, but I was beginning to mold him, too. He had less experience in the world, and he had an intense sense of loyalty. I cultivated his trust and assumed I could count on his support in the future.

After that, I always stocked beer in our prayer apartment. Ali and Mo joined me. "Come on, Wahiib," we'd say. "You've never even tasted a beer. It's good."

When we had ridiculed him enough, Wahiib would hold a can, though I doubt he ever drank more than a little. The key was getting him to take a sip at all. After the first sip, he was quiet and went along.

Mr. Hartwood's secretary called in January to invite me to lunch with Mr. Hartwood and Dr. Forger, President of Penn College. I had forgotten our conversation at Thanksgiving, and Mr. Hartwood's idea that I needed to develop college friendships.

The following Thursday at the faculty club, I was seated between President Forger and his big donor, Everett Hartwood. The fourth person at our table was Fhad, the Shiite Arab. My relationship to Fhad was like Protestants and Papal Catholics in the European wars. I was not very religious, but he was a dangerous heretic anyway.

"Everett tells me that you haven't met many other students," began President Forger.

"I have met a few here," I replied. "I have gone up to Kansas City and I have a friend from high school who goes to the University of Missouri."

"We'll have to fix that," Dr. Forger continued, "It won't do to be strangers among Friends. That's why I asked you here." He gestured to Fahd. "Fhad and I have been planning a Penn College Organization of Arabian Students."

"When I told Paul about you," Mr. Hartwood cut in, "he told me about this new group he was already working on."

"We're planning an open meeting in April with some announcements and gatherings," continued Dr. Forger. "Fhad is the chairman. From what Everett tells me, you'll be a valuable addition."

Fhad joined in, "I'd like to have Sayiid help. It would be

good for Arab unity." He turned to me, "You can help plan the evening seminar."

I smiled.

At the end of April, the student convocation at Penn was a program about the relationship between the Middle East and the United States. President Forger moderated the discussion. Mr. Hartwood spoke about his business experiences, Mrs. Hartwood tried to make the desert sound tolerable for women, and a sociology professor, Dr. Bauer, who had been instrumental in persuading President Forger to encourage Arabs to come to Penn said, "We're proud that Penn is one of only six American colleges and universities to offer an Arabian Student program."

In the weeks after the convocation, some men who ignored me before would nod and say a few words, but the girls were evasive as they had always been. The exception was a girl in geology class.

After the convocation with Dr. Forger, the student newspaper, *Penn Life*, ran an editorial, "Arabs Plan Friendship." The girl was reading the editorial when I came into the lecture hall. I sat one seat away, not to be too close, and commented, "We hope our new organization works well."

I'm certain she was aware of me sitting down, but she acted surprised as she turned toward me, "Yes, it sounds exciting."

When she looked at me, I saw her amazingly blue eyes and just stared for a moment. She turned away quickly. The professor shuffled his papers and class began.

# II. American Dreams

My earliest memory is of a candle lighting up a dark place. It was one of those scary nights when everyone in Northwest Nebraska ran down to their cellar to hide from tornados. I was probably crying. My grandmother smiled and touched my face with a corner of her apron and told me I had beautiful eyes. "They're like a sunny sky," she said, "so blue.

Then she leaned back and looked at me before she added, "Your eyes make everyone feel better. When you're scared, let everyone see your smile."

Grandmother was like that. She could find a bright spot in every situation. She taught me to find something good wherever I was, and made me believe I could do special things because I was special.

I was born in Valentine, Nebraska, the county seat of Cherry County. Only 10,000 people live in Cherry County now, and in 1950 it was smaller. There's a red heart painted on the pavement at the intersection of Main Street and Highway 20. When I was a little girl, I thought Valentine's

Day was created to celebrate us.

Mom and Dad were born there, but Dad's family moved to Missouri during the Depression. They had met, but Mom and Dad didn't know each other well until they ended up in Kansas City during the war. Dad was in the Navy, but he spent the war recruiting at Olathe Naval Air Station. Mom came to the city to work at the Bendix plant. They drifted together because they were the only people they knew who understood Nebraska, and, after bad experiences with a couple of guys, Dad was the only guy Mom felt safe with. After the war, they got married and moved back to Valentine. I came along in 1946.

The first time I was sure I was growing up was when Mom let me walk to my grandparents' house by myself. I felt I'd joined the adults—who greatly out numbered kids—as they would until the post war baby boom took off. I was safe because everyone knew everyone else and, before they widened the highway, people drove slow in town.

On Saturdays, after I emptied the wastebaskets, I'd go over and watch my grandfather. He'd worked on the railroad and then on a ranch, but now he did projects around the house. I don't remember anything he ever finished, but he always treated me special, like the times we'd go to the café to get ice cream. He never asked if I wanted ice cream. He simply said he was going and asked me to come along.

Once he got his ice cream—which was always chocolate, my favorite—he'd let me sit on his knee and take what he called "sample tastes." Sometimes he tickled me and I laughed real hard, but I knew he wouldn't let me fall because he held my lap real tight. Walking home he'd remind me, "Don't tell your mom. She'd want to come along, and it's more fun by ourselves." I kept the secret because if Mom knew how hard I laughed, she'd figure out about the ice cream and not let me go again.

Valentine was only two hours to Pine Ridge Indian Reservation, but not many Sioux came to town. One Saturday, while we were eating ice cream, a Lakota man and girl came into the café and sat at a table. The girl was about my age, but I'd never seen her before.

The waitress looked at them and went back to the kitchen. A few minutes later, the owner came out wiping his hands on a towel and told the Indian to leave. When Granddaddy saw this, he went up to the owner and said, "Hey, Jim. Can I have a word with you?"

They stepped over by the counter and watched the Indian as they talked. Then the owner walked back to the kitchen, still wiping his hands on his towel. Few minutes later, the waitress set two double-scoop bowls of ice cream on the Lakotas' table. "It's from him," she said, jerking her head our way.

The Lakota man smiled at Granddaddy. Granddaddy nodded in reply, and as we left, he stopped by their table. He didn't say "Hi" or anything. It was like they'd been talking the whole time, and he just said the next thing that came to his mind. "Your girl likes the ice cream?"

"I believe she does. Say 'thank you,' Claire."

"Thank you," Claire said between bites.

It was then I noticed the man's hand was curled up funny, so he couldn't open his fingers. When we were outside, I asked Granddaddy about this and he explained, "Mr. Littlepeak used to be a gandy dancer, the guys who level the tracks. Until he hurt his hand helping me in the accident."

The accident was legendary in our family. Granddaddy was riding a steam engine when it derailed. He got caught, and a cracked pipe was blowing steam right on his leg. A gandy dancer had run up and pushed the steam pipe away with his bare hand.

The one time I'd ridden a train, I'd been mesmerized to look down through the toilet and watch the ties fly by underneath. Young as I was, I knew nobody wanted to be a gandy dancer fixing tracks because they worked around everyone's poop on the track.

I don't think Claire and her father ever went back to the café. They were all right if Granddaddy was there, but everyone else thought they should stay up at Pine Ridge. It bothered me how unfair that was, especially after how Mr. Littlepeak had helped Granddaddy, so I made it a point to talk to Claire the few times I saw her in town.

She always called her father, "wa-WO-ki-a." "Is that the Indian word for 'father'?" I asked her.

"No," she said. "It's what my grandmother calls him. It means, 'A man who keeps going when a wise man would quit.'"

I was excited to start school because I wanted to read stories by myself. Only three kids my age lived in town, but three other first-grade boys rode in from ranches on the bus. That meant six first-graders shared one teacher with the five second-graders and three third-graders.

I met Harold Wilson the first day of school. Right away Harold became Harry. Harry pulled my ponytail more than once, but I kept quiet because my best friend, Jamie, told me if a boy pulled a girl's hair, it meant he liked her. One time he caught me off guard, and I let out a yelp. Then I felt sorry for Harry because our teacher turned fast enough to see him, and he got sent to the principal's office.

Harry lived ten miles out of town, but his dad came in a lot. The next summer, he led all six of us to the big rock north of the bridge. "Going to jump off?" he dared us. "Watch."

He jumped, but the water wasn't as deep as he thought, and he hit the bottom pretty hard. When he stood up, there was mud all over his shorts. "Ha!" I pointed and laughed, but I shut up when he glared at me.

Mom usually put me to bed as soon as it was dark. I'd lie awake and listen to the sounds of the night. Occasionally there'd be a truck on the highway, but mostly it was crickets until it got cold.

One night, I heard her talking loud, almost yelling, "You are, too."

Then Dad got louder. "So what? A man's got a right..."

I couldn't make out any more, but I knew something wasn't right. In the morning, there was a blanket across the sofa like I'd leave after a nap, and Mother and Daddy weren't talking. I figured they needed some sunshine, so I did like Grandmother said and smiled with my eyes open wide.

When I was six years old, I was the flower girl in the wedding of the daughter of a rancher. They hired a hairdresser up from Kansas City, and I had my hair washed and set like the bride and all the bridesmaids. Right before I walked down the aisle, the bride's mother put a gold chain with a small pearl around my neck. After the wedding, the receiving line, the dinner and the dancing, the bride found me and told me, "You were perfect."

"Here," I said and started to give the pearl back.

"Oh, no. You keep that." She touched the pearl. "That's for you."

That day is my benchmark for feeling good about myself. When I was a teenager and guys looked at me, I'd feel awkward. I wasn't trying to look sexy, only to be perfect like the flower girl who'd done everything right.

That fall, Daddy drove us to Kansas City for a horse show. We left Friday right after he got off work and drove straight through until the middle of the night. We stayed with friends of his named Hartwood, and I remember them standing in their bathrobes as Dad carried me into their house and put me to bed. The next morning, Mom slept late while Dad and I went downtown early to get a good spot to watch the parade. There were more horses than I'd ever seen, and one band after another. I wanted to be a majorette who twirled a baton in front of the band, and when a huckster came along selling toy wooden batons, I asked Dad, "Can I have one?"

"Sure," he said and lifted me up to pick one out before he even asked, "How much?"

When we got back to the Hartwoods', I was happy marching up and down in front of their house with my baton, but when I came inside my mom glared at the baton and asked, "How much did he spend on that?"

I knew I'd made her be upset at Daddy, so after lunch, when no one could see me, I hid the baton under a bush. Sunday afternoon as we packed the car to drive home, I acted disappointed like I couldn't find it.

After school let out for the summer, Mom and Dad told me we were moving to Kansas City because Daddy had a new job at Bendix. I didn't want to leave Grandmother and Granddaddy, but Mom reminded me of how fun the parade had been. That puzzled me because I knew the baton had upset her.

Daddy left in July to find an apartment. We talked to him every Saturday night. The operator would call to be sure we were home, and then she'd say, "Just a minute, please," before she called Daddy back on his end. Mom always talked first. Then it was my turn.

"I miss you," I'd say.

He always said, "I love you," and "It's great. You'll love it here."

In August, just before school started, we moved into an apartment on 39th Street. I was homesick at first, but it was exciting to explore the neighborhood with Mom while Dad was at work. There was a hamburger shop two blocks away. Mom said the place was filthy, but Dad took us there to get an ice cream float with homemade root beer in a frosty mug. Dad also said one of the stores was where President Truman had tried to sell men's hats. And there was Katz's.

We talk about superstores today, but Katz's beat everyone by thirty years. On three floors, you could buy refrigerators, toys, clothes, cameras, and tools. At the soda fountain, a Coke was either five- or ten-cent size, and for a nickel more, they'd make it a cherry Coke. There was even a pet shop. A parrot by the steps to the basement always whistled at Mom and said, "Nice gams." Mom had nice legs.

A couple blocks farther was Kelly's, a bar where Daddy stopped sometimes after work. Mom muttered about his drinking, but she still got pregnant with Freddy—which taught me a lesson she probably hadn't intended. As an adult, I've wondered if she loved Daddy, or if she was afraid to tell him, "No!" when he came home from Kelly's. But at the time, I was a little girl who was excited to have a baby brother, until I saw what he did to my life.

Freddy was demanding and made everything harder. It was all I could do to be perfect to keep Mom and Dad happy, while Freddy ran around and did things like a boy and gave them stuff to argue about. He didn't understand how hard it was to take care of Mom and Dad, and I resented how he did whatever he wanted.

I wanted to make friends in my new school, but I never saw the other kids after class let out. So I talked to the boys and girls whenever I could. Then I remember I got anxious when I went to school and worried I wasn't doing things right.

When we cleaned out my parents' house, I discovered my report cards had bad marks for talking in class. Mom had written a note at the bottom of one report card, "I will make certain my daughter is quiet in class," and signed it in her perfect penmanship. I have no recollection of anything about that.

Our first Thanksgiving in Kansas City, we had dinner with the Hartwoods. Daddy and Mr. Hartwood had gone to the same Quaker meeting, and they both graduated from Westport High School just as the war started in Europe. Mr. Hartwood was a sophomore at Penn College when the Japanese bombed Pearl Harbor. He finished the semester and volunteered to be a pilot in the Army Air Corps. He was injured during one flight, and Dad said it was a miracle that he'd been able to fly his plane back. The copilot bled to death, and Mr. Hartwood landed the plane even though he couldn't use one leg.

After the War, Mr. Hartwood went back to Penn, finished college, and started working at TWA. Dad told me he was good at his job because he knew from experience what the pilots meant when they described problems.

The Hartwoods' older girl, Carol, wasn't even in school yet, but I wished I had as many toys as she did. Kristen, their younger daughter was in diapers, and I don't remember her much from that visit.

On the way home from the Hartwoods', Daddy told Mom and me he had a surprise. "Close your eyes. Keep them closed a minute longer. " I had the sense that he was braking down a hill and then he stopped. "Okay. Open your eyes."

There was this beautiful area with hundreds of colored lights, not just around doors like I'd seen in Valentine but lights on every tree, around every door and window, and up and over every building.

"This is the Plaza," he explained. "They do this every Christmas."

I pressed my nose on the window. "They're so pretty," I whispered, and worried it was a dream that'd vanish if I blinked.

That Thanksgiving the Hartwoods lived a couple blocks south of the Plaza, but they soon moved to a town in Kansas called Prairie Village. That didn't leave Daddy and Mr. Hartwood much in common, but the Athletics baseball team moved to Kansas City, so in the summer they went to the games and it gave them something to do for an afternoon. A couple of years later, the Hartwoods moved to Leawood, and that marked a separation. Thanksgiving stayed a tradition, but I never saw them other times until I was older and started babysitting.

We moved, too, to a small house by the Plaza. That's when the difference from Valentine became really clear. Kansas City was bigger, of course, but life had still been a bit like home. We shopped nearby at Katz's on Main Street and the A&P on Westport Road, took the streetcar downtown to buy clothes, and the Plaza was a fairyland we visited every Christmas. Living near the Plaza, I began to dream about a world of nicer things than I'd ever even heard of in Valentine.

Everything was on the Plaza. There were two five-and-ten stores—Woolworth's and Kresge's—Kroger's and Wolferman's, grocery stores, and Sears. Emery, Bird, Thayer sold really nice clothes. Mom and I walked through sometimes, but it was way too expensive to buy anything. Harzfeld's and Jack Henry's were so expensive we never went in.

In sixth grade, I bought my dad a tie at Jack Henry's with money I'd made babysitting and mowing lawns. In high school, I wanted a drawstring purse from Harzfeld's to be like the other girls. I went in by myself having no idea how expensive it would be. Once I'd brought the purse to the register to ask the price, I was too embarrassed to put it back and I spent all the money I'd saved for months.

Sometimes for a treat, Mom skipped making dinner and we'd go to Winstead's, a drive-in restaurant just across the Plaza. The first time we went, I started to get out of the car as soon as we parked. Dad had to explain how the carhop would take our order and bring the food. He'd been there before, and he ordered me a Special Shake. That was like having a glass full of chocolate ice cream all to myself.

When we finished, Dad flashed the lights, and the carhop came back. As she lifted the tray of the window, he said, "Oops, I forgot," and reached into his pocket, smiled, and gave her two quarters. I felt safe because Dad knew the right thing to do. Mom didn't say much.

After we moved, I went to a new school, Swenney Elementary, west of the Plaza. Mom taught me how to walk down our hill, across Roanoke Boulevard and up to school. As we crossed Roanoke, I saw a group of women in tan skirts and jackets carrying small suitcases and asked my mother who they were. "They're stewardesses for Mr. Hartwood's airline. They fly in the planes and help the passengers."

"Where do they go?" I asked.

"All over the world, I think."

It was romantic how they flew away on planes. I dreamed I'd see the world some day, but I didn't know how. Even today, most people in Kansas City think of the world like I thought of my world around the Plaza. I knew where everything was, and I felt safe that way.

The first day I walked home from school by myself, I saw a girl about my age going the same way on the other side of the street. She crossed Roanoke where I did and then went up my hill and turned on my street. At the last corner, she crossed to my side.

"Hi," she said.

"You going home?" I asked her.

She pointed to the first house on my block. "That's my house."

I pointed down the street. "That's my house," I said. "We just moved in. My mom likes to walk down here."

"My mom works downtown."

"Oh," I said and kind of looked away as I asked, "What's your name?"

"Dianne." And just like that, we became friends.

That was the watershed, when I stopped feeling lonely for Valentine. I had a person I could play with, and we played together almost every day. We'd walk to the store at my end of the block and spend half an hour selecting one candy bar apiece. She had an allowance. I had money from chores.

One Friday, neither of us had enough to buy anything, but we went to the store and looked anyway. As we stared at Milky Way and Hershey bars, I discovered two pennies in my pocket and tapped Dianne's shoulder, "Look what I found."

"What can you get for two cents?" she complained.

I scanned the shelves until I saw the Fleer's box. "Bubble gum."

"One piece," she corrected me.

"We can split it," I said.

I bought one piece and twisted it in two, but then there wasn't enough for either of us to blow a bubble. "Here," she said, "You take my piece."

Immediately I wished I'd given her my half first, so I said, "No, you take it."

"That's okay. I don't want it anyway."

"I know. We can share." So I chewed hard and blew a big bubble and shook Dianne's shoulder for her to look before it burst. Then it was her turn, and I handed her the gum. After that, we took turns as we walked down the block until I saw Mom watching us out the window. I swallowed the gum, but Mom was already coming out. "What're you doing?" she asked.

"Nothing," I replied.

Dianne backed me up: "Nothing."

"I see," Mom said. "Dianne, why don't you go on home? We're about to get ready for dinner."

Dianne and I exchanged glances as she left me and I went inside.

"Did you put Dianne's gum in your mouth?" Mom asked.

"No," I said—because it was my gum—but that was a mistake because Mom knew what she'd seen, and she thought I was lying to her.

She dragged my arm to the kitchen. "I'll have to teach you not to lie to your mother," she said as she got a spoonful of mustard powder from a bright yellow can in the cupboard. "Open your mouth!"

I kept my lips shut, but I was too afraid to run.

She was angry. "Open your mouth." I was scared, and slowly I opened my mouth a crack. "Wider," she ordered.

I obeyed, and she put the whole spoonful in my mouth. Instantly, I looked at the sink. "Don't you dare spit that out!" she ordered.

Tears ran down my cheeks. My feet were still, but my whole body writhed. Finally I couldn't control myself, and I slobbered and ran to the bathroom. I coughed and spit and washed my mouth with water.

"You should be ashamed of lying to your mother," she called after me.

I was ashamed. Because in all the jumping around, I'd wet my pants.

Dianne moved south to 51st Street in the fifth grade. It wasn't far, but she changed to Bryant School. Mom walked me to her house once a month, but that was all I saw her until I learned to drive.

That was the year my dad got his first Cadillac. He put on a suit, propped his foot on the bumper, and lit up a cigar to look serious in a picture he sent home to his parents. Mom barely smiled in the other snapshot they sent back to Valentine. She was a killjoy about anything that involved money. Not only was she not excited about Daddy's car, she didn't give me an allowance, and she was tight with food. She watched her weight and expected me to do that, too. Most days she only fed me an egg and a slice of toast before school leaving me hungry and fidgeting in my seat long before lunch. I knew there were kids somewhere who had less than me, and I never asked for more.

My dad talked to everybody, which is how he heard that the YMCA gave swimming lessons at Southwest High School. He signed me up, and I easily earned every swimming badge—Minnow, Fish, Flying Fish, and Shark.

The next summer, he sent me to a swim camp at the Y. The last day was a program for parents, and on the way home, Dad complimented me, "You were great. I mean it. Your instructor said you should try out for the swim team at the Y downtown."

I was excited. We swam a few races in the class, but I didn't think I was good enough for a team.

Dad took me downtown to practice every Wednesday and Saturday for years. After I knew the place to go, he'd just drop me off at the door. I suspect he went to a bar over on 12th Street while he waited, but at the time I felt grown up and I loved how happy my swimming made him, even though the water was freezing and the cement floor felt grimy.

In seventh grade we had what the older girls called "The Movie." The girls went to one room with my teacher, Mrs. Howard. The boys went with the principal, Mr. Hale. The school nurse explained she was going to show us a movie about girls and boys. I'd seen enough of cows and dogs in Valentine to be really curious. One girl in the back row whispered, "and dogs and cats, and sheep and goats…"

The movie had animated drawings of breasts growing and girls getting their hair. Eggs left the ovaries and little squiggly sperm came up to the eggs. The movie showed a boy's penis between his legs. I had changed Freddy's diaper, so I already knew he wasn't like me.

The nurse asked for questions, but no one spoke until the smartest girl in the class asked, "How does the sperm get from the boy to the girl? Through the air?"

The nurse, straight backed, with her hands held at her waist, said, "It goes out through the penis and into the uterus by a process called human intercourse." No one dared ask for more details, but there were a few coughs.

On the way home, I went out of my way to walk through the Plaza and look at a statue of a boy cherub with water squirting from—as we'd been taught—his penis. I wondered how sperm got anywhere out of that little thing.

As an adult when I recall this today, I smile that in the 50s this was considered the appropriate level of information for 12-year-olds. I signed permission for my girls to have much more thorough sex education in the third grade because I believed real facts were better than the "facts" older girls were spreading. But I hoped the adult side of the "facts of life" was still beyond my daughters' grasp.

After Dianne moved away, I played with the girl down the street who went to Visitation Catholic School. She'd heard from her sister, who was in high school, "a guy has to touch your breasts before he can do anything to you. That's why you keep your bra on all the time."

I was gathering information. Like the other girls, I was interested in boys. We all wanted to know—we just didn't know *what* we wanted to know.

Mom wanted me to be confirmed in her Lutheran church. I don't think Dad agreed, but he approved of church and didn't stop her when she took me to the classes.

For confirmation itself, I wore a new white dress with a white robe and a white cap. As I repeated the Apostles' Creed, "I believe in God the Father almighty, maker of heaven and earth…" I was confident I'd do well with the added assignment to be very good to keep God happy. God was a large man who ran a house, gave directions to everyone else, drove a Cadillac, smoked cigars, and went out with his friends. It was important to act good to make "God the Father" happy, because if he got angry, there'd be hell to pay.

Sometimes Mom and Dad went to parties with Dad's work friends, but they never seemed happy when they got home. One time I heard them in loud whispers after they thought I was asleep.

"I'm not going to any of these things again," Mom said.

"I won't get promoted if I don't socialize," Dad argued back.

Mom all but yelled at him, "That isn't the issue, and you know it!"

I never heard her say what the issue was, but I thought she was being rough on him when she wouldn't support him. He tried so hard. I loved mom, but like the too-small breakfast for school, sometimes she wasn't nice.

Between school and babysitting I hardly had time to sleep because swimming took the rest of my time. I was proud of how well our team did. The most fun was relays. I swam breaststroke, or sometimes the butterfly. Not many people came to see us, so we cheered for ourselves. When Meg was swimming backstroke, we all yelled, "Go, Meg!" Then it was usually Karen on the butterfly, and we yelled, "Go, Karen!" The three girls yelled for me as I swam the breaststroke to set up the last laps for Sally. Then, as soon as could, I climbed out and helped yell, "Go, Sally," as she got to the wall. Even though we were only together at meets and at practice, I loved being with our group, but I felt awkward if guys looked at my Speedo swimsuit.

Every summer we spent several weeks in Valentine with my grandparents. I'd see Harry and Jamie, and I learned to drive. In theory, you had to be fifteen years old to get a learner's permit, but that rule was for Lincoln and Omaha. Out West, there was so much to do that when kids could see over the steering wheel and reach the pedals at the same time, they started driving errands. As soon as I was tall enough, grandpa taught me to drive, and I ran errands, too. Like walking to my grandparents' house as a little girl, it made me feel part of what was going on.

I started to babysit for the Hartwoods in eighth grade. Mr. Hartwood would pick me up on his way home from work, and I'd have dinner with their girls while they went to a movie or their club. He pointed out the Carriage Club as we drove past it on Ward Parkway.

Mr. Hartwood traveled a lot for TWA, especially in the Middle East. After one of his trips, he was really talkative. "You won't believe what those people eat," he said as we waited for a stoplight. "They roasted a lamb, and they gave me the eyeball because I was the special guest."

If Mrs. Hartwood went along on his trip, a housekeeper stayed with the girls, and I'd come over on the weekends to play. They paid me, but I'd have done it for free to hear Mrs. Hartwood's stories when she got back. I overheard her talking to my mom at Thanksgiving after one of her trips. "You have to wear this black thing that is just unbearable." Then she realized I was listening and added, "But the bazaar had such interesting things, and so cheap." I glossed over the word "unbearable." It sounded exotic to a thirteen-year-old—the women wrapped in veils, only their eyes showing—and she'd brought me a silk scarf as a souvenir.

From listening to Mrs. Hartwood, I knew there was a bigger world I wanted to see. Some people say it's shallow for travel to be the focus of your life. It offends their sensibilities that someone from Westport might want the opportunities they were born with, but that's because they've already got the luxury of not being stuck. I only wanted the opportunities they'd had given to them, but I was on my own to figure out how.

When I looked for ideas, the first thing I saw was magazines and television. It was obvious that glamorous people traveled, so I decided to be a glamorous person like a movie star or a fashion model. Mom smiled at my idea because was so far-fetched, but when I told her I'd seen an announcement for modeling tryouts, she said, "No."

I was disappointed, and I didn't want to go around Mom, but I asked Dad why she said that. He asked Mom, "What's the harm in a tryout?"

"Well, that makes it your responsibility," was all she said.

Tryouts were at the new Hilton Hotel that looked overlooked the airport. I got up early to wash my hair and put on my best makeup. Dad disappeared after he'd signed the consent form. My adult guess is he went to the bar, but at the time, I thought he was letting me be independent.

A big woman took me into a room with a lot of mirrors. "Hang your clothes here and put this on," she said, handing me a gown. Then she led me to a sink where another woman washed my hair again and gave me a face cloth to take off all my makeup. I'd thought I'd just smile and they'd take a picture, but Dad wasn't with me, and everything was too unfamiliar to know if this just wasn't how tryouts were.

After the woman set my hair and put makeup on me, the

big woman took me to a rack of black dresses and sized me up, "What size are you? A six?"

I didn't know because I usually tried on clothes until something fit, but I wasn't about to blow this opportunity, so I said, "Yes." She gave me high heel shoes and led me into a room with a lot of lights and Adrian, the photographer. "Over here," he said. Then he pushed me here and there, like touching my stomach and saying, "Hold that in" or pulling my arm, "Put your arm like this..." I could smell Adrian's cigarettes when he turned my shoulder and adjusted my chin, but this was my big opportunity, so I smiled just like he told me.

When that part was over, Adrian said to the woman, "Get her in a swimsuit. I'll meet you outside."

In the dressing room, the woman unzipped my dress and lifted it over my head. Then she handed me a striped swimsuit. I had a tank suit for swim team, but this suit had elastic in the waist and pads in the top.

I was uncertain, but the woman got impatient. "Take off your bra and put the suit on," she directed. "Then put the heels back on."

I turned my back to her, and did as she told me, but I didn't want to make their suit dirty, so I kept my underpants on. When I turned to face her, my pants showed around my legs. "Oh, God. You left your underpants on? Here." She pushed her fingers into the legs of the suit to tuck my underpants out of sight.

I was too surprised to know what to do, but fortunately she stood back and was satisfied. "Let's go," she said and led me to the pool.

My dad was waiting in the lobby afterwards. "Wow," he said when he saw my makeup, "you look all grown up."

I felt good that I'd tried something I wanted, even though I didn't get selected. One girl who was there that day had a fabulous career. I saw her on magazine covers a number of times and remembered our tryout at the hotel. Mr. Adrian sent the pictures he didn't use. The girl in those photos is naive, but she's trying hard. I planned to give a picture of me at the pool to my grandfather, but never found the right time to send it.

The night the pictures came, I heard my parents arguing after they thought I was asleep. Mom didn't usually yell, but she was yelling at Dad, "You said, 'model.' Those pictures aren't modeling. You let my daughter be a cheap pinup."

My Dad said something I couldn't make out. Then I heard my mom again, "I know cheap when I see it! And I know you. You signed her away and went to the bar. You're a damned mess!"

That was the only time I ever heard my mom swear. I was ashamed I'd caused that.

I had two backup ideas. We didn't have the kind of money to travel, so I applied to be an exchange student with the AFS, the American Field Service. I wrote my essay about how I believed in America, and I'd already taken Spanish. I said it'd be a great responsibility to represent America, but that I'd make good use of the opportunity because I had a natural curiosity about people and cultures. When Dad took my snapshot for the application, I held one of my swimming medals to show I was successful.

My other goal was to swim in the Olympics, but I had no idea what was involved. I'd won a lot of races at the YMCA, but like lots of things, you needed a coach to guide you to get really good.

On my 16th birthday, Dad let me skip my first class to get my driver's license. Right after school, I called Dianne, and that night he let me drive by myself to Winstead's. After summers driving in Valentine, there wasn't much for me to learn by more practice, and I'd worked on my studies really hard so my parents would know they could depend on me to be the most careful, most responsible, most perfect child they could hope for.

As I went to sleep, I was proud of myself. I was going to do great things as soon as I got out of Westport. Not many of my classmates knew me, but I'd worked hard to have more things going for me than most other girls, and I was a secret waiting to be discovered. In addition to being a good swimmer and applying to be Westport's foreign exchange student, I was on the honor roll. Unfortunately, I had no idea how little I knew.

At the end of September, I got a call from a senior who wrote for *The Crier*, the school student newspaper. She'd heard about my swimming and wanted to interview me. I got excited and brought along ribbons I'd won at the Y, but there wasn't any connection because Westport High didn't have a swim team. In an effort to get her interest, I said, "My dream's to swim in the '64 Olympics." There was leftover excitement from the 1960 Olympics, and that caught her attention.

"We should get a picture of you swimming," she said.

*Oops!* I thought, but there was no turning back so I asked, "Where's a place to take a picture this time of year?"

"That's no problem," she replied. "We can set it up at Southwest." Her faculty advisor, Miss Welch, could arrange time at the pool through the advisor for the student paper at Southwest.

A couple days later I met the student photographer—I think his name was Ted—before last period, and we rode out on the bus. Everyone knew Ted was a big flirt, but that was exciting and I sort of hoped he'd flirt with me.

Miss Welch, the faculty advisor for the Southwest student paper, showed me to the girls' locker room and let Ted into the spectator gallery.

The chlorine smell was familiar, and I felt the same optimism I'd gotten from my first swim instructor. Ted took photographs while I swam different strokes. I relived the fun of my swimming lessons and even forgot how much luckier the kids were who went to Southwest. Even the little houses across the street were a lot bigger than ours.

When we were done, I got out at the shallow end and thanked Miss Welch, "It was fun to be here again."

"Again?" she asked.

"I learned to swim here. Y lessons."

"Then you're very welcome."

As I walked toward the girls' locker room, I heard another click behind me. I looked around and realized that Ted had shot a picture of my butt. He winked and followed Miss Welch out.

The next day Dr. Ball, the principal at Westport, called four of us to his office to tell us we were the AFS finalists and we'd take a group photo on Monday. I was in seventh heaven, but lots happened that weekend. We lost our football game, and we almost got into a war with Russia.

After church on Sunday, I did homework all afternoon. Before bed, I ironed my best blouse and asked my dad if he'd drive me to school early. In the morning, I put on a little lipstick to look good for the photograph, but my mom didn't miss a thing. "What's that on your face?" she demanded.

Just then, Dad came in from the front yard reading the newspaper headline. "Look at the damned Russians. Putting missiles in our back yard. It's that Castro guy. We should have showed him a thing or two last year."

After that, there wasn't time to discuss lipstick, and I slipped out to the car with Dad.

One of the other four finalists was a guy named David

who swam on the boys' team at the Y. He didn't know how cute he was, or that I'd had a crush on him since eighth grade.

The photographer was Ted again, and when he got ready to take the picture he shoved me closer to David than we'd be in a slow dance. "That's it," he said and snapped a picture. "Now, one more. Smile. Great."

The four of us were uneasy being crammed together and stepped apart as soon as we could. I smiled at David, but Ted spoke first, "They're going to run the photograph I took of you."

I wasn't thinking of swimming. "What photograph?"

"The one of you swimming. The other one was for me." He winked.

I blushed. The bell rang. I looked around. David had gone to class.

That was a scary week. A lot of jets flew overhead, and we had air raid drills and went down into a basement at school that I didn't know existed. On Friday, President Kennedy gave a speech that the Russians had been trying to put missiles in Cuba, but the crisis was over.

Saturday afternoon, I looked out and watched a red pickup truck park in front of our house. I already worried I didn't fit in because I was a hick, and when Harry got out wearing his cowboy boots, I hoped no one was looking. He was in town for the junior calf roping at the American Royal, but when I asked him about it, he said, "I just got a red ribbon," and made it clear not to ask any more questions.

Harry and I talked about the Russians and Cuba. "My dad says you guys would've got hit worse than us," he said. "There's some kind of missile thing around here." Then he added, "You can always come live in Valentine."

I had no interest in living out on a ranch, but that was exactly what Harry wanted for himself. So I was surprised when he put his arm around me and gave me a peck on the cheek before he left. I didn't want to be his girlfriend and live on a ranch. I wanted to be special.

In November, Dianne asked me to go to the Southwest versus Southeast football game. Dad didn't watch football, so all I knew was that guys ran up and down the field and made touchdowns, but it was fun. Southwest won by one point, and the players carried the coach off the field.

After the game, we went to a youth center at the Baptist church on 39th Street because they gave out free hamburgers. Most of the kids had blue Westport jackets with "TIGERS" in gold letters, but some wore green jackets for Pundit, one of the Westport literary societies. The Westport kids were nice to Dianne because Southwest beat Southeast, and no one liked Southeast.

Exchange student interviews were on Saturday before Thanksgiving. I arrived the same time as David. "You ready for this?" he asked.

I was excited that he was talking to me and so nervous that I could barely speak. I probably turned scarlet, but I answered, "Yes."

We immediately remembered there were four of us competing for one spot, but we wished each other luck.

The interview was with two teachers, a woman from the AFS office for Missouri, and Dr. Ball. I thought I was doing well until the woman from the AFS asked me, "You have a swimming award in your picture, but how will that help you if we send you to a country that doesn't have swimming pools?"

I wasn't quick enough to give any one of a hundred answers that would have worked. All I could think was, "I'd tell them about swimming and show them how to swim outside the water." After that, I wanted to sneak out before they laughed at me, but I waited while David and the other candidates were interviewed. Then Dr. Ball came out and told us how well we'd all done and how he wished he could send every one of us.

David and I walked the same way afterwards and he ended up walking me home. On the way, we passed a store that had been remade into a coffee shop with a sign that read, "The Point." "That's such a cool place," he said.

"What's The Point?" I asked.

"You drink coffee while a guy plays folk songs. Like Peter, Paul and Mary. I'll take you some time," he said. "It's like a bistro in Paris."

"You've been to Paris?"

"Yeah. My dad works for GM, and we've traveled all over."

"Where else did you live?"

"Pretty much everywhere. London, Rome. We even lived two years in Japan. Right now he's working at the Buick Oldsmobile Pontiac plant over in Kansas so I can go to high school in the US."

The Cuban Missile Crisis was old news by the time we went to the Hartwoods' for Thanksgiving, but it came up after dinner. "I don't like the man's domestic politics at all," Mr. Hartwood said about President Kennedy, "but I'm with him one hundred percent on this one."

Dad agreed, "Yes."

"We had to stand up to them, but the funny part is that most of us don't know a thing about 'em...or the rest of the world." Mr. Hartwood motioned to himself and Dad. "We were in the war. We saw the world, but most of that was looking down the barrel of a gun."

"I didn't see that much," Dad replied. "They kept me here in Olathe."

"Right." Mr. Hartwood paused to remind himself that Dad hadn't been on a ship even though he was in the navy. "Take the Middle East. Americans have no idea what that place is like...and we already make half our gas from their oil. If we don't understand them, we're at their mercy."

"We certainly didn't understand the Russians in the last war," my dad said. "One minute they're our friends. The next, well, look at Cuba."

"Yes." Mr. Hartwood nodded. "That's why I'm bringing the son of one of my colleagues to go to school at Penn. He's at an American school in Switzerland to buff up his English. Real nice young man."

There was an early snow in December. David asked if I wanted to go sledding. I said, "Yes," and he said, "I'll borrow a sled and pick you up."

I thought we'd go to the hill near our house, but David said that was too tame. "We should go to Suicide Hill."

"Where's that?"

"I'll show you."

Having been on Colorado ski slopes, I'd describe Suicide Hill as a very short bunny slope, but it was big for Kansas City. We went down on two sleds, and then we went down double. My toes got numb and my ears stung, but I was having so much fun that I wasn't going to quit before I had to. On the way home, we stopped at Winstead's but went inside instead of sitting in his car. I didn't have full-blown frostbite, but for months my ears burned every time they got cold.

The next Saturday we walked on the Plaza and mugged at the camera in a photo booth at Woolworth's where you put in a quarter for four pictures. I still have two of the pictures. I began to think of him as my boyfriend.

David got selected as foreign exchange student, not me.

It was a setback, but there was still college. I babysat for the Hartwoods on New Year's Eve. Carol had friends sleep over. They were old enough to be on their own, but they giggled and called a lot of boys. I was there to be certain they didn't sneak out.

I was also there to be with Kristen because Carol would ignore her. I was too embarrassed to tell my friends I was babysitting on New Year's Eve, but fortunately no one asked. At least it was better than staying up with my parents to watch the ball in Times Square on television. Mr. Hartwood drove me home about 1:30 a.m. "What are you doing after high school?" he asked.

"I want to go to college. I don't want to just be at home."

"Where do you want to go?"

"Probably KCJC, and Kansas City University if my grades are good."

"You should think about Penn."

"That's a really tough school."

"Oh, you could do it. You're a junior now, right? Let's talk about it when you're applying. Next Thanksgiving."

The other girls on the swim team went to different schools, so we weren't school friends and swimming didn't translated into recognition at Westport. No one at school said anything to me about my swimming picture in *The Crier* or the exchange student picture either.

In January, the swim team sort of melted away. Sally quit first. She was a senior at Paseo High School. The girl who replaced her—I don't remember her name—came from Southeast High School and never acted like we were a team. If we didn't win, she exploded at the rest of us like it was only our fault. Meg, Karen, and I didn't plan what we were going to do, but we all quit on the same day.

I replaced the swim team with small jobs. I didn't have an allowance, and I wanted to have money to spend on makeup and things. I worked in a card shop and one afternoon a week as a hostess seating customers at a new coffee shop on the Plaza called Putsche's.

I liked Putsche's. The customers were nice, and after a while Ken, the manager, asked me to babysit for him and his wife. They lived south of the Plaza, near Dianne. I'd walk to their house early in the evening, and Ken would drive me home when they got back. His wife was nice, and their little boy was cute.

When Ken decided I was ready to wait tables, I made money on tips. He told me I didn't need to split my tips with the busboys because they were paid better. But they were good guys, and it seemed the right thing to do.

All but one of the busboys were Mexican. They could have tried to get fresh, but they didn't. I tried to talk my Spanish with them. It reminded me of Claire and how she liked it when I tried to use the Lakota words she told me. I also did it because the other waitresses were standoffish, and having moved there from a small town, I knew how it felt to be an outsider just because of who you were.

One of them, Manuel, had a sister my age who went to Argentine High School in Kansas. When she visited, I talked to her to make her feel welcome. There weren't a lot of Mexicans on the Plaza.

That summer Kristen started steady dating her guy named Sam. She was fourteen years old. I hoped someone at school would ask me out.

The Sunday after I started my senior year in high school *The Kansas City Star* ran an article called "Love in 1984." Like any teenager, I was curious about love and sex, but Mom pulled the article out before I could read it.

At lunch the next day, the girls talked about the article and one girl had brought the magazine to finish reading it. After she was done, she let me read it while the other girls said things like, "I don't believe it," "Why would one take that kind of chance?" or "My sister, she's in college, she says you have to be careful not to get P-R-E-G-N-A-N-T."

The author claimed that by 1984 most girls would have sex before they were married and some girls would have sex with a boy they wouldn't marry. About the only thing I'd learned about sex since the seventh grade was that you had to be careful with guys. I didn't feel I could ask the other girls my questions, but I did wonder why a girl would choose to be bad.

My second period class was Spanish. In early October, right after class started, Dr. Ball's secretary came into the classroom and spoke to the teacher, who called my name. "You need to go to Dr. Ball's office right away." She was so serious I knew something was wrong.

When I got to the principal's office, Dr. Ball's secretary knocked on his door and led me in. Dr. Ball stood up and said, "I'm sorry to tell you that your grandmother has died. Your parents are coming to pick you up in a little while. I'll let your teachers know you won't be in class this week."

I was stunned, and then I started to cry.

Dr. Ball let me wait in his office until my parents arrived. Mom had packed a bag for me, they'd picked Freddy up at Swenney, and we left straight from school.

A lot of folks came to the funeral. We stayed with Granddaddy in their house. I got up early the next morning to make pancakes. Granddaddy was already in the kitchen. "What you doing up so early?" he asked.

"Thought I'd make breakfast before anyone else was up."

"You know, your grandmother tried to get up before me one time, but I just got up earlier. It got to be a sort of competition. I'd get up earlier and then she'd get up earlier, and we kept getting up earlier and earlier 'til we were so tired we barely got any sleep. We were both getting up at 3:00 or so. What a mess." He laughed. "Then one day she slept in 'til 7:00, and neither of us ever said anything about it."

I didn't know whether that was a story or a hint to go back to bed. Then he had tears in his eyes. "I wish to god I'd let her get up before me just one time. I was so stubborn...and so was she." He looked at me. "I'll go back to bed and doze a bit if you'll make some hotcakes before I come back."

"Deal."

I found out in English class that President Kennedy had been shot. The vice principal walked in and spoke to the teacher. He was usually pretty definite about things, but this time he didn't quite know how to act as he turned to our class and said, "President Kennedy has been shot in Dallas. Class is dismissed."

No one said a thing. Like everyone else, I was pretty numb and had no idea what this really meant. We gathered our books and walked into the hall. That night, my family watched television that showed crowds of serious faces and our new president. Three years before, we'd been in Valentine listening to the Democratic Convention on the radio when Johnson lost out to Kennedy for the nomination. Now, just like that, all the voting at the convention had been turned around.

My parents had planned to go to Valentine for Thanksgiving with Granddaddy. After Kennedy was shot, nobody was getting anything done, so they decided we'd leave Tuesday. It was the first Thanksgiving I could remember we hadn't been at the Hartwoods'. I think Daddy missed that as much as I did because he called Mr. Hartwood Monday night to wish him a good holiday.

On Daddy's end of the conversation, they talked about the Peace Corps and getting to know other countries better. "What will happen now?" I asked after he got off the phone.

"Things'll be all right. Like Everett says, we just need to learn as a country. We're ignorant about a lot of people."

David and I talked between classes, and we walked home together sometimes. I wanted so badly for him to ask me to the Valentine's Dance. The week before, he brought up the dance while we were walking. "Do you think Kathy would go with me if I asked her?" he asked.

I choked, but I smiled and told him the truth, "*Every* girl at Westport would be very happy if you asked her." He didn't get my hint, but in a way it made sense. Kathy had visited London so she and David had exciting things to talk about. I was sad for a couple of days, but I made the best of it.

The night of the dance, Dianne and I went to the Waldo Theater and saw *The Prize*. In the long perspective, that film broke ground with a major star, Paul Newman, openly trying to get Elke Sommer to bed. But we didn't see changing morals. We saw a handsome actor we all had a crush on. And it was set in Sweden, where all women were beautiful blondes with blue eyes.

After the movie we went to Dianne's house and ordered pizza from Antonio's. Her parents were out, and if we'd been older, we probably would've sneaked a beer, but it was exciting enough to have the house to ourselves. When Leslie Gore came on the radio singing, "You don't own me," we held Coke bottles like microphones and sang along. "You don't own me, I'm not one just one of your many toys" We belted out, "I'm young and I love to be young" And we sang to an imaginary audience in the living room, "To live my life the way I want/To say and do whatever I please." We knew we could grow up to be who we wanted to be.

At the end of March, I got a letter from Dr. Bauer, Director of Admissions at Penn College, offering me provisional acceptance. I was excited beyond belief when I saw the word "acceptance," but then I read the letter more carefully. I had no idea what "provisional acceptance" meant, so I called Penn and asked for Dr. Bauer's office.

He answered himself, "Provisional means your grades need to be good enough the rest of your senior year to demonstrate you'll be able to do college work," he explained. "Who told you to call me?"

"No one," I said. "You're the one who signed the letter."

He chuckled. "Maybe you are ready for college."

A week later I received a letter accepting me without restrictions.

I got a small scholarship from Bendix that they gave to all employees' kids, and my parents said they'd help for the first year. I worked four days a week at Putsche's to save money. It was minimum wage, but I got good tips if I worked hard and was friendly.

I quit work the second week of August so we could all go to Valentine. Dad let me drive an hour at a time, but he still sat right next to me in the front seat.

Harry talked me into going to the river to swim. As we were splashing around he tried to kiss me, but I ducked backwards. "Harry!" I protested as I stumbled where the water was deeper, but I wasn't alone in the water. I bumped into something that felt like a big fish, but it didn't swim away. I stepped back toward Harry. He started to put his arm around me again, but I said, "Harry, I'm not kidding. Something bumped into me there."

"Where?"

I pointed. "There."

He strode into the pool, and the water was up at his chest when he jumped back, too. He pointed to the shore. "Give me that stick."

He prodded into the water and finally caught something. I could tell it was big from the strain it took for him to move it. Then a man's face broke the surface. It looked terrible. "Oh my god," was all I could say.

The face was bloated, but the shirt had red beads like an Indian's. Harry took a step back. "Holy shit. They meant it..."

"Who meant what?"

"Never mind—let's get the sheriff.

We grabbed our shirts and drove back to town. Harry found the deputy and led him to the body. Then the three of us stood around silently as we waited for the sheriff and the doctor who doubled as coroner.

The deputy recognized the shirt. "Looks like the one that Indian had, your grandfather's friend. What's his name? Littlepeak."

By the time the sheriff found Claire and drove her out, there must have been fifty people who'd heard about the body and come out to see. The sheriff pulled the tarp back for Claire to look. She couldn't recognize him either, but it was definitely the shirt her grandmother had beaded.

The man from the state police lab arrived about two hours later, loaded Mr. Littlepeak's body in the ambulance that doubled as a hearse, and took him into town. The sheriff led Claire to his car, and they followed the ambulance.

I waited outside the sheriff's until Claire came out. She was the only Lakota on the street, and I could only guess how lonely she felt. I couldn't think of anything to say, so I took her hand and led her to the café. Everyone looked the other way when we sat down. I wanted to buy her a soda or a sundae, but I didn't have the money so I bought each of us a scoop of ice cream. Granddaddy would have said that was the right thing to do. I didn't eat much. Claire just moved the top of the ice cream around with her spoon until it melted into a puddle.

The sheriff found us and spoke to Claire. "I called your chief up in Pine Ridge. They'll take care of you. The deputy will drive you up there."

The deputy put her in the back seat, the seat with the bars on the windows so a prisoner couldn't get out. But Claire wasn't trying to run away.

After eight years in Kansas City, I knew what it was like to feel out of place. Coming from a small town, I didn't know the right things to say in different situations. My clothes were bought on sale. I got hungry at school and felt lucky if a guy noticed me. But at least I was white. It had to be worse if you were poor, didn't know how to fit in, and had dark skin in a white town.

I asked Harry who'd made a threat, and all he could remember was he'd heard that Gus offended someone and they were angry. He told the sheriff, but Gus's murder was never solved. Daddy told me the coroner found a lot of whiskey in Gus's stomach, but there was no alcohol in his blood. The whiskey had been poured into him just before he was drowned.

The next week was quiet until Wednesday, when they started to set up for the Harvest Fair. Valentine was too small for a rodeo, but the Fair dated back to when the town depended on the railroad and everyone came.

I rode the Ferris wheel with Harry, and when we stopped at the top, he kissed me. Not that I really wanted to date Harry, but it was the first time a boy ever kissed me, and that was exciting.

It was a small town, so everyone knew everyone else, and it was okay for kids to go out on the dance floor. Harry asked me to dance, and afterwards we drove out by the river. We talked about Claire and her dad. He put his arm around me and kissed me again but not too mushy. When he put his hand on my blouse, I pushed back. "Harry, no."

"Come on. We're going to school tomorrow. I want you to be my girl before I leave."

"Your girl before you leave, but you go to Omaha and I go back to Kansas City. No way."

"It'll be our secret. Come on."

"I don't want to."

We didn't, but the next morning some of the guys watched me different, and Jamie asked, "Was it as good as they say?"

I was furious at Harry, but there wasn't anything to do. He'd gone ahead and told everyone a big story, and people always believe whoever starts a rumor, especially if it's bad and about someone else.

My first day at Penn felt like the start of a whole new life. Mom and Dad surprised me with a brand new Smith-Corona portable electric typewriter and drove me out to freshman orientation. I had a clock radio, a dictionary, and a bunch of records. My roommate, Lynn, was bringing a phonograph.

In the early 60s, girls spent hours rolling big curlers every night. We sat around talking and playing get-to-know-you games organized by the upper class girls. We made lists of favorite records and movie stars, and once we found out whose birthdays were in September, we drew handmade cards for the birthday girls. These games filled the time after the dorms were locked at 10:00 p.m. until we drifted to bed an hour or so later.

Penn bragged they didn't have sororities and fraternities, but they had societies, which is a euphemism for exactly the same thing. It was exciting to get the invitations to their teas, but I knew right away they weren't for me. The girls talked about how they focused on serving the community in the spirit of Penn College, but they dressed in a way that showed they had money to spare. It was pretty obvious I couldn't afford to waste tips on extra clothes. When societies invited girls to join, I wasn't asked. There were more of us who didn't get invited, but we didn't have anything to brag about, so we each felt left out by ourselves, instead of finding company with all the others who would've been just like us.

I'd expected not to be in a society, but I expected to do well in the physical education class we had to take. The first day was a swim test. If you couldn't swim the length of the pool, swimming would be your first semester physical education class.

I'd gained weight after I stopped swimming, so my suit was ridiculously tight. I tripped as I came into the pool and skinned my knee. Everyone stared at me. Thank god there were no boys. The woman instructor, a coach named Lorel, shook her head. "Need to develop some balance, do we? Can't graduate clumsy girls, now. Can we?"

It would have gone easier if I'd cried when Lorel called me clumsy, because she'd have gotten her pound of flesh. But I forced myself to step up to the edge to get ready. When it was my turn, I dove in, and she went wild on her whistle and chased me down the side of the pool. "You, the clumsy one. No diving. Get in at the wall and swim the whole length."

I started to breaststroke back, but she yelled again. "Don't swim back. You're in everyone's way. Get out and walk. Let everyone keep going." So I climbed out and walked to the end of the line.

I was the last person to start, and, when no one was looking, Lorel splashed water in my face just as I took my first breath. I choked, but I'd choked before, and I knew how to handle water in my throat. I flailed as I coughed and then swam my best stroke down the pool. I concentrated to act like I wasn't bothered at all.

Spanish was a bigger challenge. I knew the grammar, but I had a Mexican accent from talking with the busboys at Putsche's. The professor wanted Castilian, and I couldn't get my tongue to lisp the "th's" right.

English class overwhelmed me. The department head, Dr. Notpu, was from India and spoke with a clipped accent. Notpu had been at Penn for years, and he had the idea that we'd be better writers if we spent hours on his idea of the beauty of the language and why words meant what they meant.

We used a textbook that was all about syntax and how words change meanings. There was a chapter called "GHOTI spells fish." Simple: G-H as in enough, O as in women, and TI as in fiction. That was supposed to make us appreciate phonetics.

I write reasonably well, but Notpu gets no credit for that. I write well because professors and others—even my husband eventually—looked at what I wrote and suggested what might work better.

I did, however, sit between David, a townie from Jackson City, and a Middle Eastern student named Wahiib. David was cute, and I made excuses to talk to him. Wahiib always sat down just as class started, and he was never there long enough to make talking to him seem casual.

On a Saturday, a couple of weeks after I didn't get invited into a society, I was trying to come up with an idea for a three-page English paper on how we know what the word "know" means. This was before everyone learned in high school how to write a basic, five paragraph essay—hypothesis, three paragraphs of supporting arguments and conclusion.

My door was partially open, and Christie, a sophomore girl, knocked.

She saw my English textbook. "Boy, do I remember Notpu's assignments. They're legendary."

"Yeah..." I shook my head.

"I've got an idea," she said. "Do you want to go to the football game with me? I don't have anyone to sit with."

I said, "Yes," just to get out of the dorm.

Everyone knew Christie was dating a football star, and that made her popular. So although I wasn't in a society, I had a great seat on the fifty-yard line.

Christie helped me understand football. "They move the down marker—that's the pole with a circle on it—because the team got a first and ten," she explained when I asked what the men in black and white were doing on the side of the field. "Carl explained it to me."

So Christie explained downs, teams, the center, the quarterback, and running backs. Especially Carl, who was a running back.

I couldn't see Carl's face because of his helmet, but Christie knew his number and got excited when he ran toward our side of the field carrying the ball. After the game, I waited with her for the team to come out of the locker room. The crowd thinned out and a few guys came out, but everyone else was someone's girlfriend, and I felt out of place. "I gotta' go," I said.

"It won't be much longer. I want you to meet Carl."

"That's okay. I will sometime."

I cut class the day before Thanksgiving so we could leave early for Valentine. We weren't rich by Kansas City standards, but driving directly up from the city we could bring fresh lettuce, cranberries, and sweet potatoes. The store in Valentine was the biggest for one hundred miles, but fresh food never got that far in the winter, and it was already winter there.

Mom brought a frozen turkey from Kansas City with the idea it would defrost during the trip, but it was still icy when she put it in the oven at 6:00 in the morning. I made cookie dough while the turkey cooked. Mom left the turkey in until 2:00, but when Dad started to cut it, he pointed to the red juice and said, "This isn't done. Whoever thought it would thaw out?"

I didn't want an argument to spoil dinner, so I chimed in, "I have the oven on for cookies. If we bake some of it in a pan, I'll have time to get the cookies ready."

I'd found Grandmother's turkey-shape cookie cutters. After the turkey was out, I quickly baked two sheets of cookies while Mom improvised gravy as everyone got ready to sit down to dinner a second time.

I met Jamie for ice cream after lunch on Friday. There wasn't much else to do. She was a senior and one of the three cheerleaders for Valentine High School—division D for really small schools.

"Do you ever see Claire?" I asked.

"Not since that happened with her dad. The Indians don't come to town except in groups, and they never stay after they get what they came for."

I saw Harry, too, but it was a short conversation. He was going back to Lincoln that night. He played for the Nebraska Cornhuskers and was a running back, too.

My roommate was a know-it-all. She liked Notpu's class, and when I said I didn't get it, she shrugged like I was an idiot. This was before I learned that the best sign that a person doesn't know what they're talking about is that they can't explain it to anyone else.

I would have flunked the whole course except that our

last assignment was to read *King Lear* and explain our favorite part. We'd read *King Lear* in high school and written a paper about it then. That paper was good, but the teacher put lots of suggestions on it, and I used those suggestions. I got my paper back from Dr. Notpu with one comment. "You should work this hard every time." As if I didn't.

The first day of class after Christmas, David and I compared our vacations. "I delivered groceries right up to Christmas Eve. You'd think people would plan ahead," he said.

"I worked every shift no one else wanted," I said, "including New Year's Eve. I'd have missed Christmas Eve except they closed to let the busboys go to mass."

Wahiib came in at the last minute and sat down without saying a word. He reminded me of Claire. I never saw anyone talk to him, and I felt uncomfortable leaving him out of the conversation, so I turned and asked, "Did you go home for vacation?"

"Yes," was all he had time to say before Notpu came in.

After class, Wahiib hurried out before I could ask anything more. I guess he thought I was one more student trying to do the minimum to be polite. Eventually, I asked him what his major was.

"Political science. I will be a diplomat and represent my king."

"You really have a king?" I asked. "Like the King of England?"

Wahiib nodded. "You Americans know very little about us. I'm here so at least we will know something about you." He laughed as though he had revealed a state secret. He seemed like a nice guy, very intelligent and polite. If I'd known how much money he had—all the Arabs had—I wouldn't have felt like I needed take care of his feelings so much. But being an Arab, he was more on the outside than me, and that couldn't feel good—money or not.

The week before finals, Christie knocked on my door just

to talk. She'd stopped wearing lipstick, and her eyes were dark. Something was wrong, but I didn't know what to say, so I asked, "Want to get a Coke at Le Pois?"

"Thanks, but I don't want to go there. I might run into you know who." I had heard she'd broken up with Carl, and I was sad for her, but I'd never met him, so I didn't know what to think beyond that. Then she abruptly changed her mind. "You know what? Forget it. I really should try to study."

The last day of class, Dr. Notpu wandered off into talking about beat poetry and Alan Ginsberg. "They read poetry like that at The Point," I said to David as we left the classroom.

"What's The Point?" he asked.

"It's the coolest place. On Main Street, by the Plaza. Everyone goes there." Even though I'd never been there, I told him everything the David in high school had told me when he walked me home. We'd talked almost every day for a semester so I decided it wouldn't hurt to stick my neck out. "You have a car. Let's go up there tonight. I'll show you where it is."

He made excuses, but in the end we drove up. There wasn't anyone reading poetry that night, but we had coffee and listened to a guy who played a guitar and sang songs he'd made up. I knew David had a good time, but like mine, his plate was full and he didn't have time for much else. We faced the same challenges, but neither one of us knew how to slow down to find others who'd be supportive because they lived with the same problems.

The Saturday after semester break, Christie asked if I'd show her how to take the bus to downtown Kansas City. "Yeah. That'll be fun. We can see all the stores."

"Actually," she said, "I need to get a passport photograph."

"Wow. Are you taking a trip?"

"Yes. Mom and I are going to London for spring break."

I thought that was odd because both her parents worked

in ordinary jobs and you had to be rich like the Hartwoods to travel to Europe.

We got our first semester grades soon after that. I didn't even get a C average. College was really hard. The worst part was that I got only a C in physical education, and I thought I was a good athlete.

Second semester, Dr. Notpu assigned us to read *Rabbit Run* by John Updike. The sophomore girls talked about this all first semester and told us in a knowing way it'd be our education. I saved a dollar buying a used copy in the bookstore. As I read, I realized I was going to learn stuff I'd wanted to know. More important, I found that starting where Rabbit and Ruth leave Tothero, someone had written in the book, not in the outer margin where the used book buyer would see the marks when you tried to sell it back, but in the inner margin, near the binding, like a secret message from the last reader. There were comments like, "Bitchin'" and "Wow."

It was more complicated than the sex education movie at Swenney. I didn't understand the part at the beginning where Ruth got wet to have sex with Rabbit, but I was too embarrassed to ask anyone to explain it to me.

Wahiib was nervous and blushed a little when class discussed what Updike was saying about going all the way. David asked a lot of questions, but that was so he wouldn't get called on to answer anything. I tried to look so unprepared that Notpu wouldn't call on me. Not because I hadn't read the book, but because I had no idea what I'd say if he asked me about Ruth. I didn't know if she was a prostitute because he paid her money, or if she was a friend because she and the other girl knew Rabbit and his friend before.

A couple of days after spring break, I went by Christie's room to ask how her trip was. The door was open, and Betty, Christie's roommate was talking to someone. She was pretty loud, but she didn't make sense. "I could tell she was fast, but going all the way with that football player. What a skuzz."

"She sure got caught, didn't she? But going to England to take care of it must have cost an arm and a leg," said a voice I didn't recognize.

I didn't understand what they were talking about, but I knocked and asked if Christie was there.

"No, she's not," sneered Betty. "And I don't think she'll be here much longer." She added with a knowing smile, "Your friend's gotten herself into some big trouble. My guess is you'd better look for a new friend."

As far as I could tell, she was talking in riddles.

I returned from the library before dinner and met Christie coming out of the dormitory with a box of her stuff. "Where're you going?" I asked.

A man—thinking about it now, I guess it was her father—stepped between us and said, "I don't think Christie wants to talk right now."

But Christie touched his arm and said, "She's okay. She's about the only friend I have here."

I was really confused. Christie was popular and talked to everyone, but no one was talking to her today. I took a step toward her, and she burst out crying, "He never even called to see if I was all right. He never called."

I learned over the next few weeks that Carl got Christie pregnant, and her parents had taken a loan on their house so they could take her to England where abortions were legal. But Christie suffered with her secret and when she spilled just a little bit to her roommate, Betty turned on her and spread the gossip like wildfire. College girls can be sharks when they smell blood.

The administration found out and told her to leave.

When Penn was founded, they had a mandatory weekly

meeting for all students. This had evolved to non-religious convocations on topics that fit with Quaker beliefs.

At the end of April, the convocation announced a new Arab Student Association at Penn. The president of the college, Dr. Forger, spoke about "various aspects and consequences of an Arab population on campus." Dr. Bauer, head of the sociology department—who'd admitted me—made a plea "for integration on a friendship and mutual understanding basis." Mr. Hartwood spoke as an alum because he knew about business opportunities in the Middle East.

As students filed out after the program, I thought the polite thing to do would be to go up front and say hello to Mr. Hartwood.

Several students waited to ask him questions, but he recognized me and called me by name. Dr. Forger joined us, and Mr. Hartwood introduced me. Fortunately, I had to excuse myself for class, so I dodged any questions about how I was doing in school.

As I left, I thought about how Penn had given me a wonderful opportunity. I hadn't succeeded in making good use of that opportunity so far, but I could give back something if I supported their project to make the Arab students feel accepted by the student body. I decided to befriend Wahiib and two Arabs in my geology class. One was a senior named Fhad and the other a sophomore named Sayiid. I made it a point to talk to both of them after our next class.

# III. Weeks

The second week in May, geology class had a three-day field trip around Missouri. The day before we left, Sayiid sat beside me in the lecture hall. "Aren't you excited about the field trip?" I asked.

"I can't go," he said. "I have to meet with a friend of my father."

"I'll take some extra pictures for you," I volunteered.

I was disappointed Sayiid couldn't go, but I could still make Fhad feel included if the other students avoided him. Besides, he was funny and polite.

As I walked out of class, Fhad called to me, "Hey, Sayiid." I wanted to ignore him, but he was speaking in Arabic and I could not pretend he was not talking to me because I was the only one who could understand him.

"Yes," I replied in English. I was not about to play his game.

"That girl in class. What's her name? The girl who's gotten so talkative," he said. "She told me you're skipping the field trip."

My face must have revealed some involuntary reaction to Fhad discussing the blue-eyed girl because he jumped on my reaction even before I spoke, "Oh. Wow." He pointed at me. "Look at him. You like her."

All I could think to do was say, "Fuck you!" and walk away.

The field trip was fun, and when we got back, Fhad asked me out to dinner. It was a school night, but I was flattered that a senior asked me out, so I said, "Yes." We ate at Jasper's in Waldo. He knew just the right things to order. It didn't bother him that I didn't want any wine, and he got me back to my dormitory ten minutes before curfew.

Sayiid called right after I got back, but I didn't recognize his voice, and he just started in telling me what to do. "Don't trust him,"

"Who's this?" I asked.

"This is Sayiid," he said. "Don't trust him."

He was as confusing as Betty. "Don't trust who?" I asked.

"Fhad, that's who," he said, and then he gave me a talk about how I should be suspicious of Fhad. I was annoyed he was lecturing me, but I did wonder how he knew I'd told Fhad I'd come to a swim party at his apartment on the weekend. I figured Sayiid knew because he'd been invited, too.

Fhad picked me up in his BMW and took me to his apartment. It was a new building and looked expensive. "The others will be here soon," he said as we walked in. He pulled back a curtain revealing a glass door that opened to a deck. Sunlight flooded the room. "The pool is out here." He indicated another door. "You can change in there."

It was a bedroom. "I'll wait until the other girls get here."

"No problem," Fhad said, and he breezed by me to a door on the far side of the bedroom. "Private bathroom. You can change here." He made a great show of closing the drapes so the room would be private, but he lingered as though there was something else, and I felt uncomfortable.

"Hey, Fhad," came a loud voice as the front door opened. Another Arab walked right into the room as though he'd been there a hundred times. He stopped when he saw me. "Oops! I didn't know you had company..."

"Hi, Saad," Fhad said. "I was showing my friend where she could change for the pool. We need to let her dress." But as he left the room, he paused and brushed his hand on my hair like he was going to say something.

What'd happened? Wasn't I thinking the worst just because Sayiid had warned me? I peaked around the curtain at Fhad and Saad on the patio. Then I pushed the button lock, changed into my swimsuit, and other couples got there. It turned out to be a fun afternoon.

I saw Fhad on Sunday afternoon as I was getting gas. He looked askance at my car and pantomined that he couldn't even begin to compare my Buick to his BMW. Then he started talking about the girl with the incredibly blue eyes. From what he said, I assumed he had gotten the blue-eyed girl to bed with him. I wanted to strangle him, and I frowned involuntarily before I could force a smile. Fhad saw that, and he pounced, "Sorry. I got there first."

Again, "Fuck you," was all I could say.

"She's a nice girl, Sayiid, but she's out of your league. She needs a mature man." He could see my anger. "Tell you what, little brother. I'm out of here in two weeks. You'll have another chance."

I was doing well in geology. My grandfather had spent hours showing me how the Niobrara River cut through layers of rock around Valentine, so the course remined me of summers at home. My roommate Lynn was taking the same class, but this time she was the one having trouble.

Monday of finals week we had to turn in a project listing the eras of the rocks we saw on the field trip. It counted for a third of our grade. Sunday afternoon, Lynn was in a panic. "I don't know how to do this."

I thought if I helped her she'd be nicer to me so I volunteered, "I'm almost done. Do you want me to help you?"

"Oh, yes. That'd really be great."

It was a simple assignment, but we didn't have computers back then and typing anything took hours. I helped Lynn until about 10:30, but when I started typing my chart, Lynn asked me, "Can't you do that in the morning? I've got to get up at 8:00 o'clock."

"Sure. I'll have time," I said as I set our alarm clock.

But Lynn woke up early, turned off the alarm before it sounded, and left without waking me up. I barely had time to start on my chart before I had to run to turn it in. Lynn got a B+ in geology. I got a D-. She never asked me my grade, she didn't thank me, and she was still mean.

I saw Sayiid at our geology final, but he ignored me. I figured he was upset that I went swimming at Fhad's, but I couldn't understand why. Fhad was a nice, and when I told him I had to earn part of my money for school, he gave me his used books for classes in the fall.

Soon after I arrived home in the desert for the summer, my brother Jabir called from Germany to tell my parents that he wanted to marry a German girl named Elke. My mother immediately worried he would dishonor our family. She believed that all Western women were promiscuous, and by definition a promiscuous woman could not be a virgin. A bride must be a virgin so that she cannot compare her husband to any other man. How else can a man feel secure in his home?

The American idea that a pregnant girl might "need to get married" would be a joke in the desert. A good family would never allow their son to marry a girl who was not a virgin, no matter what the circumstances. In the same way, to prove their daughter is a virgin is a mark of honor for a bride's parents—as important as her dowry. To prove virginity, representatives of both families inspect a girl's hymen.

Jabir anticipated Mother's reaction, so he asked Elke's parents to escort her on the trip. In addition, he arranged an examination by the midwife who had delivered us. The nurse who cared for us as children was the witness for my family. Elke's mother did not want to watch her daughter's humiliation, but Elke begged her to be present so she would not be alone.

Elke's father was insulted, but during the War he had dealt in military supplies and when Germany lost, he lost everything. He could never give his daughter as much as my wellborn brother, even if he was an Arab, and it was better than losing her to a drunken American GI.

I tried to imagine how Elke felt with her legs apart for everyone to get a good look. It was her choice, and it surprised me that a Western woman loved an Arab enough to put her vagina on display for his family. Over the years, however, it has surprised me even more how openly Jabir has loved her.

Elke's hymen was intact, and my parents had no other reason to object. Jabir and Elke married and returned to Germany. After they had gone, I wondered if I would ever defy my parents to marry a Western girl. The idea of the girl with incredibly blue eyes briefly entered my mind, but after she had gone to Fhad's apartment, that would not be acceptable. Fhad did not say she had sex with him, but it was enough to know that she had been alone with him. I would never consider any situation where I was second to a Shiia.

Just before I returned to Kansas City for my junior year, the Egyptian government arrested Sayyid Qu'tb for treason. Qu'tb was a secular Egyptian writer who had changed to become very religious, and his arrest sparked many conversations.

Based on a visit in the 1950s, Qu'tb described American culture as crass and offensive. He could not get a decent haircut, Americans drank tea without sugar, and women exposed the shape of their bodies to excite men's lust. He never explained why he was troubled by the arousal of his lust. Perhaps he embarrassed himself in front of some Americans, but whatever the reason, his obsession with the behavior of American women was reminiscent of the pretend piety of Rev. Dimmesdale in *The Scarlet Letter*, one of the few American novels I bothered to read.

Qu'tb proclaimed that secular rulers of Egypt were leading people away from the true beliefs of Islam—or allowing them to depart from Islamic law, it made no difference whether it was an active or a passive process—and that displeased God. For this reason, it was the duty of Muslims to replace the government with a theocracy that adhered to a strict interpretation of the Qu'ran. He would not compromise with the government, so he was hanged a year later.

The followers of Qu'tb were like supporters of the younger President Bush thirty years later. They supported his policies in direct proportion to how ignorant they were about the countries their leader criticized, so that his most vocal supporters were those who knew the least about America.

Several weeks after Qu'tb's arrest, my father gathered many of his friends at our home to wish good fortune to Wahiib and me as we returned for the next school year. This was my father's way to express satisfaction with my accomplishments thus far. He even invited his superior, the Prince.

In the tradition that older men would counsel younger men, my father and his friends dominated the conversation. Late in the evening, the Prince asked if I agreed with Qu'tb that American women tried to arouse men's lust.

"I cannot answer your Highness with authority," I fumbled as I remembered Carol and Kristen Hartwood, and Tina, and women in shorts. "I do not know their intent, but," I warmed to the question, "the women dress as Qu'tb says. They expose skin and show the shapes of their bodies. There are many temptations in America."

I added the latter to claim by inference that I had been tempted but resisted. My father, at least, might believe that.

I decided to spare my father telling the Prince about swimming with the Hartwoods' nearly-naked daughters. That story would lower everyone's perception of the Hartwoods' morality and adversely affect my father's reputation with anyone, the Prince included, who had been a guest with the Hartwoods in our home. If my father's reputation suffered, mine would also.

The Prince listened. There was nodding of heads among the men. Then the Prince turned to Wahiib. "Cousin. Do you agree?"

Wahiib hesitated as though he had not expected the question. "It is difficult to know, cousin. I agree that their clothes are provocative. They show their legs, and their hair is not covered."

After several months being around no young women, even these words excited me. I remembered the warmth of Tina in the back seat.

"But it is not easy to interpret," Wahiib continued. "Here, a woman who allows her skin to be seen says something about herself. She should only dress that way for her husband. If other men see her, it is clearly wrong." He chose his words carefully. "I think America is different. Even women who are old, or fat, show their legs and wear shirts that show the shape of their breasts. It is difficult to believe these women are trying to arouse lust."

Everyone chuckled. A man waved the shape of a woman's body in the air and pantomimed "she" was hobbling with a cane. Wahiib continued, "They have different rules, and we cannot be certain what they intend."

One of the other men challenged him. "Surely you do not contradict the Prophet who wrote that women should dress modestly."

"I agree," Wahiib answered, "but modesty is different in America. Here, if a woman exposes herself she is trying to attract attention. In their country, all women expose their arms and legs, so a person who dresses like that will not stand out and thus she may not be immodest."

The man waved him off. "You argue too much like an American."

I silently asked myself, *Does intent matter?* Is it better when a woman intends to excite you? Come to think of it, it was more exciting with the Hartwoods' girls who did not intend to be exciting. It was more exciting when the girl was naïve.

Ali and Mo arrived as my father's friends were leaving. The four of us were traveling together the next day, and they were guests in my father's house that night. As I went to sleep, the blue-eyed girl was again on my mind. Fhad had gotten to her to bed, and that angered me.

My father arranged First Class tickets. On the flight from New York to Kansas City, the crew served a meal and champagne, and there was only one passenger besides us in the front cabin. To Wahiib's disapproval, I had another glass of champagne. As the stewardess set the second glass on my tray, I tried to pick her up. "Where are you from?"

"Chicago," she replied.

"Do you still live in Chicago?"

"No. I'm domiciled in Kansas City."

"What's 'domiciled'? It sounds painful."

She smiled. "It's the word they use to mean I have a home there and fly out of Kansas City. They say I'm domiciled there."

"I'm domiciled in Kansas City, too," I said.

The other passenger rang the call bell. I could not see if it was a man or a woman. The stewardess smiled and went to answer. Mo watched from across the aisle and gave me a thumbs-up like we had seen in war movies.

After the stewardess removed my tray, I asked for her phone number, but she said she didn't date passengers. "But I'm not just a passenger," I said. "I'm a special friend of Mr. Hartwood. You know who Mr. Hartwood is? Mr. Everett Hartwood?" She didn't believe me.

"Everyone knows who Mr. Hartwood is."

"He and my father work together. They've been setting up a new airline." After the champagne, I was speaking broadly. "I've known Mr. Hartwood since I was that tall," I said and reached my hand toward the aisle to show her, which happened to be below her waist. She dodged back as though I was going to touch her pussy.

"I met him in my father's house. Mrs. Hartwood was there, too."

"I've got to check the other passengers." She picked up the last trays and got on the intercom to remind everyone to fasten their seat belt low and tight. As she walked down the aisle for her final check, I caught her hand. "Come on. Just your phone number." She smiled.

As we stepped off the plane, she slipped a piece of paper into my hand.

Our fathers decided that Wahiib and I would live in the apartment we had gotten for prayers. The building was not old, but the carpets and furniture were poor quality and badly worn. Since we would live there two more years, it was a good investment to make it nicer and my father provided a generous budget. Mrs. Hartwood took over the project. The landlady was a Quaker, who went to the same meeting, so she let Mrs. Hartwood do what she wanted.

Mrs. Hartwood had the carpet replaced and took me to Jones's Store where we bought a sofa bed, two chairs, and two dressing tables. Then we went to the Hawn Bedding Company to buy beds for me and Wahiib. I remember the slogan on their sign, "Yawn time is Hawn time."

I stayed with the Hartwoods while the work was completed. Carol still dated Sam, but now the Hartwoods let her stay out until 1:00 a.m. After our day of buying furniture, they had a barbecue to welcome all of us back. The next day, furniture was delivered, and we moved into our apartment.

I had to wait one more day for our phone to be connected before I called the stewardess's phone number. After three rings, a man answered, "Antonio's Pizzeria. How can I help you?" It was the phone number for an Italian restaurant that delivered pizza.

After classes started, I often met Wahiib at Le Pois. Compared to Europe, midwestern coffee was swill, but skirts were shorter, and if a girl wasn't careful, when she sat down, you could see her panties. The blue-eyed girl talked to Wahiib if she was there at the same time. I talked to her occasionally. She believed almost any story I told her. Like the Hartwoods' daughters, she expected she could trust people.

Pam, my new sophomore roommate, was from Herman, Missouri, which gave us something in common because Herman was as small as Valentine. I'd found reasons to go to Pam's room last year after Christie left, but I didn't dare tell her I was on probation because of bad grades.

I saw Wahiib on campus and asked him how his summer had been. Sayiid was with him a few times, but he was weird, like he was angry about something. I couldn't guess why because we barely knew each other.

Every year, Penn had a backwards dance right after Halloween. It was originally a Halloween dance, but after some guys demonstrated pretty poor taste in costumes, the administration changed the theme to Sadie Hawkins. I asked David, the guy who'd driven up to The Point with me, but I was nervous, so I added, "If you want to go with someone else, I'll understand."

His answer was, "I'd like to go with you."

The dance was the first week of November.

I told Pam. Then panic set in. I'd had a few lessons in waltz and foxtrot in grade school, but this was 1965 and the girls were dancing to songs like "The Name Game" and "Wooly Bully."

"You just get up and bounce," Pam said.

"Bounce how?"

"Sort of side to side, and then a bit like screwing standing up," she answered and began to move her hips around like Elvis Presley did in one of his movies. Her demonstration was doubly informative because, even though I'd read Rabbit, Run I only had the vaguest idea of what screwing was like, standing up or lying down.

I ran into David more often, and I wondered if he was

trying to be where I was to say "Hi" and talk.

I asked my mom to mail me my good dress. She said she would bring it down, but instead she bought a new dress at Emery, Bird, Thayer on the Plaza and brought it down the Saturday a week before the dance. It was on sale, but it was from Emery, Bird's.

In American history class I'd gotten the second highest grade on the midterm. If I did well on the final, I'd get off probation, so I spent a lot of time in the library. In the middle of Sunday afternoon, Betty, the girl who'd been Christie's roommate, found me and said, "I've got to talk to you."

"I can meet you after dinner," I offered.

"No. I've got to talk to you now. It's an emergency."

I couldn't think how I'd be involved in an emergency with Betty, but after what she did to Christie, I was afraid to make her angry at me. So I followed her out of the hall.

"You asked David to the backwards dance didn't you?" she demanded.

"Yes." I smiled involuntarily. "Why?"

"I've got to go with him."

"What do you mean?"

She shot back, "Do you love him?"

"What?" My mind tumbled over words like, *I like to spend time with him...he's a nice guy...he's good looking*. But love? All I could reply was, "I don't know."

"Don't know?" she exclaimed, "and you're standing between us? I love him. You can't make him go with you if you don't even know."

"But I've already asked him."

"Tell him you can't go. Tell him you've got to go home to help your mother. I don't care. Just tell him." She had me on the defensive; I worried what she could do to me, and in the end, I promised I'd call David that night.

I already worried he was going with me because I was the first person to ask, but I felt awful when I called him. "David, I can't go to the dance with you. I'm sorry. I wish I could."

"Why not? I was looking forward to it."

"I have to go home that weekend."

"I've got a car. I can pick you up at home and then take you back. It's not that far."

"I don't think that would work out." It sounded like he cared, but it'd be too embarrassing to change my mind because that would be like admitting I was making up a story in the first place.

I felt like the world's biggest loser, and I was too ashamed to tell my mom or Pam what really happened. So I made up a story for them, and I made excuses to tell myself, like, we were only friends from class. I didn't believe he wouldn't be a lot happier with Betty.

When I did a year in Bern—and Brad and I spent hours deciphering *Playboy*—I told him I was a prince. He believed my story and worked to maintain our relationship. His family had the connections and money for a prestigious college, but Brad was not a student at heart and his parents realized he would do better at a school where getting average grades was less difficult. They chose the University of Missouri, better known to students as Mizzou. Brad was studying journalism.

Columbia, Missouri, where Mizzou is located, is in the middle of Missouri. Besides the University, there were two all-girls colleges, Stephens College and Christian College.

I spent a couple of weekends at Mizzou that fall. Brad introduced me to his friends as an Arab prince. Most of them had never left the Midwest, so Brad's sojourn in Switzerland made him an expert on international affairs. Some of them may have known that the gas they burned in their cars at twenty-five cents per gallon had originated in the Middle East, but none of them even began to comprehend how much money they fed to Arab princes as they sped at seventy miles per hour on the interstate.

Brad was dating a "Susie," a girl from Stephens College. She set me up on a date with her roommate. Girls from Stephens had a reputation for coming from families with a lot of money and for being rebellious because their parents had parked them in the middle of Missouri. My date was blonde and blue-eyed, so my dark skin made a date with me an extension of her rebellion, and having been told by Brad that I was a prince made me exotic.

We went to a keg party where guys and their dates sat around an open fire drinking and roasting marshmallows. Gradually, couples got up and carried blankets into the shadows away from the fire.

I stood up and pulled the blonde girl's hand. She was compliant, and we walked about fifty meters from the fire, stepping around some other couples who were so involved in each other that they did not notice us. I spread a blanket on the ground, and we kissed and then lay down.

Coming from a place where a boy would never even be alone with a girl, this was nearly too much. I met this girl two hours earlier, and we were rolling on the ground in the dark with only a few flickers of light from a fading campfire. I looked at the stars. "Same stars here as at home."

"Very romantic," she said. "Like the Arabian Nights or something."

After a while, I kissed her again. She let me kiss her, and then she opened her mouth and kissed me back. I thought, "This girl wants me."

I kissed her deeply, and she responded. I pulled her close and edged my hip into the soft place between her legs. It was warm, and I slid my hand under her blouse at her waist and rubbed her breasts through her bra. I don't share the American fascination with breasts, so I quickly put my hand on her upper thigh and grabbed her butt through her jeans. Then I rubbed her between her legs, and she kissed me more.

She let me slide my hand under the waist of her jeans to touch the bare skin of her ass, but when I moved my hand around inside her panties toward her hair, she pushed back. "No," she said.

I stopped moving, but I didn't remove my hand.

"I said 'No!'" she repeated. Then she got louder. "Let go of me."

I worried others would hear her, so I tried to put my other hand to her mouth to calm her. But that left me open, and she jerked her knee hard up between my legs. I stifled an intense, "Agh..." and let go.

She jumped up and walked back to the fire without a word. I lay there holding my crotch and remembered that, with Tina, I kept going. It was a mistake to pause. I also saw the importance of having a place where I would not be afraid of noise—and where the girl could not walk away. All of this was reinforced when I looked at myself the next day and saw a large bruise.

My family drove to Valentine for Thanksgiving and missed dinner at the Hartwoods' again. I loved my grandfather, but it was a crazy, wild rush to get up there late Wednesday night. Then we got up at dawn on Thursday to cook a turkey, had dinner, and ate leftovers Friday and Saturday.

Mom and I spent Friday and Saturday cleaning the bathroom and the kitchen while Freddy and Dad visited Dad's friends. Harry wasn't home because of a big game.

On the drive home, Mom commented that she thought Granddaddy might not be able to stay in the house much longer. All Dad said was, "I don't see that it makes much difference. We clean the house in the summer and at Thanksgiving. He's happy. Leave him where he is." It was unfair that Dad said "we" and didn't give Mom credit for all her work.

In movies, I learned how Americans talked, shopped, drove, and ate. I learned their slang, and James Bond showed how to act when a man was alone with a woman. *Goldfinger* was in a second run, and the four of us saw it that weekend. Later, we met Masoud and Khalid at Arthur Bryant's. Bryant's did not serve beer, but they did not object if we brought our own. We bought a six-pack at Berbiglia's. Wahiib was squeamish as usual.

We talked about how Bond knew how to handle women. "That's like me," I said.

"Oh, right," chimed in Mo. "One girl in two years. Right."

"I'm saving my energy," I continued. "I'm going to date a girl at Penn." The blue-eyed girl popped into my mind. She was the only Penn coed who'd even talk to me. "Just wait."

The editor of the student newspaper, *Penn Life*, fanned my dreams. For example, a front page in October read, "Are student values changing?" Two Penn students were scheduled to discuss everything from religion to sex on a local television program called "College Update." The editor predicted they would reveal great changes in student values.

The editor, David Le Coste, never said girls should have sex before marriage; but he said old ideas were up for debate and gave a clear idea of how he would settle the debate. A few weeks later, he wrote about the sexual revolution:

> "The administration should be more realistic in how they try to control the problem of the so-called 'new

> morality,' because perhaps, for the students, the ones whose lives are actually affected by the change, there isn't really a problem."

I looked for opportunities to be with Wahiib when the blue-eyed girl stopped by. One time, Wahiib was in class, and she asked me where I was from. I told her. "Like Wahiib," she observed. "It must cost a lot to come this far to school. Are you rich or something?"

I used the same story. "I'm a prince." Which was only partially a lie. The King and his forefathers have been very vigorous and the majority of men are related to the King in known or unknown ways. I actually knew that I was a fourth cousin by marriage through my mother's grandfather.

She asked me what I was doing for Thanksgiving. I told her I would be with friends, but I did not mention Mr. Hartwood's name. Had I realized that her parents knew the Hartwoods, I might have done things differently.

In December, my former roommate, Larry Davis, called. He got right to the point. "I want to invite you and your friends to hear the *Messiah*."

"Why?"

"Because it's the holiday season. Because if you want to understand Christmas, you should hear the *Messiah* at least once." He had obviously rehearsed prior to making the call. "And because I feel I should ask you."

I had forgotten that Larry sang in the school choir. I wanted to ask if this was an apology for being such a judgmental prick, but instead I said, "I'm surprised. Let me talk to my friends."

I was glad I saw the *Messiah*. Of course, I was disappointed when we stood up to leave as they sang some chorus, but then sat down to listen for another forty-five minutes. But all together it was educational. That was the first time I heard several melodies that are iconic in the West.

I saw the blue-eyed girl on the other side of the crowd as we were leaving. She saw Wahiib and worked her way toward us. "Don't you just love the *Messiah*?" she asked.

"Yes," I answered.

"It puts me right into the holiday mood." She smiled awkwardly and then asked with genuine curiosity, "Do you go home for the holidays?"

"Sometimes, but this year we're going skiing."

"Wow. I've never been skiing. What's it like?"

"Neither have I. We're driving out to Colorado to try it." I had an impulse. "Would you like to come over to our place for a Coke?"

She was startled, and then made a little face that was like an apology. "Uh. I don't think I should."

"No one ever comes to our parties," I complained. Then I reassured her, "Wahiib will be there. You can go with us in my car."

My accusation put her on the defensive, and when Wahiib became part of the invitation, she accepted. On the ride over, she sat between me and Wahiib in the front seat. Despite her winter coat, I could feel she had more—what did the guys say?—"meat on her" than Tina, but not enough to be embarrassingly fat.

Sayiid shared an apartment with Wahiib, so I figured he'd be nice, too. And not going would have been counter to my plan to make the Arabs feel that Americans accepted then.

Actually, Sayiid and I were both outsiders at Penn, but Sayiid was less bothered than me and his approach to life was more attractive. He had all the confidence I didn't have. He did what he wanted, while I didn't have the confidence to say what I wanted at all. While I struggled, classes were easy for him. When I worried about grades, he laughed and said I could do it. He'd been to school in Europe, and he was so cosmopolitan and sophisticated. He had a protocol about him, like knowing the right thing to do in every situation, and he was incredibly neat in style. He was fun-loving and seemed, to me anyway, like he had the world at his feet. I could dream of one big trip to Europe someday, but he had enough money to fly beyond Europe just for vacation. And he was flirting with me. I was going to ask if he was the son of Mr. Hartwood's friend, but I never got around to it.

The day everyone left for vacation, Sayiid asked what I was doing for the holiday. "We're going to Valentine," I told him.

"I thought Valentine's was in February."

"That's the holiday. We're driving up to my grandparents' in Valentine. It's a town in Nebraska."

"Never heard of it."

"Most people haven't." I added, "It's a real small town. I lived there until I was eight."

"What's there?"

"Mostly ranches."

"Your grandparents own a ranch?"

"I wish. They live in town now. Grandpa worked on the railroad. That's where he met Nanny. She was a cook. Then the railroad shut down, and he worked on a ranch. He still rides really well. Sometimes he borrows horses and takes me riding." I liked telling Sayiid about my hometown.

The four of us had a great time in Colorado. I was the first one to ski black diamonds. It is ironic that you cannot ski well if you are overly cautious. Trying too hard interferes with control.

We drove back early because a storm was expected. This left us in our apartments for the last two days of the year. We decided to see *Dr. Zhivago* because it starred Omar Shariff who was an Arab like us even though his movies were banned as immoral in the desert.

The film excited me. I thought of Tina as Komarovsky seduced Lara. He and I understood what we wanted. We had the money to impress women. We led them to where we were in control, and took the pleasure we needed.

At first I did not understand Lara and Dr. Zhivago, but as their paths crossed, I saw that, despite his quiet façade, Yuri was intensely passionate. I also hid my passionate nature. Lara tried to deny her attraction to Yuri, but when they were alone, they went to bed. I thought about Wahiib's friend, the blue-eyed girl. I was not going to find a wife in America, but there could still be conquests. James Bond never got married. Zhivago never married Lara.

"What a good looking woman, Lara," said Mo as we drove back to my apartment. "I'd love to fuck her, too."

I was too involved in my fantasy of Lara and the blue-eyed girl to allow him to besmirch either one. "She's not a fuck. She loved that guy, the doctor. Zhivago. He just didn't know how to love her at first."

"What do you know? Why are you suddenly the expert?"

"I know a lot," I protested. "I know a lot."

"Oh, like all the girls at Penn who are just running after you?"

"Shut up." But I was in a corner and my unplanned response was to throw down my daydream as though it was fact. "There's a girl who likes me. I can tell it. I just need some time alone with her."

"Are you guys proud of how you're talking?" Wahiib interrupted.

"No. No." Mo cut Wahiib off. "I want to hear. What are

you saying, Sayiid? Let's be out in the open."

I knew immediately how stupid it was to mention the blue-eyed girl, but I was out on a limb so I decided to be really daring. "I said I've met a Penn girl who's hot for me. I just need some time alone with her."

"Cut it out, Sayiid," said Wahiib. "You sound like a desert rat."

"No," Ali disagreed. "Let's see what the big man can do. Bet, Sayiid? Polish my shoes for the next year? If you lose, polish my shoes?"

"No bets. I'd feel sorry for you. I know what's going to happen."

The Hartwoods invited all four of us to their party on New Year's Day, but I did not pass along the invitation. I told the Hartwoods they had other plans. I think they watched football with Masoud and Khalid.

There were about thirty guests. Carol was a senior in high school, so she and her friends talked about colleges. Again, it was so unfamiliar. In the desert, women this age would gossip about who was getting married and who had gotten married and was already pregnant.

The entertainment was an afternoon of football. The big focus was on Missouri against Florida in the Sugar Bowl. I was bored, so I wandered into the kitchen where Carol was spreading crackers on a plate. Even in the safety of her parents' house, being close to her excited me. In the desert, I would never be alone with the daughter of any friend of my father. When she saw me she hurried out another door.

Men cheered in the other room. Missouri had scored.

"How was Valentine's Day?" I asked the blue-eyed girl back at Penn.

"Not Valentine's Day," she protested. "Valentine,

Nebraska." She blushed slightly. "What was skiing like?"

"I had a great time. I'm actually pretty much a natural."

"It must be fun to do stuff like that, go to Europe and ski. You know such interesting people."

This gave me an opening to ask her to go somewhere with me. "Would you like to meet some of the European students?"

"I'd love to. I applied to be a foreign exchange student in high school." She paused as though admitting a failure. "But I didn't get it. I was a finalist, though."

"The Arabian Student Association has a gathering for international students Friday night. You can be my guest."

The blue-eyed girl arrived at the party late. Everyone was involved in their own conversations. There was a light rain, and she stood by the door in a trench coat with her arms folded across her chest as though she was cold. I understood why Fhad was attracted to her. She had a trusting, sexy vulnerability. I let her stand for several minutes before I crossed the room and said, "I thought you were going to stand me up."

"I wasn't trying to stand you up." Then she added, "I didn't realize this was a date. I'm sorry."

I was annoyed. "What else would it be?"

"I don't know. You said 'gathering,' so I thought it was a meeting of some kind. I'm sorry."

I sighed slowly to let her know I was displeased before I asked, "Should I get you a Coke? That's all they have."

"Yes, please."

I poured half a glass of Coke, and when no one was looking, I added a small, airplane bottle of rum to fill it up. When I returned, she was talking with Wahiib. "I was surprised to see you here," Wahiib said to her, as he glanced at me with disapproval.

Before she could reply, a couple of other students pulled Wahiib away to settle an argument about life in the desert. When he was out of earshot, I said, "You've got to watch him. He's quite the ladies man, you know."

It was almost too easy. She did not anticipate how some men are excited by an unchaperoned girl, and she stared at Wahiib to try to see what clue she had overlooked. "Thank you," she said and took an anxious gulp from her glass. She coughed once and immediately leaned forward and backwashed the rest of it into her glass. "What's that?"

"Coke," I said flatly.

"That's Coke?"

"Trust me—it's Coke."

"Oh." She seemed relieved. It was ironic how taking the initiative to insinuate something bad about Wahiib made her trust me more.

As our Quaker hosts put away the ice and unopened Cokes, I called Mo aside. "Wahiib's a bit of a problem. Can you…uh…keep him away?"

"Sure." Mo winked. "I'm betting on this. Don't want to give you any excuses." He asked Wahiib to join him and Ali for a hamburger. "We'll be gone less than an hour," Mo assured him.

I'd been okay after the *Messiah*, so I didn't think it was risky going to Sayiid's apartment. I thought he was interested in what was good for me because he encouraged me and said I'd do okay in school. I may also have had something to drink at the party which was a new experience for me because I hadn't drunk anything in high school—or before at all, for that matter.

You can bet I was vigilant anyway because—even though *Penn Life* said a girl had a right to go to a boy's apartment—

I knew what could happen if she did. I figured if Sayiid tried anything, I'd be out of there in a flash. That wouldn't be an issue anyway because Wahiib would be there, and despite what Sayiid'd said, Wahiib seemed okay. He was admired by the rest of the Arabs.

Sayiid's apartment was dark, and this time there wasn't food set out like anyone else was coming. I felt awkward. "If you haven't got anything ready," I suggested, "maybe we should get a hamburger or something."

"You Penn girls are all alike," he said sarcastically. "Just because I'm different." I didn't get what he meant, but I didn't mean to hurt his feelings.

The blue-eyed girl talked like she expected to discuss the party, so I played along and told her stories about the countries other students had come from, and when I didn't know real stories, I made them up. I had traveled enough to know how large the world was. She lived in a city, but her understanding was limited to a small town. She only dreamed of what was over the horizon. Years later I took my daughter to see *The Wizard of Oz* and realized the blue-eyed girl was singing "Somewhere Over the Rainbow" all her life, even if she did not know the words.

I got two Cokes from the kitchen and made a point of opening them in front of her to assure her I had not added anything. "Do you want to watch TV?" I suggested as I handed one bottle to her.

I sat on the floor and leaned against the sofa ignoring that she stayed on the couch. "What should we watch?" I asked, not waiting for her to answer.

"I don't care."

The television warmed up and the sound came on. Eventually she gave in to the awkwardness of sitting on two levels and slipped off the couch to sit on the floor beside me. As she did, her skirt caught on the cushion and pulled up showing her legs. She quickly pulled it back down.

I thought to myself, "It's like getting Wahiib to drink beer. The first step was to get him to drink a Coke."

We watched some of "Gomer Pyle" and the beginning of "The Smothers Brothers Show," their early situation comedy the network dropped after one season. "Not very good, is it?" I said.

"Not really."

I knew she was trying to decide whether to leave, so I set my empty Coke can on the carpet and put my left arm around her shoulder. We were about the same height, so I had to sit straighter and almost force her to slouch down. She did not snuggle like Tina, but she did not pull away either. I think she was uncertain what to do because she was surprised.

During a commercial, I turned her face toward me with my hand and kissed her. It was a short kiss. She looked into my eyes, not with fear or anger but to question why I had done that. In the 60s girls still debated whether to kiss a guy on the first date, and I was a classmate she hardly knew.

I was annoyed. She was toying with me. After Fhad, what was the big deal? I kissed her harder and probed her lips with my tongue. She parted her lips just a bit, but she didn't respond like Tina. It was like she wanted to say, "Okay, a little, but then let's stop."

But her reflex to breathe made her open wider, and I seized the chance to probe her mouth with my tongue. She wiggled again, but that moved her toward the floor. A small squeal, a lost attempt to say, "No."

Any moment she might sit on the sofa, or worse yet, leave. I leaned back on my elbows and took a couple of deep breaths. She stared ahead, too. All that ran through my mind was Mo's smile and the realization that, at this rate, nothing would happen. And I remembered Fhad.

So I did what I had to do. I opened the zipper of my trousers. She probably thought I was scratching my crotch because she looked away. I had an especially hard erection, but I didn't wear tight trousers like most guys, so I easily got myself out in the moment she wasn't looking.

I pushed my tongue into her mouth. She tried to pull back and turn her head away again, but this time I stayed on her. In one motion, I went from lying beside her on the floor to straddling her with one knee on the floor on either side of her. She could not push me up, so she wiggled further down on the floor. The carpet caught her skirt and pulled it up so her panties were exposed. She tried to lift her hips off the floor so she could pull her skirt down. I prevented that and put my hand between her legs. She froze, but I did not pause. I leaned on one arm and backed toward her feet just enough that I could get myself under her skirt by her panties.

"What are you doing?" she managed to ask.

"I'm not doing anything." Denial confused her for a moment, and I wondered who she was trying to kid as I found the edge of her panties with my free hand. "Just hold still," I ordered as I worked my fingers around the slippery cloth until I could feel her hair.

I was really hard, but her legs were together, and I could only get myself to the edge of her panties. "I just want to feel what it's like to be here."

She tried to wiggle toward the safety of the sofa, but I leaned on her shoulder with one hand and kept my other hand between her legs. I moved too quickly for her mind to catch up, too fast for her completely to give up her belief that somehow I was still her friend. She managed to plead, "Can't we slow down?"

If her thoughts got organized, I would lose my advantage.

I had one chance before "Stop!" and a struggle.

With my free hand, I jerked her panties aside. I was by her hair. Like skiing black diamonds, I pushed hard between her legs.

She made a little jump before she froze. I remembered how the calf stopped struggling when the cowboy had tied her legs. I came. It had been less than one minute. I was a champion.

# iv. Months

⁚⁚⁚⁚⁚⁚⁚⁚⁚⁚⁚⁚⁚⁚⁚⁚⁚⁚⁚⁚

:I:I:I:I:I:I:I:I

I was too stunned to speak.

Ed McMahon barked, "Heeeeeeer's Johnny!" on the television. Light from the screen flickered between the bumps in the ceiling above me. Sayiid got up and went to the bathroom without saying a word, like I'd upset him. He left the door open, and I heard him pee. Water ran into the tub. There was a metal noise, rings of a shower curtain, and he started humming above the sound of water.

I got up and shook my skirt down. When I looked at the floor, I saw my blood, and I was ashamed like I'd peed on the carpet. "Cold water," I told myself as I looked in the kitchen for something to wipe it up. "Cold water," I repeated as I got on my knees and scrubbed the spot. It helped that I could do something right, but I wanted my back to a wall, and when the shower stopped, I ran out.

When I turned on the light in the bathroom, there were

streaks of blood on me. "Oh," I realized, "It's her monthly flow.

"She wasn't pushing me away," I told myself as I ran hot water. "She was embarrassed because of her period. She was helping me stay clean."

As I rinsed in the shower, I remembered *Dr. Zhivago* and his blue-eyed girl. *You're the next Omar Shariff,* I thought, and before I walked back to the living room, I wrapped a towel around my waist and wiped away the steam to look in the mirror. "Fit, like James Bond," I said to myself.

I walked down the hall. The outside door was partly open. There were wet towels beside the sink, but she was not there. My impulse was to go to bed, but I had not expected her to leave without a word. I wondered if she was upset because I left her alone while I took a shower to clean myself.

Pam was at her desk when I got back to our room. I must've looked a mess because she asked, "What happened to you?"

I gave her some explanation, but I didn't want to get into a conversation. I was obviously soaked from the rain, so I used that as an excuse. "I'm freezing. I'm going to take a hot shower."

I sat on the toilet with my legs apart and looked at myself with a hand mirror. I could see an edge like ripped tissue paper where Sayiid had hurt me. The world fell on my shoulders as I turned the water on hot and got into the shower. I needed time to think, but Pam knocked and cracked the door a bit so she could talk to me. "That guy Sayiid is here," she said. "He wants to talk to you."

"Tell him I can't talk. I'm trying to warm up in the shower."

"Okay."

I turned off all the cold water and let the water run as hot as it could, like I hoped it would burn something away. Pam knocked again, "He's pretty pushy. He says he needs to talk to you."

"Tell him I won't talk to him."

"I'll try."

The room was so steamy I could hardly see the door. Pam didn't come back, and I felt safe enough to turn the water off and wrap my hair in a towel. Then I heard a car horn. Right outside. I left the light off and pushed the curtain aside. Sayiid had pulled into the parking space below my window and kept blaring his horn.

I left the light off and tried to put on clothes, but the noise scared me. What was everyone else thinking? Why wouldn't he stop? Everyone knew about Christie and Carl. They'd jump to the same conclusion about me. It was like his horn was yelling to everyone, "I screwed her. I screwed her. I screwed her." All I could hear was Betty pronouncing, "What a slut." Except it'd be, "If she didn't want it, why'd she go there?" I imagined heads turning every time I walked into a room. And I panicked.

I kept pounding my car horn. Lights came on in two other rooms, and I saw her curtain shift. Then she was standing beside the driver's window with her arms folded across her chest, no coat, no hat, no umbrella. I reached across and opened the passenger door. She hesitated before she stepped through the headlights and got in the passenger side.

"Let's not leave it like that," I said.

She stared and said nothing as I backed out of the driveway.

At my apartment, I brought the umbrella around and opened the passenger door. She did not move until I pulled her shoulder, "Come on. It's warmer inside." A casual observer might have thought I was being careful from the way I tried to keep her dry, but I was remembering a movie of a cowboy trying to break a horse. The cowboy spoke gently at first, and that seemed the best thing to do.

Sayiid opened the door to his apartment. I felt corralled and looked to see if anyone was watching. He tried to act like everything was a normal as could be, but I was still in a daze.

He brought me back to the dorm just before midnight. The light was off, and Pam immediately said in a groggy voice, "Don't put the light on. I'm almost asleep." Then she rolled over and asked, "Where'd you go? One minute you're here and the next you're gone."

"I went up to the store," I said, "and ran into a guy from class. We talked for awhile."

"Oh," she mumbled as she turned back toward the wall.

I lay in bed and stifled tears until the sky began to get light. I'd blown my chance to say anything when I panicked. From the moment I got in his car, anything I said would look like Sayiid and I'd had a spat—and I'd be the student in trouble trying to blame someone for my bad choice. At 8:00 a.m. I realized I could catch the 8:45 bus up to Kansas City if I hurried. Pam woke up while I was gathering books. "Where're you going?"

"Home to study for finals."

"When you coming back?"

"I'll call you."

I walked into my parents' house just before lunch. Dad was in the living room and stood up to greet me. "I didn't know you were coming home. You here for the weekend?"

I stuck with the truth. "I decided to come home to study for finals."

I got nothing done that week. Every day I smiled at breakfast, but after Dad took Freddy to school and Mom left for work, I'd put my face in my hands and sob. I looked at my swim trophies and wondered what had become of me. I wasn't that girl anymore. It was all I could think about—but I couldn't think. The story I couldn't tell anyone boiled through my mind, dragging me through a montage of Sayiid and running away and the blaring of his horn. Always the horn until a sound or motion jerked me back. Then I'd blink and find myself an hour later staring at a blank sheet of paper with only a word or two at the top. My period started early. When I saw the blood, I was certain I was bleeding all over, like I'd picked off a scab or something. Maybe I'd scratched myself in my sleep.

I forced myself to eat, but then felt nauseated for hours. I watched television with my dad. He mimicked the Nazi soldiers in a show about World War II, but I got confused and didn't even know who the bad guys were.

Friday night, I sat at the end of our kitchen counter and watched Mom make beef Stroganoff. Just before she stirred in the sour cream, she picked up a yellow can of mustard powder. "It's my secret ingredient," she explained as she dusted a heaping teaspoon-full across the meat, "but don't add it 'til the cooking's done. That keeps the flavor sharper." The first dollops of sour cream sizzled as she stirred.

Out of curiosity, I touched a finger into the mustard. Mom turned at the moment I put it on my tongue, but before she could speak, I was at the sink spitting and using my hand to cup water.

"Oh, dear," she said as if I wasn't already in pain, "you shouldn't take mustard straight. It'll burn like the dickens."

On Sunday, Mom invited me to go to church with her. It was communion Sunday. At the part where we talked about our sins, I knew God was looking right into me, and I couldn't sit still. I whispered to mom, "I have to go to the bathroom."

"You okay?" she whispered back.

"Sure. Time of the month. I'll meet you at the back." I knew the stuff about forgiveness, but I was beyond that. I was the prodigal daughter who'd wasted my parents' hopes—and betrayed myself.

My first final was Monday. Dad drove me out to Penn on his way to work. Someone told me professors tested on what they said in class, so I'd tried to study my notes, but I knew I did poorly as soon as I walked out. Exams on Tuesday and Wednesday went a little better. My last final was Thursday afternoon.

Wednesday night, I stared burning horribly when I went to the bathroom. Then I had a pain in the bottom of my stomach and needed to pee all the time. Thursday morning, I shivered and began to sweat.

The professor was handing out the tests when I got there and took the last empty seat. I knew most of the answers, but as soon as I started writing, I had to pee again. I made my way down the center aisle to the front of the lecture hall and asked the professor if I could use the john.

"I can't let you do that. It wouldn't be fair to the other students."

"I'm not going to cheat or anything."

He shook his head, "Sorry. You should've used the bathroom before."

I coughed right after I sat down again and suddenly felt warm between my legs. I hoped no one was watching as I edged my finger around my skirt to check. I wasn't certain what I'd touched, so I pretended to scratch my nose as I smelled my finger. Oh, god, pee!

I gathered my purse and test and put my coat over my arm. Before I stood up I squirmed a little to wipe the seat. I walked back to the front, and forced a little smile as I handed the professor my test. I was afraid he'd say something, so before he could see the blank pages, I ran out the door.

I showered, but I still felt dirty. I was on fire when I peed, and I leaked in my pants when I coughed even a little. I was embarrassed to go to the nurse on campus. Then I remembered a doctor near campus on Maler Road.

I walked in and told the nurse I'd wait as long as I had to if he'd see me. He gave me pills that made me pee orange and took the pain away. He also gave me antibiotics. It cost me $7.00, but I only had $5.00 with me, so I promised to bring the rest on Monday. I thanked him, but he mumbled something about an "early honeymoon" as I left. I didn't know what he meant, but it sounded mean the way he said it.

On Saturday, I got a letter from Penn saying I'd been dropped from school. But, in typical Quaker fashion, I could reapply at the dean's office on Monday morning. It was an accreditation thing. They couldn't keep a student who was on probation and flunked a class, but there was no rule that they couldn't let me reapply—which is what I did on paper—and accept me on the spot.

But even though I was back in, I didn't know how to stay in. Then I remembered President Forger seemed like a nice man when he spoke to our class. I could ask him what to do. I walked over to his office, and his secretary said I could see him the next morning at 10:45.

Dr. Paul Forger, former anthropology professor, wasn't your typical college president. He wore baggy clothes and hung out in Le Pois, the student union café. The alumni loved their memories of Dr. Forger. He could be at ease with everyone from a banker to a guitar player. His thesis, "A Study of the Role of Women in Healing," was in the library. He'd done research in the Amazon, and rumor was he took a drink called *ayahuasca* and witnessed cannibalism. Everyone said he learned to be at peace with himself as he listened to the drums at night, wondering whether he'd be their next meal.

I was comfortable I'd made the right decision as soon as Dr. Forger's secretary left and closed the door behind her. He turned through a few pages of my file and then looked up, "What can I do to help you Miss..." He glanced back at the file to get my name right.

"I have a problem..." I began.

His eyes drifted to his desk enough to tell me he was remembering something he'd just read. "I know," he answered in a neutral voice. In an instant, I imagined Christie sitting in the same chair, hearing him say the same things. Everyone said Dr. Forger was so nice, but kicking Christie out was mean—and he was getting ready to do that to me. I wasn't pregnant, but in my mind sex and pregnancy were equally bad. I didn't intend what Sayiid did, but I'd let it happen.

I had to change the conversation. "With classwork," I burst out. "I'm having trouble with classwork. I don't know how to do this," I added, thinking that was a colossal understatement. "I study all the time, but I don't seem to study the right things." He let me go on, and he didn't kick me out.

When I ran out of steam, Dr. Forger picked up the phone. From what I could hear, he called Dr. Baker who taught my sociology class. They chatted and finally came around to talking about me. After he hung up, Dr. Forger flipped through a few pages before he closed my file. "That was Orville Baker. You took his class."

I nodded, because I was too scared to find any words.

"I want you to go over to his office and tell him what you

said about not being able to guess what'll be on exams." Then he smiled, "You're right you know? You can't learn everything, and there's a trick knowing what to study. He'll help you."

I walked out hardly believing that I was still in school, and that began my relationship with Orville Baker, "OB" to Penn students and "Orv" to president Forger, that eventually led to my master's in sociology. He helped me see why nothing made sense and helped me save my college dream.

I bragged to my friends about sex with the blue-eyed girl, but I had a problem. The other Arabs noticed she was never around and I was never with her. I thought of calling her, but her silence made me wonder if that might provoke her to do something that would make people gossip about me.

In the next edition of *Penn Life*, the editors fired another salvo in what had been called the Sexual Revolution. A front-page picture showed a student waving a poster with a circle with an arrow to symbolize a male and another circle with an "x" to symbolize a female. The caption read "Double Standard???" and the article quoted the dean of women, "Perhaps we don't need fewer rules for women, but more rules for men."

The second page had a cartoon that might have been in *Playboy* a few years earlier. A college girl stands in her room. Her hair is tousled. A sleeve is torn loose at the shoulder. Her skirt is ripped, her slip shows, and the top of a stocking is pulled down. Her roommate looks at her with alarm as the girl says, "And he was captain of the DEBATE team!"

I doubt the blue-eyed girl laughed at the cartoon, but I saw two guys in Le Pois the day that issue came out. One saw the cartoon, chuckled, and poked his companion to show it to him, and they laughed together. They looked "clean cut." Perhaps they were on the debate team.

It was two weeks before I saw the blue-eyed girl walking across campus alone. She held her books close to her chest like protection. I did not approach her until she had gotten a drink and sat down at Le Pois.

"Hi," I said.

"Oh," she looked around to see if anyone was watching.

"I haven't seen you around."

"I've been studying really hard."

"It's too soon to work that hard. You'll burn out. You should get out."

"I can't. I'm in real trouble."

"Studying doesn't solve trouble."

Then she just burst out in a loud whisper, "I flunked out."

"What do you mean 'flunked out'? You're still here."

"It's a long story," she said, but she didn't explain as she gathered her books. "Got a class."

I called several times, but the blue-eyed girl's roommate always said she was unavailable. Finally, I left a message that I would pick her up at 7:00 in the evening. That got results. She called back a few minutes later and said she would meet me at a cafe near campus on Maler Road.

When she arrived, I already had a cup of coffee. She waited to see what I would say. It was obvious she was there because I had said I would come to her room, but I did not acknowledge that. Doing so would point out to her that she could avoid me if she chose.

"How's class?" I asked

"Okay," she answered.

"You in another sociology class this semester?"

"Yes."

"Which one?"

"Dr. Baker's class."

"He's kind of a crazy guy, isn't he?

"I don't know."

Another student came in and got coffee to go. He didn't say anything, but he looked at her, then at me, and he looked surprised. The blue-eyed girl pretended she did not recognize him, but I could tell she knew him. I tried to recall why he was familiar, and then remembered that he was a townie. To take the initiative, I said, "Let's cut the library and go to a movie."

"If that's what you want to do."

"That's what I want to do," I said. "There's an 8:00 show at the Rockhill. A French film. *A Man and a Woman.*"

The theater was in a marginally bad part of town, but we found parking only a few meters from the door. The movie was romantic. I took her hand, but she did not hold mine back. It felt like touching my sister.

The show let out five minutes after ten, later than I had expected. Her weekday curfew was 10:30 so we had to hurry, and I was doing about forty when I saw a red light flashing in my rear view mirror. "Damn! A cop," I thought as I slowed down and pulled over.

Sayiid was speeding when he ran a speed trap. When the policemen tried to flag us down, Sayiid pushed the accelerator to the floor. His car had a big engine, and the tires squealed, but just as quickly, he pulled over to the side of the road. The officer was irritated because he had to walk farther to where we stopped. As he approached the car, Sayiid opened the door to get out. The officer paused with his hand by his gun and ordered, "Stay in the car, boy. You were doing forty-two in a thirty-five-mile zone." He wasn't trying to be polite. "Let me see your license."

Sayiid reached into his pocket and pulled out a big,

folded document. The cop looked at it. "What's this, boy?"

"It's from your State Department...sir!" Sayiid replied sarcastically. "It says I'm a diplomat, and I can drive anywhere I please. It means you can write me a ticket, I'll throw it away, and nothing will happen." Sayiid was doing everything he could to irritate the officer. "So, I suggest you return it, and we'll just go on our way. This young lady is late as it is."

The officer looked at me and asked, "You okay, miss?"

I managed a weak smile, "Yes...yes..." I didn't want to be there, but if I left now, there'd be no way Sayiid wouldn't just make a scene the next time I showed my face at Penn.

The officer didn't give up so easily. "You okay being with him, you want to be, I mean..." His voice trailed off.

I suppressed tears. "Yes, officer. I'm okay. Thank you for asking."

The officer hesitated. Then he said, "I'm going to call my sergeant." A few minutes later, he came back and tossed the license in the window without a word. Then he turned off his flashlight and walked back to the patrol car.

"How do you do that?" I asked.

"What?"

"Throw away a ticket."

"Diplomatic immunity. I'm registered as a diplomatic dependent. They can kick me out of the country, but they can't do anything else to me. I could kill someone, and they'd just send me home."

"I thought your dad worked for an airline."

"He does, but he has friends," he said smugly. "He did this for my safety. He doesn't totally believe I'm safe here. I don't know why."

I've come to understand why. In the Middle East, everyone smiles for appearances' sake, but you never trust anyone who isn't a blood relative. When laws work according to who you know, it's a survival skill. It was one of many desert rules Sayiid brought to Jackson City.

I got so many demerits for being late that I was campused the next weekend. At least the school kept me safe from 7:00 Friday night to Sunday afternoon. After that, Sayiid was more powerful than a policeman again.

Sayiid called the next Thursday and said he'd be over to pick me up at 7:00 on Friday. I didn't want to be seen with him, so I told him I'd be out and it'd be easier to meet at the café again. I don't think he believed me, but he let it slide. "We can hang out at my place," he said.

I didn't want to go anywhere near his place, but how else could I get him to leave me alone around the other students? "You know my roommate, Wahiib?" he continued.

"Yes."

"He will be there." I couldn't think of a reply quick enough before he said, "That's agreed. I'll see you then."

Friday night I met the blue-eyed girl about 7:15. I told her I forgot something at my apartment and had to go by there. She wanted to wait on the porch, but I reminded her Wahiib was there, so she came inside.

I pretended to look for something in my bedroom, but it pissed me off that she and Wahiib were laughing together when I came out. "Cutting in on my girl?" I said.

"Oh, no," Wahiib answered. "We're discussing class."

"We have the same sociology class, just different sections," she added.

"You shouldn't be flirting with my friends," I said to her.

Wahiib quietly withdrew to where the television was, but he asked us if we wanted to watch television with him. Before I could make an excuse, the blue-eyed girl said that would be great.

We watched television for about two hours. I ordered pizza and drove her back to her room earlier than I had planned. "I'll pick you up at 8:00 tomorrow night," I said as I stopped in front of her dormitory.

"I can't go out tomorrow night."

"Why not?"

"I just can't."

"I asked, 'Why not?'"

"I have plans."

"What are you doing? Going bowling?"

"No. I just have plans."

"Who are you going with?"

She was defensive, and I was irritated. "I have plans," she insisted.

Then I realized, "You have a date. You little bitch. You think you're going out with some other guy. Who would that be? Huh?"

"I'm just going out."

"Yeah. You're going out with me."

"I can't. I have plans."

"No. You don't have plans! You know what I think of your plans? I'll stay right here and find out who you don't have a date with. Then you watch. You don't have a date because I'll tell him that you're mine. My girl isn't going to go fucking with some other guy."

"I'm not..." She tried to be determined, "I'm not going fucking..."

"You're right. You're not going anywhere with anyone."

She was shaking and tears rolled out of the corners of her eyes. "Look," I said, "don't make me say these things. Call the sucker. Tell him you can't go. Say your Mother's sick. I don't care. Just be ready at 8:00."

The students who wrote for *Penn Life* seemed to take

Sayiid's side against me. They kept pushing for students to live off campus and freedom for women—which meant freedom to screw around for men.

> The basis for Penn's Victorian policies on women's housing and women's curfews seems to be the assump tion that women's minds change in some way at mid night...something—whatever something is might happen after midnight that could not just as easily happen between 1:00 and 3:00 p.m. ...sexual behavior can only be controlled by the persons involved...always a personal choice."

I wonder if David LaCoste who wrote those words ever sits in his law office and thinks about what he accomplished. It was fun to rebel, right up to the moment it got violent. His pontificating didn't explain that a girl had to expect to be raped if she went to a friend's apartment. And I doubt he had a clue what it meant when a girl's only personal choices were either to go someplace else with a guy to keep him off campus, and feel awful in private, or to hide so he wouldn't humiliate her on campus.

Sayiid got more aggressive. He'd threaten to come over, so I'd pretend I was going to be out anyway and it'd be convenient to drop by his apartment. I always hoped Wahiib would be there because he seemed at least to suspect what was going on, maybe even what Sayiid did to me in the first place.

One night Wahiib wasn't there, but that was my fault because I'd forgotten to check. I didn't want to stay, but Sayiid was prepared. "I've already made coffee. Real Arab coffee, not that green piss they drink in the East. And the pizza will be here in a few minutes. At least have something to eat. Then we'll go to a movie or something."

A pizza delivery guy showed up, but before I'd eaten even

one piece, Sayiid put his hand around my head and kissed me hard. I didn't like what he was starting, so I tried to move away casually, and stood behind a chair in the kitchen. But he pulled my hand toward his room with enough of a grip I couldn't stop him. "Let's watch TV," I said.

"No," he said. "Let's go to my room."

I couldn't find in myself the courage I needed to just get angry at him and leave. So I made an excuse. "I can't. I'm on my period."

"What does that matter?" he asked.

"Don't Muslims not make love with a woman on her period?"

"Oh, those rules. They're not unbreakable." He paused. "And you were on your period before."

I had no idea what he meant.

"Before," he repeated. "When we were here before. You were on your period then, too."

"No, I wasn't."

"Of course you were," he contradicted me. "I got blood all over me. You definitely were on your period."

"That wasn't my period."

"Then what the hell was it?" he demanded.

"I never made love with anyone before you," the blue-eyed girl said.

The simplicity of her words burned like a flashbulb in a dark room sizzling through its plastic coating.

The blue-eyed girl could have been my American wife. But how could I have known she was a virgin? She indicated what kind of girl she was when she went to Fhad's apartment, and she went there long before mine. Pleading with me to slow down was just an act.

I wanted to scream at him, but I couldn't find the words. He guessed what I was trying to say and ridiculed me, "Don't try to tell me you were a virgin?"

I nodded and my eyes filled with tears.

"Who are you trying to fool? You were a whore for every man on campus, and I'm taking a chance trying to make you better."

"I was a virgin," I insisted.

"You liar."

"I was a virgin." The shame of keeping it all secret drove me to say it again and again. "I was a virgin. I was a virgin."

"You lying whore."

"I was a virgin. You broke my thing...my cherry..."

"You liar."

"I was a virgin," I yelled at him.

But he was like talking to a rock. "You liar", he said.

I slapped him as hard as I could.

My first impulse was to laugh at such a feeble gesture, but I could not let that stand. I slapped her hard, and she spun and fell crying to the floor. Then I kneeled and coaxed her to sit up on the floor. "You shouldn't make me do things like that, "I said.

Like a tango leader, I cupped my fingers behind her shoulder and guided her to my bed. I did not hide my intent. I removed my trousers and laid them across the chair at my desk. She did not move from where I put her, and my bare ass was in her face.

I pushed her to lie down. With one hand I pulled up her skirt, but when I started to remove her panties, her muscles tightened, and she rocked back and forth, as though her body was saying, "No," that I could not do.

So I straddled her left leg and used my fingers to guide myself, but when I pulled her panties aside and pushed to enter her, she was totally dry. I prodded with my fingers to find some moisture to spread around, but as I tried to massage her vagina to make it wet, nothing happened.

"I'll get something," I said, because even very hard, it would be painful for me to fuck her this way. I had no Vaseline or ointment of any kind. Then I saw my tube of brushless shaving cream.

"This is a special cream," I said as I squeezed half of the tube onto two fingers and spread it around her hair and into her vagina. It was not wet like Tina, but it was slippery enough.

As I entered her, I forced her right leg up with my knee. She tightened her muscles to keep her leg flat, but I was stronger.

I tried to find a rhythm that would get a response, but she did not move. I came; and then as I relaxed, I felt my penis burn. "Oh, god," I realized, "Menthol shaving cream! Shit." And briefly, I also thought, "Her vagina must really burn." But she did not move.

After that, she came over whenever I called, and I could brag to my friends. I often gave her a beer because if she relaxed, I enjoyed it more. If she hesitated when I called, I said I would pick her up, and she would decide to come over herself.

Sayiid said nasty things out of the blue. For example, one of his friends got an XKE. He borrowed it and insisted I go with him so people would see me with him. I rationalized that, if anyone saw me, I could say he was giving me a ride. Fortunately the windows were so low it wasn't easy to see who I was.

As we drove through the Plaza, I watched a guy in the

crosswalk. "Want to fuck him?" Sayiid asked.

"What?" I had no idea why he asked me that.

"Want to fuck him? You looked at him like you want to fuck him."

"I did not."

"I bet you'd fuck every man for ten miles."

"Stop. Please, stop."

"Why? Don't you like the truth?"

"I just looked at the guy," I protested, but that was admitting I'd looked.

"See. That's what I mean. You were sizing him up. You'd go down with every guy at Penn if I let you."

The Saturday before I went home for the summer, Masoud and Khalid organized a picnic at Lake Jacomo. That's some Missourian's idea of a clever name for Lake Jackson County Missouri, Ja-Co-Mo.

I told the blue-eyed girl we would leave at 10:00 a.m. She arrived with a rolled up towel. "You forgot a bathing suit," I said.

"No, I didn't." She unrolled the towel to show me a limp nylon suit.

"That's a bathing suit?"

"It's all I have. I wore this on the swim team at the Y."

"What?"

"I was on a swim team in high school."

"You never told me you were on a swim team."

"There was never a time for me to tell you."

I looked at the suit. "You can't wear that with my friends."

"I don't have anything else."

I took a deep breath. "Let's go." She followed me to my car.

On the way to the lake, I drove past our turn and went

to a shopping center where I'd seen a department store. The blue-eyed girl asked, "Where're you going?"

"You'll see."

The woman at the first counter quickly directed us to women's swimwear. When the blue-eyed girl understood that I expected her to buy a new bathing suit, she objected, "I didn't bring enough money."

"I'll loan you the money."

"I can't pay you back right now. I don't need a new suit. I don't go swimming that much."

"I want you to look good for my friends." She looked at one-piece suits, but I pointed to the other rack. "Try one of these."

"I won't look good in a two piece suit."

I was explicit. "I want you in a two-piece suit."

There wasn't a dressing room at the lake, so we took turns changing in the back seat of my car. Wahiib suggested we rent a boat. That was not what I had in mind, but I said, "Sounds good to me."

We ended up in two rowboats. Wahiib, the blue-eyed girl and me in one boat, and Ali and Mo in the other. Khalid and Masoud weren't interested.

It was bright and windless, and we were sweating by the time we rowed across to the shade on the far side of the lake. I got out and waded toward the shore. The bottom was mud and rocks with slippery green slime.

Mo got out, and splashed water at the blue-eye girl, who was still in the boat. She splashed back and got some water on me. All I could think of was the Hartwood girls and how much I wanted to fondle a girl's ass, the blue-eyed girl's ass, in a wet bathing suit.

Sayiid got pushy for some reason. He dragged me out of

the boat and started splashing me. When he grabbed my butt, I said, "Your friends are watching," but that didn't stop him.

My stomach rolled over the waistband. I squatted to hide in the water so they'd stop staring at my fat and sort of automatically floated back with only my head above water.

"Hey, your girlfriend's getting away," said one of his friends.

Sayiid lunged for me, so I took a stroke back. The others thought it was a game, but Sayiid didn't laugh when I stroked backwards again to stay out of reach. "Okay," he yelled. "If that's the way you want it, get back on your own. See if I care."

I turned and could just see the trees on the other side of the lake. I could swim that far, but I worried they'd catch up. Maybe the boat would force me under as I took a breath, or I'd choke on a gulp of water, or they'd knock me out, and they wouldn't have any idea how to save me. But anything would be better than how I felt.

They were such klutzes. I was on the beach when they got across. It was funny watching them try to row their boat, but I didn't dare laugh. At least my swimming impressed Sayiid. "That was quite a swim," he said.

I didn't dare brag. "It wasn't really that great. Olympic swimmers do that three times a day. I…anyone can learn to do that. It's just practice."

Masoud and Khalid had a fire in the picnic area and we cooked strips of meat directly on the iron grate. After lunch Sayiid made me stand for him to take a picture of me in my bathing suit. I felt like his trophy.

I had a photograph of the blue-eyed girl in a bathing suit in my pocket when I went through Customs in the desert. I might have kept the picture, but I had hidden a *Playboy* magazine in my suitcase. The Customs agent ignored it, but the officer from the Commission for the Promotion of Virtue and the Prevention of Vice, what I like to call the Vice/Virtue squad, found it. Then he insisted on searching every piece of my luggage, every book, and all my school materials. Finally, he went through my wallet and found the picture.

"What is this?" he demanded. "This is not even from a magazine. You made this picture yourself. Is this your favorite American whore?"

I wanted to tell him to fuck off. No one took him seriously, but neither did anyone want to accept responsibility for saying his ranting was ridiculous.

My father watched from beyond the security barrier. Even through his friends in the airport administration, he could not say anything until I was though Customs. "I'm glad your Mother was not here to see this. What was the picture? What have you been up to?" I did not try to explain.

I worked at Putsch's that summer and watched Ken's kids occasionally. They'd had a second baby, a girl. My report card arrived a week after I got home. I got two A's, a B, a C, and a D. At least working with Professor Baker had helped. If I kept it up, I'd stay off probation.

Harry called the last week of June. We hadn't talked more than to say, "Hi," since he lied about us just before we started college. He was going to be in Kansas City with his dad, and he was trying to make up for being such a jerk. "I hear the University has a theater right in the middle of the city. He tried a joke. "It's part of Mizzou, but I guess a Cornhusker can visit as long as it's not in Columbia."

"I hope so," I replied.

"There's a play about the Marquis de Sade. I can get some tickets. Do you want to go?"

"Sure." Even Harry's attention was welcome now.

Performing *The Persecution and Assassination of Jean-Paul Marat as Performed by the Inmates of the Asylum of Charenton under the Direction of the Marquis de Sade*, usually known as "Marat/Sade," was a coup for Missouri Rep, but no one in Kansas City knew what to expect, certainly not me, and Harry even less.

The lights went down, and screaming people wandered down the aisles. A narrator told us these were mental patients who'd present the play. Marat sat in a tub bathing his sores. Harry tried to be romantic and took my hand, but then Marat stood up, naked, facing the audience—everything showed—and Harry's hand went limp.

Afterwards, Harry couldn't stop talking about the nudity. "That guy stood up in front of god and everybody. And that girl, too. Crazy people take their clothes off, but did they have to show that?"

I caught similar conversations around us, and I heard later that some people walked out when "Marat/Sade" opened in London. I tried to say it was okay, but Harry continued, "I'm sorry I brought you here. I didn't mean to embarrass you."

He was a friend, and I'd wondered if I could ever talk to him about Sayiid, but he was more embarrassed than me by the play. Football player or not, he was a virgin. He thought I was a nice girl he could take home to his mother. We were at very different places in our lives.

I spent most of my vacation in the American compound with TWA staff. I could take the men to what fun spots there were, even though there would be no women, and I survived by being around women who did not cover themselves in the compound. I heard my parents were arranging a marriage, but I would be celibate for years if having sex had to wait for them. I had too much energy to wait that long.

Mo and Ali asked if I got letters from the blue-eyed girl. I received two but told them I got two or three a week. In their eyes, I became legendary. I had made good on my bragging. I was knowledgeable about sex and women. I was building a reputation that would make them look up to me for the rest of our careers.

Before fall semester started, my family went to Valentine to help Granddaddy sort out Grandmother's stuff. Freddy loved trains, and there were lots of old schedules and snapshots of locomotives. His favorite picture was a steam locomotive with eight wheels, lying on its side, down an embankment.

"I remember that one," Granddaddy said. "There was a loose track and the southbound derailed." He pointed. "I ran one of those cranes and that Indian guy, Littlepeak, was my helper." Granddaddy glanced at me because he remembered that I'd found Mr. Littlepeak's body in the river.

It was hard to be around Granddaddy because he was so supportive, and I was so ashamed about Sayiid. The day we'd left for Valentine, I received a letter from Sayiid saying he'd been thinking about me and was arriving in Kansas City Labor Day weekend. He gave the time and number of his flight...

> Pick up my car and meet me at the gate. I will have been traveling for almost 24 hours so do not be late. I look forward to being with you. I know you have missed me. We have a lot to make up.

The blue-eyed girl met me at the gate for the simple reason that I had told her what I expected, and let her decide if she wanted to disappoint me.

We went straight to my apartment, and I led her to my room. Fueled by images in a *Playboy* magazine that had not been caught by the Vice/Virtue squad, and the memory of her half-naked in a swimsuit last spring, I was excited and ejaculated almost immediately. It never occurred to me that I never touched her breasts or even her bra. I ignored so much of her.

I dropped her at her parents' house late that night. Her street had small houses mixed with small apartments, the kind with six or eight units on three levels, much like my own apartment in Jackson City. At the end of the block was a small market with a Coke sign.

When I came back after lunch the next day, the blue-eyed girl answered the door. I stepped forward to squeeze her, but she held up a hand to stop me. "My Mom's here," she warned.

"So?"

"I thought she'd be at Dad's office picnic, but she stayed home."

"Okay." I tried again to squeeze her ass.

"Wait," she said as she twisted away.

Her mother was in the front room. "Who's there, dear?" she asked, as though she expected someone had rung the wrong doorbell.

"It's for me," the blue-eyed girl replied.

"Oh," her mom said as she saw me.

The blue-eyed girl introduced me as we entered the living room. "This is Sayiid. He's from Penn. He just got back from summer vacation."

Her puzzlement gave way to dismay at my dark skin, but I could charm almost anyone, which is why I am a successful diplomat. Even as I thought, *You prejudiced American bitch who drives her big gas guzzling car on our oil,* I nodded politely and said, "Your daughter has told me so much about you."

"Say-dee?" she asked. "I've not heard that name before..."

"Sayiid," I softly corrected her. "Sayiid is a Muslim name."

The blue-eyed girl's mother did not flinch. I think it was because of her experience meeting all types of customers as a bank teller. I was an impersonal interaction, just like any white or black or Mexican at her window that she spoke with in the course of her work.

"Pleased to meet you," she added as she glanced at her daughter with a question even I could see in her eye.

I drove the blue-eyed girl out to my apartment. As soon as we went in, I kissed her and started to slide my hand under her skirt.

"I can't today."

"Why not?" I demanded.

"It's that time I might get pregnant."

"But I want you." I rubbed my crotch. "We want you."

"Please, I can't take a chance."

Sayiid opened his zipper and shook himself out. All I could think of was Christi, and I didn't have any money to go to England if I got pregnant. I tried not to look, but he was obvious even in the corner of my eye.

"Here." He put my hand on his penis and wrapped my fingers around it. "That's it. Now squeeze lightly and moved back and forth."

"Oh, god," I thought.

"We don't want to do anything that could get you pregnant, do we?" he added sarcastically. I had no idea what he meant until he'd wrapped his grip into a wad of hair on both sides of my head.

Sayiid walked into the bathroom and washed his hands. I waited until he was done and then went in, closed the door and scrubbed my face. Even with lots of soap, I felt filthy. I took off my blouse to rinse out the oily stuff. As I rubbed, I realized he'd opened the door and was staring at me in my bra.

Without a word he put one arm around my shoulder, kissed me deep in my mouth, lifted my skirt, and shoved his other hand into my underpants. He didn't take them off. He ignored them.

I didn't dare make him angry. He finally took his hand out of my pants, adjusted the waistband like he was tidying up and left without saying a word. He was in charge.

Granddaddy had a heart attack and died at the end of September. I missed school for three days to go to the funeral.

A couple of weeks later, my mom called me early Friday morning. "Ken, that guy from Putsch's, called me just now."

"What'd he want?" After I quit Putsch's to go back to school, Ken would only schedule me when no one else was available.

"He asked if you wanted to work tomorrow. Some girl up and quit last night. I told him I wasn't sure, but I'd call you right away."

It was like finding the secret escape hatch in one of those old movie serials where the heroine is about to get crushed in a room with moving walls. "Tell him, yes. And find out what time. Okay? And thanks, Mom."

"Don't thank me. He's the one who called."

"Thanks for finding me right away. You'll never understand...it just means so much right now..." I left a note for Pam and caught the 3:00 o'clock bus. Mom made dinner and the four of us went to a movie. I didn't hear a word of it. I was just so happy to be with my family.

When I called the blue-eyed girl on Friday night, her roommate said she wasn't there. "Where is she? She knew I would call."

"I don't know. She didn't tell me. She just left a note."

"What's the note say?"

"'Won't be back tonight.' That's all."

"Where'd she go?" I demanded.

"I don't know."

That night I read *Playboy*, but it was not as good as the real thing. When I called Saturday, her roommate told me again, "She's not here."

"Has she been back?"

"Wait a minute." There was a pause as the roommate checked. "I don't think so. Doesn't look like anyone slept in her bed."

"When she gets back, tell her to call me right away."

"Does she have your number?"

"Yes! She's got my number!" I slammed down the phone. Sunday afternoon I called earlier. "Did she sign out to go somewhere?" I asked.

"Maybe," the roommate replied, "but I can't look at her sign-out card. That's private. I'd get in trouble."

I wanted to yell how stupid she was, and that she could easily look because everyone's cards were in one little box. But I knew she would not do it. I called again at 10:35, five minutes after she had to be back from the weekend. "Is she back now?"

The phone had that hollow silence it has when someone puts their hand over the mouthpiece, and then the roommate returned. "She isn't back yet."

"You sure?" I challenged her. "You just talked to someone."

"Oh, her? She's from next door. We're studying together."

I knew she was lying, but I didn't want to betray my anger.

I'd look foolish if I stood around campus watching for the blue-eyed girl, so Monday night I asked Wahiib if she had been in class. "Yes. Why do you ask?"

"She did not feel well when I talked to her," I said. "I wondered if she was better. Sounds like she is."

On Wednesday, I walked with Wahiib to the class he had with the blue-eyed girl. They met in an old Quonset hut put up as a temporary lecture hall in the 40s.

I created reasons to talk until Wahiib said he'd better go in. Almost at the same time, the blue-eyed girl hurried up the path from the student parking lot on the far side of campus. That was why I could not find her. She walked all the way around campus on side streets.

"Missed you," I said. "Where were you last weekend?"

She didn't answer. I blocked her way. "Where were you last weekend?" She did not answer, so I grabbed her arm.

She shook her hand free. "I've got to go to class."

"I'll be here when you come out," I promised, and I was.

Wahiib asked why I was there when class was over. I told him I was meeting the blue-eyed girl. "She was in class," he said. "I saw her."

"I'll wait," I said. The Quonset hut had only one door to go in and out, and I stood there. An old—what do they like to be called?—black woman carried in a bucket. And I went in to find the blue-eyed girl.

I hid in the lecture hall until the maid came in to clean toilets. "Is he still there?" I asked her. "The guy? He's Arab."

"Yes, honey, he's still there."

"Oh, god," was all I could manage.

The woman took my hand and led me to a toilet stall. "Now you get in there, and get your feet up so they don't show if he looks under the doors."

I was terrified, but she seemed to know exactly what was going on and how to handle it. There was a lot of noise. I heard Sayiid talking nasty to her. I even heard his shoes scuff on the floor in the women's john, but then he left.

The woman hummed to herself as she cleaned and let me stay huddled where I was hiding. Finally she whispered, "You doing well. Keep it up just a minute longer. It's almost over."

She left the bathroom, and I could hear her humming in the hall. Finally she came back. "He's gone."

She took off her gloves, and pulled some paper towels to wipe the tears on my face. "You be all right?" she asked. I couldn't speak, but I nodded. "I get off in twenty minutes," she said. "Where you live?"

"On the other side of campus."

"I'll drive you there."

Dad found out that Johnny, the man at the McCall's gas station on Main Street, was selling an old Rambler. Johnny had rebuilt the engine for his son, and then his son joined the navy. Dad talked him into selling me the car for a hundred dollars down and fifty dollars more for the next two months.

After my last class on Friday, I caught the 1:00 bus up to the city and took the Country Club bus out Main Street. I met Johnny at the gas station, gave him five twenty-dollar bills, he signed the papers, and I had a car.

I overheard Mo tell Wahiib he saw the blue-eyed girl drive out of the student parking lot. I pretended to be occupied opening a can in the kitchen. The rules allowed her to have a car as a junior, but I could not imagine where she had gotten the money to pay for it. I bluffed. "Yeah, she just got that."

"But," Mo continued, "who drives a Rambler?"

I was quick. "Yeah, they have a pretty bad reputation, but that makes them cheap." I was guessing, but old and cheap seemed logical.

"Come to think of it," Mo replied, "I'd guess it was several years old."

I remembered other jokes about Ramblers. "That model has the front seats that fold down…very convenient, yes?" We chuckled. I wondered why she had not told me, but only for about three seconds. She did not want me to know.

There were no Ramblers in the student lot on Saturday, and none on Sunday afternoon, so I returned about 9:30 on Sunday night. After fifteen minutes, a white Rambler station wagon hit the driveway, bounced and swung into an empty space. I waited in the shadows while the blue-eyed girl gathered her stuff and locked the door. As she hurried toward the dorms, I stepped out of the shadows. "Have a good trip?" I asked sarcastically.

She jumped. "I wasn't on a trip." She tried to walk around me.

I grabbed her wrist. "Wait a minute. I just want to talk."

"I don't have time. I'm due back in ten minutes."

I did not let go. "I'll walk with you."

When I did release her wrist, she shook her hand with a gesture like she was shaking off water. There were a few other students as she hurried across campus, so I could not grab her again. She moved quickly. "Where'd you go?" I asked between my breaths.

She did not answer. At her room she opened the door and turned her head only slightly to say, "Good night."

I knew she meant "Good bye," but I would not accept that.

Friday I cut my afternoon class and parked off the main road outside the parking lot. As I anticipated, about 2:30 she drove out of the parking lot and headed toward the city. I followed a few cars back. She was speeding, and she did not notice me.

I recognized her parents' neighborhood and pulled over, half a block away, and watched as she parked and walked inside. I was about to leave when the door opened and someone came out wearing a tan dress with a blue apron. It took me a moment to recognize her. She paused at the door and looked back. Then her mother stood in the door and watched as the blue-eyed girl walked down the sidewalk toward the Plaza—and toward me.

I recognized Sayiid's car down the street. He slouched behind the steering wheel, but I tapped on the window. "What are you doing here?"

"I'm just sitting."

"You followed me. Didn't you?" I was late so I started walking.

"Don't make me follow you like this," he called as he got out of his car, but he didn't seem as confident as when he was at Penn.

"I'm not making you do anything," I said over my shoulder.

I got to 47th Street. When the light changed, I crossed and opened the door of Putsche's. "What's this?" he asked.

"This is where I work." I was feeling brave because for once he seemed unsure of himself. "Unlike you, some of us work to get through school, even a little college in Missouri." I went inside, and eventually he left.

Now my weekends were safe, but he pestered me to come

by his apartment on my way back Sunday night. "Can't," I answered. "I need to be in by 10:30, and there isn't time. I don't get off work Sundays 'til 9:30."

"I'll drive in Saturday night. We can go to a movie after your work."

I pretended to consider that. "Saturdays are hard. I work from 2 until 10. I'm usually pretty tired."

But he didn't give up. "Why don't you get a job in Jackson City or Grandview?" he demanded. "There are lots of places to eat near the airbase."

"Service men don't have any money. If they tip, they're trying to pick me up." I thought for a moment about whose life was worse. "I'd end up tipping them. They volunteer for the Air Force to stay out of the Army, but it's a shit job either way. Makes my life seem pretty easy."

"Whatever happened to your girlfriend?" Mo asked.

"What do you mean 'whatever happened'?"

"I just noticed..."

"You noticed what?"

"The weekends. She's not...her car's always gone on Saturdays..."

"And...?" I challenged him.

"I don't know."

"You're right. You don't know pig dung." Then I gave him reasons. Her scholarship was for freshmen. She needed money. There wasn't a job near campus. And on and on until it was clear that he should never ask again.

Ali, however, made the comment that inspired me. "Why don't you give her money? Your allowance is three times her tips. Your personal 'waitress' of sorts...if you get my drift."

I laughed, but it gave me a plan. Suppose I was out of money?

The next Wednesday, I waited outside the auditorium where she had class with Wahiib. When she saw me, she darted toward the parking lot. But that helped because there was no one else there in the middle of the day. "Wait a minute," I called. "You're trying to avoid me."

She stopped, but she did not look at me. "What do you want?"

"You don't have class tomorrow morning. Let's see a movie tonight."

"Okay. We'll go to a movie."

At the theater, I feigned surprise when I opened my wallet, "Damn! I forgot. I only have two dollars left. I get a stipend, but sometimes it runs out. Can you lend me ten dollars? I'll pay you back."

She reached into her purse, and I got a hook into her that she did not even perceive. She would come back for the money because ten dollars was enough to mean something to her.

At the first of the month, I called that I had her money. She could come by my apartment and pick it up, but I wouldn't be home until 7:30 or so. That's what I said, at least, because Wahiib usually left for the library by 7:00.

My birthday was in October. I planned a party for Saturday night, and I needed the blue-eyed girl there so I could show her off to my cousin, Jalal, who was sightseeing around the United States.

"I work 'til 10:00," she said. "That's too late."

"That's not too late. You sign out to your parents' anyway so you won't need to worry about getting in. We can party all night."

"I work Sunday."

"You can promise to come," I told her, "or I'll be there to pick you up."

Mo brought a girl from Grandview, a secretary in a law office. She had very blonde hair, and she loved his car. Ali was there to celebrate. Wahiib did not accept alcohol, but by the time the blue-eyed girl arrived, I had drunk enough for both of us. “Hey, look, guys,” I said. “She’s here.”

I held out a beer to her. “Have a drink.”

“No, thank you. I have a long day tomorrow.”

“Don’t want beer? Mo, get her a girly drink. A rum and Coke.”

“Okay. I’ll have a beer.” She accepted the can but didn’t drink from it.

“Can’t just hold it,” I said. “It’ll get warm in your hand… Your hand is so warm.” I had not seen Mo walk up behind me, so as I turned around, I knocked his hand and her drink splashed on the floor. “Damn it,” I said.

“I’ll get it.” The blue-eyed girl hurried to the kitchen and returned with a towel. The spill was right in front of the television, and she paused for a moment when she squatted down as though none of us were there.

When I kneeled down to wipe up a spilled drink, the spot gave me feelings of pain. Then I realized it was the same place, on the same floor.

After that I could barely stand still, so I started nervously taking glasses to the kitchen and wiping tables. Sayiid’s friends took that as a signal to get their coats, and his cousin went with Mo. As the last of them left, I started to wash dishes, but Sayiid grabbed the washcloth. “I’ll do this.”

“I can do it,” I objected.

“No. I want it done…”

“Your way?” I completed his sentence, but that was a mistake.

“You are such a…look. There’s cake left. Have some.”

I got some cake on a napkin and brought it back to the

kitchen. But I touched the icing with my finger before I started drying dishes, and I smudged a glass. Sayiid caught me wiping the glass extra hard to get the icing off. "Give it to me. I'll wash it again." Then he lectured, "Why don't you do things right in the first place."

"I'm sorry. I was just trying to get it done."

He was so conceited he assumed he'd make me feel better with a kiss. Right away he slid my skirt up and put his hand on my pants. I didn't close my eyes, and I made a little noise when I saw Wahiib come in. Sayiid realized it was a sound of alarm and let go to look around.

"Excuse me." Wahiib held something. "I'll put this in the fridge."

In the confusion, I grabbed my coat. "Gotta' go. Long day tomorrow."

Sayiid insisted I come over to his apartment Wednesday night because his cousin was visiting. It turned out to be the same guy, Jalal, who'd been at his birthday party. Right after I arrived, Sayiid left to run an errand.

"I'll come back later," I said.

"No," Sayiid said, "You keep Jalal company."

Sayiid was gone over an hour, which was awkward because I had no idea what to say to Jalal. We pretty much sat and said nothing.

When we could hear Sayiid parking his car, Jalal pulled out his shirttail and made a point of tucking it in as he opened the door. "Hey, Sayiid," he said, "thanks for sharing your girlfriend." And he looked at me and winked.

I was caught totally off guard, but I managed to say, "Nothing happened." But I could tell from Sayiid's face he wasn't buying that, so I started to get defensive. "He's just saying that."

Sayiid pushed Jalal on the shoulder in a sort of camaraderie, and said, "Hey. You wouldn't do that to me, would you? My own flesh and blood? We're buddies, aren't we?"

I put in my two cents. "Honest. We just talked."

Sayiid turned on me. "Is this what happens when I turn my back?" I got frustrated, and it showed. It was like they were working together to make me feel bad.

Then Sayiid and Jalal started laughing. "See what I mean?" Sayiid asked Jalal. "She takes everything so seriously."

It wasn't easy to believe the sudden turnaround, so I just stared. Sayiid slapped my back. "What's the matter? Can't you take a joke?"

After Granddaddy died, we went to Thanksgiving at the Hartwood's for the first time in several years. Their house smelled of turkey and pie. Kristen and Carol were helping in the kitchen, but the real work was being done by their colored maid and the girls' contributions were non-essential. Then the doorbell rang.

"I bet that's Sayiid," said Mr. Hartwood.

My heart sank, and Mom's expression said it all. She knew but kind of hoped it wasn't true herself. I greeted Sayiid. Yes, we knew each other at Penn. "I didn't know you'd be here," I said to him.

"I didn't know you'd be here either," he said.

Mrs. Hartwood seated me next to Sayiid. He took an active part in the conversation, but while he talked, he slipped his shoe off and rubbed his foot on my foot. Later he pretended to adjust his napkin and put his hand on my leg. I looked across the table just as Carol averted her eyes.

Mr. Hartwood introduced me to the blue-eyed girl's father and two more men from TWA whose jobs depended on working with my father. He served me cranberry juice, assuming that, as a Muslim, I would not want alcohol. As a consideration to my father, I thanked him for the juice.

Mr. Hartwood reminded the blue-eyed girl's father how he tried everything to avoid being sent to the Middle East because of how hard it would be on Mrs. Hartwood. Finally, TWA told him that he could go, or he could find another job.

He described the day I met them. Mrs. Hartwood's fears were underestimates of the real misery they faced, but she appreciated how my mother helped her adjust to the heat and that created the friendship between our families and brought me to Penn.

"Your father is a special man," Mr. Hartwood continued. "He loves your mother. He told me he worried what it would be like when his parents arranged his marriage. But he thinks he's the luckiest man he knows."

"Thank you," I said. "You honor me."

"I also honor your mother," he replied. "She's a wonderful person."

I replied, perhaps saying too much. "Islam allows a man to have more than one wife if he treats them equally. Many men take a second wife informally. My friends point out the second wife of their father. My father is unusual because he does not have a second wife. My friends marvel at this."

To the blue-eyed girl and her mother, the Hartwoods represented the best of society. They belonged to the Carriage Club, and their daughters would be presented at the debutante ball at the Nelson Art Gallery. The blue-eyed girl and her mother did not know how to act in society, so they watched Mrs. Hartwood's every move, but they watched differently.

If Mrs. Hartwood picked up a salad fork, the blue-eyed girl's mother picked up the same fork a fraction of a second later. She was terrified of missing a cue. It was a comedy to watch her.

The blue-eyed girl, however, watched to learn. She followed the lead to pick up her salad fork, but she also watched how everyone else picked up their salad forks. And then she put her fork down and picked it up again as though memorizing the opening gambit in a chess game. She was thankful for the opportunity to learn how to dine from someone who knew the right way.

After dinner, we went to the den for the American tradition of Thanksgiving football. I enjoyed the skirts that flew up to show the cheerleaders' legs. At halftime, the blue-eyed girl's father asked me, "What will you do after graduation, Sayiid?"

"I will return home and enter the Ministry of Foreign Affairs. My father has arranged it."

"Arranged..." He pondered the word. "And will your parents arrange a marriage for you like your grandparents arranged for them?"

"You bet," cut in Mr. Hartwood. "Sayiid's father told me he's working on that." The blue-eyed girl gasped.

"I don't know," I said cautiously. "Many of us do not think our parents should make such decisions for us any longer."

Mr. Hartwood continued, "But it's not like here. Boys and girls never meet in your country. How would you ever meet a wife?"

I could sense the blue-eyed girl shrinking into her seat.

"This will be a challenge for our generation. Like your students in California, we are challenging the old ways."

Then I changed the subject. "My goal is to return to the United States as our ambassador." A worthy goal, they both commented. I knew that was boastful, but I was the best choice of all the men of my age, and my father was also a cousin to the King. But I wondered if the blue-eyed girl's father had asked that question to elicit exactly that answer in front of his daughter.

I could not guess what the blue-eyed girl took from the conversation, so I did not call until the next Friday afternoon. When I called, I invited her to join Wahiib and me for pizza. She said, "Yes," but she'd be late because she was picking up a present for her father. She may not have wanted to be with me, but she still did not have the confidence to end our relationship.

To project a different image, I made sure Wahiib stayed. We watched Johnny Carson, and during a commercial I asked her, "Why didn't you tell me you knew the Hartwoods?"

"I never even guessed you'd know them, too." She continued, "I've been to their house so many times, Carol and Kristen are like my little sisters. Mrs. Hartwood has a whole table covered with perfume bottles in her bedroom. When I baby sat for them, after the girls went to bed, I'd put on touches of her perfume." She laughed. "I must have reeked of perfume when Mr. Hartwood took me home. She has things from all over the world, and she always said nice things about people she visited." The blue-eyed girl looked at my eyes for some reaction, but she did not mention my parents directly.

There are no significant hills between Kansas City and the North Pole, neither are there any natural barriers between there and the Gulf of Mexico. Storm systems move quickly up and down the Mississippi and Missouri River Valleys. Air temperature can rise forty degrees one day and drop forty degrees the next day. The Thanksgiving snow melted in a warm spell.

I convinced the blue-eyed girl to go to a movie on Thursday night. It was drizzling as we drove toward the Plaza. For some reason, I had crossed over to Wornall Road.

"That's where I learned to swim," she said, pointing to a

brick building.

"There? It doesn't look like a swimming pool."

"It's Southwest High School. Westport didn't even have a pool, but they did. The Y gave lessons there on Saturdays. It was my dad's idea."

"Is that where you became such a good swimmer?"

"Yes. We had a great relay team, but we only practiced one day a week in the winter. Every summer we spent half the season getting our wind back. The country clubs' girls practiced indoors all winter.

"I dreamed I'd be an Olympic swimmer." She thought for a moment. "Gave that up, didn't I?"

It was drizzling when we went into the theater, but there were three inches of snow on the ground when we came out. As I paused under the marquee to button my coat, the blue-eyed girl took two quick steps and slid forward on the snow. "Let's go sledding," she called back to me.

"We don't have a sled."

"We'll get one at my parents' house."

"You have to get back."

"The roads are too slick to drive back. I'll call in and sleep at home."

"Where will I sleep?"

"On the couch."

It was too slippery to drive even the few blocks to her parents' house, so we walked. She went in and called, "Hi, Mom. You remember Sayiid, don't you?"

"Yes," her mom said calmly and turned to me, "How are you, Sayiid?"

The blue-eyed girl did not give me time to reply. "We saw a movie at the Plaza. Now there's too much snow to drive back. We're going sledding, and Sayiid's going to sleep on the couch."

"I'll get some blankets."

"I'll get them, Mom. We won't be long. I don't have boots."

It was only a few blocks from the blue-eyed girl's house to a park in a small valley. My feet were freezing, but the blue-eyed girl was excited. After a few short runs, she said, "If we had warmer clothes, we'd go to Suicide Hill. That's the best sledding in the city."

"Where's that?"

"That way." She pointed to an abandoned railroad track on the other side of the street. "Suicide Hill is at 57th Street and that old street car track."

She fell back in the snow and moved her arms and legs back and forth to make what she called a snow angel. "I love the snow. It's a fresh, white start. I thought swimming would be my start to get out of Westport."

"Westport?"

"This is Westport, all this area north of the Plaza. Everyone here thinks they'll graduate from high school and go to work, maybe be a nurse or a teacher or something. I just want out of it.

"Of all my friends, no one's parents ever went to Europe, except the dads who went in the War. When I realized I couldn't be an Olympic swimmer, college was the only way that was left. That's why Penn's so important. I'll do anything to get a degree. I just can't be stuck here."

She walked a few steps and fell backwards to make another angel. "No matter how bad things are, snow lets you start all over." She grabbed the rope on the sled and ran. "I'm freezing. Let's go back."

At her house, we took off our shoes and socks and warmed our toes over the vent in the living room. The blue-eyed girl made hot chocolate and insisted that I take a shower to warm up. I borrowed a robe while her mother put my clothes through the dryer and laid a blanket on the sofa for me. Then the blue-eyed girl said goodnight, took a long shower herself, and disappeared behind the door of her bedroom.

It was a small house. All the rooms opened on to one hall, and I heard her parents shuffling in their room as I fell asleep. I could not imagine four people living in such a cramped space. I could never be that close to anyone.

In the morning, I drove back to Jackson City. The blue-eyed girl stayed because it was Friday and she worked that afternoon.

When we got our first television, I was fascinated by the gimmicks to sell to children. You could send in labels from Ovaltine to get a Captain Midnight Decoder Ring, and Freddy sent in box tops from Wheaties for a set of metal car logos. When I was in high school, I sent away for a booklet entitled, "Do Cows Have Neuroses?" and learned that there were special people who helped people with emotional problems.

Driving back on Monday morning, I thought about how I'd been hiding Sayiid for close to a year. I was depressed. I avoided everyone I could at school, and I didn't like to brush my hair because all I saw in the mirror was a bad person. I remembered the booklet about neuroses and wondered who could help me.

For some reason, I decided to go out Wornall Road and then east on 95th Street. I cursed mildly when road construction forced me to detour through Grandview. I got lost and knew I'd be late for class. Waiting at a stoplight, I found myself staring at a storefront sign that read "Grandview Counseling Center." I wondered if God himself had put up the detour sign.

"May I help you?" the receptionist asked.

"I don't..." I hesitated. "Oh god..." and I started crying.

"Riley," the receptionist called. Another woman came out from the back. "Let me help you," the second woman said as she put her arm around my shoulder and led me to a room to sit down.

"I have a boyfriend..." I said.

"We've all had a boyfriend," she said. The receptionist laughed a short grunt of agreement. I was crying, but then I looked at them. They were so normal. They'd never understand about Sayiid.

"So, why are you here?" asked the second woman. "I'm Riley, by the way." She was kind, but I couldn't find the courage to tell her about Sayiid forcing me to have sex with him and how I gave in to keep him away from me at school. What I was doing was too bad for anyone ever to believe I was a good person. All I could do was give her little hints. "My boyfriend keeps borrowing money. I don't know how to tell him to stop."

"Anything else?"

She knew the answer before she asked. By coming in the door, I'd let her know that, but I stuck to my story about lending money and never got around to asking them for the help I needed. I wanted desperately to stop Sayiid, but even in the counseling center, sex was a taboo subject for me.

Sayiid went skiing at Christmas but got stuck in a snowstorm, so I babysat for the Hartwoods on New Year's Eve. This time Kristen's friends were coming over, and I made popcorn in the kitchen with Carol while she waited for Sam to pick her up. "Do you like that guy, Sayiid?" she asked.

I couldn't think of anything else quickly, so I said, "I guess so."

"He's creepy," she said. "When he first came here, he tried to feel me up, and he was always staring at me."

"Maybe you misunderstood him."

"I don't think so. Mom says women over there are wrapped up all the time. The men stare at any woman, and there are police who hit women if their arms show. Daddy didn't disagree, but you know how he is. From what Mom says, women's lives there are shit. She swore she'd never go back."

Kristen and her friends went to bed at 1:00 in the morning. They wouldn't go to sleep, but that was the instruction from Mrs. Hartwood. The Hartwoods weren't due home from the party at the Carriage Club until 2:00. I didn't know when Carol would be back, but that wasn't my concern.

I listened to WHB play top songs in January going backwards from 1967. Before long the DJ announced, "Now Leslie Gore with 'You Don't Own Me,' number two for five weeks after 'I Want to Hold Your Hand' by the Beatles." He laughed. "That would've been tough competition."

My world had fallen apart since Dianne and I had sung "Don't tell me what to do/And don't tell me what to say/And please when I go out with you/Don't put me on display."

Friday after we got back from Colorado, I did not have an appetite at lunch. About 3:00 or so, my stomach hurt. At 6:00 I vomited. I told myself it was probably the leftover hamburger for breakfast. I was running a low fever. Wahiib, Mo and Ali had gone into the city, so I called the blue-eyed girl. She told me I should go to the infirmary. The infirmary had a bad reputation. "That hell hole?" I asked.

"What am I supposed to say then?"

"Okay," I said. "What do I do?"

She told me how to get there because, in four years, I had not been sick. There was fresh snow on the ground as I walked over. The entry hall was open, but the infirmary itself was locked. A sign by a wall phone said to call the operator for emergencies. The operator said I should wait by the phone.

There was just one wooden chair, and the heat had been turned down for the weekend. I was cold by the time the phone rang.

I told the nurse what was happening. She told me to stand and asked, "Does your stomach hurt?"

"No."

"Hop a little bit. Does that hurt?"

"Not really."

"Okay. Stand on your right foot and hop one time. Be careful. You might fall."

What sort of an idiot did she think I was? But the pain was immediate and sharp. My right leg collapsed under me and only grabbing the back of the chair kept me from hitting the floor. "Shit!" I yelled in the empty room.

The nurse was concerned. "Are you okay?"

"I'm okay, but god did that hurt. Why did you ask me to do that?"

"Mr. Algedda, you probably have appendicitis. We don't have a doctor on the weekend. Can you get a ride up to the emergency room at the Baptist Hospital? I'll call and tell them you're on your way. It's not a big operation," she added. "You'll be out in time for finals."

I called the blue-eyed girl and told her to drive in with me. She asked if I wanted her to drive, but she had never driven my car, and she was not going to start now. "No. I'm better already. I think this is a lot of worry for no reason."

Sayiid was afraid to drive to the hospital alone. I offered to take him in my car, but he was too stubborn for that. On the way, another car ran a stop sign, and we almost got into an accident. Sayiid jammed the brakes and his car slid sideways until it lodged against the curb. He floored the accelerator and tried to drive on, but all that happened was the wheels spun in the snow. He let the engine slow down and tried again, but he couldn't get it out.

He yelled and made it a point to cuss in English so I'd know how angry he was, "Fucking snow. Fucking car. Fucking roads. Fucking Missouri. Fucking Americans." I was scared he'd take out his anger on me.

After a couple more failed efforts, I asked if he wanted me to try. "Daddy showed me a way. It might not work. You'd do the same thing if your stomach didn't hurt." I said everything except 'a woman can't do anything right.'

He gritted out, "Okay."

He slid over, and I crawled over him. I was ready for him to put his hand between my legs, but I guess he was really sick.

I shifted forward and reverse with my foot on the brake to get the feel of his car. Then I revved the engine, put it in drive and rocked the car forward. Before the wheels began to spin, I flipped into reverse and gently accelerated again. The car rocked forward and then back, and I repeated this until I sensed the moment to use the momentum to go forward. The car got into the middle of the street on my first try. Sayiid didn't say a thing.

At the hospital, the nurse wouldn't let me stay because I wasn't a relative. "Here," he handed me his keys. "I'll get my car in the morning."

When I stepped out of the emergency entrance, six more inches of snow had fallen. Sayiid was shut up in his hospital room and couldn't come after me all night because I had his keys. I was free for the first time since September. I got in his car and remembered my father taking me to a parking lot like this and teaching me how to drive in the snow.

I accelerated away from the entrance, across the lot. Then I jerked the wheel to the left and hit the brakes. The right side of the car skidded around into a spin. I tapped the gas, and the car finished the circle and faced back toward the emergency room. You could skid older cars just the way you wanted.

After a second, I drove back and did the same thing again and came to rest facing away from the emergency room. "That's it," my dad had said. "That's as good as any guy in Valentine could ever do. It's a bootlegger turn... if you're carrying moonshine."

I imagined headlights in my rear mirror and pretended I was escaping bad guys. Then I saw it was only fifteen minutes to curfew and left the lot and drove back to Penn. The housemother didn't give me late points because the nurse backed me up that I'd been to the hospital.

I hobbled to the window and watched the blue-eyed girl leave. There was defiance in how she careened around the parking lot. I was amazed at how good a driver she was. Better than most men. Better than me. But I'd never tell her that. Women aren't supposed to drive cars.

The surgeon coming in to remove my appendix was in a minor accident and did not arrive until almost 8:00 a.m. I was feeling better. He urged me to go ahead with the appendectomy, but I'd had enough.

Several years later, I had exactly the same symptoms just after my wife said she suspected me of seeing another woman. That time I stayed for the operation. The new surgeon marveled at the scarring of my appendix and said I must have had an infection some time in the past. When I told him this story, leaving out the blue-eyed girl of course, he said he had heard of chronic appendicitis and that must have been what I had.

After the second semester started, Ali convinced me to try a karate class. Like many small men, he felt larger if he knew martial arts. The men who taught these skills understood that their clientele liked to act like they were associated with military sites, so Ali's karate class was in a studio near the air-base a couple of miles from Jackson City.

I liked twisting my wrists as I air-boxed in practice, but pushups on my knuckles were more work than I wanted. After class, we were pretty sweaty, but I had not brought a change of clothes, so we got in his car to drive back and shower at my apartment. As we did, I saw a white Rambler pulling into a space further along the street. White Ramblers were not common.

"Hey," I asked Ali, "can you drive back the other way?"

Ali edged to the right lane to make a U-turn. "Sure," he said as he waited for traffic to clear, "What's up?"

"I thought I saw a new McDonald's down there and want to check it out." I feigned looking ahead, but my eyes were trying to identify the person who hurried into the building in front of the white Rambler. As we passed, I read the sign, "Grandview Counseling Center." The car had the distinctive purple and white sticker for the Penn student parking lot. It had to be hers.

"I guess I was wrong," I said. "We can go on back."

What the hell was a "counseling center"?

That night I asked Wahiib if he knew what a counseling center was. He explained it was for people who needed help with problems, like drinking, for example. "It's probably there for the air base."

"What do you mean?"

"Soldiers have wives and girlfriends. Sometimes they fight and the soldier hits his girlfriend. Americans are sensitive about men hitting women. I'd bet the center you saw was put there by a church group. They help women when men pick on them."

I was amazed that Wahiib had learned so much about a part of America that had nothing to do with either Penn or his classes. "Only in America," I said as I got a beer from the refrigerator.

The next afternoon, I called the Center to ask what services they offered. "We're a family counseling service," the woman answered

"What does family mean? Is that men and their wives?"

"It might mean a lot of things," she said, but she seemed to sense something evasive in my questions. "I'm sorry, sir. What did you say your name was?"

I hung up.

Two days later I called and a different person answered the phone.

In the 60s, very few women or men knew about counseling, so it was easy to say I was calling for my sister who needed help with an airman she was dating. The woman explained that they matched girls in groups with similar problems. As the groups met, the girls learned to trust each other, and then they shared their problems and helped each other find solutions.

"My god," I thought. "What story is she sharing with this group?" But I also realized I knew something that the blue-eyed girl thought was secret. I didn't know what to do with that, so I decided I would not say anything until it would really catch her off guard.

The dorm housemother was the only person who knew how much time I was with Sayiid, and she never talked about it. If I'd told Pam anything, it would have been all over campus in a day. She wouldn't be trying to be mean. She just wouldn't think what she was saying before she spilled the beans. No one saw me with Sayiid, so no one ever guessed my horrible situation, and if anyone even thought about me, I was just gone a lot.

Sayiid was politer after the hospital, but it was over a month and he hadn't paid me back my ten dollars. On the other hand, I felt safer at his apartment because Wahiib started studying there on weeknights. Wahiib and Sayiid were the only people I talked to outside the Counseling Center. I couldn't bring myself to tell the group about my real problem with Sayiid, but I was learning skills that came out in a surprising way.

One evening when Wahiib let me in, I sat down and casually looked at some old envelopes on the sofa. One of them was from the Savings and Loan where my mom worked. "I didn't know you banked there," I said. "Isn't it kind of far? Their closest office is up in the city."

"It's just a savings account," he replied. "It was Sayiid's idea. Our government allowance is way more than we need, and that bank pays the best interest. Sayiid is really tight. He must have saved $2,000."

"How much do you get a month?" I asked.

"Three hundred dollars. It's there on the first. Like clockwork, as you Americans say."

I asked Wahiib to tell Sayiid I'd forgotten something, and I left.

I waited for the blue-eyed girl after class the next day. "Wahiib said you were over and left before I got back. What was that all about?"

She took a big breath, "Sayiid, how much is in your savings account?"

"I don't know exactly, but I'd guess over two…" I caught myself. "Oh, it's about the ten dollars. I was going to pay you back."

I got out my wallet, but that was a mistake because it was full. I still pretended there was nothing wrong and handed her a ten-dollar bill. "Here. Now we're even."

"Why didn't you pay me back before?"

"I just don't carry money around with me all the time."

"You've got a lot now."

"I just cashed my allowance."

"You waited a week to cash your check? You borrow my money just to carry more around in your pocket? You get more in a month for doing nothing than I make in three months working my butt off."

"I'm sorry I upset you…" I said.

But she didn't ease up. "You're so spoiled. You expect people to do everything for you. You'd never make it in America. We have jobs, and we earn our money. You're just a spoiled rich boy. It's just like they said."

When she said "they," her Tuesday afternoons at the Counseling Center flashed in my mind. They gave her the idea to talk back to me, and I did not like it. I had to let her know that nothing she did could escape me. "Who's 'they'?" I demanded. "Your little girls' group?"

That startled her, but only for a second. "You followed me there."

"No. I did not."

"Then how'd you find out? Huh?"

"That is not your concern," I replied. "But don't let me interfere. You probably need mental help."

That was the closest we came to discussing the Counseling Center, but that confrontation led me to do something I regretted almost as soon as I did it. I took a job as a gas station attendant at the Mobil truck stop in Blue Springs, Missouri. I was going to prove she was wrong. I could hold a job as well as any American.

It had to be a secret, however, because I could never admit I took a job to win an argument with a woman. In the desert, a man tells a woman she is wrong, and that settles the matter. The other reason for secrecy was that only Palestinians and servants do manual work. A menial job would be in my skin and forever lower my status in the desert. I chose the truck stop because no Arab would ever stop there. They would fill up before they left if they were going down to the University.

When Sayiid told me he had a job, I assumed he was responding to me asserting myself. I wanted to see him at work, but I waitressed Saturdays. I figured he'd intentionally created the time conflict to force me to skip work to see him, but I told myself that was being too suspicious. What happened was I arranged with Ken to split a shift on Saturday so I could drive out just after Sayiid started in the afternoon. And I decided to surprise him.

When I pulled into the gas station, Sayiid walked up to my car and didn't even look before he snapped out, "What do you want?"

"Is that how you always talk to customers?" I asked.

"I'm sorry," he said when he recognized me. "It's been so busy I haven't had a break for at least an hour." After that, he put on a show of smiling as he pumped gas and wiped the windows, but I figured "What do you want?" meant, "Why in hell are you bothering me?" and was what he usually said. Nevertheless, I was impressed and got out my camera.

I cringed when the blue-eyed girl snapped a picture of me, but decided it would not matter. She did not know my friends well enough to show them the picture. I was leaving soon, and after I abandoned her, sharing a photograph of me was the last thing she would do. So I grinned in the filling station shirt, borrowed from another employee, with "Red" embroidered over one pocket and their red, flying-horse logo in a bold circle on the sleeve.

After she drove away, I worried that I could never explain the photograph without humiliation. Unlike America, where corporate executives brag about their first job at McDonald's, in the desert bragging begins at birth. Everything a man does remains a part of him.

When I showed Sayiid the pictures, he got real serious. "Don't ever show those pictures to anyone."

"Why?" I asked.

"Because…"

"It's just a couple of snapshots."

"Here." He reached for the prints, and before I knew what he was doing, he ripped them in two and stuffed the scraps in his pocket. "Now we don't need to worry about them."

Grabbing the picture was so like a lot of the other unpredictable things Sayiid did that I didn't pause to reflect on it. As an adult, I see that Sayiid was angry about the picture because Sayiid was afraid. He and his friends acted like everything between them was copasetic, but if any of his friends had seen the photograph, he would've been the object of ridicule from which he could never recover.

Instead I internalized the immediate threat that if I

embarrassed him, I'd experience the same fate as the photograph. On the other hand, if I let myself be part of his image—if he appeared to have his woman in tow—I wouldn't feel pain. I couldn't imagine what he'd do if I openly tried to embarrass him.

I dreamed everything would end when he graduated, but if he just left, I'd feel used. So I ignored the obvious and told myself he cared, and it wasn't as bad as I knew it was. And I'd stop feeling dirty when he acknowledged how much he really cared for me. I am mortified at how much I compromised myself, but I was trying to survive in the middle of hell.

As my graduation approached, the blue-eyed girl let me pick her up after work on Saturdays. Curfew did not matter because she signed out to her parents' home for the weekends. A couple of times we bought food at an all-night market and picnicked in Loose Park until 1:00 or 2:00 in the morning.

She usually drove back early Monday morning. Once when Wahiib was on a tennis team trip, she told her parents she was going back but slept on the couch at my apartment. I felt she was testing to see if I had changed or if I would coerce her into sex. I slept fitfully with an unrelieved erection all night.

She confused sex with love and tried to convince herself everything would all be all right when we got married. I was no longer a controlling boy who threatened to humiliate her. Instead, she thought I was so passionately in love with her that I could not stand to see her even talk to another guy.

A skeptic might ridicule this interpretation, but I have proof. I know the conflict the blue-eyed girl felt that spring—because she wrote it down.

The last Friday before exams, her class ended early, and she came by my apartment. Half my books were in boxes. The sofa was covered with clothes I had laid out to decide which ones to take home and which ones to leave. I was surprised, and I think she mistook that for humility. "I can't offer you much of a place to sit," I said.

"I see..."

She offered no resistance when I put my hand behind her shoulder like we were going to dance. I kissed her, and when I pushed up her skirt and touched her bottom through her panties, she did not become tense. I took her hand, and led her to my bed. She watched as I caught the waist of her panties and pulled them down, and she watched as I slipped off my pants.

Sayiid had been so much less demanding that when he hugged me, I figured one time more or less wouldn't make a difference. I hate to admit it, but women are hardwired for sex to feel good, and I did for a moment. But when he lay on his back and sighed, I realized everything was about him, and I felt like the dirtiest person in the world.

I sat bolt upright. "Oh my God. I'm late for work. Gotta' wash off."

I shook my skirt down to cover my butt and ran to the bathroom hoping Wahiib wouldn't come back. I washed, but I still felt dirty. I ignored the sting and lathered soap in my vagina. I wanted him out of me.

While the blue-eyed girl showered, I idly looked through one of her textbooks. A note written on pink paper fell out. I picked it up and could see it began, "Dear diary..." but I heard the bathroom door and stuffed the paper in my pocket as she came out of the bathroom fully dressed.

She was nearly running. "Have you seen my clogs?" she asked.

At home, I glanced at my bra and pants as I changed for work. I checked the clock and had time for another shower, so I grabbed a towel.

I scrubbed all over again but still felt dirty. I stood there and ran water on my face and chest, but I couldn't get him off. When the hot water ran out, I curled up on the bottom of the tub and shivered. The cold water kept going until Mom came in.

"Oh, my goodness," she said grabbing towels and rubbing my shoulders. "I saw your car, but you're supposed to be at work...I've been in the garden...I'm so sorry." She helped me to get out of the tub and walk to my bed. "Whatever happened?" I thought I would die. I wanted to die.

Mom put a kettle on. "I heard the water running when I came in..." she called from the kitchen. "What ever happened?" she repeated as she came back with another blanket.

A lie couldn't make anything worse. "I had a bad argument with Sayiid," I stuttered through my shivering. "He pushed me into a bush."

Mother looked at me not knowing what to say. I was cold and confused. But where'd a bush come from?

After the blue-eyed girl left, I read the note.

Blowing up Sayiid situation to monopolize
my time so I can procrastinate further &
not do my thesis

If I do my thesis
1. done by end of April
2. teach for 1 ½ mos for money
3. able to go to Europe
4. get job with gov't

If I married Sayiid
Only because—but I can't say only,
because many feelings are raped up in it also.
Reasons
1. funny kind of love
2. position
3. status
4. money

The word "marriage" was never spoken between us, but the only way she could be a virgin for her husband was if I were her husband. I vacillated between ignoring this fantasy and screaming at her to see the world as it really was. It would not be a pang of conscience that made me do this, but rather a cry to stop because she sounded so tedious.

It was her spelling, however, that caught my attention. The blue-eyed girl was a perfect speller. She could tell me how to spell almost any word. So spelling "wrapped" without the "w" and just one "p" jumped out with its own meaning.

She could not say that feelings were "raped up" in her decisions because it would have been her word against mine. In the worst case, my Diplomatic Immunity would let me go home. For her, the best case would still mean that everyone at Penn knew, and Penn was her only way out of a small house north of the Plaza. Even though she suppressed the thought, some part of her screamed out loud on that paper.

There was never a question that my parents would attend graduation. In the desert, we celebrate when our children return.

I had four tickets to the ceremony. I gave one to the blue-eyed girl, and I have used the other three as bookmarks. She sat at the back of the auditorium because she was running to the bathroom again. Her illness fit with how I felt that week. Arabs had just been routed by the Jews in their so-called Six Day War.

I did not realize how many Jews lived in Kansas City until I saw blue and white flags and yarmulkes everywhere. I was tempted to wave a Palestinian flag to annoy them, but America was buying the idea of a preventive war, much as they would accept the creation of a ghetto on the West Bank forty years later.

My landlady gave a graduation party for me. She made a great show of being uninterested in my relation to the blue-eyed girl. *Penn Life* agitated for girls to have freedom, so perhaps my landlady wanted to be in tune with the times.

I have a snapshot of me in a white dress at Sayiid's graduation party. Sayiid has set his drink on the table so he wouldn't be holding it in the picture. He touches my arm as I laugh. There's another girl in the picture, but I can't see who she is because she had the foresight to turn away from the camera.

I had so many emotions. If I hear songs from those years, the feelings come back. More than anything the tiredness of it all. I was better able to say, "I'm not lending you money." And I was better able to say that I wouldn't come over to his apartment on Sunday evening after work. Still there was a gigantic part of me that was relieved because his going would take a lot of pressure off me.

I keep the graduation photograph so I won't forget how much I compromised myself. In Sayiid's culture women have two options. Be angry at their complete lack of control, and be angry all the time, or find a way to live with what they cannot escape. I laughed with Sayiid because I could not get away, and I could not live in a continual state of anger. I smiled to survive.

I helped Sayiid's landlady clean up afterwards. "Mr. Algedda is such a nice man," she said. "I hear his father works with Mr. Hartwood."

A couple days later, I drove Sayiid to the airport. I had no desire to watch him take off, but he'd started talking about grad school, and if he was coming back, it wasn't over. I'd be better off if I could say that I waited until he left. So I found the bar and ordered a martini like in the movies. I took it in a single gulp, choked, and ordered another.

As my plane took off, I remembered the blue-eyed girl driving away from the hospital in the snow and wondered if she had waited until I left.

From English class, I appreciated how a metaphor could intensify a description by drawing in the feelings from other events. I thought through the last four years, and my mind stuck on an old black man riding a tractor lawn mower the morning I drove by Penn for the last time. It rains, the sun comes out, and the grass grows. Then the grass is mowed, and it is the size it is supposed to be, and everyone is happy—unless the grass gets too big, and then it is cut down to size again. Grass is always mowed. I think of that black man every time I hear a mower or smell freshly cut grass.

My parents invited the whole family to celebrate when I returned. A degree from an American college was remarkable, even if Penn was only a small Quaker college in the Midwest.

As I dressed for the party, I recalled the whole cacophony of my experiences in America—sounds, sights, tastes, simply, as Qu'tb said, an abundance squandered in a way an Arab would never dream of wasting.

My mother, who had never left the desert, could not begin to imagine the expanse of green. Once, we visited her relatives in Islamabad and drove up to the Swat Valley. When I described America to my mother, the green of the Swat Valley was my point of reference, but she said I exaggerated to brag about my experience. Allah would not bless unbelievers with a country as big as the entire desert that was green over half the year.

The celebration was different from the party given by my Quaker landlady. Families arrived, but women, wives "in chador" as my friends and I would say, went to separate rooms where they removed their black covers and relaxed. It would be several years before they bought expensive European clothes to wear under their chadors and show to friends when they were alone. Adopting European fashions in secret confirmed what an American student had observed in my freshman dormitory. "Women dress to impress other women."

My father's boss, the Prince was one of the guests, and he asked me when I would begin at the Ministry. I told him in a month.

"We expect a lot from your generation," he continued. "We have invested in your success, and your success will be our success."

"Yes, sir," I replied.

"I was one of those who selected you. Did you know that?"

"No, sir, I didn't. Thank you."

He asked about my experiences in America, what I found most interesting, and what I did when I was not in class. I said I studied.

"But there were other times." The Prince had lived in America for ten years as a secretary in our embassy in Washington.

"Well, I did enjoy their drag races."

"Drag races?" he asked. "I have heard this word, *drag*. Surely they do not run races with such men?"

I chuckled because he was showing off his American slang.

"And what did you think of American women?" he asked in a tone that invited me to confide in him.

"They dress immodestly." I paused. "It was so unfamiliar."

"I know what you mean."

I wondered if he had memories like mine, or if he had simply been surprised by Western women. My father served at his will. I could never ask.

After the last guest had left, and out-of-town relatives had retired to their guest rooms, my father knocked on my door. "You bring honor to your mother and me," he said.

I noted how unusual it was for a man to include the opinion of his wife, and even more unusual a man to mention his wife before himself.

"I saw you talking to the Prince," he said. "He has an excellent family." Then he said good night.

As I tried to sleep, I was already restless for the freedom I had in America. I wished I could celebrate with the blue-eyed girl in bed. But why did my father comment on my speaking with the Prince? I had only talked with him for a few minutes.

The next morning, I found my sister Fatima in the courtyard with a glass of juice and bread. She was wearing a modest skirt and a long-sleeved white cotton blouse open at the neck, and looked like the high school girls I saw in uniforms when I drove into Kansas City.

Fatima was ten when I left for Switzerland. She had grown, and although she was my sister, I noticed her breasts and her exposed knees as she crossed her legs. I remembered her playing in this courtyard with her friends. Several of these girls had come with their parents last night, but they wore chadors now and they also went to the womens' rooms. I could imagine my sister's friends in skirts and blouses, but I would never see them without a chador, except perhaps if they married a relative and even that would be rarely. I could only guess until they were too old for me to care.

Fatima wanted me to be her male escort so she could go shopping. I tried to say I could not do that, but she reminded me, "I only have to be with a man from the family. You are an adult. You can take me just as well as father."

"Won't you be bored with only me?"

"We can call Wahiib and Nasra," she said, adding Wahiib's sister to the conversation. "He came back for the summer. He was on your flight."

"How do you know that?"

"I talked to Nasra yesterday."

I made a mental note that she had cornered me. She was perfecting skills that would make her life less difficult. I felt protective of my own flesh and blood, as I would eventually love and care for my own daughter.

We met Wahiib and Nasra at the market. We could have demanded that our sisters walk behind us, but Wahiib and I let them walk ahead. They were conscious that this was a privilege and repeatedly looked over their shoulders to be certain they had not gone too far.

When they stopped at a stall and started looking through a pile of lace, the shopkeeper became nervous. The Vice/Virtue Officers would charge him as well as them if he talked to unchaperoned girls, but they were already rummaging through a second stack. I caught Wahiib's arm so that we kept back a moment to watch the shopkeeper squirm, but then Fatima turned and spoke to me and he breathed a sigh of relief.

"How much?" I asked as I picked up a shawl at random.

He quoted a price. "Sir, that is very nice, but perhaps you would like to buy something finer for your wife and her friend."

I choked. *My wife?* But it was possible. I looked old enough to have a wife, and once she was in a chador, any observer would assume that my sister had begun her monthly flow and thus could have been married off by my parents. She was dressed modestly, but the front of her chador did not fall flat. Her maturity was obvious to anyone but a blind man.

"Perhaps," I said.

He showed me other scarves, but they were all fitting for a married woman, not the schoolgirl I escorted. We left and browsed at other stalls.

"Wahiib," I said. "I forgot to ask the man something. Watch my sister for a moment, I'll be right back."

"But I'm not…"

I cut him off. "Of course you're a relative, you are my brother student." And I was off.

The shopkeeper was surprised but happy to see me. I selected his best shawl, handed him the asking price and said I would come back the next day. When I collected it the next afternoon, it was wrapped, and the shopkeeper said, "Sir is good to his wife. She will appreciate the surprise."

"I'm sure," I said. But I thought to myself, *Idiot.*

Early in the Israeli war, the Jews attacked an American spy ship, the *Liberty*. After that, Arabs realized how closely they were being watched, and the foreign minister decided that important documents should be carried by couriers. He also decided that being a courier gave me a low profile to visit our European and Asian embassies. On every stop, the consul accompanied me to the foreign ministry where I received diplomatic credentials from the host country. I had done this in America as a charade before going to Penn, but now I was a genuine diplomat.

I celebrated accordingly. In London, I went to shows and

clubs in the West End. In Sweden, I visited various bars. In Paris, I went to the Lido and had my picture taken with a nearly naked dancer in my lap. My driver made discreet inquiries, and I spent the night and most of the next day with her.

I also returned to the United States and would have called the blue-eyed girl, but this was before cell phones or calling cards. Direct dialing was only available from the embassy phones, and I did not want to explain the call.

The blue-eyed girl sent several newsy letters. The hot weather, the drought, her job at Putsche's. She asked me to tell my parents "Hi" for her, which was ridiculous because they did not know she existed.

When school started, Wahiib gave me a lace and silk scarf from Sayiid. What was I supposed to do with it? No one I knew wore scarves.

The year before, Sayiid brought back a watch with snap-on metal pieces to change the color of the face. That sounds odd now, but they were a fad in the 60s, like the sunglasses with interchangeable frames or different dresses on cutout dolls we had when I was a kid. I thought the watch had value, but when I learned how cheap it was, I kept it so I wouldn't forget how much I'd been manipulated.

When I brought the gift back to my room, there was a note from Professor Baker asking me to come by his office.

"I think you should write a senior thesis," he said.

"What?" I stared at him.

"A senior thesis. It's not that hard. Truth is, if everyone knew how easy it was, we'd be drowning in PhDs."

I asked him meekly, "How do you write a thesis?"

He explained the basics and insisted that writing one was

easy. After all, sociology is just looking at how groups of people behave.

But what to study? Professor Baker had an answer for that. "Get some groups together and get them to talk. It'll be interesting." He liked hearing himself talk. It was like *Jeopardy*. He gave me an answer, and I was supposed to guess the question. "Think up some ideas and we'll talk about them next week. We have until April to get it done."

As an adult, I realize the thesis idea was an excuse for him to spend a lot of time with me. He never forced anything on me, but he spent hours telling me about his mistresses. That issue aside, if I'd understood the work I was getting into, I'd have run the other way.

My cousin Alice visited from Cleveland that weekend. She wanted to go shopping, and I volunteered to spend Saturday afternoon with her daughter, Christine. It was perfect Indian summer. Leaves had turned color, and the air had that dry smell that I associate with the lower sun and the shorter days.

Our first stop was Winstead's. We could still order from my car in 1967. As we waited for our malts and steakburgers, Christine told me about school. "I don't want to go to college," she said.

"Why not?"

"Because the boys all drink and play football."

I tried to sound wise. "What would you want them to do?"

"There ought to be parties and pretty clothes. But everyone knows you can't dance when you've been drinking."

"Where'd you hear that?"

"Mom told Daddy that after a party at the club. They were arguing about something."

"And what did your daddy say after that?"

"I didn't hear. My show came back on after the commercial."

I suggested we go to the zoo in Swope Park. The park wasn't as safe as when I was a kid, but I figured we'd be okay on such a wonderful afternoon.

Our first stop was the sea lions. When I was Christine's age, they'd built a large concrete pool filled with salt water, like a giant washtub set in the ground with a concrete island in the middle. Sea lions swam around it in big circles, never changing direction until they all changed at once. I always tried to pick out the leader who decided the direction to swim.

"Auntie." Christine called me Auntie even though I was technically a second cousin. "Mom says you went swimming with her one time, and some boys teased you. You bet a boy you could beat him to the end of the pool. She said you were out sitting on the wall before he even got there."

"That was a long time ago," I replied.

In the monkey house, a male monkey was trying to mount a female, and Christine asked, "What're they doing?"

If one of my children had asked me that when they were eight years old, I'd have been certain they were trying to be funny, but I don't think she knew. It was a different time, and her family hadn't been around a farm for two generations.

Before I could think of something innocuous to say, the female turned and gave the male a big smack across the face. The male rolled back, sat a moment, and then ambled up to the female and started stroking her head.

I ignored the lead-up and replied about what was happening in front of us. "That's a boy monkey and a girl monkey. The girl monkey got angry at what the boy monkey was doing, and now he's trying to make up to her."

"What'd he do to make her angry?"

I wasn't going to answer that one. "I don't know."

"Do you think they were arguing about sex? Mom says that Daddy never does anything for her unless it's about sex."

Back at school on Monday, I told Pam what Christine said at the zoo, and we both laughed.

"It's all so simple to kids, isn't it?" I said.

"Yeah. They don't know what they've got to watch out for..."

"Or how to respond, even..."

"Like if you get pushed in a bush," Pam added. I was startled. Where'd a "bush" come from? "You know," she went on "how we respond is so influenced by if we think we can say something, or if we feel we can't."

I felt a twinge of anxiety that she understood more than I'd told her, but it wasn't like Pam to hint that she knew my secrets.

When I knocked, OB yelled for me to come in. He was writing and waved for me to be quiet. I said I could come back, but he said, "Just a minute." He tapped the pencil down the page as he read what he'd written, then set the pencil on the desk and looked up. "Have you decided on your thesis?" he asked.

"Uh..."

He cut me off. "I see, no ideas at all. What'd you do on the weekend? You saw groups of people, didn't you? It's not that hard to wonder what they're doing. Look around you. A thesis is easy. The only hard part is keeping at it until you're done."

I looked blankly at him as I realized how wrong he was about me. I had no idea how to finish anything. But he read right into my thoughts. "Think you don't have the drive to do it? You went in to see Paul Forger, didn't you? You had the desire to graduate. You just didn't know how. Most folks know how, but don't bother. It's easier to help you learn how, than to get you to want to do it. Now, what did you do this weekend?"

"I took my niece to the zoo."

"And...?"

"It was sunny, but it was cold and there weren't a lot of people."

"And animals? People are just animals. What about the locked-up animals?"

I told him about Christine and the monkeys.

"And you couldn't get any ideas?" OB could hardly contain himself. "So what groups are you going to study?"

"What do you mean?" I asked.

"What groups? The girls you're going to get to talk about how they feel when a guy pisses them off. That's who."

And so my thesis, and eventually much of life, was built on my niece asking me about sex between monkeys.

Professor Baker's idea grew into a big project. It was fascinating, and I didn't notice time passing while I was doing it. Only that I had no time to myself.

I organized four groups of women, met with each group four times, asked questions and let them discuss the answers. That was only sixteen hours. The catch was that on one of his African trips, OB had bought a tape recorder in the duty free shop, an early model with tape that ran between little spools. He wanted me to record everything and make transcripts for each session. Group meetings were easy. Typing the material was a back-breaker.

I ran into Wahiib at Le Pois as I was getting coffee. He asked if he could sit at my table and insisted on buying for me. "I receive $300 per month. I don't know why they think I would ever use that much."

I shrugged and made no comment.

His English was excellent, but he didn't do well with slang yet, and he stopped me to explain even simple things I said like, "OB told me not to sweat it," or "I scarfed down my lunch in a hurry." I realized he wasn't trying to take advantage of me and tried to recall where I'd gotten the idea I couldn't trust him.

How I'd misjudged him was on my mind as we left for class. "Wahiib..." I said, but then didn't know what to say next.

"Yes?" He waited.

I had to say something. "You're really like I thought you were in freshman English, aren't you? Somehow, I had a wrong..." and I trailed off.

He ignored my comment. In fact, we never talked about that again, but he did say, "Talking helps my English. Perhaps I might buy coffee for you again next Wednesday. It helps me to practice my conversation."

Wahiib lived in the apartment he'd shared with Sayiid. He was studious, and he always sat in the front row and asked the best questions. He kept to himself, but everyone knew who he was because he was a star on the tennis team and his picture had been in *Penn Life*.

The next week I brought a copy of *Better Homes and Gardens* from my mom. I told him it'd help him understand American homes. If I were doing it today, I'd bring a copy of *Sunset* because it'd be more impressive, but *Real Simple* might be even better to let him know what wives think about.

Sayiid sent me a telephone number to call him on his birthday. He said it'd be better for Wahiib to place the call because the operators only spoke Arabic, and I'd waste a lot of money trying to get through by myself.

It was best to call Sunday morning his time which was

Saturday night at Penn. So I met Wahiib at the student union at 10:00 p.m. After Wahiib made the connection, I fed in $40.00 in quarters. Wahiib spoke to Sayiid for a few minutes, some of which didn't sound friendly, though he did turn a couple of times and smile to reassure me.

I remember nothing of what I talked to Sayiid about that night. In fact, I remember few things we ever said at all. Asking him to slow down is very clear. That he called me a liar for saying I was a virgin. His orders to meet him at the airport. His insistence that I go to the hospital with him even though he was driving.

Wahiib's uncle died the next week, and he went home for the funeral. I asked him to carry a note to Sayiid.

The night after the eulogies for his uncle, Wahiib and I had a long conversation. It was easy for him to stay awake because his biological clock thought it was the middle of the day. It was easy for me to stay up because I was alert for details about the blue-eyed girl.

Wahiib told me that the blue-eyed girl worked with Dr. Baker most of her free time. He saw her on Wednesdays when they had coffee, and she still went home on weekends.

"Tell me, what's she like now?" I asked.

"You know," he replied, "very much the same."

We talked about Wahiib's classes, the thesis he was doing for honors in economics, and his plans to enter the diplomatic service in my footsteps. The title of his thesis, "Analysis of the Effects of Air Travel on the Shifting Economy in States Formerly Dependent on Limited Surface Travel"—"Getting off camels," for short—made it easy to lead the conversation back to the blue-eyed girl. "She wrote that she's doing a thesis. What's that all about?"

"It came out of working with Orville Baker. He's taken

an interest in her. I wondered if he was chasing a skirt, but I don't think so. He has some connection with a counseling service over by the airbase. Did you ever notice that Air Force base over near where Mo took karate? She's doing a survey on what women think of how men behave toward them. It sounds, oh, what's that American word?" He paused to remember. "Oh, yeah, 'heavy.'"

Wahiib tried to explain some story about the blue-eyed girl going to the zoo with her niece. I didn't understand, but Wahiib laughed. "At first I thought I was laughing at her story," he said. "But I think I actually laughed to keep her company. Something was more important to her than just her niece asking about a couple of monkeys."

It angered me that she discussed monkey sex with that dirty old man Orville Baker. Such a bitch! But I did not put that in the letter I gave Wahiib to carry back.

My father was tolerant and worked with some Shiia. On a business trip, he met Fhad's father and learned that Fhad was doing a master's degree in California. That rekindled my plan to go to graduate school. I missed America because it rained from time to time, women were not wrapped up in heavy cloth, and I could take up where I had left off with the blue-eyed girl. I began to look at college catalogues, and I wrote to the blue-eyed girl that I was coming back for certain.

Wahiib read the magazines I lent him. "I understand America much better," he said.

He returned the favor next week by giving me a flier he'd seen on campus while I was in KC for the weekend. "These went up Monday morning. I thought you might have missed it."

The flier announced that Penn was organizing its first

ever women's swim team. Tryouts were that week. I looked at him for an explanation. "You should try out," he said.

"Me? Not on your life. I haven't been in a pool in years."

"You swim very well. You swam across the lake." He paused as though embarrassed to bring up that day. "I've seen many people who think they swim well. And..." The future diplomat paused for emphasis. "You swim better than most men."

I waited to see what else he'd say. Then I gave him all the excuses I could think of, including that I didn't have time.

Wahiib politely ignored my objections. "Please go to tryouts. It will let me think that I have done something for you and earned your respect."

Tryouts were miserable. I only had my suit from junior high, which I didn't even know I had with me. I think I'd put it in the back of my car one weekend, and it'd found its way to my room at school.

The coach was Lorel, the same woman who'd made me take the freshman swim test over. She took one look at my suit and stifled a laugh.

We swam in heats. I had great form and was ahead for the first two laps, but I got winded fast. After that, I swam like a dying trout. As I got out, Lorel made a snide comment about my suit being left over from junior high school. When she posted the team, I wasn't on the list.

I left tryouts without drying my hair. By the weekend I was getting a cold, so I slept over at home and cut my Monday morning class. When I got to our room after lunch, Pam said Coach Lorel was trying frantically to find me. I wondered what that was about, but students didn't question a teacher's authority, even when you weren't in their class. So I called back.

It was simple. The star swimmer for individual and relay breaststroke was no longer able to be on the team. Lorel had decided I was her best alternative, and practice was in thirty minutes. I explained this to Pam as I rummaged to gather things and run to the locker rooms.

"I bet it's the cheerleader who fell doing a flip at the game Saturday," Pam said. "They took her away on a stretcher."

This time there were no nasty comments. Lorel introduced me to the other girls. "This is our new breaststroker."

I wasn't in shape, and Lorel hounded me as I struggled at the end of practice. "Feel your breasts push the water...make them feel for yourself...no man can push 'em like you can... men never understand like a woman ...feel your legs push the water...push it out...push it out like an old lover..."

As everyone got out, she called me aside. "You've got a lot to make up. I expect you in here every day at 4:00 to swim laps. Weekends too."

"Coach," I said in my most respectful voice, "I'll work really hard. I'll come in at six every morning, but I can't be here Saturday and Sunday."

"Why not?"

"I work. My job's in Kansas City. I'm paying my own way. I had a scholarship, but I flunked some courses and lost that."

"Humm!" she said, but added, "We'll see."

At the end of practice on Thursday, Lorel asked, "How much do you make at this job, whatever it is?"

"I waitress on the Plaza and make $40.00 if I work three shifts."

She did the mental calculation, "That's less than $2,000 a year. How do your afford school? Penn isn't cheap."

"Loans."

"This'll help you more than I expected. I'm making you instructor for the beginning swim class, two hours a week. You don't need a degree to teach PE, and I've checked, you don't have class. You get half tuition for "family" if you teach here. See you Saturday at 4:00."

"I can't."

"And why not?"

"I'm already on the schedule this weekend. I can't leave Ken in a lurch. He's the manager. He won't have time to find someone else."

Lorel looked at me very hard. "Okay. Then I will see you Monday afternoon and every afternoon after that, Thanksgiving included, since you live so close by, until I think you are in as good a shape as the rest of my girls.

"And..." She addressed me by my full formal name that she would only know if she had really looked at my transcript. "I allow everyone on the team to disagree with me exactly one time."

I did extra laps after every practice and ate a late meal in a side room off the cafeteria that was empty by the time I got there. I could see that I didn't make it as a swimmer in high school because the Y team only practiced twice a week. I felt good, but life was crazy. I swam, taught, went to class, studied, and in the time that was left, I typed transcripts for my thesis.

The groups for my thesis were very different. Pam helped recruit a group from Penn. The second group was Mexican girls that Manuel's sister helped me find. The third group was black girls I lined up through Jimmy, the one black busboy at Putsche's. His sister worked with the Girls Club, and after I had explained my project, she helped me meet some high school seniors.

The fourth group was wives of servicemen getting ready

to go off to Vietnam. That was OB's suggestion. I asked how to find such women, and he referred me to a friend who was director of the Grandview Family Counseling Center. He winked and said, "I know everyone. Didn't they tell you that at orientation?" Fortunately, she wasn't one of my counselors.

I improved enough that Lorel cut my workouts to only five days over Christmas vacation, which was great because I had only transcribed a couple of the tapes. Ken gave me a couple of shifts, but I don't know what I'd have done if I'd had to work every day at Putsche's. Transcribing was mindless, except that you had to pay close attention so you couldn't listen to the radio.

I intended to write to Sayiid, but I couldn't find enough time to write a long letter. If I wrote a short letter, he'd get nasty and say I mustn't care if I hadn't put any more effort into it. So time slid by with fewer letters.

Between trips carrying documents, I was often included in conversations between my father and the Prince who would ask my opinion on what I'd seen. Eventually a rumor reached me that my father was negotiating with the Prince that I would marry his daughter. The Prince's daughter had played with my sister years ago, and I assumed she had developed much as my sister had. Of course, she would be in chador any time I saw her, so I would see very little of her.

When Wahiib came home for midwinter break, I asked him about the blue-eyed girl. He replied, "Very much the same."

"And...?" I prompted.

Wahiib hesitated.

"What aren't you saying?" I insisted.

"I don't know how to put a finger on it," he said. 'Put a finger on it' jumped out at me. He was using American slang in our conversation. "We talk," he said. "She always asks about you."

"Is she with another guy?"

"I don't think so. She'd have said something or I'd have heard."

"Has anything else changed?"

"Only the swim team, but she must have written you about that."

I thought *Swim team! What the hell is that all about?* but I replied to Wahiib, "What difference does swimming make?"

"She loves it. It's like that time she swam across the lake. Remember that swim test everyone had to take freshman year?"

"What a pain," I said, and we talked about the bitchy woman who gave the test. That woman was now the girls' swim coach, and she had made the blue-eyed girl the instructor for freshman who failed the swim test.

Wahiib had become her friend, and I wondered for a moment if he told this story to irritate me. When he returned to America, I asked him to carry a small silver tray as a gift for the Christian holiday. We worked as usual on December 25th, and I realized I had not seen the blue-eyed girl for six months.

Wahiib gave me a Christmas gift from Sayiid, but I was so focused on swimming and my thesis that I barely had time to write a two-line note.

Our first meet was a tournament for all the women's teams from Missouri and Kansas. I swam well in 200-meter breaststroke, but I bungled a turn and came in second.

As I waited on the block for my teammate to tag the wall in the mixed relay, I knew we were even, and if we were going to win, I had to pull ahead. I was twenty-one years old, and I was as good as I'd ever be.

My teammate was coming—stroke, stroke, stroke. I hyperventilated. I'd pass out if I timed it too soon, but if I timed it right I wouldn't have to breathe for over half of the first lap. That'd make a difference.

In breaststroke, you only see a person who is about to pass you when their hands reach ahead into your field of vision. Out of the turn, I saw a hint of a splash and decided it was now or never. I usually breathed every stroke, but I could push myself to every two or even every three for a sprint.

So I did, and we won. We stood on the blocks to be recognized, and a photographer for *Penn Life* snapped our photograph. I remembered Sally and Cheri and wondered if they ever had an opportunity to swim and feel as good again.

"Nice trick," said Lorel as we walked back to the bench. "Breathing every other stroke. Risky if you burn out before the wall, a solid second versus a try at first. Maybe I should say gutsy. I don't know how I'd have played that one." Our team photograph was printed on the front page of *Penn Life*.

Wahiib sent me a clipping of the blue-eyed girl. Fortunately, the newsprint was so thin that the Vice/Virtue censors did not inspect the envelope. From the photograph I understood how much the blue-eyed girl had changed, and how much it said about Wahiib that he did not notice why.

The photograph shows the blue-eyed girl and three other women from their knees up. The wet tank suits reveal more than would a padded bathing suit. Their nipples are erect in the cold, and their groins are delicately outlined. They each hold a ribbon, and the blue-eyed girl glows. Her thighs are slender and muscular, and I wondered if she knew I would see that.

I held that picture so many times it eventually broke apart. Then I scotch taped the rips and kept it in my English-

Arabic dictionary. I looked at that picture many times hoping that the thought of her young body would arouse me, but it never did, and I wondered why. When I looked at the picture recently, I understood why it did not excite me. That was the first time I could see that she was not smiling because she had lost weight and looked sexy in the close-fitting tank suit. She was smiling because she had won. In the picture, she knows she can win.

I hurried to complete my graduate school applications and convince the Prince that I would be more effective if I returned to America and earned a master's degree like Fhad. I wanted to go back to America. I wanted the freedom. I wanted the excitement. I wanted the blue-eyed girl. I wrote to her that I was coming back. Then her letters stopped.

Shortly after the beginning of second semester, I got a letter from Sayiid. It was a jolt to realize I hadn't written to him about the swim team. I didn't want him to be part of my life, but he wasn't going to allow that.

> So I will get my master's in economics at KU, and that will be close to Kansas City. I'm going to write to Wahiib that I will need my car back. I know you will be glad we can spend more time together..."

"Together?" I felt ill. I could try anything I wanted, but Sayiid was coming back and I hadn't found an ally to help me deal with my secret.

Sayiid's letter was on my mind when I met Wahiib for coffee the next morning. My name was in *Penn Life* again. Wahiib's first comment was, "You're quite a celebrity."

"Right," I replied sarcastically.

"No, I mean it," he assured me.

I smiled and our conversation moved on to other things until we were interrupted. "Wahiib, why haven't you introduced me to your friend?"

I looked up and found a handsome, athletic guy standing behind me.

"You never asked me to," Wahiib said.

"I'm asking now."

Wahiib introduced me, then said, "This is Karl Anderson. We've played tennis together—what is it—our fourth season?"

"Four years. I can't beat him consistently, but he can't beat me consistently either."

"Actually, I've kept count," Wahiib said, "The tally is 901 to 893."

"Okay. Who's ahead, wise guy?"

"I am. I would never have mentioned it otherwise." Wahiib smiled.

Karl made a mock sneer. "The year's not over yet." He turned to me. "That was quite a feat in the swim meet, barely breathing the second lap."

"How'd you know that?"

"It was in *Penn Life*. I asked the guy who wrote the article why he noticed. He didn't. He said Lorel pointed it out to him. That was a surprise in itself." He changed the subject. "So what society are you in?"

"I'm not."

"Come on. You've got society written all over you, and your performance on the swim team. Why aren't you in a society?"

"They didn't ask me."

"I've got some friends. They have three years to make it up to you."

"Not actually. I graduate in four months."

"What? Where'd you transfer from?"

"Didn't. I've been here all along."

"I've never seen you before."

"They didn't have a swim team 'til this year."

"But come on, where've you been hiding?"

"I work weekends up in KC."

"You a day hopper?"

"Of sorts."

Karl looked at Wahiib. "Is she telling me the truth?"

"We sat next to each other in freshman English," Wahiib replied.

I cut in. "Dr. Notpu? *How English Means? Rabbit Run?*"

"My gosh," Karl exclaimed, "She really was there." He pulled up a chair.

It never entered my mind to wonder why a guy who was such an obvious prize didn't already have a girlfriend. I just found it exciting that a guy was taking time to be in a conversation with me.

I met Karl at Le Pois on Friday and felt a part of the student body at Penn for the first time. He told jokes, whispered comments about everyone who walked by, and when I told him I thought people were looking at us, he said they were looking to see who I was.

When I got back to my room, Sayiid's letter was still on my desk, and I got an idea. Karl was strong and athletic enough to intimidate even Sayiid, and that'd keep Sayiid away if he came back. Of course, Sayiid could start bragging to Karl about what he'd done with me, and that wouldn't go over so well. So my plan had holes, but it was better than no plan.

I found a big difference between my thesis groups over the holidays. Girls on campus and the black and Mexican girls expected to have a say in what they'd do with their boyfriend, and if a guy made every decision, they'd dump him. They'd tell their boyfriends what they didn't want to do, including not getting too intimate if they didn't want to.

Girlfriends of servicemen preparing to ship out were a different story. Facing death made the guys want sex now, and their girlfriends gave in to them. One girl all but told us she'd gotten pregnant because she felt bad that he was so scared.

Dr. Baker was happy with the first draft of my thesis. "This is fascinating. Just fascinating. Women adjust to their boyfriends' stress. Think how a guy could manipulate that. This ought to be required reading for every woman on campus." He thumbed through the pages before he added with more thoughtfulness than usual, "Just don't let the guys in on it."

But writing itself wasn't my strong suit. After he started to reread what I'd written, he said, "I don't have time to work on this right now. Why don't you leave it for me? I'll make some comments and drop it in your mail box."

What he meant was that he didn't have the heart to rip it apart in front of me, but that didn't stop him from ripping it apart. I got it back two days later with red marks and pencil edits in every blank spot on both sides of all pages. His not-so-subtle demand for an extensive rewrite was disheartening, and I was at a loss. I talked to Karl about it, but he got by on tennis, not his writing.

I mentioned it to Wahiib on the next Wednesday.

"Would you let me look at it?" he asked.

"I guess," I said, " but do you really want to?"

"Yes. After all, I've listened to your worries about this for, hummm..." He pretended to count on his fingers. "Almost six months."

Wahiib may have been learning slang from me, but he'd

mastered formal English. His first comment said it all. "You've said everything you need to say. You just have your ideas out of order. Here..."

He handed back the manuscript with a number by each sentence for all thirty pages. The sentences on the first page were numbered like this: 1, 2, 4, 7, 27, 28, 29, 16, 207, 209... etc.

"You should retype it rearranging the sentences in the order I marked. Sentence 3, for example, is on page 14. It really belongs in the introduction. But what you have as the ninth sentence, I've numbered 207. It belongs much later. I'd guess it will end up on about the tenth page."

The amount of time he had put in! "Thank you so much. This must have taken hours."

He was gracious. "I learn when I do something new, so I should thank you." He took a minute to find the right words. "I learned something about life in America that I would not have learned anywhere else."

"What's that?"

"In my country they say that American women are immoral, but what they mean is that women in America expect to have a say in what happens in their lives. People say American women are spoilt by money and that's why so many of them believe they should make their own decisions.

"I expected women at Penn to feel entitled because they come from wealthy families. It is the same at home. A rich man allows his daughter a little authority to impress his subordinates. But she knows she must always confine her orders to employees or servants.

"Your thesis taught me that even poor women, Mexicans and Negroes, believe they have a right to decide for themselves. I will remember this."

A week or so later Karl surprised me after class. "You

told me about that coffee shop up on Main Street," he said.

"The Point. Yes."

"My 8:00 o'clock class is cancelled for tomorrow. You don't have a class in the morning. Let's run up there tonight. Pick you up at 6:45?"

When we got to 43rd and Main, The Point was closed and had been long enough that the tape at the top of the sign that said "Closed" had come loose and fallen over the lower tape like a hinge. I was embarrassed.

Karl patted my leg and said, "That's okay," but when I thought about it later, I remembered there was no surprise in his voice. "I've got an idea," he added. "Have you ever heard Milt and Bettye?"

"Who are Milt and Bettye?"

"Ohhhhh. You'll see." He took me to the Horseshoe Lounge over on Troost Street. That was the first time I'd had a drink in a bar, and Karl ordered Tom Collinses. All I knew about alcohol was that it was an acquired taste, and there was a lot of pressure to acquire the taste. I'd drunk alcohol with Sayiid, but that was only to make him tolerable.

Bettye had the deep voice of a large woman who has experienced trouble in her life. I thought of Mehalia Jackson. She was that good; she just never got the right break as it turned out. But that didn't stop her from putting soul—as the word was coming to be used at the time—into her music.

My second drink was about half done when I saw it was 10:00. "Karl, it's an hour till I need to be in." Seniors could stay out later, but they still had curfews. We were going to the big spring dance in two weeks, and I didn't want anything to ruin that.

As Karl drove south on Troost, I said, "You better watch your speed. They love to put a speed trap up here." He slowed a little, and as we came over a small rise, there was a police radar unit pointed at us. I glanced at a policeman writing a ticket. He seemed familiar, and I wondered if I'd seen him before.

"You're right," Karl said. He squeezed my leg, "That would've blown my budget for the dance. I knew there was a reason I liked you."

By 10:45 he was opening his car door for me. "That was so much fun," I said. "I didn't know jazz sounded like that. All I've ever heard was Dad's Dixieland."

We stood in a shadow away from the door. There was only one other couple. Most girls had 10:30 curfew, and most seniors, who could come in later, were finishing their year-end projects so they wouldn't need to take finals—which was where I should've been.

It was a warm night. Karl kissed me and put his hands on my chest, one on each side, carefully not on my breasts. It was a long slow kiss that couldn't lead to anything in the next five minutes, so I felt safe. I was beginning to think this guy loved me, and I kissed him back. It is difficult to explain after all that happened next, but that was the first time in my life I enjoyed a kiss. I wanted to do it again, but he left me at the door as I rang the bell to get in.

I went shopping on the Plaza with my mom and found the perfect dress at Harzfeld's. From a distance it looked white, but it was pale pink, the kind of pink that made my eyes glow. I planned to carry a shawl my grandfather had given me.

The dance was downtown at the Meuhlebach Hotel ballroom. I signed out to stay at my parents' for the weekend. When Karl picked me up, I introduced them. He'd brought a corsage that I put on in the bathroom.

My mother called, "Have a fun time," as we left.

Karl's only comment was, "That coffee house is real close, isn't it?"

Since underclass students came to the dance, alcohol was

forbidden. To get around this, Karl and several of his friends rented a motel room for a pre-party. "Mood adjustment," they called it. The room was close to the hotel, so no one would have trouble driving to the dance.

When we got to the Meuhlebach, I was nervous about dancing. Despite a drink and despite what Pam and told me about screwing standing up, it was difficult to relate the soft lights and music to being coerced in Sayiid's room.

Karl, however, was a great dancer, and when he led me it was easy to follow. He was the kind of guy that the girls would look at to judge me, but I felt okay with him.

Late in the evening, Karl suggested, "Let's go back to the motel afterwards. There's still some champagne."

"I don't know," I replied. "Maybe that wouldn't be a good idea."

"Why not? I already asked Rick and Susie. They're coming."

I was still reluctant, but told him, "Well, okay."

When I saw Susie in the powder room, I asked, "Are you and Rick going to stop on the way back, too?"

"Yes," she answered. "We can party a little more and still have time to get back. I took a late sign-out." She went into a toilet stall, and it got awkward to talk.

"See you there," I said, and I left. But we hadn't talked about exactly where we were going.

There were dirty glasses in the motel room and a couple of empty champagne bottles from before. One bottle was unopened in a bucket with ice that hadn't melted yet. A towel was neatly tucked around the bottle like a waiter had set it there. Karl turned on the television. I sat at the end of the bed while he popped the cork with a great flourish and poured a glass.

"Where are Rick and Susie?" I asked.

"They'll be here."

Karl started to kiss me. I felt safe at first because we were sitting, and because Rick and Susie were coming. Then Karl started rubbing my breast through my dress, and Rick and Susie didn't show up. I was anxious, and when he put his hand on my leg, I tensed. "What if they walk in?"

"They won't."

"Why not?"

He hesitated. "Uh, Rick had to get gas. They'll be along. We'll just have a drink. There'll be here in no time."

I understood. God, I understood. I moved to stand up, but Karl didn't let go. "I've got to pee," I said.

He looked at me as though he was weighing my words before he took his hand off my leg. I made a point of leaning toward him as I laid my shawl on the bed. I'd told him it'd belonged to my grandmother.

I made lots of noise to take time in the bathroom. Then I had an idea. I left the bathroom light on and walked toward the outside door. "Did you double lock the door?" I asked. "So no one walks in…"

"No," he replied, exasperated because, I realized, he knew no one was coming anyway. "No, I didn't." For some lucky reason, he turned to pick up a glass. In a moment, I opened the door and was out. Never mind my shawl on the bed.

I ran to the corner and crossed Broadway. Behind me, I heard Karl yell, "Hey wait," but he was struggling to get his shoes on.

I ducked into the arched doorway of the Catholic church across the street. If I was lucky he'd think I'd gotten farther than that. The all night restaurant on the corner blocked his sight as he got into his car, and he had to wait for the light.

In a few moments, I saw him drive east on Linwood. He was looking around, slowing up to double check and then speeding up to get to where he thought I'd gone. He circled back once more, very slowly, and I was glad I'd anticipated his return. He'd eventually give up.

I waited an hour before I ventured out of the doorway and walked south to my parents' house. I used side streets so I'd see lights of any approaching car, and I prayed Karl wouldn't cruise with his headlights off.

Karl told me he'd played football, but that the weight training improved his tennis game, and tennis was a lot less work. As my stockings wore through, it dawned on me that Karl was probably Carl who'd gotten Christie pregnant. In my mind I'd spelled his name two different ways, so I'd thought he was two different people.

On Monday, Susie asked if I felt better. She and Rick had gone to Putsche's with several other couples. Karl had told everyone I didn't feel well, and he was taking me to my parents' house. I said I was fine.

On Wednesday, Wahiib asked how the dance had been. He smiled when I said, "Let's not talk about that. I had to walk home."

I was back to square one. I hadn't written Sayiid for months. He'd be back for grad school, and I couldn't risk he'd be angrier than he already was. So I wrote a newsy letter about classes and my upcoming graduation. I ignored the time since my last letter and filled in details about my thesis and typing the manuscript with no typos. Trying to depend on Karl had been a wild dream anyway.

I received the first letter in months from the blue-eyed girl as I was waiting for my parents in the front hall. Negotiations had gone well with the Prince, and that day I was going to meet his daughter for the first time since she had been my sister's playmate.

A servant had gone to our mailbox earlier, and I recognized the blue-eyed girl's meticulous cursive writing on a pink envelope. I held it and contrasted my experiences in America with the contract I was about to sign for a marriage arranged by my parents. Then I heard my mother and my father on the stairs and put the letter in my pocket.

We were not of the same social class as the Prince, but I was bright, my father served the King well, and the airline thrived. The Princess could reject me, though the Prince had assured my father that would not happen. She sat at one end of a long, formal hall in her parents' house. I arrived with my parents, and her parents escorted me to her and introduced us. Then the four parents retired to the far end of the hall and watched us as we talked. We would never be alone until our wedding night.

She was pretty in a dark kind of way. And she had a childlike smile that let me know that because of my father's reputation, she immediately trusted me. "You have studied in the United States," she said.

"Yes," I replied. "Have you been there?"

"No, but my father has. I have seen many pictures of the United States."

"Ever see American movies?"

"Oh, yes. I love *Mary Poppings*."

"*Mary Poppins*," I corrected her.

"Yes. *Mary Poppins*. I have seen it many times. I can even say 'super-cali-fragil-istic-expi-ali-docious.'"

I thought to myself, 'What would she think of *Tom Jones* or *The Graduate*, movies that I'd seen in London. Such a child. And she has brown eyes.

After two hours of contrived conversation, I retired to the

other end of the room. Her parents spoke to her quietly, I saw her nod, and then the three of them walked to the middle of the room. She sat on one side of a table; I sat on the other. As our parents watched, we signed a contract that specified that we would be married in the winter, the dowry her parents would provide, and my commitment to provide for her and our children.

I knew she was a virgin. My old nurse had watched the examination to be certain on behalf of my family. No one was offended by being asked to prove her virginity. It was assumed she would be asked, and it was a matter of pride to her parents to prove that formally. I would own their daughter. She had to come to me as a girl so I could make her a woman.

Such meetings are exhausting. When we got back to our home, we went to our separate rooms to rest, and I opened the blue-eyed girl's letter. She ignored the long time she had not written and said she would be traveling in Europe with a girlfriend. She remembered my brother in Germany, and she hoped that we could meet while I was on one of my diplomatic trips. She included the dates she would arrive in Europe and return to the United States.

Jabir called that night to congratulate me. He joked that he would have to give me pointers on sex. My parents sat across the room and heard only my side of the conversation. I said things like, "You're right," and "I can't wait."

Jabir understood they were eavesdropping, and for a moment we were two kids harmlessly misleading our parents with him saying things that would mortify my mother and me saying banal things in reply.

Toward the end of the call, I was caught up in the daring aspect of our telephone banter. "Jabir," I asked, "I have friends from Penn who are traveling in Europe. Could they stay with you for a couple of days?"

"Sure."

I could have told the blue-eyed girl to meet me any number of places, but I wanted the excitement of introducing her to Jabir. I sent a note that I would be traveling, and she should write to me at my brother's address in Homburg. It was already planned that I would visit Jabir in August.

When Wahiib came home, I found out why the blue-eyed girl had not written.

Wahiib had played number one or number two on the Penn tennis team for four years. He played a mental game in which he actively tried to appear uncertain or confused. This ability to mislead opponents related to his ability to be so unobtrusive that people spoke in front of him as though he was not there. For this reason he overheard Karl, his co-captain of the team, and Jerry, another senior, discussing the blue-eyed girl in the locker room.

Jerry joked to Karl that it was unfair for a senior to take advantage of a freshman woman. When Karl said she was a senior, Jerry insisted he would not have missed such a woman for three years. Karl turned abruptly to Wahiib and said, "Tell him she's a senior."

"I wasn't certain whom he meant," Wahiib said, "so I asked. Jerry cut in, 'The one with the blue eyes. The *blue eyes*.'"

Wahiib had no idea my girl was dating Karl, so it took him a moment to understand what Jerry meant. "Karl told Jerry all about her," he continued, "working on the Plaza and going home for weekends. And then competing on the women's swim team."

"And what else?" I asked. I knew he was hiding something, and I waited. I am good at waiting when I know my question has hit a nerve.

Slowly I got from Wahiib that Karl bragged to Jerry how he planned to get my girl alone in a motel room after a dance. I have talked about enough women to understand what Karl planned and how he would make it happen. The blue-eyed girl might be in better shape for swimming, but she would still be no match for him. I wondered if Wahiib remembered virtually the same conversation between me and Mo just two years previously.

Monday after the dance, however, Karl was fuming because, when he made his move, she outsmarted him.

I estimated that was one week before I received my first letter from her since February. It might seem strange that the blue-eyed girl wrote to me after that experience, but in her system of morality, she belonged to me and returning to me was an effort to recover her self-respect.

She had tried to humiliate me, but I'd settle that when I returned. In the meanwhile, I wrote back as though I knew nothing about Karl.

Wahiib also brought a copy of the blue-eyed girl's thesis entitled "Signs of Love as Perceived by Women." There were strange ideas in the abstract.

> Women whose boyfriends were facing combat felt that their boyfriends loved them despite intolerance of differences of opinion, intense jealously if they spoke with another man, or anger and forced sex if the woman did not want to be intimate...women can love domineering men if they believe the men are under extreme stress such as facing the risk of death.

I could not understand what facing death had to do with a man taking charge. It was some American thing. I put it down and never finished it.

Wahiib's parents were easy to spot at graduation. His mother's head was wrapped in a scarf despite the heat and ninety-five percent humidity.

After the ceremony, I introduced Wahiib to my mom and dad. He introduced them to his parents, and then he introduced me to his parents.

I reached out to shake his father's hand like I'd usually do. His father seemed to be caught off guard, but he reacted quickly and shook my hand. Wahiibs' mother, however, was like a stone and folded her hands in front of her when I reached to shake her hand.

Wahiib immediately said something to his father in Arabic. They talked for a few moments, and then his father spoke to his mother. She extended her hand, but she did not flex even the tiniest muscle. It was limp. She was doing as she was told, but she did not look at me.

While this was happening, Mr. Hartwood came up and said "Hi" to my dad, but his real purpose was guide Wahiib's parents away. "Sorry, we've got to run," He pointed to his watch. "Dinner reservation at five." He turned to my mom and dad and said tersely, "Nice to see you." Then they were gone. He didn't speak to me at all, and for the first time I saw he didn't give a damn about me. His only concern was his job at TWA.

Despite that awkwardness, it was a proud day. My GPA never recovered from my freshman year, but OB sponsored me to receive departmental honors for my thesis. I thanked him, but he wasn't through yet. "I've decided you should go down to Columbia and get a master's degree," he said, referring to the University of Missouri graduate school.

"I'd love to," I answered, "but I've barely had time to get

anything done but this project. I haven't even thought about applications."

"Don't worry. I sent a copy of your thesis to the admissions director for the sociology grad program. She's a longtime friend of mine." He smiled so I'd know she was a special friend. "She'll take good care of you, but you'd better call her Monday."

"Let me take a picture," said my dad as he pulled my arm to pose me beside OB. "We know how much you've helped our graduate. Now smile."

My father asked if I knew of the woman who was Wahiib's friend at Penn. "I don't think he knew any women at Penn," I replied.

"It was a young woman he drank coffee with every week," my father explained, and I realized it could only be the blue-eyed girl.

"There was a girl in some of his classes," I said. "Why?"

He explained that she had met Wahiib's parents, and his mother worried about how he knew her. She attended school in the same classes with men; she spoke directly to men, and had even reached out to touch Wahiib's hand.

I understood her reasoning. In the desert, an unmarried woman never meets a man without a chaperone. In the eyes of Wahiib's mother, the blue-eyed girl acted like a promiscuous woman. Even my mother would never have understood the Hartwoods' daughters going on a date or the freedom American women thought was normal.

My graduation present to myself was a trip to Europe. In 1968, the only Americans who'd been to Europe besides soldiers were rich. I wanted to be one of those Americans, and

I'd saved money all year.

Pam had signed up to enter the Peace Corps in July, so I convinced Barbara, another girl in our dorm, to go. We read *Europe on Five Dollars a Day*. I brushed up on my Spanish and gave my parents a list of American Express offices where we'd pick up mail. Knowing how I panic when my kids don't at least email, it amazes me how calmly my parents let their twenty-one-year-old daughter head off to Europe with a Eurail pass and a book that told how to find rooms through the tourist desk in the railroad station.

Sayiid wrote that we should meet at his brother's in Homburg. I couldn't even pretend to think he wasn't coming back, or that he'd leave me alone when he did, so I figured if we met him at his brother's, it'd be easier on me in the fall. And, I was curious to meet someone else in his family.

In Europe, I was free. I didn't know anyone, and no one knew anything about me. Our first big city was Salzburg. Rooms were tight because of a music festival, but we found a room in a private home. Our host suggested we take a tour of the salt mine that gave the city its name.

We were the last people on the tour, so we had to crowd between other tourists on the little train cars. I almost literally sat in the lap of the guy behind me, but he didn't take advantage of the situation. After the tour, I found out that Will, the guy, was from Missouri, too. He'd just graduated from a Baptist college on the other side of Kansas City from Penn. He was touring with the college choir and they were singing that night. "Do you want to come hear us?"

Barb was skeptical about a college choir from Kansas City, but it was fun. About150 local people showed up. Will saw us come in and looked right at me until I smiled and gave him a little wave.

It rained during the concert, so outside the pavement sparkled from the streetlights and the lights on the castle across the river. Will bought wursts from a street vendor, and he and I walked for several hours. We would both be in Bern in two weeks, so we promised to leave messages at the American Express office when we knew where we were staying.

Barb and I took the train to Venice and Rome. An American couple in Rome advised us not to spend the night in Naples, so we got up early and took a day trip to see Pompeii. Our guide got a little creepy when he showed us some sexy mosaics, but it was fascinating to get a feel for Roman life.

I forgot Sayiid had been in Bern until I saw a brass plaque by a door that read, "English American School, Founded 1927." I cringed. I'd been sending cards to Sayiid so he'd have less to get angry about, and it was possible he'd eventually see whatever I wrote in my travel diary, so I'd put in lots of references to missing him to cover that base.

The next morning there was a note from Will that he'd meet me under the clock tower at noon. We explored the old part of town and took the cable car that went up to a park that overlooked the city. At the top, we followed the Wander Path until we left the families and older folks behind. Will spread his coat on the ground, and we sat and ate in the sun. For years, I had a snapshot I took that afternoon. The sky was very clear, and some kind of grain was yellow for harvest. I knew this was what I'd remember of Europe.

Will's choir left for Madrid. They were going home from there. We met two girls from California, and the four of us went to Costa Brava, near Barcelona. We watched the performers at a flamenco club and danced a little. Afterwards Barbara walked on the beach with one of the dancers, but I went back to our room. I had enough to think about. I felt less excited about the rest of our trip, and I began to wonder what it'd be like if I didn't visit Sayiid.

In Barcelona, we left our stuff in a little hotel just off Las Ramblas and took off to see the Sagrada Familia cathedral. There was no roof, and it was like seeing them build a cathedral in the Middle Ages. I got in line for the gallery and found myself in a group of Americans with one of Will's friends. "What are you doing here?" I asked.

"Our travel agent screwed up the flights. We spend a night here and then fly to London tomorrow night. Will's shopping. He'll be glad to see you," the friend said. "Hey, why don't you join us for lunch? We're all supposed to meet up in about an hour."

Will's choir gave an impromptu concert in a park that night. The next morning, Barb went to the Picasso House Museum, "I figured you'd have other plans," she said in a good-natured way as she left. She was right of course. Will was coming by at 1:00.

I sent a postcard to Sayiid at his brother's address that my flight got changed and I couldn't meet him. But I didn't sign it "Love."

Then I ran back to our room, took a bath, and put on the fresh skirt and blouse I'd saved to wear in Homburg.

Will knocked as I was dressing. I let him in, and we kissed as we sat on my bed and kept kissing as we lay down and kissed side by side. He hugged me. Finally, he lay back, looked at the ceiling, and said, "Wow."

I was nervous, but I felt close enough to make love. "I wish I had something to drink," I said.

"Why?"

"To relax. So we...we could..." but I trailed off as I realized he wasn't even understanding my hint.

"I want to see you when we get back, but I don't want

to…" He stopped and looked at me as though a light had come on and he saw I was telling him I wanted to sleep with him. He tried to hide the change in his expression, but his face filled in all the details. The midwestern boy knew the good girls at his Baptist college didn't have sex at least until they were nearly engaged. And we weren't—so I wasn't.

I couldn't stand the silence, so I jumped up and hopped on one foot and then the other to get my shoes on. "Let's get something to eat. There's a great place down the block." Will didn't move. The room had drapes thick enough to make it dark at midday. I sat down in the one bright spot where light came in between the curtains.

Finally he stood behind me with his hands on my shoulders. "I want to see you when we get back home."

He was trying to be nice, but I knew I'd never be okay with a guy who had to think that long to decide what to say. Also, Sayiid was coming back, and any guy I knew would eventually meet Sayiid. I was still as corralled as when he honked his car horn.

I knew I was somehow tied to Sayiid. Like Karl, Will had been a bad idea.

My sister-in-law, Elke, met me at the door when I arrived in Homburg. Jabir got home from his office soon after, and the three of us had wursts and warm beer for lunch. After lunch, Jabir wanted to show me something in his office. He closed the door behind us and handed me a pile of letters in the neat handwriting of the blue-eyed girl. Every one had been opened. "Why are my letters open?" I demanded.

He answered with his own question, "Is this your friend?"

We quickly escalated into an argument. To keep Elke from overhearing us, we argued in Arabic, which would roughly translate as:

"What the fuck are you doing?"

"I asked you. Why did you open my letters?"

"I didn't open the first ones. I just saw the postmarks from all over Europe. The postmarks and her name on the return address. It's a girl, Sayiid. Your friend is a girl."

"So, why did you open the letters?" I demanded again.

"You are such a fuck up."

"What business is it of yours?"

"When she sent the postcard, it became my business." Jabir picked up a postcard and read sarcastically,

> Dearest Sayiid,
> We are on the Costa Brava. I miss you so very much. It has been over a year since I have seen you. I hope you have not changed much. I wish you would write...

"And she signs it 'Love'..." He paused to let his words sink in. "After this came, I opened the letters to see what else she had written."

"You know what, Saad?" I always called him by his formal name when I was really angry. "It is none of your fucking business!"

"It's my business when it's my home. You are using me as a mail box for your American whore."

"What difference does it make?"

He exploded. "It's the honor of my family. It's not just yours."

"I can have a girl if I want."

"You don't get it! You met the Prince's daughter. In his mind, you might as well have had your hand in her panties. He won't take kindly to you running around with your American whore while you go home weekends to plan a wedding."

"Oh, shut up."

"She plans to be here for two days. You told her you'd see her."

"And I will."

"You idiot. Your future father-in-law's cousin lives in Homburg. It is a small city. I used to see him all the time, and he'd just walk by and pretend he didn't know who I was. Now he speaks to me because we'll be family. Don't even dream he won't tell the Prince if he sees you two snuggling somewhere."

"Who's going to stop me?"

"I will. I'll call father and tell him. If he can't talk sense into you, he will go to the prince and break the contract to save his honor."

"You wouldn't dare!"

"Try me. Father is an honorable man. He'll cut off his right hand before he gives up his honor. Are you ready to be cut off, little brother?"

Father would never mention the blue-eyed girl, but he would tell the Prince he had learned something about me that might embarrass him, and it was his duty to let the Prince know as soon as he knew. If Jabir called now, father would go to the Prince in the middle of the night.

Father would lose his job, but it would only be a loss back to neutral value for his life. If the Prince learned that I had even appeared to embarrass his daughter, he would take vengeance on my father and cast him much lower than an abruptly unemployed airline manager. My father would be lucky to find a job herding camels.

If I were out of the desert, I could escape; but I would be just another refugee with a college degree. I might find a job translating business documents, but my dreams of being a diplomat would be over forever.

"When she gets here," Jabir continued, "I'll have Elke find her a cheap hotel. I'll pay for it if I need to."

"You can't do that to her."

"Oh yes, I can. I'm not getting involved with your American whore."

"She's not a whore."

"Right..."

"You can't cut her off like that." I did not want to explain everything to Jabir, but consequences would be greater if word came back to my father through his friends the Hartwoods. At least Jabir would keep secrets to spare our parents.

Jabir realized my pause meant there was more, and he waited.

My anger was exhausted. "You can't cut her off," I said again.

"Why not?"

"Because her father is Everett Hartwood's best friend, and I've already told her they could stay here. If we back out, Father will hear about it."

Jabir's face slackened as he listened.

"Mr. Hartwood and her father have been friends since childhood. They go to the same religious thing, a *meeting* they call it. When I went to dinner at the Hartwoods', she was there with her family. Mr. Hartwood told her dad all about working with our father."

"You've met her parents? What have you done?"

Jabir knew it was an inescapable quandary. I agreed to stay in a hotel. My brother assumed I was a man of my word, but I spent the afternoon watching his home from a café down the street. I drank at least six cups of coffee, but it was not the coffee that kept me awake that night. I had seen the blue-eyed girl walk past, and I remembered the smell of her.

Sayiid's brother had a family similarity, but he was kind to his wife. They didn't know anything about me like I would if I had been the host, so gradually I understood that Barb and I, and even our visit, were a curiosity.

I was embarrassed because I'd assumed we'd automatically be their friends, but there was a more important bit of information missing in the conversation. There was no mention of Sayiid coming back to America for graduate school. And when I asked when Sayiid would arrive, Jabir said that unfortunately he wouldn't arrive until after Barb and I left.

We went to a Middle Eastern restaurant for dinner, and I watched how Jabir held the door for Elke and pulled out her chair at our table. He listened to her. When he put his hand on her leg, she playfully pushed it away as though embarrassed that he touched her in front of strangers—and he didn't get upset. She was sweet, but her face said she was hiding something she didn't dare to tell us. When I gave her a hostess gift, she acted even more guilty.

"So will you visit again?" Jabir asked.

"Maybe at Christmas. I have two weeks off from school."

"School? I thought you graduated already."

I explained starting graduate school in three weeks. Jabir couldn't understand why a woman would want more school.

Jabir came to my hotel room after the blue-eyed girl and her friend Barbara had gone to bed.

"You didn't tell me you said you'd marry her," he said.

"I didn't tell her that. She just assumed."

"God, Sayiid. She's just a kid. She's not a womanly woman."

"Yeah," I said wistfully.

"She introduced you to her parents, Sayiid."

"So what?"

"You are such a jerk," he said, as he realized I did not

care. "When is this going to end? Your wedding approaches, or have you forgotten?"

"It's over. It was just temporary."

"Oh, so you're telling me she was your wife according to prescription. How convenient! Did she know that?" Only he used the archaic Persian, *nikah-el-monkese: Arnsi-sighei,* "A wife according to prescription." This is the Muslim practice that allows a man the convenience of a temporary wife when he travels somewhere for a long time. It makes fornication acceptable.

I had vaguely made this excuse to myself so I could do what I wanted, but it did not sound as simple when he said it out loud. I became defensive. "So what?"

"We aren't in a tent anymore, little brother. These people trust, but they have rules." Then he paused. "How long do you plan to keep this up?"

"I was going back for graduate school. But I'm so busy, I may not."

"You're right you aren't. You stay out of America, and I won't tell father. You go back to continue this, I will tell father."

"I'm not going back. I'm working for the Ministry."

"Have you thought about what the daughter of Everett Hartwood's best friend will do when you abandon this marriage by prescription?" Jabir asked with a sneer.

"She will remember me fondly and never tell anyone. She will do what American women do—find some fool to believe she lost her cherry on a bicycle seat. The idiot will be happy to get laid and never ask questions."

I couldn't find my travel diary as I was packing.

"Perhaps you dropped it in the restaurant last night," Jabir suggested.

"No. I wrote in it before I went to bed."

We took my room apart but couldn't still find my diary. Jabir insisted that we go back and check the restaurant even though it couldn't be there.

We missed the express train to Frankfurt, so Jabir drove us.

"If I find your diary, I will send it," he promised.

I still couldn't understand where I'd lost it.

We checked in for our flight and went to the departure lounge. In the duty free shop I saw a watch like the one Sayiid had brought me as a gift. It was marked "Special Watch/Many Faces/$2.00."

I moved down to Columbia a week after I got back. Will tried to call like he promised. He talked to my mom once when I wasn't at home. Mom took his phone number, but I didn't call back. He also wrote a couple of letters that Mom forwarded after school started.

He hadn't judged me as much as I'd judged myself, but it was too late to go back. I didn't have the haziest idea how to restart a conversation without being overwhelmed trying to guess if he thought I was a bad person because of what I'd done with Sayiid. And Will couldn't help me if Sayiid came back. He was nice, but not that kind of guy.

Sayiid wrote me, but I was happy not to see him. My life was a whole lot calmer without him. Not seeing him in Europe had been a relief.

I didn't have anywhere else to live so I stayed in the dormitory my first semester. The other girls on my floor were freshmen. They talked about guys and making out. If they came in drunk at times, I became the older sister who cleaned them up and put them to bed.

As girls returned from sorority rush parties, I heard the screams of those who were happy beyond belief to pledge Beta, or "DG," or some other girls' club. And I wiped the tears of those who came to my room after all the other girls were quiet and who cried because they'd been left out. As best I could, I tried to reassure them that they'd be happy again.

My scholarship wasn't enough to cover my car, so I took a job waitressing at the Heidelberg. Not a great restaurant, just the nicest one in Columbia. It had reopened after a fire the year before, and it was hard work.

A week or so after I started, I came back dead tired and went right to bed, but just as I started to go to sleep, one of the freshman girls knocked on my door. "Telephone call for you."

"Oh, god," I thought, "that could only be my mom. I wonder what's wrong."

As I pulled on my robe and walked down the hall, several girls watched me. They acted casual, but even they'd noticed I never got calls except from my mom on Sunday nights. "It's from a guy," one of them said.

"Who's this?" I asked.

"Hal."

"Hal?" I was puzzled.

"Hal. Harry. Harry Wilson. I go by Hal now."

"Oh, my gosh, how did you get my number?"

"My mom called your mother. Hey, you coming to see me Saturday?"

"What's Saturday?"

"Nebraska against Missouri in football. Should be good."

"What'll you be doing?"

"I'm playing?"

"I thought you'd graduated by now."

"No. I got redshirted for a year."

At the University of Nebraska, Harry had become Hal Wilson. I didn't know what redshirted meant. He explained a guy could only play four years of college football. *Redshirted* meant he didn't play freshman year so he could take five years to finish college and still play when they called him a senior. The athletic department squared it with his draft board. He started at offensive back.

I told Harry—Hal—I'd be honored to watch. He left me a ticket at the box office, and the usher seated me in the middle fifteen rows up. Harry was number 24. Several times he ran around the side of the field near where I sat. At least once, he looked straight at me after the referee blew his whistle.

The Heidelberg was swamped, but the manager liked me and let me off at 8:00. I ran back to my room, changed and ran back to the Heidelberg to meet Harry for dinner. It was really the only choice in Columbia.

We were joined by Larry, another guy from Valentine, and his friend Brad. Larry was only a junior because he'd spent two years in the army before starting school. Brad was in the last year of a five-year journalism program that had taken him six years. There were some jokes about that. Brad's fiancée Francine, a graduate of Stephens College, worked in St. Louis, and she'd come down for the weekend. After a few drinks, Hal teased us because Nebraska had won handily. We promised we'd protect him from angry Mizzou Fans. Over dessert, conversation came around to me.

"I'm getting a master's in sociology."

"Have you been at Mizzou all along?" asked Francine.

"No. I got my bachelors at Penn. It's a small school up by Kansas City. Have you heard of it?"

"Oh, shit!" Brad blurted out, spitting beer back into his mug as he did. He looked at Francine. "Pardon me. Oh, damn..."

"That Penn?" she asked.

"What?" I was puzzled.

"That Penn," Brad answered.

"Sorry," he explained. "It's a long story. There was this piece-of-shit camel jockey named Sayiid Algedda I met in Switzerland. Almost cost me the love of my life." He put his hand on Francine's shoulder. "He went to Penn. He visited one time, and I set him up on a date with Francine's roommate."

"He tried to rape her," cut in Francine. "Sorry, but there's no other word for it. Did you know him?"

"I knew who he was," I answered.

Harry walked me back after dinner. "Are you all right?" he asked.

"Yes. Why do you ask?"

"I feel like something upset you. You were having fun, and then you weren't."

"Oh, just girl stuff. Time of the month, I guess," I said, and then couldn't believe I'd said something so intimate.

After Hal left, I sat at my desk and knew Sayiid would be back and that I couldn't hide from him. 'Better if he's not pissed off,' I told myself as I started to write him a letter.

I continued to live in my father's house, and he was in the hall when I returned from one of my diplomatic trips. "Sayiid, could you come in for a minute please?" he asked as he opened the door of his study.

When he closed the door behind us, I had the premonition that I knew what he was going to say. He opened his desk and took out a pink envelope that had been opened. I saw the blue ink and felt cold. My father, too?

"What are you going to do about this?" he asked.

I put on my most puzzled expression. "I don't know what you..."

He cut me off. "Don't pretend with me! Jabir told me you promised to stop this." He held the letter in my face. "But this letter talks about your letter two weeks ago. You did not stop. You are still doing this."

"But..." I tried to interject.

"No! You are still doing this."

"What did Jabir tell you?" I asked.

"What he said is none of your business." He shook the envelope at me. "This is my business. Your brother cares about our honor. I could have arranged for him to marry the Prince's daughter, but he married that German girl. I should never have allowed it."

I saw determination I had not known my father had.

"This girl's father is a friend of my friend. I work with these people. I need them to remain my friends. I can't have my son dishonor their friend's daughter. What have you been doing?"

"It's not what you think," I protested. "We just spent time together."

"Do you think I'm stupid?" He went to his desk, pulled out a small notebook, and read from it, tearing pages as he turned them.

"Rome. 'I miss him so much. I do love him.' "

A page almost tore out of the diary as he turned to the next passage.

"Paris. 'He doesn't answer my letters. I do hope he hasn't gotten married.'"

Another page nearly ripped out.

"London. 'Still no reply to my letters. Suppose he's hurt or something. I can't be angry at him.'

"Copenhagen. 'Two more days and I'll see him in Homburg.' That is not a friend!"

I was unprepared for how much he understood.

"Everett told me that you had spent time with the daughter of his friend. Is this the same girl?"

I nodded.

"I hope you have been a good representative of our family, but I doubt that." He wasn't going to let me get a word in. "The Prophet, peace and blessings be upon him, says a man can have four wives, but the Prince thinks his daughter is equal to four wives. He will be displeased, and he will respond! I make you the promise that I will do exactly what Jabir warned you of. You will end this now, or I will go the Prince and end your engagement. Do you understand?"

I nodded.

"I expect you to keep your word," he said, and he left the room.

I looked at the last letter from the blue-eyed girl. She had quickly lapsed into calling the college Mizzou. She described a football game that she'd enjoyed, and I longed to be around her optimistic way of looking at the world.

She included a picture taken with Jabir and Elke. In it, she sits leaning toward Jabir in that way people crowd together for a snapshot. Jabir's arm is draped around Elke's shoulder. I remembered watching the blue-eyed girl from across the road as she arrived.

Jabir had given father her diary to refute every excuse I could make. I understood the Prince's anger if he found out. But I wanted the blue-eyed girl to want me so I could cut her off, not just fade away because my father told me to drop her.

I read every entry from the time she got on the plane in Kansas City. Her excitement was palpable in her writing, and I visualized her writing just before she turned out her light. The diary gave as clear a view into her mind as the pink paper that fell from her book in my apartment. It was the last entry that I read and reread...

> Wonderful day in Homburg. Jabir took us shopping. I bought a Hummel for Mom. It is so good

> to watch Jabir and Elke together. He is so considerate of her. It reminds me of my parents. We are going to dinner tonight at an Arabic restaurant. We have talked of coming back for Christmas. That sounds so exciting, but I know I will stay home.

I wished I could do as I pleased, but in the end, my father had the power. At this one moment in my life, my ambition had more influence than my desire to control another person. I could not control the Prince, and it was too risky to take chances.

I wrote a letter that talked in a vague, general way about the pressures on me from my family and closed the letter,

> I agree with your thoughts that things were less binding and thereby possibly more enjoyable a few months ago. I treasure as I always will the memories of our always-good times together, with the hope that somehow we will remain lovers even if we are to be limited by our social obligations.

A letter arrived from Sayiid just before I went home for Christmas vacation. I remembered Mr. Hartwood saying Sayiid's parents were arranging a marriage, and I wondered if he'd met the girl beforehand.

I felt like when I swam across the lake, when I left him in the hospital, and when he flew away after he graduated. Those were times he'd set me free, even the swim across the lake although he'd said I'd have to get back across on my own. I could never have done anything myself that would have made me feel as free.

An Arab has to feel in control. God help her if a woman tries to escape. I'd only be safe if Sayiid truly believed everything I did was with his permission.

I read once about an Arab man in Buffalo who beheaded his wife when she threatened to get a divorce. This was thirty years later, and that man didn't have diplomatic immunity. I'd gotten myself into the quagmire of a culture with a man who thought he could behave in America just like he could in his own desert.

My mistake when I got his letter was to think I'd never hear from him again.

# V. Years

There was blood on my nuptial sheets, duly observed and reported to my parents by the old woman who had been my nurse. They were pleased. I was disappointed. The Princess never ventured the slightest complaint—so unlike the blue-eyed girl who tried to escape every way she could imagine. To control a person who is resisting is exciting. Driving with the blue-eyed girl, sex with her, anything with her was exciting. The Princess was boring.

The buzz was that Harry was good enough to go pro, but late in the season a bad hit tore up his shoulder. After that, scouts stopped looking. The only consolation was that he became 4-F, and fortunately, the Nebraska coach offered him a job as a recruiter. That fit. Harry had a knack for recognizing talent. He also recruited for basketball, and in January, he came to Mizzou for a high school tournament and asked me out to dinner.

"I was kind of a jerk," he said, "that time I told everyone

we went all the way."

"That's true. You embarrassed me so much I had to leave town," I joked.

"I owe you an apology. You're not that kind of a girl."

I patted his hand. "That was a long time ago, Harry."

I lived off campus second semester, and I let him come in when he walked me back to my room. We had a glass of wine, we kissed, and this time I let him touch my breast through my blouse. I felt safe he'd stop when I asked him to.

"Do you want to make love?" he asked.

My impulse was to laugh and say, "Harry we're friends. I've forgiven you, but that's what we are—friends." But I looked before I spoke. The football player who'd face a 220-pound defensive back was hanging on what I'd say. And, if I'm honest, I was making a devil's bargain with myself. I wanted to know what it felt like to say *yes* when there was no threat if I said *no*.

"Yes," was all I said as I gulped the rest of my wine and led him to my room.

Psychologists say if you force yourself to smile you'll feel happier. But having the choice to say no didn't make me feel any better about saying yes. For Harry, it was different. He assumed we'd reached an understanding, and when he was home, he told his mom we were dating. In a small town that means all that's left to do is set the date.

When I married the Princess, I did not anticipate being stuck in the desert all the time. To father an heir, however, being home was essential. I also think the Prince sensed that my attentions might wander, so I worked full time at the Ministry of Foreign Affairs.

The Princess did not become pregnant, she wanted to be

close to her mother, and I stayed in the desert. Jabir sent letters and small packages from Germany, but I could not tell if these were sent in kindness or to remind me that his words had prevailed.

This was before home video, but the Prince had a movie projector. In addition to *Mary Poppins* for the Princess, he had a pirated copy of *The Prize* with Paul Newman and Elke Sommers. The plot quickly lost its freshness, but the Princess was always embarrassed when Paul Newman lay on Elke Sommers as they hide in the back of a car, and she asks, "Do you know what you're doing to me?' And he replies, "I guess we'll have to get married." Embarrassment made her more interesting. It was the closest she ever came to resisting me.

As graduation approached, I saw on the job bulletin boards that Planned Parenthood in St. Louis was hiring a social worker. They wanted an MSW, not a sociology degree, but I applied and gave OB as a reference.

He wrote a two-line letter of recommendation:

> This is the girl you want.
> This is why.
> Orville Baker
> William Penn College

...and sent it special delivery with a copy of my thesis.

They assumed I'd be a great counselor and offered me the job without even interviewing me. And I am a great counselor. I can always see the solution to everyone else's problems.

That summer, NASA put a man on the moon, and I got an apartment in a neighborhood called DeMunn near Forest Park. The brick buildings were already old, but the area was popular with students.

My second day at Planned Parenthood, I met with a nurse in clinical services to update me on pregnancy rates with different contraceptives. She compared everything to eighty percent pregnancy after one year of unprotected sex. It wasn't lost on me that after a year and a half with Sayiid, only luck had made me different from Christie. My eyes must have looked like I was miles away, but I think she was just making conversation when she asked, "What kind of birth control do you use?"

All I could think of was "Rubbers," which would have been okay except that I forced a smile, and it came out like a child trying to guess the right answer. "Rubbers?"

My question hung in the air. "You're not a virgin are you?" she asked.

"No," I answered. "I'm not."

"Oh, my god," she backtracked. "Please forget I asked you that. It's none of my business."

"That's okay," I answered.

She went on talking about fifteen percent pregnancy with condoms, five percent with the pill, and I was certain she assumed the circumstances were always, "independent young woman making her own choices." But I'd only known force, fear, and mostly pain.

She was the kind of woman who would've found a way to help me if I could've started the conversation. But at the time I thought I was the only girl who'd ever been so stupid, and I let the moment pass. I split myself into two people, a young woman trying to do the right thing by helping others, and a scared girl living in terror of anything that might expose her horrible secrets. I wanted to put Sayiid behind me and forget him, but of course, the more I tried to sweep him under the carpet, the more he became a lump I tripped over.

Harry and I stayed in touch after I started work. Occasionally we'd have a few drinks and he'd sleep over. He wanted to go back to his father's ranch, but I had no desire to be a rancher's wife. I didn't meet anyone else. I sort of drifted.

At Planned Parenthood, I heard lots of stories. Guys were wonderful, but they left for Vietnam. Guys were wonderful, but they were still in school. Guys were wonderful, and she knew he loved her. Guys were wonderful, but they were married. Occasionally, some guy was wonderful with no "but's."

But the story that changed my life, I heard at my apartment, three months after I started work.

A couple moved in downstairs with their two-year old child, Louise. I met the girl, Cindy, in the laundry room. She was eighteen, and her husband Charles was nineteen. He went to Washington University on a scholarship.

Cindy was lonely, and she pretty much told me her life story right away, as though it would affect what I thought of her. "I got pregnant with Louise. Charles said it was because I wasn't careful, and it wasn't his baby anyway. My dad didn't let him get away with that, but what happened after we got married was I moved away and lived with my grandmother until it was my time. Charles carried on like everything was normal. He even had a date to the prom."

I could sympathize, but had no idea what to say, so I asked, "Do you want to come up to my apartment for a change of scenery?"

Louise took to me, and pretty soon she was playing with my pans on the floor. Cindy saw where I'd been trying to sew a jacket. "You sew? I love to sew. I learned from my grandmother," she said.

"I like to sew," I answered, "but sewing doesn't always like me." I pointed to the pattern and added, "I can't figure out what they mean by 'ease in the sleeves.' It's like it's a secret code word."

Cindy picked up the jacket. "The problem is the words don't tell you what they mean." She held the sleeve next to the shoulder hole. "It's not a straight line or a thing you sew. You just start at the bottom and make it fit. The funny thing is it doesn't make any difference how you do it. Whatever you end up with, you adjust the cuff, and you're done."

She made it sound simple, and once I saw how it worked, it was.

Charles was always in the library. Jogging was coming into vogue, and sometimes I watched Louise while Cindy went for a run. Despite that, I watched Cindy gain weight over the first couple of months.

One evening I came home and there were police cars and a fire truck. One of the neighbors said Louise drank something, "The mom freaked and called the police. The kid looked fine, but they went to Children's Hospital."

I visited that evening. Charles had only stayed a few minutes, and Cindy was by herself. I sat beside her and watched the crib.

"He..." Cindy stifled a sob. I knew she was talking about Charles, "He said our apartment was a mess. So I got some furniture polish to clean it up." She looked at Louise and sobbed out, "She drank it while I had the cap off."

Louise was asleep after the ordeal of coming to the hospital. Cindy reached into the crib and stroked her hair. "She looks so rested."

"I'm sure she'll be fine," I tried to reassure her, but the nurse on the other side of the crib gave me a look that told me to shut up. I leaned over the crib to pat Louise's back before I left. She breathed out lemon smell even after they'd washed off the furniture polish and changed her clothes.

I worked late the next night, but the following evening I found Cindy in the waiting room. "Where's Louise?" I asked.

"They put her on a machine. They stick needles in her, but she doesn't cry any more."

"What's going on?"

"I don't know. I asked to talk to a doctor, but they're all busy."

I didn't know any clever words to say. In a while, a young man in a white coat walked in and spoke to me, "Mrs. Marshall?"

"I'm Mrs. Marshall," Cindy told him.

He introduced himself as the intern. I started to leave, but Cindy asked me to stay.

"Mrs. Marshall," he began, "we're not making much progress. We see this with kids who drink furniture polish. They look good for a couple of days, and then it gets bad."

"She'll get better, won't she?"

"We're trying real hard, Mrs. Marshall." He changed the subject. "Is there anyone I should call? Mr. Marshall?"

"He's in the library."

I took the day off to go to the service for Louise. Besides Charles and Cindy, there were four other adults that I assumed were the grandparents. There was a lot of mutual reassurance that Louise was with God now, and somehow that was good.

Cindy's mom kept her off to the side and stood between her and everyone else, but Cindy saw me and made a little wave. I think it helped that someone cared enough about Louise to come to her funeral.

I heard a lot of shouting from their apartment for the next few weeks, then it ended abruptly, and I saw a middle age woman moving in. Cindy's mother let slip to the landlord that Charles went off with another girl, and Cindy went back to live with her grandmother.

Except for an occasional visit by Harry, I had no social life, so after Louise died, I started to volunteer answering calls at Poison Control. It was there I learned about Olde English Furniture Polish. Adults love the smell, but they don't drink it. Kids love the smell, and they drink it. The chemicals take about three days to destroy the lungs from the inside out. It's that simple.

Most calls to the Poison Control hot line were shared between St. Louis Children's Hospital and Cardinal Glennon, but the schedule had gaps. Volunteers answered calls at those times. After the first few months, they asked me to teach new volunteers how to calm parents over the phone and get the information you need before you can help.

In November, the Princess and I were temporarily posted to Madrid. To my relief, my chauffeur understood the needs of a bored husband and introduced me to a woman friend who satisfied those needs discretely. The chauffeur's friend spoke only a few words of Arabic, and no English, so this created an opportunity to call the United States in private.

The blue-eyed girl's mother answered the telephone. "Mr. Algedda, how are you?"

"I want to wish you a Happy Thanksgiving. It's that time, isn't it?"

"Yes, it is. How kind of you to remember."

"And will they turn on the lights on the Plaza?" I remembered the lights on every building and loved the knowledge that America's thirst for power fueled their need for our oil. They had a slogan, "Light a light, stop a crime." As long as they were afraid of each other, electric companies would sell electricity, and we would sell oil to feed the generators. Light more lights, America. We love the business.

The blue-eyed girl had moved to St. Louis, but she would

be home for the holiday. "Why is she living in St. Louis?" I asked.

Her mother lowered her voice to a conspiratorial tone. "She took a job with Planned Parenthood."

"What's Planned Parenthood?" I asked.

"It's a…I feel funny saying this. It's a birth control organization," she burst out. "They give out birth control pills. There's even a rumor they do abortions. Goodness, I wish she wasn't involved with those people."

"How did she get into this?"

"Something about feeling sorry for girls who…well…got themselves pregnant."

As the call ended, she said she would tell Mrs. Hartwood I had called, but I said I was going to call her myself. I had not planned to call the Hartwoods, but I made the call to head off the gossip that would be generated if the blue-eyed girl's mother called first. I spent twenty minutes telling Mrs. Hartwood about my wife and my career.

I was so frustrated after the call that I threw the chauffeur's friend across the bed and ripped her clothes off to satisfy myself. Then I paid her several times the cost of the call. If she said anything, the chauffeur would demand most of the money, so I knew she would not say anything. The chauffeur waited knowingly at the car. He would forget as he was paid to do.

One of the Poison Control administrators who was going to a conference in Los Angeles had a family emergency. Her ticket was nonrefundable, so she asked if I wanted to go. Poison Control would cover my room, and there wouldn't be cab fare because the meeting was at the airport Hilton.

The first day of the conference, a man hurried in at the last minute, sat in the empty seat beside me, and began taking pages of notes on yellow pads.

At the break, I excused myself and stepped past him. I had a vague sense that he looked at my legs, even though my butt was closer to his papers.

A few minutes later, he stepped up to get a cup of coffee as I was stirring in sugar. "You writing a book, or something?" I asked.

"That?" he said. "My boss wants lots of notes."

"What for?"

But the bell rang to start the next session before he could answer.

I saw him at the late afternoon reception and introduced myself.

"I'm David," he replied. "David Miller."

"Pleased to meet you, Mr. Miller." I shook his hand.

He took a big breath, "I know it's kind of forward, but do you want to get dinner when this is over?"

"There isn't anyplace to eat around here. I checked last night. I figured I'd eat some extra snacks here," I said.

"I was thinking of going up to Santa Monica. I have a car."

"A car from LAX to the Hilton! What do you do?"

He told me he was an attorney from St. Louis. He'd been in LA for a few days before the conference and used the car to visit clients.

I accepted his invitation. Later as we waited for a table at the restaurant I said, "Funny. I've never seen you at Poison Control meetings."

"I don't work for Poison Control."

"Then why are you here?"

"I represent Johnson & Johnson. They make Olde English Furniture Polish."

"Oh my god." I told him about Cindy and Louise.

"My boss is working on that case." As though it made it okay, he added, "They're coming out with a new bottle. Hard plastic with a special top. A child can't get the cap off, and the liquid comes out so slowly you can't take a big gulp. It should be on the shelves in two years, three at the most."

"Three years! How many kids will get hurt in the meantime?"

"These things take time...use up old stock..." and his voice trailed off.

We drove back on the Pacific Coast Highway, through Venice and down to the airport. The next morning, David showed up without a tie and searched around to find me.

We went to dinner that night in Beverly Hills. When he brought me back to my room, he kissed me at the door—behind my ear—and I giggled. He didn't try anything funny, and I smiled as he walked away from my door.

The conference ended the next day, and we drove up to Hollywood to a restaurant his boss recommended. Over dinner, David told me he realized he was representing the wrong people. I asked if that meant he'd quit, but he said he had to finish some things first. "I need to get them to change the bottles right away. They won't respond to a bunch of—pardon me—do-gooders, but maybe I can persuade them it will save money on legal defense to do it quicker."

I wanted to be with David for no other reason than to be with him, and I was certain he felt the same about me. We kissed in his car. Again he didn't try anything, but I'd have let him. I wanted him to touch me like he'd already touched my heart. But he was shy, and I guessed he'd spent a lot more time with books than with women. When he walked with me to my door, I spoke first. "Want to come in for a minute?"

"I need to work on my report."

I wanted to see him in St. Louis, but we'd only just met, and if he knew about Sayiid, he'd probably break it off. Better to leave this all in California. I took a big breath and blurted out, "I've had sex before."

He looked at me like he didn't know what he was supposed to say.

"It wasn't my fault," I added nervously.

There. I'd told him. In the 60s some guys still cared about virginity. He might be like that, midwestern and all, and if it were up to me, he'd find out pretty soon. I didn't want either of us to be embarrassed, but his response was, "So...?"

We stood there for the longest minute of my life. I had no idea what to say next, and I didn't know how to even begin to hint how dirty I felt after Sayiid. He broke the silence, "What time's your flight tomorrow?"

"I'm on the red-eye to Kansas City. To stop by and see my folks."

"Have you been to Disneyland?"

"No. I've wanted to go since fourth grade."

"Good. Pick you up in the morning at 8:00? I'm on the red-eye, too. We must be on the same flight. I go through Kansas City."

I was relieved, but never tell a lawyer half a story.

It rained at Disneyland, but that made the lines shorter. There was a new ride called "Pirates of the Caribbean," and by the time we rode it the third time, David was singing, "Yo, ho, ho, ho, a pirate's life for me..."

David almost missed his connection in Kansas City. After his gate closed, I ran outside where Mom was picking me up. She'd barely started to fish out change for the Broadway Bridge when I announced, "I've met the man I'm going to marry."

Her first thought was, "What about Harry?"

"I like Harry, but this is different."

I could never imagine Harry singing, "Yo, ho, ho, ho, a pirate's life for me," and when I pretended to stop David's singing by putting my hand over his mouth, he gently gnawed my fingers before he kissed them.

"I know why you live up here," David said as we reached the door of my apartment back in St. Louis. "After three flights, no guy could give you trouble."

"Works, doesn't it?" I smiled. He pretended to glare at me as he caught his breath. "Sounds like you need a rest," I added.

We kissed on my couch, and he pulled the collar of my blouse to one side to kiss my neck. I bent my head the other way to make it easier. Gradually he undid buttons and pulled my blouse away to kiss my whole shoulder. Then he put his hand in the small of my back and hugged me to him. He didn't ask if it was okay, but he didn't assume either. He went slowly and paused long enough for me to accept his actions, or to say that was enough.

I wondered if he was thinking it wasn't a big deal because I'd done this before. Then I shocked myself. "Do you want to lie on my bed? It'll be more comfortable."

He didn't say a word, but he stood up.

"Let me get a drink," I said, needing to relax myself.

"What?"

"I said a drink to relax, but..." I thought about how comfortable I felt with him, "I don't need that."

We just kissed that night, but we made love several days later. I worried how that would develop, but he pulled a condom out of his pocket and asked "Are we ready for this?"

"Is that to protect you from me?" I asked. I was joking,

but also doing what David would say was forever putting myself down, like I was a source of contamination.

"No," he replied, "It's so we won't get any surprises from me."

David said we were a perfect couple and asked me to marry him. I called Mom. "Are you sure?" she asked. "You've only known him a couple of weeks."

I wanted to tell Harry myself, but I couldn't figure out what to say over the phone, and I couldn't get to Omaha for a while. As it was, my mother told a friend from Valentine, and the friend told Harry's mother. He sent me a postcard two weeks later. There was one word on it. "Congratulations."

When I think about those weeks, the word that comes to mind is *joyful*. David and I've had problems, but I've never felt as happy any other time in my life, and the joy carries me through. I wouldn't confuse this with the passion people feel when they say they're in love. It was simply happiness, and it's more addicting than any drug.

Two weeks later, I got a horrible bladder infection. The doctor at Planned Parenthood wrote me a prescription for the same two pills, the antibiotic and the pill that made my pee orange. I felt better in a couple of days, but it brought back memories of running to the bathroom as I tried to take finals my sophomore year.

"Girls change their mind and then they lie about it."

"Come on, George. What do you mean?"

"It's very simple. A girl goes to a party, has some drinks, goes home with a guy and has sex. Then she sobers up and says, 'Shit, what've I done?' So she cries 'Rape.'" George was an attorney friend of David's boss. We were at a cocktail party given by his firm in the suburb of Town and Country. This was my first time to meet anyone from David's office, and I needed to make a good impression. He'd introduced me to our host, a senior partner in the firm, "This is my fiancée."

From how the partner glanced at my neckline, I had his attention even if that wasn't what I'd intended. "When do you plan to get married?" he asked.

"Before the end of the year," David replied.

"What do you do?" The partner looked me in the eye this time.

"I'm a counselor at Planned Parenthood, and I volunteer answering phones at Poison Control."

"Very commendable," he said, but I doubted he was sincere.

George continued telling his story in a voice so loud that I couldn't ignore him. One of the men asked, "So, George, what do you do with these cases?"

"I start by asking her to repeat her story. That makes her feel she's on safe ground because it's what she's already claimed. Then I whittle away."

George enjoyed having an audience, like we were a jury. "I start with the little things. 'Where had you been that night?' 'Did you know him before?' It lulls her into thinking my questions won't be too hard. After she's let down her guard, I get more direct. 'Did he force you to come to his apartment?' The answer to that is always 'No.' I build from that to turn her thoughts back on her and make her doubt the logic of her own story.

"One of the odd things is that the more I can get her to say about herself, the more the jury is likely to acquit my client. Doesn't matter what she talks about, school, her job, she likes basket weaving, whatever. The jury seems to get tired of her voice and then everything she says loses its force."

He was into it now. "I know how to get stories out of

people. I was a psychiatrist before law school. A good psychiatrist can actually control how the patient remembers the story. Did you know that?"

"No," another man said, "but it sounds time-consuming."

"It takes preparation to figure out how to approach each girl—like choosing what kind of candy to tempt a child with. I have a whole team. I have an investigator who interviews other guys she's dated and a psychologist who did his PhD studying rape."

"That's a lot of resources."

"I do charge, you know? And it beats the $50.00 an hour I'd make listening to the same girl talk about her guilt." George had become the center of attention, and as he rattled on, I got anxious.

"I've saved quite a few young men from prison. Their families pay quite happily." While everyone paused to take in what he'd just said, George added, "I'd never thought about it, but all the boys come from families with a lot of money. Funny, huh?"

"I'm sorry that came up," David said after he'd tipped the valet and closed the car door. "He sounded like a creep. Using psychiatry like that."

"That's all right. It didn't bother me. Really it didn't." I changed the subject. "Do you think I made a good impression on your boss?"

"I know you did. I knew you would."

"I hope so."

"Well, he's a man." David squeezed my leg in a teasing way.

I glanced down at the neckline of my dress and wondered if that's how David's boss saw me. Then I wondered if that was what David saw, too. I'd wanted so much for this intelligent man—who paid attention to what I said—to be different. Maybe I'd imagined that. "It wasn't only my dress, was it?"

I said. "You saw how he looked at my front."

"No," David said. "He's that way with every woman."

We talked about other things. But in my mind I heard George over and over again, and I wasn't surprised. The moment I ran out of Sayiid's apartment I knew everything would be just like George said if I'd ever tried to get anyone to listen to me. Sayiid had money and a whole government behind him. Nothing would've happened to him. Only to me.

A month later, I got another bladder infection. David said something must be wrong and got me the name of a urologist.

After he took my history, Dr. Manley explained, "Sometimes the symptoms go away but not the infection. We say it's 'subclinical.' I'd like a sterile specimen to see if it's cleared up with the antibiotics. Then the next step is to look and see if there's a physical problem. We can do that today."

I found myself in an exam room with my pants off and my legs apart while a nurse wiped me down with disinfectant and put a tube in my bladder. I was cold, and I was embarrassed. Then she put me in stirrups with my legs up and wide apart and left me with just a white towel between my legs.

She came back with Dr. Manley who used a numbing cream and looked in my bladder with a metal tube. "Everything looks fine," he pronounced. "Why don't you come into my office when you're dressed?"

I felt safer with my clothes back on.

"I don't see anything wrong. The culture will be back in two days. Miss Waters will call you if there's any infection. If there isn't, let's have you come back in a week or so to talk about what to do next."

"Okay."

He added, "Do you think you could come up with a list of when you've had infections in the past?"

I still had notes on my study planners and calendars.

"I think so."

There were no bacteria in my culture.

At my next appointment, Dr. Manley studied my list of infections spread out over four years. "I need to ask a personal question."

"Okay."

"How old were you when you first had intercourse?"

I gulped. Why'd he asked that? But you didn't lie to your doctor. "Nineteen years old," I said.

He didn't raise his head, but he looked up over his glasses. "Was this something that went on for a while?"

I was squirming, but I answered, "About a year and a half."

"Have you been having sex with your fiancé?"

"Yes."

"And when did that start?"

I told him about three months ago.

"Were you having sex with anyone else before you met your fiancé."

I was mortified that he was reading my life history from a list of dates.

"Yes," I said, barely audibly.

"I see."

He had a waiting room full of patients after me, and it wasn't more than a minute, but it seemed an eternity before he spoke. "A history, the story, often gives us better information than another test." He was trying to be kind. "You get bladder infections when you have sexual intercourse, when you make love. The year you weren't sexually active, you didn't get cystitis."

I would've slid out under the door if I could.

"Some women get bladder infections when they have intercourse. Fortunately, the way to treat this is fairly simple."

"He said I should pee after we make love," I told David that night.

"That's it?" David asked.

"He said there isn't anything else to do. I'm normal as far as he can see, but this happens some times. Some doctors call it 'honeymoon cystitis' because girls get it on their honeymoon."

"How'd he figure that out?"

"He had me make a list of every bladder infection I ever had. Then he asked me how old I was when I started having sex."

"And you told him…?" David didn't like that I'd told Dr. Manley anything about other sexual relationships.

"I couldn't lie, could I?"

David looked up at me exactly like Dr. Manley had. I would've died if that could've made him feel better. This was the Midwest, and it was barely the 70s. David knew what Dr. Manley thought about me, and thus what Dr. Manley thought about him.

Things got awkward after that. I was embarrassed because Dr. Manley made me remember everything about Sayiid I'd never explained to David, and my reaction was to get really quiet. David didn't say anything. For all I know, he was preoccupied with a case, but I interpreted his silence to mean that somehow he knew what I couldn't say and judged me for it. I wondered for a couple of weeks if our relationship would simply fade away. Then he surprised me with a bunch of Easter eggs he'd dyed at his apartment.

"Be gentle with them," he warned me. "You can't use a whole basket of hard boiled eggs, so most of 'em are raw." After he went home, I found a stuffed bunny on my pillow with a note reading, "I'm here to keep you company when David can't."

The Princess did not become pregnant, and the Prince decided we should consult a specialist in London. We stayed at the ambassador's residence. I was going to be posted in London for a year, and ostensibly this was a trip to find an apartment. We dutifully looked at flats in Kensington and Knightsbridge. The Princess wanted to shop at Harrod's, but despite the bustle on the street, we were both thinking about why we were there.

After a late lunch, we took a cab to the clinic of a fashionable fertility specialist, Dr. Assam, on Marylebone Road. I acted as though I did not know who he was, but the Embassy staff had already been briefed concerning his practice, though not for fertility issues.

Arabs generally do not trust each other, but there are types of information, most often gossip, we do share. In this case, the Algerian Consul learned about a gynecologist who was doing hymen repairs. As more Muslim women spend time in the West, some enter into sexual relationships of their own choice. When they want to be married, the need to prove virginity for the groom's family creates a need for the appearance of virginity. And where there is a need, someone will meet that need.

Finding the practice was simple for a woman, but the combined Arab embassies needed a year to learn that these "repairs" were done by Dr. Assam in a converted flat near the Baker Street tube stop.

Dr. Assam was a small dark man who spoke with a clipped Indian accent. I suspected he was Hindi and laughed privately at the foibles of his mostly-Muslim clientele. "Mr. Algedda," he said to me, and then, turning to the Princess, "Mrs. Algedda, I'm Mr. Assam." I remembered that funny English thing where surgeons are called Mister, rather than Doctor.

He asked many questions. How long had we been trying to become pregnant? Eighteen months. Did either of us have any illness? No. Had either of us had any infections? No. Had either of us ever had any injury or trauma? I thought about the keg party at Mizzou, but answered, "No."

"Very well, the next step is to examine both of you. He indicated the nurse standing silently in the room. "Mrs. Algedda, if you will accompany Sister Claire, I will show your husband where to undress."

"We're here to check my wife," I said. "I'll wait here." I was not going to be prodded by this Hindu.

"Okay," said Mr. Assam, but like all his people, he was arrogant, and his face betrayed a hint of condescension at my refusal to be examined. My response was to wonder what it would be like to poke around different pussy every hour, all day long—and get paid very well to do it.

"Mrs. Algedda appears to be normal," Dr. Assam began after he and the Princess returned to the consultation room. "Sometimes infertility is not an insurmountable inability to bear children. It may be in the situation. Your wife's hormones must work together, like a symphony, and sometimes even a beautiful orchestra can be out of tune. In such cases, it is important for the musicians to relax and to start again from the top."

*What the fuck is he talking about?* I thought, but I kept my peace. I needed my wife to tell the Prince that I paid attention to every word.

Mr. Assam said her temperature would go up slightly on the mornings she ovulated, and her eggs would be fertile for about forty-eight hours. We should have "intercourse" twice on days her "baseline temperature" was elevated. As I paid his fee of one hundred and fifty pounds in cash, I wanted to ask the cost of repairing a cherry, but I could not do that with my wife present.

In October, we moved to London and took a fashionable flat. We had two maids, an old Arab woman who had been a servant in the Prince's family for years and a middle-aged Scottish woman. I savored the thought of the young Welch girl we interviewed but had the wisdom not to say a thing.

The staff assumed I would be an ambassador some day, but for now, I acted the charade of a junior secretary who arrived early to open the Consular desk at 8:00 a.m. When my wife got out of bed at 9:00 or so, she would take her temperature. If it was elevated, I was called home for an emergency. Our life became erratic, like the Keystone Cops in an American silent movie.

The staff eventually realized that this happened about every four weeks; but when gossip started, Wahiib, who was also posted in London, squelched it. He was a loyal friend, but the Princess did not become pregnant.

David and I got married the Saturday after Thanksgiving.

Freddy had a part time job and asked if he could take me out to dinner before the wedding. There was a new restaurant at the airport.

We sat by a window, and Freddy enjoyed talking about the times Dad had brought us here to watch planes. He'd repeated two grades in school, and was struggling to get through any class at Westport. My parents had him taking shop and art as much as they could. Eventually he got a certificate that he'd attended all his classes.

As our steaks came, he asked me, "What happened to that Sayiid guy? He came to our house. I thought you were going to marry him."

This was beyond an easy explanation. "David is so much nicer than him," I answered.

Freddy was satisfied. "That makes sense, then."

I wanted a wedding in Mom's Lutheran church. Bridesmaids, a march down the aisle, a receiving line, cake, and a party. My dream was fueled by Carol Hartwood's wedding after the end of her sophomore year in college. She dropped out of school to have her baby, but my parents said she was going back to finish. I don't know if she ever did. But she had a big church wedding even though they were Quakers.

Dad wanted a Quaker wedding. I didn't fight him on it because I'd heard the story a dozen times. He'd given in to being married in Mom's church and had always missed the tie to his community.

The difference is that the whole meeting presides over a Quaker wedding. Members of the meeting stand in a circle. Non-Quaker guests are outsiders in a way because it's the Quakers who know how it works.

The bride and groom walk into the circle from opposite sides. I got to wear a white dress, but there was no organ music and no role for bridesmaids. David and I met in the center, took hands, and talked. I said I loved him and would stay with him always. He said the same to me, but no minister pronounced us man and wife. Instead, everyone lined up and signed a large certificate that said I married David on this date. Each person both witnessed the wedding and pledged to support us as a couple. The ceremony had origins in early America where it was the community that made a marriage real.

The guest I had not expected was Sayiid's landlady. My wedding was a function of our Quaker meeting, so it was logical for her to be there. She stared at me for a long time—as though she was judging something—before she signed the certificate.

David and I went back to St. Louis after the wedding. We both had to work the month of December.

I had a driver in London, but I also enjoyed excursions on the Underground. One time, I got out at the Baker Street stop and walked past Regency Park all the way up to Swiss Cottage. It was a cold day, and I watched several young women with prams. Many were blue-eyed.

I also learned to make international telephone calls from St. Pancras train station and called the blue-eyed girl's home on Christmas Eve. Her mother answered, "Mr. Algedda, good of you to call. She isn't home yet."

"From St. Louis?" I asked.

"Yes," she said, "they're driving up today."

"Really. Why did she move?" I did not notice she had said "they."

"Let's see, she moved home three months ago. It was too complicated planning the wedding from St. Louis, and she'd already decided to leave Planned Parenthood. Something about a college student who died. Frankly, I think she took their stories too seriously."

Her babbling covered my shocked silence.

"Wedding?" I asked.

"Mr. Algedda, you sound like me. She stopped by on her way back from Los Angeles and told me she'd met the man she was going to marry. I reacted just like you. She was dating this nice man in St. Louis, and now she's talking about a man she'd known two days."

I was stumbling, but I managed to ask, "What kind of conference?"

I only caught parts of what followed as she kept talking. A neighbor's child had died. Did I have children? Wasn't it expected I'd have children right away? I was polite to camouflage that all I really wanted to ask was why the blue-eyed girl got married. Eventually I brought the conversation back to that.

"Here they were a thousand miles away from home," she said, "and just sat down next to each other and started talking and it went on from there. When he visited they were so in love." She dragged out her story. Was she happy for her daughter? Happy to be telling me the story? Or both? "He's a lawyer for a company that makes furniture polish. She bent his ear on that, but he listened. She liked that a lot—that he listened."

I stepped into the icy air on Euston Road. The last traces of Christmas were in shop windows. Most of the English were with their families. We would have dinner at 8:00, but it was just another day for us. In the desert we would have worked, but in England, we recognized the local custom.

As I approached the Baker Street tube station, I wondered how she told this David about me. No man would marry a woman who was not a virgin. How did she explain that? If she tricked him—a lawyer of all people would sense if a woman tried to trick him—he would kick her out.

Then I remembered Dr. Assam's other clinic. It would have been expensive for her, but she must have found someone to repair her cherry.

But, I thought to myself, no Dr. Assam could take away the memories we shared. And not only would we always share those memories, she would never tell her lawyer about me. Between us, she would be my American wife in fact, if not in name. It was exciting again. We were bound by our secret, and a hint that I might reveal it would always get a response from her.

So it was better than my first thought. Our secret was the Achilles' heel of her marriage, and I controlled that secret. I looked at my watch and calculated it was almost noon in Kansas City. I smiled to myself as the train pulled into the underground and I got into an empty car.

When David and I arrived, Mom was fidgety, like something was on her mind. I assumed it was nervousness about adding a new family member, and she was less anxious when there was time to sit around the tree after dinner. My family usually went to bed early Christmas Eve, but David wanted to go to a midnight service. The Quakers didn't have one, and I had no idea if mom's Lutheran church did.

"No problem," David said. "I got the name of a church from a partner. It's on that divided street that goes out parallel to State Line."

"Ward Parkway," I told him.

We arrived just before 11:00 p.m. A few other people were arriving at the last minute like us. The blue glow through the arched stained glass windows and the dark wood inside reminded me of Westminster Abbey. People nodded to each other, but I didn't recognize anyone. An usher seated us and gave us each a candle.

Teenagers read the Bible about the Virgin Mary and her child sleeping with the animals. I thought about the night before the Christmas holidays in the dorm at Mizzou. A lot of girls got drunk, and after hours, one girl said boisterously, "I won't be giving birth to any messiahs this year. I, uh, don't qualify for the job any more," and then laughed with her friends.

At the end, an usher with a candle came by our row, and we lit our candles from his. The lights dimmed and the choir sang "Silent Night."

When we got to "sleep in heavenly peace," I touched David's hand. I hadn't been in church for four years.

After donuts and opening presents Christmas morning, Mom and I cooked all afternoon. David made mashed potatoes, and Dad read in the living room. Freddy played with his model train under the tree and wandered in and out of the kitchen using his finger to sample almost everything.

We sat down to eat around 4:00. As Freddy finished his second helping of mashed potatoes, he looked across the table and said to David, "You make great potatoes." He inhaled another mouthful, and while he still had food in his mouth, he looked at me and asked, "Did Mom tell you that your friend Sayiid called yesterday?"

Mom gave me a look that apologized for not warning me.

"No," I replied. "She didn't."

"Mom talked to him," Freddy continued.

I looked at my mother. "He wanted to say 'Hi,'" she said. "I told him your big news. He said to tell you, 'Congratulations.' That's all."

There was an awkward silence.

"How long did you date him?" Freddy asked even though he knew the answer.

"A year or so," I answered in as even a voice as I could manage.

"Funny," he said. "I thought it was longer than that. Oh, well..." and he reached for the jam to put on a roll.

We had pie for desert. I helped Mom clean up afterwards.

"I'm so sorry," she said as I dried her mother's china. "I meant to tell you, but there wasn't the opportunity. I had no idea Freddy would...you know..."

There was no point in getting angry, so I reassured her, "That's okay." But I got agitated talking about it again and chipped a saucer as I put it on the shelf.

When we were getting ready for bed, David asked me, "Who's Sayiid?"

His question was logical after Freddy's making a big

thing of it, but I was so awkward, it showed. "A guy I dated," was all I could say.

"What kind of a name is Sayiid?"

"Middle Eastern."

He thought for a moment. "Is that the guy who...you know...forced you?"

I nodded.

"So you dated him for a year and a half, then he raped you?"

I couldn't lie, I couldn't say the truth, and I couldn't even begin to explain Christie being kicked out of Penn, Sayiid's car horn, the abuse, the unpredictability, the pain—my fear of Sayiid.

I took so long to not answer that I might as well have put up a sign that I was hiding something. David guessed. "So he raped you, and then it went on for a year and a half?"

I felt horrible, and all I could do was ask him, "Please don't say, 'rape.' No one wants to think they were raped. He wasn't a bad person. There were some good times."

"What?" David was incredulous. "By definition, rape makes a guy a bad guy, a very bad guy, unless you..." his voice trailed off.

I was humiliated. "I told you I wasn't a virgin," I said as defiantly as I could muster, but in a way I was begging. "What else matters?"

David never said I was a bad person because of what I'd done with Sayiid, then or any other time; but Sayiid had called, and Freddy had been a jerk, and David had blundered into a mess that was impossible to explain. He was trying to understand, but even his simplest questions put me back in a dark place where I felt buried alone.

I had no clue what else to say. I concluded then—and I believed for years to come—that David felt cheated that I hadn't been a virgin for him. But I'd told him so at the beginning, I'd warned him, so I didn't understand what else there was to say.

In fact, it was me who was cheated—and to that degree, David was cheated—because I lived within the boundaries of scars I couldn't see. I'd adapted so completely to the fear that I might do something to resurrect the shame of Sayiid that I put my emotions, my voice, and especially my sexuality, on a kind of leash. Those scars distorted how I participated in sex even with this man I loved with all my heart.

The scars became evident only when I wondered why other women felt different in their lives from the way I felt. But that would happen years in the future.

As we went to sleep, David put his arm around me, but it was like the hug of a stranger. That was probably all in my head—like with Will in Europe, I judged myself more than he did—but it didn't matter. I assumed I knew what he thought about me, because that's what I thought of myself.

It snowed overnight. Freddy left early to drive a snowplow for a friend. Mom and I walked to the after Christmas sales on the Plaza. There weren't a lot of people since streets weren't cleared yet. David helped Dad with something around the house and acted as though nothing had been said.

In St. Louis, everything was back the way it had been, but I couldn't tolerate even the new lower dose birth control pills. So David used condoms, and the result was I was expecting almost as soon as we held hands. I uttered a prayer of thanks that I hadn't gotten pregnant with Sayiid.

The Princess missed two periods, but she wrapped unused Kotex in toilet tissue and left them in the trash so that the old woman would not report this to the Prince. Dr. Assam used a glass rod to place a drop of her urine in a yellow circle on a small black card. He swirled the urine with a stick until greenish-yellow flecks appeared in the liquid. "Congratulations, Mrs. Algedda. You are going to have a child."

I felt a great relief. After two years, the Prince and my mother would be happy. The Princess was also relieved. We had champagne, and she made love in a way that felt like a mistress. I wondered where she had gotten such ideas, but I did not care. I liked what she was doing, even if she was my wife, and her father had the power in our relationship instead of me.

The Prince was genuinely excited and said he was pleased I had given him the hope of a grandson by his daughter. He joked that he had been thinking I might need to divorce his daughter so she could marry another man to give him grandchildren. But I knew this was not a joke to the Prince.

There was an air of celebration at the Embassy the next day. My wife's pregnancy was a secret, but that only meant that no one could talk about it or congratulate me even though everyone knew. Two weeks later the Princess had cramping and bled heavily. Dr. Assam said it was a miscarriage.

The Princess's mother came to London to console her. She tried to make me comfortable about having intercourse with her daughter while she slept in the next room, but I could not keep an erection knowing that my mother-in-law heard every squeak of the bed. If my friends were listening and I had a girl in my bed, I would be as stiff as a horny camel. But when my sexual desire was welcomed, all I wanted to do was go away and find a challenge.

I think the Princess's mother told the Prince because my driver was replaced, and the new driver insisted on taking me everywhere. Nothing was said, but I was not allowed to be on my own at all.

Eventually my needs took over, and I came to the Princess

two or three times a week. Her mother smiled the mornings after I had been with her daughter, but we were in an odd alliance. Both of us would be off the hook if the Princess had a baby, but that did not happen.

I could not call the blue-eyed girl that Christmas.

I took visa applications, talked to our citizens who had money troubles, and arranged solicitors and barristers for those who needed legal help. I accompanied one man to prison as he began a life sentence for killing his daughter. He had found her with an English boy in their living room. They weren't even kissing, but he called her a whore, grabbed a knife, and slit her throat to preserve his honor. The boy escaped.

When Scotland Yard arrived, the man was holding his daughter's body in a pool of blood, wailing and asking why she had made him do such a thing. I had to help him understand that the English did not allow a father the same right to defend his honor that he had in the desert.

After a year of regular sex, the Princess had not gotten pregnant again, and we visited Dr. Assam. When Sister Claire had taken the Princess for her examination, he asked me to sit down and proceeded to suggest the time had come that he should examine me, "to consider the possibility that the problem might be in you."

"Bugger you!" I exclaimed in my best British insult. "Bugger you!"

I got up to stalk out of the room, but he said one more thing. "As your physician, I must tell you that your wife's father has been making inquiries."

He said it very quickly, as I already had the door open, and then he watched as I stopped and returned, almost as a primitive hunter might watch a large animal slowly collapse as a poison dart took effect.

"I told him that as your physician I could not reveal anything. But as your physician, I must tell you he has inquired."

So while Assam examined my wife, I masturbated with Swedish porn that made *Playboy* look like church literature. I looked at my specimen and remembered Miss April 1966. I would have prayed if I had believed outside of the mosque where I had to appear to believe when I was around other men. He also squeezed my testicles, poked my rectum with his crude Hindi finger, and shoved it so far up my groin that I gasped.

We returned a week later on the pretext that he needed to assess the eggs in my wife's ovaries. During the procedure, he was called out on an "emergency." The Princess waited with Sister Claire while Dr. Assam talked to me. "You have what we call oligospermia," he said.

"Ol-ee-go-spermia," I repeated.

"Oligospermia."

"What's that mean?"

"We found only a few sperm in your semen last week."

"So? What difference does that make?"

"Conception is like evolution, Mr. Algedda. We need many sperm so that one can survive. If there are few, it is unlikely that any will get through."

"But she was pregnant!"

"Yes, but that was a miracle, a one in 10,000 chance. Such a chance is unlikely to happen again while she is still young enough to have a child."

Then he outlined three possibilities: continue the same course with about a one in 10,000 chance of another pregnancy; gather my semen on many days, concentrate the sperm, and put them into the Princess on the optimal day based on her morning temperature; or mix sperm from a select donor with my sperm in the hope that my sperm would make a baby. At the last suggestion, I exploded.

"Bullocks! You're saying put my sperm in with some other guy's sperm and then pretend she's pregnant with my child. Bugger you!"

Dr. Assam sat quietly while I vented my frustration.

"I want another doctor. You're a buggered Hindu quack."

Several days later, a card arrived addressed to me in Dr. Assam's neat, public school handwriting. It had a name, an address, and a telephone number. He had probably seen reactions like mine before.

The second consultant, a professor at Hammersmith Hospital, did not see patients privately. I was examined in a cold, white-tiled consultation room, by a medical student, a registrar, and a senior registrar before the professor entered the room. They each palpated my testicles, poked deep into my groin, and did a rectal exam to feel my prostate. The registrar was a young blonde. As she rubbed my prostate, I had an urge to urinate and then I felt an erection. I think she noticed, but she just flipped off her glove and left without saying anything. She exuded an English disdain for Arab dignitaries, and I wondered what it would be like to play with her anus but quickly lost that thought as the senior registrar squeezed my testicles. The professor was just as thorough.

This time I turned in a specimen when I arrived. The laboratory did the analysis while the professor finished his exam. The results were the same, and the professor gave me the same options. He also suggested that, if I were uncertain, I could at least begin to collect specimens that could be concentrated to try my own sperm again.

I waited a few weeks before I called Dr. Assam. I would do this in a private setting if I were to do it at all. To explain the visits to his consultation, he drew blood samples on the

Princess and did exams to try to diagnose her problem. I played the patient husband—and masturbated to produce semen.

Dr. Assam was clearly troubled by keeping the truth from the Princess, but he pursued the greater goal of getting me to cooperate because he knew that being pregnant would make the Princess's life less stressful. He understood that even if the Prince had me divorce his daughter, he would only be able to arrange a lesser marriage a second time. She would always be considered a failure, even if she had a child by another man.

He told the Princess that her vaginal secretions were toxic to my sperm and that he would put my sperm into her uterus directly. She was scarlet with embarrassment, but I acted supportive and said I accepted the affront to my honor so we could have the child that we both wanted so much. She did not notice how clumsy was the act that Dr. Assam and I performed to convince her of our good intent, and to keep my secret.

The Princess missed her next period, but we kept that secret. About three weeks later, she had very heavy flow, and we visited Dr. Assam that afternoon. She still had on a pad when we arrived. Dr. Assam inspected the blood, and then had a look of recognition. He took the pad into the other room. When he returned, he said one of the spots was a tiny embryo.

He spoke kindly to the Princess, "Mrs. Algedda...you were pregnant again...and this was a miscarriage." Each muscle in her face sagged. A tear appeared in one eye, and then she sobbed. I sat beside her, but it was Dr. Assam and Sister Claire who held her hand and patted her shoulder.

The Prince called me the next day. "Sayiid, when will my daughter have a grandson for me?"

"I do not know, sir," I replied.

There was an uncomfortably long silence, before he added, "The good Dr. Assam has his ethics of privacy, but his lab technician is not well paid."

He let that sink in.

"She was pregnant, but she miscarried two days ago," I admitted. I could not lie to the Prince when he already knew, and I worried how much more the lab technician had told him.

I called Dr. Assam. He fired the technician, and I told him I was ready to try the third option. He suggested an anonymous donor matched for skin color, religion, and age. I did not want a stranger, so I decided to use Jabir. To do this, I invented a story that the doctor wanted to test his sperm to see if there was something that ran in the family. We went together to Dr. Assam's repair shop four blocks away and gave specimens at the same time. There were no women there to make him suspicious, and Jabir thought it was a regular laboratory.

Our specimens were mixed and stored overnight. The next day, Dr. Assam again went through the charade of putting my sperm directly in the Princess's womb to bypass her toxic vaginal secretions.

The Princess missed her next two periods. I thought briefly of taking steps to assure that Dr. Assam would be permanently unable to tell my secret, but, after consideration, I realized he would not reveal anything because the Princess would suffer more than me. He had become protective of her, and in the desert, a problem would always be her fault.

About the time we announced our pregnancy, the Arab world was shaken by Egyptian President Anwar Sadat's attack on Israel. The English were stunned but focused on the Zionists fighting back. We knew, however, that the war was far more successful than the Zionists wanted to admit. Egypt reclaimed enough territory to reopen the Suez Canal. More importantly, Sadat proved the fabled Zionist intelligence service was fallible when he launched a nearly perfect surprise attack. Egyptians beat the Zionists until Zionists—flying American planes—shifted the balance.

In the middle of the two-week war, the Organization of Petroleum Exporting Countries imposed economic sanctions on the West for their support of Israel. The OPEC ministers embargoed oil exports to the United States, and cut oil production by ten percent.

David put a lot of money into developing new cases, but we weren't poor. Ironically, he often faced lawyers he'd worked with a couple of years before. I went back to Planned Parenthood again, but we'd had twins, and managing them was a full time job. I went part time and finally quit.

As the kids grew, David reluctantly agreed we needed to have a yard and a place for them to play inside in bad weather, but getting him to do anything was a different story. I looked at nearly thirty houses and narrowed it down to three. He took a day off in the middle of the week, but by the time we made an offer on the house he liked, it'd been sold. We settled for one of the other two houses and became homeowners at the end of October.

In November, President Nixon gave a speech explaining that Arabs weren't shipping us oil and we needed to drive fifty-five miles per hour to save gas. Gas prices went up seventy percent, and David and I agreed we were lucky we hadn't bought a house further out because we'd use more gas.

We considered not going to my parents' for Christmas, but in the end we drove up two days early to avoid the gas lines. Every time the phone rang, I was terrified it'd be Sayiid and made myself busy so I couldn't possibly talk. There were a lot of sudden baths and spur-of-the-moment walks to Topsy's on the Plaza for a popcorn treat.

When we drove back to St. Louis a couple of days after Christmas, it was a glorious sunny day. I was thankful that Sayiid hadn't called and wondered if he'd finally leave me alone.

The Princess had a son. She was relieved. My mother was happy. I joked with my friends, but I avoided Jabir when he visited with Elke and their twins. He was unusually fond of my son, more than our father's affection for his nephews, more than my father's affection for any of his grandchildren.

I thought briefly about the fact that the blue-eyed girl had not used anything to prevent pregnancy, and of course I did not wear anything any more than I had for Tina. I had wondered why she did not become pregnant, but when I sensed the answer, I forced myself to think of other things.

In 1978, I was appointed Vice Consul at our embassy in Paris.

There were more Arabs since immigration was easier from Algeria. I loved the Lido and other clubs, I loved that my chauffeur could always find women, and I loved the men's gossip in tea houses that did not yet exist in London. I occasionally saw women in chador walking behind their husbands, but it was more common to see them in the back seat of a Mercedes while their husbands raced, then braked, from stoplight to stoplight.

I called the blue-eyed girl's mother on Christmas Eve afternoon, figuring it would be her morning. We exchanged our usual niceties. When I asked if her daughter was at home, there was a brief muffled sound as though she had covered the mouthpiece of her telephone, and then she came back on.

"She's not coming home this year. She's expecting her third, and...well...it's so hard to travel with the twins...being pregnant and all."

"She has twins?"

"Yes, and they're so cute. They're almost seven. They hadn't planned a family so soon, but it just happened. The twins came along eleven months after the wedding. If it'd been sooner, the neighbors would've been talking." She paused, "So how are you? Do you have children?"

"A son," I said without excitement. I added, "I'm in Paris now. Vice-consul."

"Vice-consul? Is that some sort of assistant ambassador? I remember you wanted to be an ambassador."

I was annoyed that this woman remembered. "It's a step toward being an ambassador. One waits for an opportunity as senior persons retire."

"Like union seniority? Is that it?"

"Sort of, I guess." I told her it was a big promotion, and within a few years I should have a more senior post. As I locked my office safe that night, I wondered why I still called and resolved never to call again.

In August, my father died of a heart attack. He was only sixty-seven years old.

The Princess and I took our son home as the family gathered. The first night in my parents' house, I got up at 3:00 a.m. and went to my father's library. It was a large room, but it had only one bookcase and one desk. Father read widely, but he kept only books that added to his understanding of life. Everything else he passed along to friends.

The books were mostly Western—a King James Version of the Bible and copies of *Hamlet*, *Macbeth*, and *King Lear*. No comedies or histories, only tragedies. There were Churchill's history of the English people, novels by Hemingway, Dickens,

Fitzgerald and Updike—the same Updike who had written *Rabbit, Run*—and one science book, *From Fish to Philosopher*. The last book argued that there could never be a philosopher until kidneys evolved to allow life on dry ground, where there could be paper on which to write. One thing must change before another can.

I opened my father's desk, something I would never have dared to do while he was living. He never locked it, but the fear of his disapproval kept all of us out of his private things. A letter from the blue-eyed girl was there, along with her travel diary and a letter from Jabir.

> I regret the necessity of bringing these things to your attention. I tried to reason with him, but I have not been successful. He watched the American girl come and go from a cafe on our street. The owner told me an Arab man was watching my house. He thought I was in danger. I told him my brother was...

I thumbed through her travel diary. Pages were partially torn where my father had ripped from one place to another in his anger.

I heard Jabir's voice. "You caused him great pain."

I looked up and wondered how long he had been watching me.

"How?" I asked.

"He worried about how you treated the daughter of his friend's friend."

"What business was it of his?"

"Sayiid, we are one family. If one is wronged, we all are wronged. If one does wrong, we all do wrong. If one is dishonorable, we are all dishonorable."

"Maybe in the desert, but not there."

He paused and then continued as though his was father's

voice. "Mr. Hartwood arrives tomorrow. Did you know that?"

"No, I didn't."

"Please, do not ask him anything. Do not tell him anything."

"What makes you think I would?"

"I watched you reading that girl's diary. You are here with your wife and child, but your mind is there."

I challenged his assumption. "What would I want with her?"

"I didn't say your heart was with her, only your mind. That was a polite way to say your prick."

"My what?"

"Your prick. Your cock. Whatever you want to call it."

I was as surprised as I had been by the strength of my father's threat to tell the Prince not to allow his daughter to marry me. My jaw dropped as he continued, "I would never harm you, little brother, but I ask you not to dishonor our father's memory. Let this stop now. Don't call her any more."

How did he know these things?

"Don't act so surprised. The Prince knows almost the time you will crap next. He talked to father more than once. Father asked me what I thought he should do on the telephone an hour before he died."

He stared into my eyes until I had to look aside. "You caused him great pain." As he left the room, he cut off the light with a sense of dismissal. I stood there in the dark. The light from the hall was not enough for me to read by, so I put her diary in my pocket and went back to my room.

David was invited to speak on consumer safety litigation at a conference in London. Mom agreed to take care of the kids, which I've since learned, caring for my own grandchildren, was a bigger gift than I realized.

As she and Dad dropped us at the Kansas City airport, she said to me, "That friend of yours, Mr. Algedda, lives in Paris. You should call him."

"If I have time," I said, but I was furious that she chose that time to remind me. I wasn't really angry at her. I was angry that Sayiid had called at all. My mom just didn't get that I didn't want a thing to do with him. I hoped David hadn't heard her.

After the conference, we flew to Frankfurt and used Eurail passes to get to Homburg. Everyone thinks I mean Hamburg, but that's a big city up north. Homburg is near France, and it's known for hats. David wanted to buy a Homburg in the city where they're made. I didn't want to dampen his enthusiasm, so I didn't tell him I'd been there on my trip with Barbara.

I had no idea where he'd use a hat, but it was cute how excited he got as he tried on different styles. Finally he selected one. The clerk boxed it and tied it with a string.

As we turned and started toward the door, I bumped into an Arab man with a woman in tow, his wife I assumed, who was wrapped in black except for her face. He was the image of Sayiid's brother. I froze.

"What's wrong" David asked.

"I don't know," I said. "Maybe something from lunch," and I pretended to look around. Of course it wasn't Jabir, because I was remembering a man from ten years ago—but I must have looked pale as a ghost. David stepped in and asked the salesman in his broken German, "*Haben sie ein toilet für damen?*"

The clerk led me through the back storage area to a room with a toilet and a sink. It was clean, but looking in the mirror, I realized how close I'd been to being that veiled woman, and how lucky I was to be with David.

"Better?" David asked when I came out.

"More than I know how to explain," I said, but David was focused on thanking the sales clerk. I didn't say anything more. To explain how good I felt with him, I'd have to explain to David how truly bad I'd felt with Sayiid. I couldn't allow myself to go there.

When we returned to our hotel after dinner, David was a little tipsy, and I was feeling brave. As we got ready for bed, I wanted to feel close to all of him, so I didn't bother with a nightgown.

My nakedness surprised him, but he welcomed it. I was much more likely to change in the bathroom, or behind a screen if we were in a hotel with a shared bathroom. Or if he tried to catch a glimpse of me undressed, I'd say, "Don't look."

"I don't get you," he'd protest. "It's not like we haven't been naked together. We have three kids already."

But my body had changed with three kids, and in my heart I was afraid of what he might think about me. What would he assume about me if I ever hinted I was the kind of girl who liked sex because it felt good?

I always had the same answer. "A girl has to have her secrets."

Ironically the more I tried to hide my sexuality, the more he probably wondered who I was thinking about, perhaps even Sayiid. Especially after my next stupid idea.

We took the train to Rome and then to the Costa Brava in Spain. I thought about my plan in Barcelona, long ago, to ditch Sayiid and stay with Will. That didn't work out, but my life with David still proved how wrong Sayiid was about me. I wanted Sayiid to know that life with David was wonderful. But I couldn't begin to figure a way to talk to David about this, and besides, it seemed like something I had to do myself.

Naively, I began to hatch a plan. My thought became the idea that I could say something to Sayiid that'd impress him. I wanted to show him my life was good—that I was good—despite how he'd treated me. I wanted to confront him and say, "I'm not interested in your life. Leave me alone. Stop calling my mom."

I decided to do this in Paris.

We arrived on an overnight train and found a small hotel. I told David I didn't feel like touring and would do laundry. He volunteered to help me. "That's all right," I said. "I saw Notre Dame with Barb. I don't need to see it again." He shrugged his shoulders and gathered his camera.

After he left, I asked the man on the desk about a Laundromat and how to call Sayiid's embassy. He was Arab, possibly Algerian. He waited a moment and then looked out the window, pretending to crane his neck to see if David had returned. I hadn't realized how much sarcasm there could be in looking down a street as though he was helping me do something behind David's back.

"The Laundromat is on the second street to the right. You will need franc pieces. Do you have change?" He thumbed through his notebook. "This is the number of the Embassy. You can call from the phone in the corner." He pointed across the small lobby. "I will not charge you."

A woman answered. "And what is your business with Mr. Algedda?"

"I'm a friend from Penn College in the United States."

"Mr. Algedda is not here now."

"Please ask him to call me if he comes back in an hour or so." I left the number of the hotel.

Wahiib and I returned to Paris a week before the Princess. The respectful quiet because of my father's death had faded, and the staff enjoyed the warm autumn days. Discreet plans were being made for short trips to Munich for Oktoberfest. For the record, no one was going to drink beer; these were opportunities to observe the culture of non-believers.

The Princess was remodeling our flat a few blocks from the Embassy. Wahiib walked with me when I went to lock it after the workmen left. On the walk back, we joked about how to spend a bachelor evening before my wife returned, and I suggested the Lido.

"I'll pass on that, but perhaps the opera," Wahiib said. "I hear 'La Boheme' is risqué."

We laughed as the guard saluted, and we went to our separate offices.

The Embassy staff was all men except for carefully vetted women who answered the telephones and sat at the lobby desk as a sop to French sensibilities, so they could not say we restricted women to the home or the harem. All other Embassy business was carried out by men—male couriers, male secretaries, male transcriptionists, etc. At times the Embassy took on the air of a college fraternity house. This was one of those times. As I went up the stairs, everyone smiled like we shared a common joke, but I had not been let in on the punch line.

On my desk was a message the operator had taken from the blue-eyed girl while I was out. It read, "In Paris for 24 hours. Call if you have a chance," and gave a number. My impulse was to telephone immediately, but fortunately I went to close my door and found half the staff waiting to see what I would do.

"I checked. That hotel is on the Isle de la Cite. Truly a

*bon marche*!" said a voice.

It was the other vice-consul, neither my superior nor my subordinate, performing for the crowd. "Honestly, Sayiid, couldn't you be more careful than to have your women call here, and from such a seedy place? Where is your respect for the King? We can chip in to get her a better hotel."

I was at him in a minute. "I've had it from you..." I took a swing for his face, but he had been a boxer, and he simply dodged me.

I swung again, and again he adroitly moved aside. He was laughing. Everyone else was moving back into an unplanned circle.

"Stop that!" It was Wahiib.

He held the note from my desk and understood that the staff assumed it was a call girl who had taken the liberty of calling me. Everyone knew the chauffeurs made arrangements and were the persons to call if a girl was ill, or needed help with a pregnancy.

"Sayiid," he asked, "why is she calling you? Were you trying to prepare a surprise for me?" Everyone stared at Wahiib.

"She's a friend of mine from school in the United States. In America, a man can be a friend with a woman. But I have no idea how she knew I was here." He watched my face for an explanation. "She must have tried every embassy in Europe."

No one would suspect Wahiib of anything bad. The other vice-consul apologized, and I had the wisdom to laugh it off.

"You missed a wonderful view." David gave my waist a squeeze and kissed me as he walked in. "I climbed to the top of Notre Dame."

"David." I stopped folding a shirt and paused to get

his attention.

"Yes. What is it?"

"I need to warn you I might get a phone call."

"From who? Who do you know in Paris?"

"Sayiid."

"Sayiid?"

"Sayiid from Penn."

"How does he know we're here?"

"I tried to call him."

"Why? You guys keep up a little correspondence on the side?"

I realized how bad a mistake the call had been. "David, he calls my mom at Christmas and talks to her. She reminded me that he was in Paris when we left the kids."

"Isn't that cute."

"David, please."

"Please what? What am I supposed to think? You send me off so you can call—what euphemism should we use here—an old boyfriend?"

"It isn't that way."

"Then what way is it? Tell me."

I paused because I didn't know myself. "I want to tell him that my life is good despite him. I want to say, 'See, I'm better than you thought.'"

"Well, I thought our life was all right until now. What do you want to do, have a nice quiet dinner with him?"

"No," I insisted.

"Then tell me?"

"Why do you keep asking questions?"

"Because I don't get answers."

"I don't want him. That was all over before I met you."

"If it's over, why'd you call him?"

"I can't explain. I wanted to talk to him when I wasn't..."

"When you weren't what? When you could wait until I

wasn't around?"

"My life is good. I wanted him to know my life is good despite how he treated me."

"Why does it matter what he thinks?"

"Okay." I was frustrated. I couldn't say what I meant because I didn't know. "Can we drop it?"

"No, we can't just drop it."

"Why?"

"Because you don't end it."

He paused, the lawyer gathering his facts to make his argument. "I'm not naïve. Do you want the list of girls who've spilled their stories to me?" He started counting on his fingers. "One got drunk and then the guy dumped her. One got drunk and then decided the guy wasn't for her, but he wouldn't let go and she married him the last I heard. One slept with a guy when they were engaged, but he broke the engagement and she went out and picked up another guy in a bar. She never even knew that guy's name. Lots of girls have sex for the wrong reasons, but it's never over 'til you deal with it."

"What's left to deal with?" I challenged him. "I told you everything when we met. What difference does it make? You've got me, don't you?"

"Got you? You tell me. Do I have you? I'm not certain."

Our tickets home weren't for three days, but our trip ended that night. We talked politely and laughed at a few obviously funny things, but we didn't make love and there was no closeness. When we stopped in Kansas City to pick up the kids, I was sick as a dog. It was two more weeks before I realized I hadn't had a period for eight weeks. There was no problem getting pregnant with David. It must have happened in Homburg, when we were so in love for a night.

He was busy at work. I didn't have a paying job, but I still read the product safety reports. Sometimes I found an article David had missed and teased him that he was losing his edge. That shared interest held us together for the next few months.

At Christmas, my parents were excited about a new baby, but as we were washing the dishes, my mom asked, "Do you really want another one right now? With the others still so small?"

"Yes, mom. David and I talked about it. I was at Planned Parenthood long enough to know there're options. They're legal now. Can we drop it?"

"Okay," she said.

After dinner, the adults opened presents. David had bought a pair of Villeroy & Boch teacups in Homburg as my present. As we got into bed, I said, "The cups were very nice. Thanks, again."

"They're our other souvenir of Homburg," he said patting my stomach.

That overrode Paris, and life was better again.

I waited until January to call the blue-eyed girl's mother so it would not look like I was responding to her daughter's call. We went through the same formalities. My son was walking. The blue-eyed girl's twins were in third grade, and their baby was a year and a half old.

"I got a message that she tried to call me in Paris," I said.

"She didn't tell me she called you. But things have been so busy since she came back, with the twins' birthday and then the holidays. She must have remembered I told her you were in Paris. You told me that last year."

"Yes, I remember," I replied. "Why was she in Paris?"

She told me about a trip they'd taken while she took care of their grandchildren. After a meeting they'd attended, the blue-eyed girl and her husband had traveled around Europe.

"I think they had a great trip. As a matter of fact, I'm sure they did."

She was bursting to tell me something, so I asked her why.

"Because they're expecting in July."

When I had received her message, I assumed the blue-eyed girl wanted to see me, perhaps to remember our always-good times over dinner. But another kid brought her husband into the picture and told me her reason was not that simple. I wondered what was on her mind when she called me.

I tried to sew a dress for our daughter at Christmas, but with four kids it was all I could do to keep ahead of the rush, and that project got lost. Most of what David and I shared got lost the same way. But even when there wasn't time for anything fun, even to go to a movie, he still wanted sex. That was exactly how Sayiid had seen me, too, as a warm body for sex. I began to believe that's all I was to David.

David interviewed for a job at UCLA. He was upbeat when he returned. I asked, "Do you really want to raise kids in Los Angeles?"

"Why not? It's sunny all year round. Look outside." He pointed to the window. "There's not a leaf anywhere and there won't be for months, but when we drove through the campus in LA, it was green everywhere."

It was a couple of years before I knew enough about California to point out brown in the summer when there's been no rain for six months.

My parents came with us to care for the kids while we moved into a house in San Marino, a suburb of Los Angles. It was one of those Spanish stucco houses with a tile roof.

I found the house, I loved the house, and I loved San Marino.

David was immediately consumed with preparing lectures, grading papers, and consulting on cases he'd left in St. Louis. I set the kids up in school and with things like play dates and sports teams, now being what we call a soccer mom. The kids made friends. The timing was good for the twins, because they started junior high with everyone else.

Our Consul General in Paris had a heart attack and, after he recovered, went to New York for surgery to move veins from his legs to bring blood to his heart. The Americans called this a "cabbage." It was routine in the United States, and some surgeons did three operations in one day.

I became acting Consul General. Wahiib was only secretary for the Ambassador, so for once I was not only a year older but also outranked him.

The Consul General stayed in New York to recover from his surgery. A month later, he had another heart attack and died. I was sent to the United States to escort his body back to the desert. It felt spooky flying first class across the Atlantic and on to the Middle East knowing that the Consul's body was in a box in the cargo hold.

When I returned to Paris, I was appointed Consul General.

When our fourth child started school, I gravitated back to Planned Parenthood as a volunteer and then as a part-time counselor. I had no complaints about the husband I'd met in Poison Control, but I needed something to do where I wasn't just his backup.

My first day, I looked at the intake questionnaire. One of

the questions was, "In the last year, were you hit, kicked, or punched by someone?" So where would rape fit in? And if they asked directly, would anyone answer? Probably not. Watching Betty destroy Christie at Penn had taught me that other girls can be the worst ones to judge.

In 1985, I received a note from Dr. Assam:

> Dear Mr. Algedda,
> I have information of great value to you. Please arrange an appointment at your convenience.
> Regards,
> S. Assam, ChD

"The Hindu prick," I told myself. "Now comes the shakedown. Well, Mr. Assam, I can handle you." I assumed he was going to blackmail me, but before I arranged a solution, I decided to learn what he had to say.

It was easy to take a commuter plane to London and a hack to Marylebone Road.

"Mr. Algedda," Dr. Assam began, "so nice to see you. And how is Mrs. Algedda?" He knew better than to ask about the boy.

I made some small comment and sat down.

"I'm certain you are surprised to hear from me after all these years."

"Yes. What do you want?"

"Oh, I don't want anything. I have something for you." He picked up a paper on his desk and handed it to me. "I just returned from a urology meeting. I heard a Dr. Silver—they call surgeons "doctor" in the Americas—say he thought it would be possible to remove a single sperm from the testicle of a man who was infertile and use that to create an embryo that would be the man's own child."

"So the man was speculating. This is why you called me to London?"

"Mr. Algedda." He paused for emphasis. "Dr. Silver does not make predictions. He talks about what he has already done as though it might be a good idea, and then a year or so later he announces that he has done what he said he would do. He never shares an idea until he has done the new procedure and done it more than once." He let this sink in, but even then I was slow.

"I know this man," he continued, impatient for me to understand. "He has already done this. This is the breakthrough we've all been waiting for."

Assam was genuinely excited by the thought that someone had taken this next step to treat infertility. "Mr. Algedda, you should see if he can help you more than I could."

Two weeks later, I was in New York to carry documents. The second day I was there, I took the 6:00 a.m. flight to St. Louis where I met Dr. Silver. He put a gel on my scrotum and examined my testicles with an ultrasound. "Very interesting," he mumbled to himself as the black-and-white lines made blurry shapes on the monitor.

"What?"

"I'm sorry," he said. "I was getting carried away. Your anatomy is interesting, but you must understand I'd only say that if I thought I could help. Often, I do not know if I can help, but in your case I am certain I can."

He pointed to a black streak that went across the screen. "That dark area is your epididymis, the final place for maturing sperm. It is very enlarged. Actually, I'm surprised you don't have pain, but if it's been that way for many years, it may not have pain any more.

"Anyway, when it's enlarged like this, it's like your testicle is making sperm but the vas deferens—that's the little tube that carries sperm to your penis—the vas deferens is blocked."

"How does this 'vast difference' get blocked?"

"Vas deferens," he repeated slowly and clearly. "It can be an injury, but that'd need to be a big injury to block both sides. More likely you were born without a vas."

"Born without it?"

"Well, not born without it, because a few sperm do get through. But your vas is probably very narrow. We never really know why. It doesn't seem to be an inherited birth defect, and it's not passed along to children."

"Birth defect?" I snapped at him.

He changed the subject. "How did you say you got my name again?"

I told him.

"Dr. Assam. Or I should say *Mister* Assam. Such a quiet man. He has treated members of the British royal family and, I think, from the Middle East, too. But those are rumors. He would never say so himself. I know Scotland Yard has a virtual army of guards on his premises all the time. One looks like a nurse, I hear.

"I can remove sperm from the epididymis, but if the vas has been blocked, the sperm are probably very poor quality. I suggest we remove sperm directly from your testicle. It is a little operation, but it should work."

Dr. Silver then described a small cut in my scrotum to remove some tissue from my testicle. They would find a sperm in this tissue and put it into an egg from the Princess. In three days, there should be an embryo to put into the Princess. The only drawback was the Princess would need to take medicines to make many eggs mature all at once.

I was so relieved when I left the clinic that I asked the

driver to stop at a gas station and called the blue-eyed girl's mother in Kansas City. Being close to having my own biological child gave me the impulse to want to call to the blue-eyed girl while was in St. Louis, even talk to her husband if that was necessary. But the phone came on with an answering machine. I did not leave my name.

Four weeks later the Princess and I were back in St. Louis. I told her they needed to get an egg from her to make an embryo. The wife of a staff member had used *in vitro* fertilization in Paris, and the Princess asked why we did not use the same clinic. I told her this clinic had higher success. I could choose whether she noticed a cut on my scrotum.

We stayed in St. Louis for four weeks to allow time for the embryo to settle in before the stress of the trip back to Paris. I called the blue-eyed girl's mother from our hotel lobby and asked for her daughter's phone number in St. Louis. She told me they had moved to Los Angeles so her husband could teach law.

"He must be very good," I said.

"Yes," she agreed, "but frankly, I worry he won't make enough to support them, and he takes chances he doesn't get paid for. He goes out to toxic sites and spends time with the dirtiest people, like factory workers and the folks that clean stuff up."

"Wow," I said. "Why be around them?"

"He says it's a responsibility. I talked to her about it, and she just said she'd been exposed to dirtier things in her life. I didn't like how that sounded, but I think she was just trying to be dramatic."

Dr. Silver implanted two embryos. One of them took, and just after my forty-third birthday, I became the father of a daughter. My son was excited by his new sister, but he never understood why I stopped reading with him and, for that matter, paying attention to him at all.

I'd worked at Planned Parenthood for a year or so when the board decided to hire a director for counseling services and asked me to screen the resumes. As I read the applicant's backgrounds—hospital social worker, director of early childhood education, even a bank vice-president—I realized I was more qualified than any of them. I had experience from St. Louis and my master's degree, and I'd dealt with three, and soon-to-be-four, teenaged children.

Before my interview with the board began, a board member named Sarah introduced herself to me. She was a gynecologist in private practice who volunteered in our clinics one day a week.

"I'm Sarah," she said. "You don't recognize me, do you?"

"I'm sorry. Have we met?"

"Years ago. But I have the home court advantage. I've read your resume. You don't know a thing about me. We met at Penn."

"Oh, my gosh. I'm sorry. Did we have a class together?"

"No. I was a freshman when you were a senior."

"How'd we meet?"

"I sang in the chorus at your graduation and introduced myself after the ceremony. You were with that dirty old sociology professor. I said I wanted to be like you, and you looked at me really weird." She laughed. "You had no idea what to think.

"I swam for Blue Ridge in high school," Sarah continued. "I was on the team at Penn, too, but never as good as you." She smiled to assure me this wasn't a joke. "But that wasn't why I got the board to interview you. It was your thesis project on how women respond to men."

"I couldn't tell you a thing about that except that I wrote it."

"It was in the library, and it changed my life. I'd always wanted to be a heart surgeon, but your thesis cried out to me to do something with women's health. That's why I'm a GYN today."

As the rest of the board gathered, there was a new person I didn't know. I asked Sarah who he was.

"That's AC. I should know what the "C" stands for. The "A" is for Al. He's just come on the board. I missed the meeting when he was voted on, so I only know what was sent to us in the packet before the meeting. He gave a lot of money to our teen pregnancy program."

Spring break began the next Saturday, and one of our twins had a girlfriend sleep at our house. The friend, I'll call her Jill, had been over so many times I thought of her as my fifth child.

When they were young, the twins often slept on the floor together, but they were older now, and our son, the other twin, had long since found his own friends. That weekend he was camping with his Explorer troop.

I got up and made pancakes. The girls came down when they smelled coffee. Something was different about Jill. She wasn't as happy as usual, and I wondered why.

Both girls slept in tight T-shirts. After all, what was a T-shirt for, if not to be tight? I thought for a moment that Jill had gained weight, and she was eating pancakes like they were about to go out of style. Then she turned to pick up a carton of milk, and the T-shirt pulled around the profile of her chest. She hadn't gained weight everywhere; she'd gained breasts. I probably wouldn't have noticed if I didn't work at

Planned Parenthood, but I did notice. And I bit my tongue so I wouldn't ask if she was pregnant.

Late in the morning, Jill rode along when my daughter dropped off a pair of shoes for repair. As she got out in the loading zone, my daughter asked Jill, "You want to come with me?"

Before Jill could answer, I said, "I think it'd help if Jill waits with me. She can act like she's getting out if the meter maid comes along."

My daughter shrugged and walked toward the shop.

Jill was sitting in the back seat. I leaned forward to see her in the rear view mirror and asked, "Jill, has my daughter ever told you what I do?"

"Sort of," she replied, "Planned Parenthood or something."

"Yes," I paused, "Planned Parenthood. It's a great organization. Parents want babies eventually, but sometimes it isn't the right time."

Jill held her face as stiff as possible to hide any reaction.

"You know," I went on, "One of the most important parts of our work is confidentiality. We're like doctors. Nothing leaves the office." I tried to act as if I were speaking off the cuff. "You should drop by sometime. I could give you a tour. I'm there most afternoons after school."

The passenger door opened. "Done," said my daughter as she got in.

Jill called after school on Monday and asked if she could come by for a tour. I gave her directions and told my secretary I was expecting her.

Jill had missed two periods and she was in a panic. I didn't ask any other questions, but I told her the best place to start might be to tell her mom.

"Oh, my god, no!" she cried. "She'll kill me. My dad will kill me. I'd rather die."

"That's why we're here," I told her, "so you won't have to die."

Jill and I talked over an hour. I called her mom and asked if she'd like to come by my house for coffee tomorrow morning. I assured Jill it was important enough to cut class.

When Jill's mom arrived, I brought her into our kitchen and poured a cup of coffee. We'd met, but I had no idea how to begin, so I just said, "I saw Jill this morning."

"Oh? She was so nervous. She said there was some big thing this morning. I told her to relax, and it'd be okay."

"Did she tell you what it was?"

"No. That's the funny part. It didn't seem to be a school thing."

"Can I speak frankly with you?"

"Sure," she said to me, "Of course, but what's this about?"

"I told Jill I'd get you over here so she could talk to you in private. Would that be all right with you?"

"What do you mean, 'over here'? Is Jill here?"

"Yes."

"What's going on?"

"I think she'd like to tell you herself, but she's afraid, so I told her I'd come along, and then it seemed good to have a place that'd be private."

"I don't like this." She stood up. "My daughter's at your house to talk to me? What in the hell is this all about?"

I called into the other room, "Jill."

Jill's eyes were bloodshot, and her makeup was streaked by tears.

Her mom scowled at me as she took a step to claim her daughter, and Jill burst out, "Mom, I missed two periods."

There was a long silence as her mom took it in. Then she exploded, "You little bitch. Your dad's going to kill me."

Jill sagged on a chair and cried.

I didn't say anything. Her mom glared at me, "How long have you known this?"

"About eighteen hours."

"Why didn't you tell me? A mom's got a right to know." She turned on Jill, "Why didn't you tell me?"

Jill glared right back. "Because I'm a 'little bitch,' or don't you remember?"

Jill's mom slumped in a chair on the other side of the table. I waited before I asked her, "Are you ready to be a grandmother?"

As quickly as she had gotten angry, she looked overwhelmed. "Why does this have to happen to me?" She turned to Jill. "I've already got so much trouble with your father."

"Jill came to me," I said, "because we can help her."

We made an appointment for Jill that Friday, but it seemed best not to tell her dad. He had a temper, and there was no point in aggravating him.

I asked my daughter if Jill had a special boyfriend.

"Nope. Everyone's jealous of her. She's beautiful, but she can't see it. Every guy in school wants to go out with her, but she turns them down."

"What about that guy you both hang out with sometimes. What's his name?"

"Jerry?" My daughter laughed. "Oh, god, no. He's gay."

Our older son used my car so much that we joked it was more his than mine. He was in the shower getting ready for a dance at school, and I needed to pick up his sisters, so I called through the door, "I'm going to take the car."

"Okay."

I was gone about fifteen minutes. The girls bounded into the house, and since I also used "his car" a lot, I thought I'd better check if there was anything in the back I needed before he left. In the trunk was an ice chest with two bottles of champagne.

I held up the bottles, one in each hand, as my son came down the stairs. "Big plans for tonight?" I asked.

My son looked at the bottles and then at me. He was disappointed because I'd found them, but he wasn't contrite. "So what? You found a couple of bottles of champagne. A lot of guys get champagne for big occasions."

"What are you planning with Connie?"

"Let it go, mom."

"Just don't push anything."

He looked straight at me. "Mom, we've talked about it. You always said 'ask' so I asked. It's what we—notice 'we'?—it's what we want to do."

"Just allow her a choice."

"Why do you always make me feel so guilty? This isn't the 60s."

About two weeks later my daughter came home from school and announced, "Jill's gone."

"What do you mean 'gone'?" I asked.

"Gone. No one's seen her for a week," she explained, as she reached into the refrigerator. "I tried to call her house and no one answers the phone. Jason across the street says the police have been there two times."

My mind raced.

It took me two days to decide what to do. I wasn't supposed to share anything from the office, but if Jill was in trouble, something I knew might be the key. The San Marino police were suspicious when I asked to speak with a woman officer about Jill and wouldn't give my name over the phone. I didn't want to be recorded either, so I insisted we go to the breakfast place across the street. Officer Gonzales was tolerant and promised whatever I told her would be held in confidence. I told her about Jill being pregnant, and how she and her mom were afraid of what her father would do. She nodded and took notes. I think I was filling in details that she'd been guessing at.

"We may want to talk to you again," she said as I got up to leave.

I gave her my card, and added, "I feel better having told you. Sorry I was so weird about this. I just needed to do something. You can call me at work any time." I took the card back and wrote on the back. "Here's my home number, but please don't leave a message with your name. Jill was—I mean is—a friend of my daughter's."

Sarah was my gynecologist as well as my friend. David couldn't understand how I could go to a gynecologist who was theoretically my boss. "Isn't that some kind of harassment or something?" he joked.

"You guys don't get it. After four kids, nothing there is that personal."

"How am I supposed to take that? Not personal at all?"

"You're supposed to know that I need to do some things that may seem personal to you but that are impersonal to me. I suspect after the first twenty vaginas of the day, Sarah gets bored, too." Since he felt he was being left out, I paused to reassure him. "However, that part of me is very personal when I choose for it to be personal. Got it?"

After three years in Paris, I was appointed Consul General for our embassy in Washington. I was forty-six years old. I was well positioned to be our next Ambassador to the United States, and I was ecstatic. At almost the same time, Wahiib was appointed First Secretary of our mission to the United Nations in New York.

A month after the first President Bush's inauguration, we were invited to a state dinner at the White House. As the ranking Consular officer in New York, Wahiib was invited along with our Ambassador to the U.N. The Princess planned to attend, but our daughter was ill, and even though she had dressed for the evening, she decided at the last minute to stay with our children. The nurse from the Embassy did not seem competent to her, and the Princess doted on the children. It had taken so much for her to conceive.

After the dinner, there were opportunities to have photographs made with President Bush. This is an odd custom when you think about it, but the most prized souvenir of a visit to the White House is not a purloined napkin or teaspoon, but a photograph made personally with the President.

I took my turn. No doubt prompted by an aide, President Bush asked how Mrs. Algedda was. I told him why she had stayed with the children at the last minute. He wished a speedy recovery for my daughter. Then we smiled at the camera as we shook hands. I requested four prints that were delivered to my office by White House messenger the following Wednesday.

I had skipped my calls to the blue-eyed girl's mom because I could not keep calling without a reason. The photograph created a reason to renew our contact, and it showed me in a place they would envy. I was important enough to stand with the most powerful man in the world.

The blue-eyed girl had been recognized for her work, but her picture was taken with local politicians. I hoped her mom would skip the comparison that even though the politicians with her daughter were less important, they wanted some of the glow of her achievements to reflect well on them. President Bush, in contrast, shook my hand primarily to facilitate the flow of our oil to America through the facilities of, and for the profit of, companies that had donated heavily to his election campaign.

The Planned Parenthood board had a two-day retreat at Lake Arrowhead. I went along as senior staff. Sarah and I shared a room.

"I had no idea there was anything like this so close to LA," I said.

"This used to be a Hollywood hangout in the 30s. Back then the road up was even more winding. My guess is that driving down after a party was a good sobriety test."

The retreat topic was security. There'd been attacks on Planned Parenthood facilities in the Midwest and New York, and a board member suggested that we move termination services to separate centers, keeping our existing centers for contraception, STDs, and all other counseling services where they were. The idea was we'd conserve resources by concentrating security at one or two high-risk sites.

"I think that marks the women who need pregnancy termination, makes them too easy to identify," said Sarah. "They're having a hard enough time already. What do you think?" She turned to me.

I agreed. "If word got out that the women who went to one facility were all there for an abortion, you can bet some kook'd take pictures and make up 'Wanted' posters. These girls—young women—are scared enough as it is. We need to keep them close, not isolate them."

AC supported me in the debate. "Security is probably better managed with fewer, multipurpose facilities. It might seem logical to focus efforts on one service, but that assumes we don't need to worry about truly crazy people who don't make any distinctions."

The staff rumor was that AC had worked for the CIA at one time. I began to think that might have been true.

The motion failed, but it was close, seven against to six in favor.

"You were quite effective in the last session," AC said to me as we waited for an elevator during the break before dinner.

"Thank you."

"Are you married?"

I said, "Yes."

"Kids?"

I felt vaguely uncomfortable. "Yes."

"Love your husband?"

"Very much."

"He's an attorney, isn't he?"

The elevator came, and he let me step in first. But I asked myself, "If he knew my husband was an attorney, why did he ask if I was married?"

"Floor?" he asked.

"Three."

He didn't push a button, but I didn't think anything about it.

It was one of those slow elevators where you hear the whirr of the pump. As soon as the door was closed, he put his hands on my shoulders and kissed me. I tried turning my head to avoid him, but he grabbed my body and one arm with his right arm and turned my face back to him with his left hand. All the CIA rumors ran through my mind, and I couldn't scream because his tongue was in my mouth. Mercifully, the elevator slowed to level us with the third floor, and by the time the door opened, he'd turned toward the front and left me standing beside him, looking forward, as though nothing had happened. I was too stunned to speak. I felt horrible and had no idea how I could've stopped him.

Sarah was in the hall waiting for the elevator. When she saw me, she stepped back to let me off and said, "I was looking for you. What're you doing for dinner?"

AC stayed on the elevator and said something polite like, "Evening."

After the door closed, Sarah said, "He gives a lot of money, but he always gives me the creeps."

I was too shaken to say anything except, "Me too."

Next day, AC cornered me during the coffee break before the last afternoon session. "I know a great country music place over in Running Springs. I'll take you over there after the banquet tonight." Then he put his hand on my arm in a way that would look like a friendly pat but provided cover to brush my waist and the side of my blouse.

I didn't answer. The bell called us back to the meeting, but before the session was over, I sneaked out, bought four candy bars in the gift shop, and went to Sarah's and my room. I took a long shower and lay on my bed in one of those thick white terry cloth robes they had in the room.

Sarah came in almost an hour later. "I can't believe I got caught up so much talking to AC." She looked at me. "You're not dressed for the banquet. It starts in twenty minutes."

"I don't feel well," I said. "Time of the month or something."

"I travel with pills for that kind of thing," she said, and gave me a chance to accept her offer.

"No thanks. I'll just ride it out."

After Sarah left, I ate the candy bars and found to my dismay that the cable television didn't work in our room. I was asleep when she returned. "How was it?" I asked.

"I'm really sorry you weren't there. There was a surprise presentation for you. Some sort of staff award from the national office that the director nominated you for. Only she and AC knew about it in advance."

All I could think was that I was better off in my room.

"We have our own place farther up in Big Bear," Sarah said as we drove back to LA the next afternoon. "It's about forty miles east and two thousand feet higher. There's even skiing in the winter."

"Skiing in Southern California. They'd never believe that in Missouri."

"We'll have you and David up some weekend. You should bring your kids if any of them are interested."

Sarah had married right out of Penn, which almost ruined her chance to go to med school. She had a daughter soon after. "I was pregnant," she explained. "I make no bones about it, but I loved Peter. That was his name. Sure would have been simpler if I'd known about Planned Parenthood back then, but I didn't."

It wasn't lost on me that she'd done with Peter exactly what I'd done with Sayiid. Impulsively, I asked, "How'd you hide what you were doing?" and immediately knew how awful it was to ask. "I mean...your condition...I'm sorry. That's none of my business."

But Sarah welcomed the chance to talk about it. "Oh god. I worried something awful. You remember the dorms. Penn's a nosey place. Everyone heard the story about a freshman girl who got pregnant and then died getting an abortion in London."

I noted how Christie being expelled had become a morality tale as Sarah mused on my question. "How was it?" She paused to let her mind go to a different place and smiled.

"Wonderful. Happy. Our private game, keeping it our secret from everyone else. I've never felt as close to anyone as I felt to him that whole last year at Penn. Would I have chosen not to get pregnant? Yes. Would I have told him to wait? Not on your life. It may have even been my idea. I can't remember."

The option to choose makes so much difference.

Peter had been on an ROTC scholarship at Mizzou. Once they had a kid, he could've dodged his commission, as a dad, but he didn't. He went to Vietnam and was killed in the last week of fighting in 1975. Sarah was in her second year of medical school at the time. She and her daughter got through school and residency as a team, though as Sarah said, "She didn't have an option not to be on the team."

Her daughter lived in the Midwest somewhere. She and Sarah talked at least once a week, but they rarely saw each other. "It's easier to relate over the phone. I think that's from all the nights I was on call and the best I could do was phone home before the sitter put her to bed."

A couple of weeks later, David went to a conference in Portland. I drove him to the Pasadena Hilton to catch the shuttle to LAX. I would miss David, but I liked my space, and once I settled into my papers at work, I forgot the too-formal peck on the cheek he'd given me as he got out of the car. I only worked three-quarter time at Planned Parenthood. The kids were in school, and it felt good to have time when I didn't need to care for anyone.

David called on Wednesday and said he'd be one more day. Some work had come up that he needed to settle after the conference.

I was sad because my need to be alone had only lasted a couple of days, and the excitement of doing what I wanted, like sneaking out to a matinee or staying up late with the kids, had burned itself out. I was ready to snuggle in bed. Only he wasn't home.

When David came home, he was distant. He said the extra day was productive. When I asked what it was about, he said, "I was catching up with a colleague on a similar case. A lot easier face to face."

Our son who'd bought the champagne didn't come home until 3:00 a.m. Sunday morning. I woke up at 1:30, realized he wasn't home, and woke David up. We waited up together, but we didn't talk. David read a legal paper, and I watched television. When our son did get home, I was really upset and said he was grounded. But David took his side and said he was happy to know he was safe. After that, they went to bed, and I was left alone fuming at David for not backing me up.

David had late business meetings, worked Saturdays and started taking calls in the evening on his cell phone. That was new, but then again, he did a lot of consulting to supplement his academic salary to make ends meet with the four kids.

"It's hell trying to get it all done," he explained. "Big case. We...I've put a lot of effort into preparing it, and it's right down to the wire."

I walked round to his side of the dinner table where we were sitting and put my hand on his shoulders. We hadn't made love in two weeks. He hadn't even approached me. As I rubbed his neck, he didn't relax.

I didn't miss sex, but I missed feeling close. I could still dress up pretty well, but when I got out of the shower, my skin was loose and hanging in places. I hid from David's glances. And judging from comments he made, he assumed I was hiding from him in all ways.

"Mr. Algedda, we were so surprised to see your picture with President Bush," began the blue-eyed girl's mother.

"One of the opportunities with my new position. I'm Consul General for our embassy in Washington."

"Does that mean you're the boss?"

"Actually, the Ambassador is senior to me, but...well... it's complicated." I tried to explain that he was in charge even though I ran everything. "And how is your daughter?"

"She's busy as ever," she said, and detailed the blue-eyed girl's life, her children, her work and her husband's success.

During one of those many freshman conversations at Penn, long after the girls were in at curfew, a guy from Texas had talked about a bad date. His words echoed as I listened to the blue-eyed girl's mother. "It was like kissing your sister." I wanted to talk to the blue-eyed girl, not the woman chattering on the phone. I knew that was what I had wanted for almost twenty-five years.

At my regular GYN appointment, I asked Sarah why she didn't do a Pap smear.

"Cervical cancer is almost all a viral disease. If you've got the HPV virus, it can give you cancer. There're a ton of HPV viruses, but only two or three cause cancer. A lot of girls get HPV with their first intercourse. Most of it goes away from acquired immunity. If it lasts, we get concerned."

"Then why'd you stop giving me Pap tests?" I asked.

"If a woman's in a monogamous relationship and has a series of normal Pap smears, they're a waste of time unless she starts sleeping around."

I was surprised by what I asked next. "What would it be if...if David was sleeping with someone else?"

Sarah was professional in an instant. Yes, I should have a Pap smear then. Was I okay? Was there any way she could help?

"David takes care with the kids. He works hard. It's just that...what's that phrase kids use these days for going all the way? 'Getting together.' That's it. We don't get together anymore. And there are a lot of phone calls to somewhere up near San Francisco."

"And you think...?" She waited.

My life dissolved as I heard myself tell her that I thought David was having an affair.

Over dessert a couple of nights later, I decided to be direct.

"Are you seeing someone?

"What do you mean, 'seeing someone'?"

"What I asked: 'Are you seeing someone?'"

"Who?"

"Whoever it is you spend evenings with every couple of weeks. Whoever you talk to whose phone number is..." I looked at a paper for effect. "415.354.7603. Are you seeing this person?"

We were sitting in a restaurant in Santa Monica. David was trying to avoid saying anything, so I waited and poured myself another glass of wine. I knew the answer as soon as he'd asked, "Who?"

Finally he began, "I didn't set out to find someone. I just sat down next to her at a meeting. It was dark, and I could only make out one empty seat. It felt like when I sat next to someone else at a Poison Control meeting."

"Who is she?"

"That's what unnerved me. She and I were the class darlings in law school. I was in love with her, and then she took a job clerking for a judge in New York and that was the end of it."

"Go on."

"Then thirty years later I sit down beside her in a dark room."

"You probably saw her legs glow from the exit lights."

"Funny," he said, but he didn't know how to take that. "Look, I didn't intend anything. We just had coffee at the break."

I listened, but their meeting was too much a replay of my life to think it was cute. I was dating Harry when I met David, so I knew exactly what he meant when he said, "It just felt like something that was supposed to happen."

"Do you love her?" I asked.

"I don't know."

"Have you slept with her?"

"Yes."

"Do you want a divorce?"

"I don't know."

I surprised myself at how methodical I sounded. "I'll give you one without a fight."

"Don't you even care?" he asked.

I ignored his question. "We need to think of the kids, though, so we should plan this all out before we tell them." I didn't have a plan. I simply said what flowed from my mouth. It was where we'd arrived and had been on my mind since I talked to Sarah, maybe even before. I loved David more than anything, but I'd hidden so much about myself that I always had to be on guard. I welcomed the idea that I could relax and not care anymore.

David protested. "You talk like we're deciding this. Shouldn't we slow down? See a counselor or someone?"

"We can talk or not talk. The answer is always going to be that you've been unhappy for a long time. There's no reason to ruin two lives. You're the attorney, can I leave it to you to find us a lawyer?"

"We'll need to have two lawyers."

"Why? It'll cost more money."

"It's cleaner with two lawyers. You'll have someone to

watch out for your interests."

"I don't care. I know you. You'll be fair."

"It'd be too much like being my own lawyer. Fool for a client, that kind of stuff. Let me find two attorneys, please."

My hand was resting on the table holding a glass of wine. David reached across and touched me. "I'm sorry. Let's not leave it like this. Can we at least take some time to think about it? Please."

We got drunk, and after that, it was a random conversation. "We've had some good times…remember how mad the kids were when we left St. Louis…we've all gotten used to LA…no place else to go from here…I'm not angry, only sad… two adults…let's be friends…I'm sorry…I…I don't know anything else to say."

At midnight we took a cab home. It cost over hundred dollars, but neither of us was in shape to drive a block. David offered to stay in a hotel, but I told him that would upset the kids too much.

As Santa Monica drifted away behind us, I could almost see two excited young kids driving up there to dinner from the LAX Hilton. This time I was relieved. Some dark thing inside of me, the secrets of everything I'd allowed Sayiid to do, could be left alone again. It'd been all right when we only shared sex, but when David wanted to know my soul, I was terrified what he'd see. I could never figure out what he expected. Now I didn't have to.

I knew I'd always love him, but I was relieved to get out of the sex part of his life. I'd already spent years watching my parents' marriage up close, and they didn't get along that well either. David was a great person, but we couldn't make a go of it. Why ruin two lives trying? I hoped he'd marry and live happily with someone else.

He took my hand in the cab. "I thought you'd at least be upset."

"Why be upset? We don't love each other anymore."

"I know you say that, but..."

I cut him off. "Look, let's be friends. We'll be good to each other. Whatever happens is between two adults. No expectations. Just be where we are in the moment."

I think what I said confused him. I know it confused me. I should have been angry and kicked him out, but he didn't make a move to leave and I didn't want to be by myself. I'd been alone too much at Penn, with Harry, even in my parents' house. I just wanted to feel close to someone. Love was not required.

Just don't leave me by myself.

David looked in on the kids. Our daughter asked, "Where's the car?"

"We decided it'd be better if we took a cab home," he told her. There was no way she could have missed the alcohol on his breath.

"Where'd you leave the car?"

"Santa Monica."

"That's a long cab ride," she said, with the implication that she was enjoying her turn to comment on our behavior.

In keeping with our plan of not disrupting the kids' lives, we undressed in the same room, brushed our teeth at the same sink, got into the same bed, and lay on our backs staring at the same ceiling.

So many emotions. A tremendous pressure had been released, but emerging from all the emotions was the freedom that I didn't have to do anything. My voice was suddenly equal in what happened between us.

I turned and looked at David. From the bouncing and the sagging of the comforter, he knew I'd turned and looked back at me.

I was surprised that when sex wasn't an expectation, I saw David as a man. He wasn't fat. He worked out. He had his hair. And I was attracted to him sexually. Finally, I said, "We agreed to do what felt good to us, right?"

"Yes."

I curled my finger in the hair at his neck, unbuttoned his pajamas, and slid the sleeve off the shoulder he wasn't lying on. Then I kissed his chest.

He responded tentatively, like he was trying to figure out what I wanted, so I responded with a sigh and wiggle to let him know. Everything was my call. Not David, not anyone, expected anything of me. I untied the drawstring, pulled his pants down, and felt him react to me.

I wouldn't say it was love that night. In fact, it was a lot like sex with Harry. I wanted to do it because there wasn't any pressure, and I didn't have to. I hadn't yet realized that I could make a choice—and stay in a relationship—if that was what I wanted.

A couple of weeks later I asked David if he had the name of an attorney for me.

"Not yet," he told me. "I'm trying to decide who to call." We tiptoed around each other's feelings for months before I realized he wasn't going to call anyone.

Years later, after she was out of college, one of my daughters said to me, "We went through all the pain, but we didn't get the divorce to tell our friends about."

She meant it as a joke, but it was the kind of comment that hurt no matter how it was meant. I'd failed to protect my children. She had no idea what I'd gone through, but that didn't diminish the facts of what I'd allowed her to experience. Excuses don't assuage guilt for moms.

In December, a letter came to my office marked "Personal."

Ellen brought it to me. "I know you said to go ahead and open things like this. No secrets and all. But this seems different?"

I looked at both sides of the envelope before I opened it. The stamp was a meter from Pasadena, but there was no return address. I thought about opening it but decided to call building security. They called the police.

Two days later, Officer Gonzales came to my office. "That was quite a note you received," she said.

"What note?"

"Oh, you didn't know they sent it to us, did you?"

The Los Angeles police had inspected the envelope and then opened it. Inside was a cashier's check made out to Planned Parenthood and a note from Jill's mother. The LA police knew that Jill and her mom were missing persons, so they passed the note and check along to the San Marino Police Department.

> Sorry to leave town so quietly. It seemed better that you not know anything. We're new people now, and plan to leave it that way until Jill is a lot older. I just didn't know any other way to get away from her father. I want to thank you for being there for both of us. I don't know what I'd have done if you hadn't made me get beyond my fear and concentrate on taking care of my beautiful daughter.

Officer Gonzales handed me the check. "It's legitimate, and it's yours. We suspected her husband, but this makes it pretty certain she just up and left. None of his fingerprints are on it, and the prints on the letter and the check match ones that were all over the house, even on toilet cleaning stuff. From the mess the house is in with him by himself, we're confident the prints on the cleaning stuff are hers. They went to ground, as they say."

"How does someone do that?" I asked.

"In her case it was simple." Officer Gonzales smiled. "She took out their entire joint 401-K in cash. All of it. Over half a million dollars. The funny part is that she talked the fund out of withholding money for the early withdrawal penalty and taxes. Now her husband has to come up with that."

"But the postmark. She sent it here."

"No. She was really smart. Look at the check. It's dated two days before they cut out. And the postmark? That's a postage meter in her husband's office. Metered mail doesn't get cancelled again. She could be anywhere in all fifty states."

I was proud that I'd spoken up and helped a girl who really needed it. We put the money in our battered wives emergency fund. I kept the letter.

We went to Kansas City for Christmas. Everyone wondered when President Bush would launch the attack to take Kuwait back from Iraq. He'd been shot down in World War II, and he talked about having experienced war.

We had friends on the hospital ship *Mercy*, and we knew others whose kids were being called up with reserve units. A partner of Sarah's, a doctor in the reserves, was called to Madigan Hospital in Seattle to cover for a doctor in the army who was going to war.

I had a different problem. I was pregnant.

I'd felt okay with the new low-dose pills, but I got blood pressure problems and my primary doctor took me off the pill altogether. David didn't want a vasectomy, which always made me wonder if he thought he might want more kids, so we used condoms or a diaphragm. The diaphragm gave me yeast infections, so we usually timed sex, when we did get together, for safe times of the month. It wasn't a foolproof system.

"You sure?" was David's first response.

"Of course, I'm sure."

"Did you get one of those pregnancy test things?"

"Yes, I got one of those pregnancy tests! Do you want to watch me pee on one again? God, you can be such a jerk," I whispered loudly. It was Christmas Eve. He was arguing about whether I was pregnant, not even touching me. I wanted to run outside, but we, and all our suitcases, were crammed into my bedroom at my parents' house. The girls were in the living room, and the boys were upstairs with Freddy.

"Look. I'm sorry. You've had a chance to think about it, and you drop it in my lap after we've been flying all day. Can we go talk tomorrow?"

After the presents were opened and the dishes were clean, we walked down to the Plaza. David asked me what I wanted to do.

"I don't think I can do the baby thing again," I said. "I haven't got it in me."

"You've done a great job on the first four."

"That's sweet, but you're not telling me what you think."

"It's not up to me to tell you what to do."

"Don't cop out on me now. I sign, but it's for both of us. If you go around thinking I took an opportunity from you, that wouldn't be good."

"We could do it, you know."

"Right. I did the math. We'd be over sixty dealing with a teenager. Do you think you'd ever have the energy to do that right?" I prodded him to get him to think this through. "It'd be vanity to go ahead. What was that story about a woman who used hormones to have a child at fifty-five, in Italy or somewhere? Why have a child if you won't be around to raise it? The world certainly doesn't need spare children."

"If I'd had a vasectomy, we wouldn't be having his conversation."

"Or if I'd done something. It's a little late to blame ourselves."

We didn't discuss it anymore, but we'd made a decision.

I woke up in the recovery room about 10:00 a.m. on January 14, 1991. As my mind cleared, I wondered why January 14 seemed to strike a chord. I thought methodically back through our marriage to figure if it was an anniversary or a forgotten birthday, but I couldn't think of anything.

When I started back further, before David, I realized it was twenty-five years to the day from when I went to Sayiid's apartment. I'd marked the day with an abortion. Freud would have a heyday with that.

As I dozed in and out, I had one of those thoughts that'd never enter your mind if you were wide awake. David and I'd had no problem having four kids. We got pregnant almost by looking at each other. I'd just had to deal with that even at my age.

I never got pregnant with Sayiid. I tried birth control pills for one month, but I got too sick. That was the original high-dose pills, but obviously I didn't do well with low-dose pills either.

But Sayiid never took any precautions. I wondered why I didn't get pregnant with him. Unless he was a lot less of a man than he thought he was. There was irony in that. Trying to prove how big he was, but not having enough there. I wondered. Then I put the thought out of my mind. Life was good, and I didn't want to jinx anything.

As the Ambassador's retirement approached, staff asked my opinion on issues outside the usual affairs of businessmen or our citizens. Expatriates called to pitch their businesses. Many of these men sold oil, but others brokered food, electronics or cars. A Mercedes dealer called to point out that Arabs now worked in German factories, although he did not mention that most of their jobs were cleaning with toxic chemicals.

I thought about the qualifications of the women who worked in the Embassy's publicly visible positions. They should be young and fluent in English. The Foreign Ministry would recruit them at home, but I would personally judge whether they were satisfactory representatives of King and country.

I also arranged to have a portrait made of myself with my family. There are some in Islam who interpret any human image as a violation of the Prophet's—peace and blessings be upon Him—warnings against idolatry. Photographs, however, particularly portraits of important persons, are a necessary exception since they foster acceptance of Arabs in America. A portrait of a man with his wife and children conveys family values.

I was delayed in my office signing letters, so I arrived at the studio independently of my wife and children. The Princess had not become fat even after two pregnancies, but I was aghast at the dress she chose. It was awful, black and deep red with large ruffles around her neck. It looked like what a model might wear on a fashion runway, but by making that choice, she announced to all viewers how truly foreign she was to American life.

I thought of canceling the sitting, but everyone knew where I was, and coming back with proofs in a couple of days was expected.

In the end, the photograph portrays my life. I am in the middle, my daughter is at my left hand, my son stands behind me, and my wife sits at my right side. The Princess knew I did not like her dress, and that, in that moment, I did not like her. She leans toward me in a combination of hope that I do not mean what my eyes have already said, and hope that leaning toward me will somehow earn her a reassuring touch. But I do not touch her. My hand grips the back of her chair.

The day I brought the proofs to the Embassy, the King

made the formal announcement that he had appointed Wahiib Ambassador to the United States.

No one expected Wahiib to be the Ambassador less than Wahiib himself. He had not been interviewed and was in Boston to visit his son at Harvard. They celebrated by going to a sandwich shop.

All eyes turned to me to see how I would respond. I smiled and said he was my best and oldest friend. I could vouchsafe he would do an exceptional job. In the view of all, I called and congratulated his wife.

When Wahiib returned to New York, he was almost apologetic. "I had no idea this would happen. I was not even on the short list."

I congratulated him, but I noted that he did not join the chorus of those who said I should have been the ambassador.

I hinted that I was an obvious choice for Consul General in New York when he moved to Washington, but that was not going to happen either.

It was several years before I found out why Wahiib was appointed instead of me. He had not wanted to be Ambassador, but when I was rumored to be next in line for the job, he got concerned that I might commit some faux pas that would embarrass the King, and insisted on a private audience. Not even the Prime Minister was included. My father-in-law, the Prince, heard of the meeting only third hand—and that was from rumors, not from anyone who had actually been present. Everyone thought Wahiib was giving the King his opinion on colleges for the King's grandsons.

Wahiib suggested that the King promote our Ambassador to the UN instead of me. The King thanked him for his suggestion. Because Wahiib and I attended Penn together, our families were close, and we worked together in many diplomatic stations, he also asked why Wahiib was advising against promoting his friend.

The conversation would have remained secret except that as he was dictating his formal announcement appointing Wahiib, the King made an off-the-cuff explanatory comment to the Prime Minister, who was trying to object.

The Prince found out because the Prime Minister, a school chum as well as a relative, let slip part of the story, and the Prince wheedled the rest of it from him. On my next visit home, he called me into his library as soon as we arrived. "Your friend told the King about you and that girl in America!" he shouted.

I said nothing.

"Don't pretend you don't know what I mean. I know all about your American whore. Wahiib kept quiet when you were Consul General, but he couldn't let the King put you in charge of our affairs in America. The King wasn't worried at first, so your friend told him how you used the embassy phones to call her and told her to contact you at his embassy in Paris."

The Prince became sarcastic. "The King needed a man he could rely on, and a man who put the King above his closest friend could be relied on."

Then he yelled in my face, "You insufferable prick! What is your obsession with this girl? If it weren't for the pain it would cause my grandchildren, you would disappear into the desert tonight. Do you know she killed your father?"

I was stunned by that accusation.

"Don't look at me with your stupid mouth hanging open. Did you really think your father would keep secrets from me? Your father was a good man. He told me all about this girl, and the stress killed him."

I told myself it was wiser not to express my anger for two

reasons. First, no matter what it looked like, Wahiib had not maneuvered to be our Ambassador. He was just stupidly idealistic. Second, if he was the Ambassador, I might—as turned out to be the case—need his help.

Several weeks after he took charge, Wahiib explained over a private lunch that I was being assigned to a new post. "Your father-in-law convinced the King you could use what you learned at Penn," he explained. "It's part of our plan for the post-oil economy. You'll establish a new consulate, make social contacts, create business ties. Make friends for us." He took a sip of tea. "I've told the King you have the ability to do this, Sayiid." He paused. "But remember that you are *always* a representative of the King."

As I said, it was several years before I learned that he had advised the King not to appoint me Ambassador, but even at this lunch, I had the distinct impression he thought it unwise to allow me independence in America.

"Where will this consulate be?" I asked.

"Chicago."

Every spring, Penn College had a convocation where five alumni were invited back and recognized for their achievements. I was asked because of my work at Planned Parenthood. I wondered how Penn knew anything about me, but in my next thought, I knew it was through Sarah. My wonderful friend, my best supporter, my personal cheerleader Sarah, who I could never tell why I didn't want anything to do with Penn ever again.

Mom heard about the invitation from Mrs. Hartwood even before I got the letter. I imagined Kaye, as Mom called her now (but always Mrs. Hartwood until after both my dad and Mr. Hartwood had died) calling to tell Mom. The distance between Leawood and Westport stopped being so big once they were both widows. They had more in common than they thought, for starters the whole lifetime of memories that their husbands had shared. Even so, Mrs. Hartwood was always the executive's wife, and Mom was always the working mom.

They would get to other topics, like the Hartwood's grandchildren and my kids, but Mrs. Hartwood avoided asking about Freddy. There was never good news about my brother.

Mom told me several times how proud she was, but all I could think was how embarrassed she'd been in 1969 when Mrs. Hartwood found out I worked at Planned Parenthood. Funny how what embarrassed her then had become a source of pride.

I thought about declining, but Wahiib was to receive an honorary doctorate, and I wanted to support him. Arabs weren't popular, especially after the war in Kuwait and gas prices being what they were.

I worried I'd be asked to make a speech or impart wisdom to undergraduates, but it was much simpler. Dr. Forger had long since retired, and the new president read descriptions of the wonderful things I'd done. I worried that Sayiid would use Wahiib as an excuse to attend, but he didn't.

Wahiib introduced me to his wife at the reception before the black-tie dinner at Crown Center. She was dressed in a long, very Western dress, but with her head wrapped nonetheless. Just a wisp of very dark hair showed above her eyebrows.

When she realized who I was, she reached to take my hand. "I am so pleased to meet you," she said with a slight English accent. "When Wahiib described the honorees, he told me how you worked for women's rights. You know, he still has your paper on women thinking about their men? It is so different from home. Even when I watch your television, it is difficult to believe that your women behave so differently from ours."

Shortly after I got the award from Penn, the executive director of Planned Parenthood for Southern California resigned for health reasons. I applied for the position. I interviewed with the search committee, but that was a formality. I had worked with each of them already. I was one of the two finalists, but I didn't get the job. I was disappointed because they hired a former hospital administrator, and I knew I was better qualified.

There were not enough expatriates or visa applications to justify a consulate in Chicago, and nominally we only intended to buy grain for the Middle East, so a trade delegation would have been more logical. However, our unspoken goal to was to study the Board of Trade to find a way to gain an interest. Oil will eventually be depleted, but food will always be in demand. Technically it was not espionage, but it facilitated the work of our economists and businessmen to give them diplomatic cover. It reminded me of my diplomatic credentials when I came to Penn College.

Chicago is not Washington, but The Loop is much more hospitable than the center of either Kansas City or St. Louis. I leased space for the Consulate in a new high rise with a broad view of Lake Michigan. Living space for my family was a penthouse apartment on Lake Shore Drive, a couple of miles north. I had a chauffeur, but on a clear day I still had the energy to walk home in less than an hour.

Our team began making small purchases of grain through a broker we owned. Later, as we mastered the process, we manipulated prices with massive sell-offs to drive prices down or large purchases to inflate them, much like we had learned to manipulate oil prices through OPEC. Eventually, we organized crop tours in late August to make our own estimates of the total crop yield before bidding for the new harvest in the fall.

When Boeing moved its headquarters to Chicago, a new team bought and sold shares in the airplane giant. It was the same game to see what we could manipulate, and there was always inside information from some middle level executive who was thrilled to associate with diplomats.

The technical work was done by younger men who had been to Cambridge, Oxford, and Ivy League schools in America. My job was to be the public face of our Consulate. For this reason, I was interviewed for a magazine article about Arab diplomats who had attended college in the United States. I was amused that the reporter was named for a flower, the Daisy. "Does an American education help you as a diplomat?" she asked.

"Definitely." My gaze drifted to the open collar of her blouse. "I am much better prepared to represent my King."

"Can you explain how that works?" Daisy pulled her collar closed.

"I have better insight into what America needs and the things they hold valuable. I have lived shoulder-to-shoulder with Americans. I shared a room..." though I hoped she would not solicit a comment from Larry, "with an American." Then, as though the secure door holding my most personal secret had been loosened just a crack, I added, "I even dated a coed."

Even without saying her name, I was thrilled to mention the blue-eyed girl. I felt daring, and in an instant all my longing came back, as fresh as when I met her at Penn.

Daisy made a few notes before she asked, "You dated American women in college? That must have been a very different experience."

I knew what she was implying, so as in any diplomatic exchange, I challenged her to be more specific. "A different experience in what way?"

Daisy looked squarely at me. "In your country, your women are so restricted."

"Were," I interrupted. "*Were* restricted."

"Okay, were restricted. But in the 1960s it would have been culture shock coming from the Middle East to an American campus. Women in short skirts. Men and women next to each other in class. Socializing."

I did not want to follow her line of reasoning. "It was a change, but we were here to learn." And I redirected our conversation. "I haven't been back to Penn since graduation, but as you know, our ambassador received an honorary degree several months ago. We treasure our friends in America."

I also watched the individual staff members, in particular a young graduate from the London School of Economics. In the desert she would have been wrapped in black, but in Chicago, I could watch the folds of her suit as she walked. When we were busy she would remove her jacket, and I could see the silk outline of her breasts. One day, as I stood behind her looking at her computer screen, I put my hand on her shoulder and massaged my fingers in the soft spot, below her collarbone, at the top of her chest. She gasped and held her breath as though she had read the park rangers' instructions to play dead if confronted by a bear.

The next day she went for a walk over lunch and applied for asylum in the United States. She was from an important family, and Wahiib handled the situation personally. Nothing was ever said to me, but my conversations with Wahiib became noticeably more formal.

Living in Chicago set me free. I always worried that anything I did in public might threaten my career, but no one knew me in Chicago. I felt freer to act out my personal thoughts, but as I found out, my career could also be vulnerable to what I did in private. I wandered this new city, sometimes had a drink in the bar at the Palmer House, and decided to be more direct in my efforts to contact the blue-eyed girl.

I sent her parents a copy of the portrait of me with my family. I wanted them to see how successful I was, and I also hoped they would share the photograph with the blue-eyed girl.

Several days before Christmas I called to find out when the blue-eyed girl would be visiting, so I could call when she was there.

"I saw in the paper you're having a blizzard. How is it?" her mother asked.

I was puzzled until I realized she didn't know I had moved. "That's in Washington. I'm in Chicago now opening a new consulate. We had that storm two days ago," I explained. I asked if she had received the portrait.

"Yes. You look so distinguished. Such a nice family. How old are your children?"

I told her. She also asked about the Princess, and what she did.

"She's really a Princess?" she asked, after I had answered that my wife did not work. I gave royalty as the reason, choosing not to mention that in the desert no other women worked outside of the home either.

"Yes, her father is a third cousin to the King."

"Speaking of your King," she interrupted, "we were so excited that your Ambassador is an alumni of our little Quaker college."

"You heard?"

"Oh, yes. It was a big thing here. The television had it, and there was a big story in *The Kansas City Star*."

She went on about the public relations bragging by Penn College and how Wahiib visited and they gave him an honorary doctor's degree. She had asked her daughter if she had known him, "and it turns out they had some classes together. You must know him too."

"Yes. He was a year behind me. Our families have been friends since my grandfather. I have worked with him a lot."

"I'm impressed."

When I got around to asking when the blue-eyed girl would be home for Christmas, she said that she and her family were not coming home this Christmas.

"You know," I ventured, "I'd like to give her a call. Maybe invite her and her husband to fly up for a weekend when they're in Kansas City. Could I get her telephone number from you?

"Sure. She doesn't keep up with too many friends from Penn. She used to keep up with the girl she went to Europe with, but Barb got cancer and died. After Professor Baker died, it was like she never went to Penn at all."

I could hear papers shuffle. "Here it is. Are you ready?"

I timed my call to mid-morning on a Tuesday in January. No lawyers are at home on Tuesday, and kids are in school.

I dialed and let it ring until the answering machine came on.

When I came back from dropping the kids at school, the phone was ringing as I walked in. The answering machine picked up, and I listened. I shivered when the caller didn't leave a message. Mom had told me she'd given Sayiid our number at Christmas.

It had rained the night before so it was a cool day, but the air was clear, and I decided to walk to the coffee shop for steamed milk. I was trying to cut down on coffee, and I'd already had a cup and a half with David.

I sat by myself on the patio. There was almost no traffic, and it was quiet enough that I heard a few leaves rustle in the breeze. Looking back into the shop, I could see a boy and a girl talking, but I could not hear them. It was like watching television with the sound off. She was animated, like I'd imagine my own daughter to be.

The boy shook his head to say "No." She waved her hand as if to say she wasn't fooling and held up four fingers. I read the word "four" on her lips to match her gesture. He turned up his palms to accept her statement.

I wondered what her "four" was, and I thought of the "fours" in my life. Four years at Westport High School. Four years swimming. Four horrible years at Penn. Four kids. And meeting David four years after Sayiid.

I waited three weeks to call the blue-eyed girl again. She picked up on the second ring. I knew her voice immediately and identified myself.

"Sayiid," she said after a long pause, "Mom told me you asked for our number."

"Yes. She was excited that Wahiib's our new ambassador to the United States. Penn put on—what do you call it?—'a full court press' to make PR out of this."

"Didn't you want to be ambassador?" *Was she trying to belittle me?*

"I thought about it, but I have a special assignment to open a new consulate in Chicago. Besides, I couldn't wait to get out of Washington. It's built on a swamp. Don't you remember from history class?"

"I don't remember that class too well."

I changed the subject. "Have you ever been to Chicago?"

"I was there with my parents."

Although I had already dismissed the idea, I added impulsively, "You should come up for a weekend when you're visiting your parents. You and your husband, I mean. It's only an hour flight. You could stay at the consulate. Be our guests. I'm sure Wahiib would support that."

She did not reply.

"So, your mother says you have four children. Your husband's a lawyer? Is that right?"

"Yes."

"And you've been active in poisoning children. I mean preventing poisoning of children."

"I used to be," she replied. "Poison Control is very important."

"We have two children, a girl and a boy. They've adjusted well to Chicago. My son is ready to think about college. Are any of your kids in college yet?"

"The twins are almost through." She paused, then asked, "Why'd you call, Sayiid?"

"Like I said, I'd like to invite you and your husband to visit us in Chicago."

She was silent.

"I have a budget to set up meetings for my staff. We need better relationships with Americans." I tried to make my offer irresistible. "Come as our guests, First Class. Wahiib can invite you to Washington. Safety is important for children in the desert. And we have environmental issues..."

"And Planned Parenthood?" She knew I wouldn't have an answer for that, so she continued, "I don't think coming to Chicago will work out."

"I'd think after the hoopla about Wahiib being our ambassador, David—that's his name isn't it?—David would want to meet some of your friends from Penn. Your mom said you didn't keep up with anyone except Barbara. I was sorry to hear about her. Barbara's death that is."

I heard her take a long breath. "I don't think he'd want to spend time in Chicago."

"Has he ever been to Chicago?"

"I think so."

"Then why not?"

"I don't think he'd want to spend time with you."

"Oh?" I was surprised. "Does he know who I am?"

She was silent before she said, almost as an admission, "Yes. David knows who you are." There was another pause. "David's a wonderful person. You're the only thing in my life I've ever been ashamed of. I couldn't live trying to keep a secret like that. You're almost the first thing I told him about myself."

I was speechless.

"You know, Sayiid, this is a bad time to talk. I'm due somewhere."

I wanted to say she was just making up an excuse, because I was certain that she had, but held back. "When would be a good time to call back?"

"Please, don't call again."

"Why not?"

"Just...please don't. I don't want you to call me."

I did not dare to say anything. Then it was as though she was talking to herself and I could listen or not. "I don't want to say anything else. I've got to go now. Don't call me again."

After Sayiid had hung up, I reached to pick up my coffee, but I fumbled it. Coffee spilled across the *Times*, and I batted the cup against the edge of the counter and it shattered. Somehow I cut my hand trying to catch the cup after it broke and before the pieces hit the floor.

I bled, and I cried. The cup was my Christmas present from Homburg.

A mother never leaves danger for her children. I picked up the pieces, wiped my blood off the floor, and drove myself to the emergency room. I had five stitches but was out in time to drive the car pool to soccer, feed the kids dinner, and meet David at their school music program.

I looked at Lake Michigan from the window behind my desk. It was raining, and the pavement was gray like the lake. I had imagined a different conversation. She wouldn't come to Chicago, and she'd told her husband about me even before I knew she was married.

My secretary knocked quietly and entered. I had not turned on the lights, and he started to turn the switch by the door, but I waved him off.

"Are you all right?" he asked. "May I get you some tea? Should I call someone?"

"No." I spoke so softly that he leaned in to hear what I was saying. "I'm okay." I added almost speaking to myself, "I just had some news I need to understand."

"Oh. I didn't realize you had received any calls this morning."

The logic of his comment struck me, and I realized that I was not making sense. "Sorry," I said. "I...I called a friend. I need to think a bit. Leave the light off. There's enough light from the window."

He would not gossip, but I assumed he would check the log of outgoing calls. He might be in the employ of the Prince, always a possibility.

The rain stopped, but I sat there through lunch. In the

mid afternoon, my secretary knocked and brought in a small tray with tea and sugar. I would have preferred coffee, but tea was more within our custom, and I had demanded tea every afternoon at a precise time in order to assert control of all details.

It started to rain again, not heavy, but sullen. I opened my office door, and my secretary jumped to his feet. "I'm leaving for the day."

"I'll call your car."

"No. I'll walk."

He was already taking my coat from the hanger and holding it for me. I picked up an umbrella and walked toward the door. "What shall I do with…?" he asked. He trailed off when I glanced at him.

"Make excuses," I said, and as I left, added, "Call the Princess and tell her I have a meeting. She and the children should have dinner without me."

I could not believe the blue-eyed girl had told her husband anything even close to the truth about our relationship. A man could fuck anyone, but no man would ever have children with a woman who had not been a virgin unless she tricked him. If he did not control all of her, how else could he be certain his children were his?

I bought a copy of the *Tribune* in the lobby and walked toward the lake. The weather page predicted 80° in Los Angeles, and I imagined her standing in her California kitchen.

While we were students at Penn, she did everything possible to avoid me on campus. Yet a few months after I left, she met openly with Wahiib every Wednesday, and she had introduced her husband to Wahiib when Wahiib got his honorary doctorate at Penn.

I pondered these opposite approaches and decided the explanation was obvious. She and Wahiib were friends. The blue-eyed girl and I were lovers. No matter how she tried, she could never disguise the intensity of the mutual attraction between us. At Penn, she had to hide the intensity of our relationship to fit in with ordinary students, and she hid me from her husband for the same reason. It would be impossible to introduce her husband to a man who had already performed a husband's role in her life, and she could not risk that her David might realize she had tricked him.

I wished I could discuss this with someone. Wahiib and Jabir knew the blue-eyed girl, but they would tell me to stop thinking about her. I consoled myself with the thought that on the days I was annoyed at my wife, or jealous of Wahiib, or too tired to walk from the consulate to our condominium, I could smile at my memories of the blue-eyed girl.

I walked home. My mistake was I thought I'd never hear from her again.

# VI. VICTORIES

As we left the kids' school program, David asked, "What happened to your hand?"

"I fumbled the cup you gave me as I was getting off the phone. The one from Homburg."

"Ouch! Bad news?"

"Sort of..." After he'd backed out of the parking space, I explained, "Sayiid called this afternoon."

"God. You all right?"

"Yeah. He wanted us to visit him in Chicago."

"That's real balls."

"I didn't lose my cool, but I told him to leave me alone."

We talked about how to stop his calls, but there really wasn't anything I could do. "His government wouldn't care. They'd just think it was funny," I said. "Besides, he's a diplomat. They can get away with murder, literally."

We got home and found that Freddy had left a message on the machine that he'd taken Mom to the hospital. When

I called back, he was barely holding it together. "I went by the house and found her collapsed in a chair," he said. "They want to operate on her tomorrow."

"Okay. Okay," I said. It was like the Poison Control hotline. Get him to slow down so you can figure out how to help. "Start at the top. What happened?"

"She broke her arm. They want to do surgery tomorrow. I told them I had to talk to you."

I looked at the clock. There was time to catch the red-eye. I used my cell phone to book a flight as David drove me to LAX.

I left my bag at home and walked over to the hospital. Mom's arm was twice normal size, and the bruise made it look like she'd been beaten.

"Honestly, I just stumbled," she told me, "and when I caught myself, it popped. It wasn't even that much of a fall."

"Sometimes you just hit it the wrong way."

The surgeon, who looked right out of high school, came by before they took Mom in. "I think you have what's called a pathologic fracture." She paused looking at me. "The bone was weak before you fell. We think it might be cancer in the bone." I knew how serious it was because she'd already consulted other doctors.

Mom looked overwhelmed. To take the doctor's attention from her, I asked, "How'd she get bone cancer?"

"Not bone cancer *per se*. We think it started somewhere else and spread to her arm." The doctor was clearly happier talking to me.

"How can you be certain?"

"There are tests that we'll be doing after her surgery."

"Why run ahead with surgery when you don't know?"

"We don't know *why* for sure, but we do know *what* is going on in your mother's arm. It broke because there isn't any normal bone left." She put the tips of the fingers of her two hands together and moved them back and forth like a hinge. "Your mom's arm wiggles like this. We're lucky so far the ends are together." She slid her fingertips over each other. "If they slip off like this, it'll hurt a lot more and also be harder to do anything for her."

The doctor lingered while the nurse checked Mom's wristband, and an orderly wheeled her down the hall. When they were out of earshot, she turned to me. "When I examined your mom, I found a big mass in her breast. Maybe four inches." She stretched her finger and thumb apart to demonstrate the size. "I think that's where it came from."

I went home after Mom got out of recovery. In the morning, I looked around the house with the sense that everything was about to be my responsibility. I put water on to boil. Mom had switched to coffee when she started hanging out with Kaye Hartwood, and I had to search for a tea bag.

As I poked through stuff in the cupboard, like olive oil that she never used except when I was there, I saw the bright yellow tin of mustard powder, her secret ingredient in beef Stroganoff. Out of curiosity, I opened the tin, wet my finger, and tapped a taste on my tongue.

My mouth filled with saliva before I could spit into the sink, and I had to rinse with several glasses of water to get the burning to stop. The odd thing was that by the time I walked over to the hospital, I only had an abstract memory that even a little touch of mustard burned so horribly.

Pain is like that. The mind is merciful, and pain becomes just an abstract idea until you feel that same pain again. Then you remember why it affected you so much. I understood why I feared making my mom angry when I felt the pain of the mustard again. Sayiid was like that, too. I didn't see how much I was afraid of him until I felt the pain again.

Mom was defensive, like she'd made a mistake. "My breast started feeling different, but it wasn't like the nurse shows you in one of those plastic breast things. I thought it was nothing."

"What'd it feel like, Mom?"

She got an embarrassed grin on her face. "Promise you won't laugh?"

I was near to crying. "No, I won't laugh."

"I'd say it feels like a steak."

"A steak?"

"A frozen steak, when it's nearly thawed out." She put her hand on her good breast. "Feel this one. It mushes like a raw steak."

I touched her tentatively. "Yes, kind of…"

"Feel the other one." She put my hand on the mass. "It feels like a frozen steak."

"I see," was all I could manage because I shivered to think of her skin being that cold.

"It's metastatic breast cancer," the oncologist began.

Mom's arm had felt better almost immediately, thanks to the drugs and the surgery, and they'd discharged her the next day. Over the next three days, we walked to the hospital for a mammogram, a bone scan, and a PET/CT. The oncologist who'd taken over from the surgeon paused to look at something in his chart as though deciding whether to use it to make his point, or to spare us the visuals. I was glad when he closed the folder.

"The scan shows lesions in your back, your ribs." He made muted gestures to point around her body. "This arm of course, and your right hip. In addition, the PET/CT shows, lights up, almost your entire left breast."

"How'd it get so big?" I asked.

"Sometime things sneak up on us."

"Would a mammogram have shown this?"

"Probably. Maybe a year or so ago."

Mom's mammogram showed calcifications, little white spots, through most of her breast. Some of them would have shown up years ago, but her primary doctor followed national guidelines and stopped screening when she was in her 70s. I wanted to scream, but I didn't. This man hadn't made the decisions. They'd been made in Washington and by insurance companies.

"The difficult decision is whether to do anything for the breast where the cancer began," he continued. "It's a little like locking the barn after the horse is out, but if we leave it, more cancer can spread from there. And there's some data that breast tissue itself can make hormones."

"I went through the change years ago," Mom put in.

He turned to her. "Yes, but there're enzymes in the breast that can make hormones from chemicals that are normally in your body."

Mom had a simple mastectomy to remove the cancer, and radiation to her arm and her hip. The night before the surgery, we looked at old family albums from Valentine and the apartment near 39th Street. Dad was so jaunty with his cigar, and I remembered how I wanted to be pretty like Mom. The last album was pictures of David and me and our kids.

"You should take this one back to California with you," Mom said, before we got even a few pages into it. "You can never have too many pictures of your kids."

"That's all right," I said. I didn't want to start breaking up her house.

"No, take it." She pointed to the framed pictures on the mantel. There were of all my children. Freddy, too, but only as a child and in high school. Mom used her walker to get over to the mantel. "I've got these."

She was out of the hospital in two days and started a drug that made her hands feel stiff. I encouraged her to take the pills anyway and told her, "I think you should come to LA and live with me."

"But I live in Kansas City, and Freddy's here," she protested.

"I know, but I think I'll do a better job of taking care of you."

"But who'll watch out for Freddy?"

"That's my point, mom. Freddy needs to take care of himself now, and you need to be where I can help you."

"Let me think about it."

I carried the album of my family in my shoulder bag for the flight back to LA. When I unpacked at home, I set it on the kitchen counter. David leafed through the first pages. "What's this?" he asked.

I told him.

"Boy, these take me back," He carried it to the breakfast table.

I'd been gone for nearly a month, and I was grateful he'd driven to LAX to pick me up despite rush hour traffic. I put water on to boil for tea and enjoyed being in my own home, even though I felt guilty about leaving mom.

"Oops!" David said as some loose photographs fell from inside the back cover. He picked them up and looked at one. "Is this that couple your dad helped open a taco stand?"

I looked over his shoulder and wished I'd left the album in Kansas City. In the picture, a man posed with a woman and two, I supposed, teenage children. He was fatter and older, but I said, "That's not Maria's family. That's Sayiid."

We both stared at the portrait, but David spoke first. "That's some pretty definite body language. She's leaning toward him, but look at his grip on the back of the chair. He doesn't even touch her."

I studied this glimpse of Sayiid's wife. "She has a hard life."

Our son had come in to welcome me. "Who's Sayiid?" he asked.

I tried to lighten the conversation. "He was one of the international students at Penn. Remember Wahiib, who got an honorary degree with me at Penn a couple of years ago? Sayiid was Wahiib's roommate."

"Yeah." He nodded. David and I exchanged glances. I didn't want to explain this to my son.

"Hey, mom. Is this you?" He'd found a picture from the modeling tryout. "Heels and a bathing suit. You're pretty hot." He read what I'd written on it aloud. "To Granddad. Your granddaughter.' Wow. Who's that? Grandpa's father?"

David looked at the picture. "That'd brighten his day."

They were judging me. "I tried out to be a model. Okay?" I snapped. "It was a way out of Westport."

"And the pinup for Great Granddad?" my son asked.

"It was the picture I had. But I never sent it. See, it's still here."

David got a tea bag. Our son went on to other things. I marveled that David looked at the portrait of Sayiid and thought he was a taco-peddler, and there was more. I could see how inappropriate it was that I'd signed the modeling photograph for my grandfather. Skip the issue that it was the only picture I had, it was uncomfortable even to think of giving your grandfather a picture in a swimsuit and heels. And I made the comparison that when our daughter dropped by our house, David held our granddaughter on his knee with his hand wrapped around her waist, not in her lap. I could tell she was very safe with David, but I didn't know where else to go with that thought.

I flew to Kansas City every other weekend. David and I had no time alone except when we were asleep. I was wiped out when I went to Sarah for my annual exam.

The promise she extracted from me before she agreed to be my GYN was that I'd be treated like every other patient.

So as I dressed, she asked about David and said, "How's sex?"

I stumbled in my reply. "It's hard for him, uh…it's hard for him to have sex. I don't think he finds me exciting. Then I don't feel sexy, and I get dry. That makes it worse."

She looked up from my chart. "Do you think he's… again?"

"Not really." I checked that answer in my mind. "He's home almost every night by 6:30 or 7:00. No funny phone calls."

Sarah nodded to let me keep talking.

"I'm in Kansas City half the time. We never do anything. He watched his parents die, my dad, and now my mom. He looks at the calendar like he's planning his life, and he's running out of time to get everything done."

"As in getting things done in life, you mean?"

"Yeah, kind of like that."

Sarah was invaluable at Planned Parenthood because she thought in ways that were different from what you'd expect. And that made her a great doctor. "You might try something different. Get him interested, physically."

"What? A see-through nightie or something?"

She didn't rise to my joke. "You talked about what he does. What do you do?"

"I listen to him. I'm supportive. I love David."

"Of course you do. David's a great guy," she said. "But do you ever give him an opportunity to respond to you? Take a chance on yourself?"

"What'd you mean?"

"Men are pretty simple. Trust me, at the end of the day, they like surprises." Sarah was explicit. I took notes on an envelope so she'd think I was going to try what she suggested.

"I don't think I'd know when to try something like that," I said.

"Trust me. You'll know when."

One of the weekends I was in Kansas City, a postcard reminder came that my 35th Penn reunion was just two weeks away. Months earlier, I'd trashed the envelope with its invitations and forms to brag about my life. But David saw the card, and he convinced me we should go. I'd be in Kansas City to see my mom anyway.

At the reception, I dutifully put on a nametag and took a glass of wine. I didn't recognize anyone, and it was about to be a redo of my 10th reunion that'd been such a bad experience I'd sworn I'd never go to another one.

Then David started talking to a random classmate who volunteered out of the blue that Notpu's English class was the craziest conglomeration of ideas about writing, grammar, or anything else she'd ever seen. Thirty years later, it still bothered her that she switched majors from English to sociology after his class. I felt validated in a way, but the pain of isolation roared back when we realized we were both in Professor Baker's classes at the same time, and she kept saying, "I can't believe you don't seem the least bit familiar."

"See. You weren't wrong about your English class after all," David whispered as we drifted on through the crowd.

As we talked, a guy stood in front of me, checked my nametag, and asked, "That's you, isn't it?" He held his nametag up for me to see. "David. David from freshman English. Remember me?"

There were some familiar features. "I think you..." I began cautiously. I didn't want him kissing me like some long lost boyfriend.

He immediately launched into the story of the backwards dance that I had asked him to go to, and then backed out.

"You're that David?" I was astounded.

"You know, I never understood what happened. I thought I'd done something to upset you, and I couldn't guess what."

He turned to David, "This your husband? Lucky guy."

"She asked me to this dance where girls ask the guys," he explained to David. "I was excited, and then she called and said she couldn't go. I ended up going with this girl, Patty. What a—pardon my French—b-i-t-c-h!"

He kept talking. "You know she was this off-the-wall kind of girl." He gestured to be certain that David knew he was talking about me. "Not wild like loose or anything, but willing to try different things.

"One time she got this wild hair to go up to a coffee shop and listen to some guy read poetry. I had a car, and we raced up there and back on a school night." He smiled at me. "Barely got you back on time. You haven't been to many reunions, have you?"

"No," I replied, "This is my first."

"You sure? I thought I saw you at one about twenty years ago. You were gone before I could talk to you. You weren't there twenty minutes."

"Well, I came to one after David and I got married. But we left."

"I knew it, and boy, do I understand feeling out of it. It's the society thing. They get in their little groups and stand in the center. The rest of us stand around the edges, and we don't know how many we are unless we go looking. There's more of us than them, you know?"

On the way back to my mom's I commented, "That was weird."

"What's weird?" David asked.

"That guy, David. That stuff about the backwards dance, and knowing we'd come to one reunion twenty years ago and left right away. There was never anything between us. You can be sure of that."

"You know what he asked me?" David asked. "How

long we'd been married. When I told him thirty years, he said something like, 'She sort of takes over situations, but she's not bad in what she wants.'"

He looked at me to see if "takes over" would get a reaction. I scowled to pretend he'd offended me

"Then he said 'taking over' wasn't quite the right word. It was more like you could talk him into anything. What were his exact words? 'The kind of girl you wanted to like you.' Any guy would be happy with you. You're 'energetic...alive...' Oh, and he told me again about going to the coffee house." David was trying to get a reaction out of me, and I was determined that he wouldn't. "He said he never even kissed you, but he definitely regretted that."

"That'd never have gone anywhere. Not my type."

"I don't know." David acted like he was teasing, but I know when his teasing is serious. "I think it's pretty simple."

"What's simple?"

"He's thought about you all these years. You just confirmed what he's remembered, and he's happy because you're as special as he thought. You may think there was nothing between you, but that's not his memory." David checked both ways at a stop sign. "And he knows he shouldn't have let you uninvite him."

It took me a few days to realize what a gift that conversation was. I couldn't have convinced myself in a million years that I'd ever been the person David—either David—described. Yet here was a guy I hadn't talked to since my sophomore year at Penn who got excited as he described exactly the person I'd always wanted to be. Before I met Sayiid, I was who I wanted to be.

Eventually, I told David I'd been thinking this. He was matter of fact. "You're getting it. No one could fabricate a memory like that."

Sarah asked me to lunch the next Saturday. In the morning, my daughter dropped by with our granddaughter. She'd called to say she was coming, so I was in the kitchen slicing apples when they arrived. My granddaughter ran across the kitchen and hugged my leg as high as a two and a half year old could. She stepped back and started dancing around like I was supposed to notice something special, so I set my knife on the chopping block and tried to figure out what was different.

It was a game we'd played before. A new dress? No. New shoes? No. A haircut? No.

She started brushing her skirt with her hands, but I didn't understand the clue until she flipped her skirt higher and I saw her underpants. No more training pants. She was wearing big girl underwear. "Oh, my goodness," I exclaimed. "Such a big girl."

She beamed, proud of this milestone in her life. "You're so grown up," I said as I kneeled to give her a hug. She didn't say anything, but she put her arms around my neck and hugged me as hard as she could. "I bet Mommy's very proud of you," I said as I smiled at my daughter.

When I got to the restaurant, Sarah was sipping a glass of wine by the far window, and waiters were clearing salads and plates from the first seating. As the hostess led me between tables, I made mental notes of the most appealing desserts being served to those who'd finished their meal.

"So how was the reunion for the girl who didn't want to go?" she asked.

"I must admit I'm glad I went. I ran into this guy from my class. Actually, he found me. He looked for me."

"Ah. An old beau?"

"Not like that. You remember the backwards dance?"

"Do I ever. Anxiety city in spades."

"Well, it's too long to explain all of it, but I'd asked him and then I couldn't go and he's been looking for me ever since."

"Is he good looking?" Sarah joked.

"Not bad." We made other small talk and a glass of wine later, conversation got around to the office. "I get no respect from those kids," I said facetiously, "No respect at all."

"Oh, dear," Sarah replied in mock horror, "What's happened now?"

"Someone posted this cartoon strip in the coffee room. These kids are looking at old photos of their mom and say, 'Hey mom, you were pretty hot.' And the mom replies, 'I'm still hot, only now I'm hot in flashes.'"

We laughed together, and Sarah agreed, "No respect. Wait 'til they get where we are. Then see who's laughing."

I added words we've all said. "You know, getting old sucks without them rubbing it in."

"It sure beats the alternative."

"Yeah, but there are all the moods, and being dry when you don't want to be."

"Un huh." Sarah lifted her wine glass.

"And getting wet when you don't want." I faked a cough.

That made her laugh, and she looked at me over her glasses. "We have an operation to fix that, you know."

I rubbed my fingers like I was feeling money. "You doctors are all alike."

She changed the subject. "How's the new director working out?"

Sarah had rotated off the board of Planned Parenthood, so I didn't need to watch what I said with her now. "She's okay, but she's changed the soul of the place," I said. "It's weird having a number counter running what should be a people business."

"You'd have been the better person. It was AC who

screwed you with the board, did you know?"

"No, I didn't. What do you mean?"

"It was kind of weird. Out of the blue he made a big deal about how you were director of counseling services but didn't even have a counseling degree. It was like he took it personally. Almost like he was a jilted lover." She looked at me mischievously, "You keeping any secrets from me?"

I made a sour face and shook my head, but I immediately knew he'd waited for this opportunity ever since I hadn't played along with him at the board retreat. "Payback," I said.

My comment was so unexpected that Sarah echoed, "Payback?"

I'd wanted to forget that day forever, but suddenly I felt like talking. I told her about the elevator, and how he tried to get me to go out for drinks. "I couldn't think of any way to tell anyone that wouldn't sound like I'd led him on."

"What a sleaze," she said.

As the waiter set seafood risotto in front of me, I glanced across the room and saw a little girl getting out of a booth with her family. She couldn't have been more than three. She wiggled to the edge of the seat and slid off the cushion, using her hands to keep from falling. As she edged her feet to the floor, her skirt pulled up and her polka dotted underpants showed. I thought of my granddaughter's pride. "Funny," I said to Sarah, "how pleased little girls are when they're out of training pants."

She cut a bite of salmon. "Well, we all end up in pads again when we're older." She was the doctor again. "Something always leaks."

"No, I'm serious. It's a big thing for a little girl. When she's learned to control herself, her parents turn the responsibility over to her. We forget what that feels like to a child. It's the first big thing she learns—more personal than her alphabet or counting to ten."

"What are you talking about?" Sarah asked between bites.

"Taking care of herself..." Suddenly I felt like the faces of AC and the little girl and Sayiid were spinning around me, and I panicked.

The waiter pretended not to notice. Sarah put her glass down and asked, "You all right?"

I looked at her and forced a smile.

Sarah asked again, "What's wrong? Can I help?"

I shook my head and held my breath for fear I'd scream if I let out any air at all. I waved her off to give me a moment. When I thought I had some control, I replied holding myself tightly, "I'm okay."

I felt pressured to give an answer, any answer. My eye caught the little girl smoothing her skirt and taking her father's hand as they passed us. I nodded toward the girl and said to Sarah, "The little girl. I saw her getting out of the booth. Her dress pulled up, and I could see her panties."

"And?" Sarah listened intently.

I wiped the mascara running down my cheek with my napkin. "It reminded me of my granddaughter. One moment they're in diapers, and the next day they're out of training pants and taking care of themselves."

Sarah believed me for a moment. "Yeah, for pee and poop, anyway. That works 'til they grow up, have, kids and start coughing." She lifted her glass in a mock toast. "To The Change."

I tried to laugh, but my effort went awry and I started to sob. "Excuse me..." was all I could say as I jumped up.

The woman at the next table realized I was leaving too fast to be okay. I bumped past a waiter who thought I was going to get sick and tried to direct me to the ladies room. But I needed air. The parking attendant recognized me and started to get my key, but I could see my car across the lot.

"Do you have your check, mam?" he asked as I rushed past him.

I didn't reply. I fumbled in my purse as I ran. He had the valet key. I had the real key. But there was too much junk, and my hand couldn't recognize the key as I rummaged in my purse in the shadow between two cars. I dumped it on the ground and started tossing things around.

Then Sarah was kneeling beside me as she put her arm around my shoulder.

"My key. It's here," I said, down on all fours. "I know it's somewhere. I had both sets of keys with me."

Calmly, Sarah picked up the keys. "Here they are." She coaxed me to stand up and faced me with her hands on my shoulders. "Whatever's wrong, I'll help you."

I must have ruined her silk blouse crying on her shoulder, but she waited until I was ready. Finally, I straightened up and took half a step back. "I was raped in college, at Penn," I began. "One of the Arab students. Then he wouldn't let go. It was like I was corralled or something. I couldn't figure a way out. I went with him another year and a half."

I looked for disgust, some judgment in her eyes. Some, 'How could you be so stupid?' look, but I didn't see it. "I never realized what it did to me," I continued, "until I saw the little girl."

Sarah knew just the nod that didn't jump ahead to assume what I was trying to say.

"I was different after that, but it wasn't the sex. Everyone else was doing it. It was the 60s for god's sake. I've never told anyone but David. I told him when we first met. I used to taunt him that I wished I could've fucked every guy I dated, and then it wouldn't bother me so much.

"When I saw the little girl, I finally got it. It wasn't the cherry thing. It was the little girl in me who got lost. She was so proud. It was pride as in self-respect.

"One minute I controlled me, and the next I didn't. Rape kills the girl who's trying to grow up. That part of me has been stuck ever since. He made me like a child who isn't even potty trained." I tried to be sarcastic to regain my composure. "Yeah, I'm so sophisticated, and I work with all you doctors and business people. I look like I've got it together. But I don't!

"He destroyed my faith in me. You can't fight when you can't even be responsible for your own body. He took *me* away from me. He took away any joy in what my body could do. Gone! *Nada!*"

Sarah let me go on until she was certain I'd said all I was going to say, then touched my arm to tell me she was still my friend. "I had no idea. There isn't anything clever to say except that's a lot to carry around."

"All I want is to run away from it all. I worry this'll happen to my granddaughter, and it terrifies me."

I started going to Kansas City every week. Mom still lived at home. She had physical therapy from visiting nurses. Freddy came over every day, but she was getting weaker, and I needed to be there. I usually stayed for her doctors' appointments on Monday and caught the evening flight home.

Mom didn't have the strength to walk back if we went down the hill to the Plaza, so we walked on the level streets by our house. She talked about Valentine and dates with my dad during the war—dancing, roller-skating, swimming—but there were silences when she didn't share everything she was thinking. I got the impression she was telling me they were sleeping together, but I never asked directly. It was wartime. Everyone's life was different, like those of the girls in my study whose boyfriends were going off to Vietnam. Besides, I was a parent now, and my kids would think it was quaint if any woman had qualms about sleeping with a guy she was dating seriously.

Mom's was the last generation before birth control pills gave girls freedom to explore sex like guys had been doing for ages. She taught me that being a virgin made a difference, and because she'd taught me, I couldn't quite get over the feeling that it did. As she talked about herself and Dad, it seemed this was the only time I had left to admit to her how much I'd failed to live up to her values.

"Remember that guy Sayiid?" I asked her.

"Yes, I do. He hasn't called for a long time."

"Mom," I took a deep breath, "Sayiid took advantage of me when I was at Penn." I let that sink in so she'd have a moment to be certain she understood me. "I thought I could trust him, but obviously I couldn't."

We were both silent for several minutes. "I had no idea," she said finally, "not at all. And I talked to him all those times and told you he'd called to say hello." Her face showed pain. "I feel so bad."

"Don't, Mom. You had no way to know."

"Did you ever tell anyone?"

"Who would I tell? I couldn't tell you, because you couldn't tell Dad. He'd have gotten really upset. You know that. I felt I'd disappointed you, and I couldn't make it better anyway."

"Why'd you go with him after that?"

"He wouldn't let go. He made a scene every time I tried to get away. You know how people gossip if they get their hands on anything like that. I wasn't strong enough to face that. That's why I came home all those weekends. I had to get away as much as I could."

"And his friend, the Ambassador? You wanted us to meet him."

"Wahiib? He's a good person. Until I got on the swim team, he was the only person who talked to me. Did I ever tell you that he's the one who pushed me to try out? That's why I don't hate all Arabs. Some of them are real bastards, but some of them are like Wahiib."

"Does David...?"

"Yes." I had my own sad thoughts for a moment. "I told him about Sayiid almost as soon as I met him. I couldn't leave that loose end."

We talked longer than usual, and I almost missed my flight. I had a window seat and watched the lights of small towns become farther and farther apart as the plane flew west. And I began to think about what I'd told mom.

I realized that I trusted guys who were self-assured because they reminded me of my dad, and I desperately wanted to believe that I could trust my dad to do the right thing for me. David was one guy I could trust, but I didn't always trust him because he wasn't as self-assured as my dad and I didn't trust myself to recognize a good relationship. And I thought about trust itself.

There were a lot of people I couldn't trust. I couldn't trust my dad to be sober. I couldn't trust him to spend money to feed me instead of on his Cadillacs. I couldn't trust my mom not to hurt me when she was angry at Dad. I couldn't trust my grandfather to do things I could tell my mom about. I couldn't trust Harry to tell the truth about me. I couldn't trust Sayiid.

It dawned on me that I got into the situation with Sayiid because I couldn't trust the professors at Penn College to give me good advice. Dr. Bauer and Dr. Forger encouraged us to socialize with guys whose culture taught them that a girl by herself was fair game. Were they so naïve they didn't anticipate how vulnerable I'd be, or did they even care?

I understood that I'd never trust David to stay with me through anything if I didn't trust him to know all of me. So when we got up the next morning, I asked David to call in to the office that he'd be late and to come back after he took our youngest to school.

I made coffee, we sat in our sunroom, and I told him everything about Sayiid. There were things I'd told him before, and things I'd never told him. I needed to put everything together. Everything. I told him about having the first drink of my life. I told him about watching television and wiping the floor. I told him the details of being stalked at Penn and how I gave in to keep Sayiid away from me on campus.

I wasn't confessing. I didn't want forgiveness from David. I needed someone I trusted to listen to me. At Penn, I hadn't trusted that I could take care of myself if I said anything about what Sayiid had done. Telling David was a belated step to trust that I could tell the truth and rely on myself to get myself through whatever might happen next.

David took a legal pad out of his briefcase and took notes when he realized I had a lot to say. I wondered if he'd cross-examine me to try to get more details, but he just didn't want to lose track of what I said.

"You were set up, you know?" he said when I finished.

"How can you say that?"

"You don't see it, do you?" He patted my hand, not to be condescending, but to reassure me. "It's all about bragging. No guy wants to get caught struggling with a girl on the floor of his apartment. He doesn't care about the girl, but if she's fighting him off, he isn't much of a lover after all. He'd only try that if he was certain no one was going to walk in. You can bet he had it all set up."

"David," I said, "I know you're trying to be kind, but I don't know if I can believe that."

"There's a legal definition of rape that's been on the books since the 1920s, '...by force, fear, or fraud.'"

"But I went to his apartment. I was there. He didn't force me to be there."

"I hear your doubts," he continued, "but I know you.

You wouldn't run away unless you were really hurt. I believe in you more than you do."

It was six months before Mom agreed to come live with us in San Marino. In the middle of all this, America went to war. I wasn't surprised by 9-11. I knew how callous an Arab could be. Like most Americans, I was anxious for our safety, and I was anxious for the mothers of the men and women who went to Afghanistan and then Iraq.

In the coffee room at work, women discussed an article in the *New Yorker* about an Egyptian named Q'tub who'd been executed in the 1960s. "This guy called American women disgusting for wearing shorts," said an administrative assistant.

"Makes you wonder if that's how he feels about all women," said another.

"Oh," I added with an air of authority, "I think you can assume he felt that way about any woman who wasn't wrapped up in a black tent."

"You sound like you know."

"Let's say a friend of mine found out the hard way," I told them.

The room got awkward as though I'd tried to tell a dirty joke.

"Well, he says women arouse his lust," another woman put in to lighten the mood. "I wonder what he does with his lust when he wakes up in bed by himself." We all laughed, but I marveled at how close I'd come to telling these women how I knew about Arab men, or at least one Arab man. For some reason I wasn't as worried about being embarrassed.

I went to Kansas City to bring Mom back to California. Freddy wanted to have dinner with her alone before she left, so I had some free time and decided to drive out to Penn. I'd only been to the new auditorium when I got my alumni award, and the formal dinner had been downtown.

I got there at dinnertime, and students were gathering at the union. The building had a new wing, but it was recognizable if you looked at its setting between the older classrooms. I saw on a sign that Lorel was Athletic Director at the new gym and was surprised she was still around. I wandered to the parking lot on the far side of the campus and then went back to the student union and ordered a hamburger and Coke.

It was nearly dark when I parked in front of Sayiid's old apartment to see what I'd feel if I was at that spot again. It was a 1950s building that always seemed like it was supposed to be a motel because the doors opened directly into outdoor hallways, even in winter. I couldn't recall if his apartment was the second or the third door on the second level.

The streetlights came on. I got out of the car and walked toward campus. There were unfamiliar buildings, a small cottage and a church, for example, that were so old they must have been there all the time, but I didn't have the vaguest memory of them. I thought to myself, *You have no memory of this. Maybe your mind is playing tricks, and you weren't ever here. Maybe the whole thing's a bad dream.*

Then my foot caught where the sidewalk had been cracked by a root. I wasn't walking fast, and I made a reflexive effort to dash forward into a stumble so that I wouldn't fall on my face. But I was off balance and ran into the ground. My palm scraped on the sidewalk. Concrete ground through my trousers into my knee. And pain instantly took me back to how terrified I was of Sayiid.

I couldn't make out leaves in the darkness, but from the ground, I saw this place as it'd been seen by a panicked nineteen-year-old. The same two concrete post streetlights lit the boundaries of the shadow where I'd missed the crack. Buildings came alive with crisp shadows, like I'd been looking at them only a moment ago. I remembered the burning between my legs and looked back, but no one was following me.

I couldn't see the sidewalk for my tears and the darkness. I had to get up and run.

I sat in the car and cried until my eyes hurt. Why'd he choose me? Convenience? To prove he could?

When I could stop crying, I called David on my cell. "Honey, I'm so lucky we have each other."

"I'm lucky to have you," he said, but he sensed more in my voice, "Are you okay? Where are you?"

"I'm at Penn. No," I corrected myself, "actually, I'm looking at Sayiid's old apartment. I had to hear your voice to feel safe."

I walked across to where Sayiid had always parked his car, and spit on his place. Then I drove toward the campus until I found the place where I'd tripped. A stump was all that was left from the tree that'd cracked the sidewalk. I wondered what insight I'd have missed if the sidewalk had been repaired, and I had walked back to the campus uneventfully.

My timing was fortunate. They removed the stump and repaved that sidewalk right after I was there.

Metastatic breast cancer is a journey. Along the way you meet Vicodin and constipation. Then you add Dilaudid and Colace. When you need too many Dilaudids, you put on a fentanyl patch so you have a level of the drug all the time, and you reserve the Dilaudid for breakthrough pain. All along, you need Metamucil to keep having bowel movements, but you feel bloated most of the time and that kills your appetite. Then you need two fentanyl patches and they add morphine syrup someone squirts in the corner of your mouth with a syringe, slowly so you won't choke on it.

When Mom couldn't bathe herself, I tried to care for her, but she was embarrassed by me doing her personal care. So we added full-time staff to clean and bathe her. Eventually, David suggested I'd done enough, and that Mom needed more care than was reasonable at home. It was happening in front of my eyes, but it wasn't happening quickly.

I felt guilty the first night she stayed in the care home. Before I left, she held my hand. "You've done a lot for me. I need to have these people now. I know that." She held my hand to her cheek. "I'm so proud of you. You've done a great job. You and David have made a great home and raised four great kids."

I was teary-eyed big time.

"And," she continued, "I'm proud of what you've done with Planned Parenthood. Women have rights, and sometimes people don't give 'em to them."

Mom died in February. She wanted to be buried beside my dad in Valentine. The ground was frozen that time of year, so Freddy and I had a brief service right away and put off the trip to Valentine until late May. That would be easier for my kids to schedule anyway. Hospice found an undertaker who'd put everything on hold for three months.

In May, they told us how to arrange to fly Mom home. Trees in Valentine had started to bud, but they needed a backhoe to dig through the first couple inches of frozen dirt. The dirt underground is always warmer, even in the coldest winter.

Not many people remembered my mom. Jamie showed up with her husband and her granddaughter, who was already in grade school. Harry's widow surprised me. They had a son who'd moved to Omaha, but she liked Valentine, and she came, I think, to see what I was like. We'd never met, because she didn't move to Valentine until she and Harry were married. I told her tales of Harry leading us to jump in the river and finding a dead body, though I felt disrespectful as I turned that tragedy into an anecdote. I was happy that she and Harry had met. If I lived in Valentine, I think she would've been a good friend.

Our kids came in from all over, but they had to get back to work, or school in the case of our youngest. David and I stayed at the Best Western for a couple of days after the service.

It was warm enough to walk around town in the early evening. When you go someplace familiar, sometimes it's the sights you never thought about that catch your eye. There was still a red heart painted in the middle of the biggest intersection, and at night you could see the new neon heart at the north end of the street. But the real familiarity was the smell of dirt that'd been broken for planting on the fields with irrigation.

David took off two weeks to help me clean out Mom's house. Freddy wanted to keep it, and it wasn't worth a lot by San Marino standards, so I agreed to split our inheritance in a lopsided fashion so he could live there. We agreed that the difference would eventually be left to my children. That still left a lot of Mom and Dad's stuff to dispose of.

One of the first things we found in the attic crawl space was a couple of boxes of my stuff. My instinct was to put them unopened in the trash, but David was always an investigator. He'd won more than one case by "trawling," as he said, through piles of records to find the smoking gun he needed. He asked if he could look to see what was there, so I left that to him.

The boxes had the predictable ribbons from swimming, a class photograph from Swenney School, and some papers I'd written at Penn. Mom had added my baby book and my grade school and high school report cards with the teachers' comments. David read out loud a part where I talked too much in class. "I can believe that," he teased as I went back down the ladder.

He came down a few hours later and handed me some papers. "You might find these interesting." And I did.

Between notes from a class at Penn had been a statement from the Grandview Family Counseling Center. It was that thin, brittle yellowed paper, like the original fax paper where the paper itself had to be special to print on it. It listed a couple of months of groups. Each one was billed at $5.00 and someone had written "Pd" by each one. I knew how long it took to earn $5.00 in those days. That was more than my tips for an average night. I wouldn't have spent that money if I'd been happy.

In April 1968, I'd written a letter to Dianne about dating Karl to get away from Sayiid when he came back for grad school, but I never mailed it. It was tucked in a sociology folder, probably where I'd put it the same day.

There was another note to myself, like a diary entry, the day before my twenty-first birthday. "What will I ever do about Sayiid...I hope he meets someone else..."

What these notes proved was obvious. Even in the middle of my relationship with him, I didn't want to be with Sayiid. But what about the very first time? How could I ever know my state of mind when I went to his apartment? I wanted an untainted memory of how I felt that night, but there weren't any half-finished letters about that. That information came from an unexpected source.

Pam, my sophomore roommate, visited me in St. Louis right after I got my master's. After that we exchanged a few Christmas cards, but then the cards I sent came back, and we lost touch.

David still had cases in St. Louis, so we tied a business trip for him on to a weekend in Kansas City working on papers for Mom's estate. It was easier to drive to St. Louis than to fly. As we passed the Herman exit on I-70, I said, "I wonder what ever happened to Pam."

"Pam?" David asked.

"Pam. My roommate. She was from Herman."

"I went to the Oktober Fest in Herman before we met," he said.

"I haven't seen her since right after I moved to St. Louis." I added to tease him, "Before we met."

I watched farms fly by. "Her dad was an attorney. Pretty distinctive last name, Hofstein."

"*Eine Deutsche Freulein*," David joked, "but everyone in Herman is German."

I logged on to the Internet at our hotel and Googled "Hofstein attorney Herman Missouri." There was a woman attorney named Hofstein. There couldn't be two attorneys with that last name who weren't related.

The receptionist had only been working there two weeks and had no idea if Ms. Hofstein even had a sister, but she said she'd ask and call me back either way. I gave her my cell number.

Two hours later Pam called. She got my message from her sister. Distances weren't a big deal to her, and she volunteered to drive down to meet us at the Iron Barley, a funky place just off I-55 in South St. Louis.

Pam was quieter than I remembered. She talked about spiritual things, like crystals and how to harness power for your life.

"I'm trying to figure some things out," I said over Blender Blaster dessert. "Do you remember what I was like at Penn?"

"You were calm," she said. "You never got upset by anything. If things got confused, you tried to get everyone to be calm."

"Nothing else?" I asked.

"Not really." Then she started speaking as though another person had sat down at the table to recite something, a memory being played back on cue forty years later. "You dated this guy. His name was Sayiid." She kept going without prompting. "He pushed you into a bush... You were upset... You said you didn't like how he treated you...and you never wanted to go out with him again."

"No." I corrected her without pausing to think about what she'd said. "I dated him a year and a half before he graduated. I just kept it secret."

"I don't know about that," Pam replied, and she didn't seem convinced.

The waiter brought our check, and Pam excused herself to go to the ladies room. After she left the table, I turned to David. "What's the bush thing all about? I don't remember anything about a bush. Sayiid and I never went walking."

"Hmmm..." David responded absently as he checked items on our bill.

Suddenly it all fell into place. "I know when that was. Sayiid never pushed me into a bush. That's when I got raped."

David finally looked up from the check.

"I must have looked a mess, and I couldn't tell her what'd happened. I told her the first thing that came to my mind." I slowed a bit as my mind put it together. "After Christie being kicked out, there was no way I'd risk a rumor like that."

I couldn't believe I'd blurted out "rape" right there in the restaurant. But Pam had told me I was angry, at least until Sayiid showed up and started making a scene with his horn.

It was like easing a sleeve into a new jacket. You know when things fit together the right way. George, the psychiatrist-turned-lawyer who defended rapists, had it right. If I'd been willing, but then had second thoughts, I'd have gone for the big time and called it rape. But I wanted as little attention as possible. My sense of justice told me Sayiid had hurt me, but I was terrified to let that cat out of the bag. Yet despite my fear of being discovered, my whole attitude shouted the truth as much as I dared. "He didn't treat me right. I don't want to see him again."

"She specifically remembered you said you didn't like how he treated you," David said after Pam had left to drive home. "You know what the police call that, don't' you?"

"No."

"That's your 'outcry.'"

"What's that?"

"A guy who's accused of rape is always going to claim the sex was consensual. So the police look for the first thing a woman said to anyone...cab driver, roommate. That's her outcry. Before a woman's had a chance to make up a story. It's what she blurts out. 'Pushed into a bush' and 'never see him again' doesn't sound consensual to me. It's pretty clear what you felt at first. Everything after that was confusion and fear."

Cleaning out my parents' house took longer than expected, and David came back with me a couple months later to help me finish up.

There was always the question of the family photographs. Freddy wanted some of the pictures, but my brother wasn't too responsible, and I figured what he took was essentially lost.

The solution was that David bought a scanner on the Plaza, and I pointed out to Freddy that he could view digital pictures on his television.

There were some negatives in an envelope with photos of my grandfather. David matched most of the negatives with specific pictures because the car and a motorcycle Dad had for a while were easy to pair up, but there were a couple of negatives that didn't match any print. He scanned the negatives and inverted the image with Photoshop to make it a look like a print.

The face was unfamiliar to him. When he showed it to me, I knew who it was. "That's Sayiid."

David rescanned the negative at a higher resolution, and I realized from the Mobil gas flying horse patch on the sleeve that he'd found the negative of Sayiid at work. "What's the Mobil gas shirt about?" David asked.

"I thought I'd told you that story," I said. "It was this hush-hush, secret thing that I couldn't tell the other Arabs about. He got a job at a gas station."

David thought for a while. "That's your smoking gun, you know?"

"What do you mean?"

"Arabs don't pump gas. They sell it. It's an amazing come-down for him to pump gas and let you know it. There had to be a reason."

"I think he was trying to impress me."

"Or trying to apologize. Was this a way to try to make up to you?"

"I don't think so. I'd called him spoiled, and I think he was trying to show me he could work like I did."

"Either way. An Arab on his way to being a diplomat dirties his hands on a gas pump? I don't think so. Not without a big reason." David thought. "Looks like he was trying to convince you he was a regular guy or something."

"You lawyers," I said. "You should write a novel."

"Seriously," David continued, "he pumped gas for a reason. I've got to think about this."

In the movies, the heroine gets angry, toughens up, and kicks ass; but in real life, things unfold. We gradually see the truth, and then we slowly adjust our lives to what is true.

Without thinking about it, I changed the way I talked to people at work. I used words that were more specific. I didn't learn new words. I stopped being reluctant to use the words I already knew, and I said exactly what I meant. I trusted myself.

I was thinking these things when I got home early from work and decided to work out on my exercise bike. I rode until I was totally drenched in sweat, took a long shower and washed my hair. David came home while I was in the shower.

I wrapped myself in a towel and blew my hair dry. Then, as though it was the most natural thing, I undressed him and took him to the shower and washed him with the gentlest touch I could imagine. I led him to our bed and loved every part of his body, and when he was ready, I lay back and had him love me.

I'd always thought that during sex, the connection between our bodies made the love. This was different. I welcomed every part of him to make me feel good. For the first time I could remember, I let him see me enjoy everything he did for me. I didn't worry that because I'd had a horrible secret, he'd think I was cheap if I embraced the passion.

Afterwards we lay there until I started to feel cold and pulled up the blanket. David snuggled behind me and whispered in my ear, "Wow." And after a long pause, another, very soft, "Wow."

We fell asleep for an hour or so and then got up to make dinner. I patted his butt as we walked downstairs. He smiled and said, "Just don't tell my wife what we've been up to." I took it as the teasing he intended, and it was endearing in a way, but bittersweet. My happiness was unfamiliar, and it made me realize how I'd missed so much in my own life. I was glad that the person I was closest to was able to see how different I felt.

I was almost giggling when I had lunch with Sarah a couple days later.

"You told me I'd know when," I said barely able to

contain myself.

"When what?"

"When..." I gestured with both hands trying to coach her to remember our conversation as clearly as I did. "When..." I said impatiently.

It took her a few moments before she said, "Oh! When." She smiled. "That when?"

I relaxed. Sarah was as close to a therapist I'd ever had, and I'd met a challenge and felt better about myself than I had in years.

We talked a while, and then Sarah got serious. "I hesitate to bring this up—and if it bothers you, please forgive me and that'll be the end of it—but I had a patient last week who told me your story."

I was suddenly anxious. How did this woman know my story?

"Well, not your personal story. But the same story. And the weird thing is that it was her daughter going off to college that put her in a panic. I delivered her twenty years ago, I delivered her other two kids, I've done her Pap smear for years, and when her daughter goes to college she freaks out that the same thing will happen to her daughter. In twenty years she's never brought this up, ever."

I was catching on. "She was..." I forced my voice to be even. "She was date raped?"

Sarah nodded.

I volunteered something I didn't think was obvious to someone who hadn't been through it. "You know what the hardest part is? Realizing how rapists set these things up. Sayiid set me up, but I couldn't see that for years. It was so painful that I tried to pretend it didn't matter for a lot more than just twenty years. Sounds like she and I have that in common."

Sarah looked at me. "I know it might be an imposition,

but would you consider talking to her? I didn't tell her anything about you, but I did ask if she'd like to talk to someone who'd understand what she felt."

For a moment, I was an observer watching me discuss the most horrible secret I had, but I wasn't running away. I knew it was finally okay to stop hiding the fears that'd warped so much of my life.

"Sure," I answered. "I'd be happy to." After a pause to calm my mind as it threatened to whirl back into years of panic, pain, and fear, I added, "I think it'd help me feel better, too."

"Do you want me to come along?"

I thought about that one. "No. Thank you, but I think I'm ready to do this myself."

Sarah's other patient Diana and I met at a coffee shop near my office. We talked about where we grew up, our jobs (she was a branch manager at a bank), our kids (she had two in college) and our husbands (hers was a pediatrician). The chitchat went on until I said, "If someone knew why we were here and was listening to us, they'd have a good laugh. We've talked about everything else but."

Diana was coming to grips with how rape had shaped her life. To help her feel less alone, I told her what I'd learned about how Sayiid had set me up. She resisted believing that was anything more than a single event, so I told her about Karl, which got her attention more, and AC, which finally convinced her. "If I've learned one thing at Planned Parenthood," I said, "it's that some guys are nice and some guys are cruising to see what they can get. It's that simple, but it took me thirty years to see that."

"You feel...I feel like such a stupid loser," she replied.

"We all do. Guys depend on us feeling guilty to keep us silent."

"He tried to talk to me one time," Diana continued. "He said if he'd known I'd be so upset he wouldn't have done it. Such a piece of shit!"

Like my rape, her rape had lingered in her life. "You know how we're brought up. If something happened with a boy, it was our fault, and then the 60s took off and no one understood why we cared."

"Because it wasn't the sex," I said.

"What do you mean by that?"

Everything got clearer as I thought out loud. "Sex is way too obvious, but the people who say rape's about control aren't right either. It's really a man taking away a woman's right to choose. Not only choosing then—that'd be control—but believing she can make lifetime choices. Who can I be? What can I dare to do?"

I thought of my granddaughter for a moment. "You need control of yourself before you can grow up. A person who can't control their body gets stuck where they were when they flunked that step."

"I've been afraid to trust myself," Diana acknowledged.

"Be easy on yourself, at least you got away." I told her how Sayiid took over my life and called my mom asking questions about me for the next thirty years.

"He's a stalker," Diana said, without even thinking about it.

"Stalker?" I repeated. "I never thought of him as a third rate criminal."

"That's what he sounds like to me."

Diana's insight let me see Sayiid for who he really was, and became the final stitch to ease a new sleeve into my life. I hadn't done anything to deserve what he did to me, but my mind hadn't been able to transition directly from diplomat to rapist. It was too big a leap. Diplomat to stalker wasn't such a stretch. Once I saw that, I realized that despite his bravado, his cockiness, his ingratiating smile, even his diplomatic career, Sayiid was a common criminal.

A couple weeks later, Dianne joined Sarah and me for lunch. We'd discussed enough details about our experiences that we didn't need to go over them again, especially in public. But we talked about double standards and how no one ever criticizes what a guy does. "They just go on with their lives and feel so cocky about themselves. As long as they're in the middle of the party, life is good," Dianne said.

"What's that old line, 'I don't care what you say about me, as long as you spell my name right'?" Sarah asked. "They just want to be in the limelight."

"And spread some rumors if it makes them seem more important," added Dianne.

"That's what diplomats do, isn't it?" I said. Sarah and Diana looked at me. "It just came to me. That's what made Sayiid a diplomat. He was perfect for it. He does what he wants. And he's immune to anything I do."

Sarah completed my thought. "And diplomats are always talking about someone else and keeping their own secrets."

"And no one ever talks about them."

"Suppose." I was thinking out loud. "Just suppose..."

I'd always thought rape was the big secret between Sayiid and me, but it was my big secret. After David found the negative of Sayiid at the filling station, I realized the important secret for Sayiid was the filling station job that he'd taken to gain my approval. Sending me his family photograph might be seen as vanity by people who knew him, but a photo of him pumping gas would have to be explained.

The photo proves he had the job, and his friends and his government will wonder why a future diplomat soiled his hands that way. His diplomatic immunity can't stop other diplomats from talking about him. They will whisper for years to come.

I was tired of worrying that the horrible secret I'd kept could bust out any time and ruin my life. The most direct way to get past my anxiety was to face it, and that was in my hands if I made everything public.

I decided it was time for Sayiid to explain the filling station shirt to everyone who mattered to him. Let him explain why it was important to impress a woman by pumping gas. For good measure, I decided to give him the opportunity to explain why he'd sent me photos of himself and his family. I was sure he'd try to explain things very differently, but I'd lived with his lies so long, it was only fair for him to deal with the truth.

I typed a short note and made copies of the picture of him in the filling station shirt and the portrait with his family. Since I didn't have his address, I sent duplicates to his embassy and every consulate I could find on the Internet. Everyone who read this letter and saw these images would wonder what the real story was. People would compare notes. There'd be gossip, and he'd realize nothing was as easy as he thought.

> Sayiid,
> My husband found these pictures when we were cleaning out my mom's house. He knew my father helped a family start a taco stand and thought the portrait was from them. I had to tell him it was of you.
> I also thought you'd like to see the snapshot of you in the Mobil uniform to remind you of your job at the filling station. It's interesting how much these pictures reveal about you. Don't you agree?"

And I signed my name.

# Epilogue, Part I

After the girl from the Chicago consulate sought asylum, my relationship with Wahiib became noticeably uncomfortable. I called him with weekly reports, he visited twice a year, and I flew to Washington for major diplomatic events when it was appropriate to gather all of our senior representatives in America. But there were no jokes between us, and no discussion of anything other than official business. I am certain he would have replaced me if it was his decision, but my father-in-law used his political influence to prevent that. The Prince did not care what happened to me, but his daughter had made friends in midwestern society, and he did not want her to be embarrassed.

I was ready to get out of the diplomatic corps if I could find a way to stay in America. My goal was to live in New York City, so I settled on a plan for the Princess to ask her father if we could retire there in some part-time official capacity to retain our diplomatic status—without my having to do real work.

So that she'd come to think the move was her choice, I

initiated a campaign of trips to New York punctuated with museums, opera, shows, shopping, and parties. New York was not London, but Chicago was dull by comparison. After many comments about how exciting a place it was—and how it was closer to our children, who were in school in the American East—the Princess began to tell our friends in Chicago that she thought it would be exciting to live there. In the end, as though it was her own idea, she asked her father to help make our move possible.

I was vigorous. My hair was gray but very thick, and I looked much younger than most of my peers. I enjoyed the city. I enjoyed watching spring fashions on women. For that matter, I enjoyed watching women.

I had an office and a small staff at our embassy to the United Nations. I did not have much to do except circulate through the crowd at diplomatic events, and make small speeches that neither the Ambassador nor the Consul General wanted to make. The theme was always the same. "We are happy to do this in the name of our illustrious history...our friendship with the peoples of the United States," and platitudes like that.

In mid-April, about a year after we had settled into this life, I stopped by my office as I usually did once a week. My secretary seemed relieved to see me, and as soon as possible, he followed me into my office, stood by the door and asked, "May I close the door so we can talk privately?"

I had no idea what was on his mind, but he had been reliable up to this point, so I told him, "Certainly."

He handed me a large white envelope and said, "This arrived two days ago." It looked like a fairly typical mailing envelope, but it was marked "Personal/Confidential." As I turned it over in my hands, he added, "An envelope just like this was delivered to the Ambassador, and another one to the Consul General."

"Just like this."

"Yes, sir." He pointed. "It's the stamps. They had the same stamps." He pointed to a line of stamps of the American actor, John Wayne. "That is an old stamp. I noticed it right away."

There was no return address. The envelope was postmarked in Los Angeles. I wondered why he would notice a specific American stamp—perhaps he was a philatelist—but I thanked him and settled at my desk.

As he closed the door behind himself, I slit the fold of the envelope with an opener and had a feeling of déjà vu. For a moment I remembered my father nearly destroying the blue-eyed girl's diary, ripping pages as he read the words that disproved every claim I could make.

The first item in the envelope was a copy of the portrait of my family. Who would even have copy of that picture, and why would they send it back? Then I felt a shiver down my back as I remembered the print I had sent to the blue-eyed girl's mother. Perhaps the blue-eyed girl had found the picture and decided to return it. But I shrugged and told myself, "So what?" That was simply consistent with her refusal to visit us in Chicago.

I reached into the envelope for the note that was with the portrait. It was folded over a second photograph, and my mouth went dry when I saw my face at the gas station. Where had that come from? That photograph couldn't exist. I had ripped it into pieces. This was impossible, and the note started off talking about her David thinking my family portrait was of people who had owned a taco stand.

My throat constricted as though she had reached across time and space and grabbed my neck. The Mobil gas logo was clear on the sleeve of my shirt, and you could read the big sign for McCaully's Market that had run the gas station. I reminded myself again, "I destroyed this picture."

I laid the photographs on my desk and wondered if she knew how much these offerings of hers could embarrass me. Of course, she did. That had to be her intent, and if copies of these pictures were in the envelopes to the Ambassador and the Consul General too, I would have a lot to explain. But she failed to understand that would be the end of it. The Ambassador and Consul would ridicule me in private, but they knew better than to embarrass the King by circulating that kind of story about his diplomat, even his retired diplomat, who was also his relative by marriage.

I started to put the letter and the photographs in my desk but decided instead to shred them before I went home. I could not leave them around.

I slept poorly that night. For some reason the Princess wanted to lie close to me, so I had to go the guest room to get some rest. In the morning, I made coffee and logged on to check my email. There was an urgent message from my secretary asking me to call him as soon as I was up. That was unusual, and as I dialed the number, the pictures flashed through my mind as a possible reason for his call.

"Mr. Algedda...sir...I think you should go to the Al Jazeera website right away. There's a picture of you and your wife and children. They say it was sent to many offices. And there's a picture of you as a young man, also, sir."

It was the same pair of pictures, with an Arabic caption, "Diplomat's Secret Past Revealed." Already there were posts that reflected badly on the pride of the King. Where else had she sent the photographs? More people than just our Ambassador and Consul had seen them. Many people were talking. They were not our friends, and they were gossiping about me.

I had never tried to court the loyalty of the staff at our mission—I was senior, and they were mere staff—and when I arrived late in the morning, there were several younger men looking at a computer together. I knew it was the pictures. They had not expected me that day, and when they realized I was looking at them, they suddenly found other things to do.

I did not have any business, but I stayed in my office with the door closed most of the afternoon.

The next morning, I woke up early and could not go back to sleep. Again I logged on to my email. There were no new messages, but when I checked Al Jazeera, I found two pages of comments on the posting. Most were from Shia countries with comments like "One more reason to be careful when you shake hands with a Sunni" and "We always knew something smelled." I also checked the American version of the website. There were fewer comments, but some readers were aware of the significance of pumping gas and wondered whether the King "sent a gas station attendant for special gas sales" or "What will the Prince do about the smell of gas in his house?" One asked, "Can you scrub hard enough to get it out?" and a follow-up comment read, "I see what you mean..."

I was supposed to speak at a luncheon that day, but I called and left a message for the Ambassador that I was not feeling well. His secretary's only comment was, "He said to let you know he would cover for you," as though they already knew I would not show up.

The Princess went to bed early that night. I sat in my study and watched late night television. As the familiar face came on stage to applause, he began his opening routine, "You've all heard how bad the economy is. Homeless people in Central Park. Those who are working can't make ends meet, and they take second jobs. For example, right here in

New York, it seems that one of our local diplomats had to take a second job. You know how bad the economy is if a diplomat from an OPEC country has to take a job pumping gas."

The screen filled with a close-up of the picture of me. The shirt was clear. My face was pixelated because of my diplomatic status, but every diplomat in New York knew it was me. The audience laughed as he continued, "I guess they've fallen on hard times. We aren't buying enough gas. They always say it's up to Americans to spend to save the world economy. It's a tough job."

I clicked off the television. My heart was racing, but I undressed to take a shower with the forced calm of years of diplomatic dissembling. I stood in the hot water for a long time. I had to defuse the situation. I had to think, but I heard a knock on the door. Certainly the Princess would not dare to interrupt when the door was closed, but she called through the door. "Sayiid..."

*What the fuck? Why was she bothering me?* I yelled back, "What the hell do you want?"

"Sayiid," she said again. Her voice was very nervous, scared actually. "Sayiid, the doorman is on the phone." I'd not heard the phone over the shower. "He says Wahiib is here and he doesn't want to wait."

I opened the door. "Tell him I will be ready in a few minutes."

Everything was steamy from my long shower, but a draft of cooler air drifted in through the opened door and partially cleared one mirror. I glanced at myself wrapped with a towel around my waist and felt reassured that I still looked fit as James Bond.

Then I heard the voices in the hall.

By diplomatic protocol, my apartment was officially

sovereign territory of the King. It would cause an international incident if any American tried to enter without permission; but since it was his territory, the King, through the person of his New York security chief, had open access to everything. On this authority, our chief of security had opened the door, and I stood barefoot as Wahiib walked in. I had no robe, and I had not had time to turn off the water. "What are you going to do about this?" he demanded without even saying my name.

I shivered as the room cooled. I could not think of anything to say. When it was obvious that I had no ideas, he told me "The foreign minister and I have discussed this. We believe you should leave New York. Tonight."

I made excuses and even thought of refusing to leave, but he added, as though instructing a schoolboy, "Tomorrow, we will withdraw your diplomatic credentials. We prefer that you leave tonight."

He left me hanging for a moment so I would listen carefully as he promised what he would do. "After tomorrow, you will not have diplomatic immunity, Sayiid. Do you really want to be average in America?"

# Acknowledgments

When I was in medical school, I often tried to anticipate how I could work independently if I lost access to the modern drugs and instruments I use every day. Finally a friend commented, "Who are you trying to fool? Everything you do is dependent on other people. You will never be able to do anything entirely on your own." This is also how it is with writing. I am deeply indebted to those who have helped and who have made this project possible.

First, I thank Cyra McFadden, my severest critic and my best supporter. I would not have been able to get to the final stage of writing this book without her wisdom and understanding of what I have intended to accomplish. I thank Sandy Handsher who taught me how to tell a story. I thank the persons who produced this book. They have specialized skills I am unlikely ever to develop. Polly Lockman designed the cover, the website, and the accompanying website www.thecoldlineproject.com that offers every woman a safe place to tell her story. Kaye McKinzie organized the task of taking THE BLUE-EYED GIRL and The Coldline Project to the public.

Laurie McAndish King for editing the final manuscript. Jim Shubin for layout of both the print and the electronic versions of the book. My colleague and friend, Vladimir Lange at Red Square Press, for his constant enthusiasm and support.

I thank my wife, Janet. I would not have been able to write this book without her encouragement and support. She has tolerated my preoccupation and encouraged this venture, and she has supported me in taking this story to the women for whom it is intended.

In my years in practice, many women have trusted me enough to share their stories. I assure these women that no part of this book is based on their personal stories. Their words, however, have taught me that there are many stories like this, and these stories have encouraged me to complete this project.

# The Trouble With Scripts

Say the word for almost any activity, and a stereotypical script plays out in your mind. We only have to fill in the details to understand exactly what we *think* happened. *Baking cookies*, for example, elicits images of a mixer, cups measuring flour, and a spatula lifting hot cookies off a baking sheet. Say *riding a bike*, and there are images of feet pushing peddles, sidewalk and trees flying by, and wind in your face. Say *rape*, and we tend to visualize an ugly stranger tearing clothes off a screaming girl.

Sometimes, however, our scripts are faulty. The legal definition of *rape*, for example, does not mention strangers, ugly, or screaming. By definition rape is intercourse by force, fear, or fraud, or alternatively, penetration of a woman's vagina, mouth, or anus without her permission. Coerced sex is rape because a woman who is being coerced cannot meaningfully give permission for anything. Sex with a woman who is intoxicated or under the influence of drugs may also be rape because the woman is incapable of giving her consent. All of these can occur independent of our stereotypical script of rape.

Despite these legal definitions written in the relative calm of legislative chambers, we tend to fall back on our stereotypical scripts when we hear about rape. The more a sequence of events deviates from our personal script for what we consider rape, the less we are willing to say that rape has occurred. This applies to victims who do not report their rape, rapists who claim they have done nothing wrong, and persons who hear the story later and doubt that "real rape" occurred.

Women are often uncertain whether to call their experience rape because it did not match society's stereotypical script, and they may be reluctant to label an experience as a rape because labeling itself creates secondary stress. If they knew the perpetrator, it could not have been the stranger in their script. In fact, the more a woman is acquainted with a man, the less she is likely to think of sexual assault by him as rape. If she or the rapist had consumed alcohol or used drugs, she is more likely to accept it as a *misunderstanding*. If she did not physically fight her assailant, she is less likely to think of it as rape. But, the definition of rape does not excuse a friend, require a woman to be totally sober, or require a woman to die fighting. Sex without permission is rape.

Because of this reluctance, researchers sometimes ask women about their sexual experiences in general rather than asking if they have been raped. In a follow up of college freshmen, Orchowsky and Gidycz found that 6% were victims of sexual penetration against their wishes—a completed rape by definition—during the first 7 months of college. An additional 3% experienced attempted rape. Only half of these rapes were disclosed to friends, and only two women reported it to the police.

Rape is common. Twenty percent of teenagers between the age of 14 and 20 experience completed rape at least once. Up to 80 percent do not report the rape. This means that about one in six college graduates has had a sexual experience that meets the legal definition of rape—and never told anyone.

Rape hurts, and hidden pain does not go away. Faulty scripts lead women to blame themselves for sexual assault. Faulty scripts allow men to excuse their sexually aggressive behavior. Faulty scripts perpetuate the pain.

It is time for all of us to rethink the scripts. A society cannot reach its full potential if it tolerates violence against its greatest underappreciated asset.

www.thecoldlineproject.com is a place that invites women to share their stories. Any woman can share her story confidently, anonymously, and without charge. The Cold Line Project is based on the fact that writing about one's worst experience can be the beginning of healing.

# Discussion Questions

by

Karen Roth Ridder

1. In this story, we see the unfolding of the attitudes of two characters towards sex and sexual issues. How does each person's personal development—along with their family history, cultural understandings and expectations of how to act—shape their story?
2. Why is it so hard for the Blue-Eyed Girl to name what happened to her as rape? Why did she stay in the relationship for so long after that first incident? How did she try to downplay the importance of the rape?
3. Why is it important that this story played out over decades in the lives of the two main characters?
4. Why do you think it is hard for Sayiid to discontinue his relationship with the Blue-Eyed Girl even after it becomes detrimental to his career and family?
5. Both sides of this story are told in the first person. How does this affect the way you relate to the story? How does it shape your view of Sayiid in particular? What parts, if any, of his character or story were sympathetic? How did he turn into an abuser? Do you agree with the Blue-Eyed Girl's assessment that he was a third-rate criminal?
6. Decades after her relationship with Sayiid, the Blue-Eyed Girl and her husband go back to a college reunion. She runs into a former classmate who remembers her fondly. She is surprised to hear him describe the type of person she was before meeting Sayiid, strong and confident. She says, "I was who I wanted to be." How did meeting Sayiid change the way the Blue Eyed Girl saw herself? Why was it hard for her to reclaim herself?

7. The author uses Blue-Eyed Girl's husband David and her friend Sarah as guides to help her understand and frame what happened in her relationship with Sayiid. Why are these important choices for her? How do they help her to become herself again?
8. After Blue-Eyed Girl begins to understand she was not at fault in her rape, she becomes more comfortable not hiding it. Talk about some of the ways the Blue-Eyed Girl begins to re-frame and get a new understanding of her experience. Why are those things important in her healing?
9. In the end, Sayiid is humiliated, not by what he did to the Blue-Eyed Girl, but by the photo taken of him as a gas station attendant. Why do you think this indirect confrontation was the most appropriate way for the Blue-Eyed Girl to reveal Sayiid's character to the world? Why would that be important?
10. When the Blue-Eyed Girl is finally able to talk about her experience with Sayiid as rape she explains the detrimental effect to her friend this way; "He destroyed my faith in me. You can't fight when you can't even be responsible for your own body. He took me away from me. He took away any joy in what my body could do." How does this describe what happened in her life?
11. What parts of the Blue-Eyed Girl's story show how she turned from a victim to a victor?
12. The "Blue-Eyed Girl" doesn't have a name. Why do you think she is unnamed? How does it contribute to the story? Who else doesn't have a name? Why is that important in the story?

# Resources To Help You

Reading The Blue Eyed Girl may bring up painful memories for women and men who have been victims of rape.

The National Sexual Assault Hotline at 1.800.656.HOPE is maintained 24 hours a day by RAINN, The Rape, Abuse and Incest National Network. This hotline is anonymous unless you chose to reveal personal information.

LOCAL PLACES TO FIND HELP

You do not need to face this alone.

- If you are a student in school, you can go to your advisor or a trusted teacher.
- If you feel unsafe at school, you can call or go to your local county Social Workers' Office.
- Call or go to your local police or sheriff department and ask to speak with a woman officer.
- Call or go to your local hospital.
- Call or go to your doctor for a referral.
- Planned Parenthood will know about local counseling services.

## WEBSITES

- Rape, Abuse and Incest National Network (RAINN) has excellent resources.

  **http://www.rainn.org**

- Project Unbreakable allows women to post a photograph – showing or not showing their face - with a statement about the rape they have experienced, and in some cases to fight back at the prejudices of law enforcement offices.

  **http://project-unbreakable.org**

- About Date Rape is an excellent Australian website that discusses date and acquaintance rape.

  **http://www.aboutdaterape.nsw.gov.au**

- San Francisco Women Against Rape

  **http://www.sfwar.org**

- The Rape Crisis Center, San Antonio, Texas has an excellent website.

  **http://www.rapecrisis.com**

- The Coldline Project offers a place for woman or a man to tell their story anonymously. It also discusses the importance of what researchers call scripts and how these scripts confuse our reactions to rape.

  **http://www.thecoldlineproject.com**

# About the Author

William Goodson is a graduate of Harvard Medical School, the University of Missouri, Columbia and Southwest High School in Kansas City. Dr. Goodson has been a leader in improving the diagnosis and care of cancer and other breast diseases for 30 years. Having observed first hand the immeasurable value of women making their own decisions for treatment of breast cancer, he has become committed to the right of every woman to make all personal decisions that involve her body. The Blue-Eyed Girl is his response to those persons who would deny women this basic right. Dr. Goodson has been professor of surgery at the University of California San Francisco where he worked extensively with monitoring the quality of care and was also chairman of the curriculum committee for the Medical School. He is an author on over 100 original research articles and *It's your body...ask!*, a book that helps women understand breast cancer. *The Blue-Eyed Girl* is his first novel. He practices in San Francisco.

CPSIA information can be obtained
at www.ICGtesting.com
Printed in the USA
FFOW01n1543150314
4216FF

9 780976 039822